William Dugas Trammell

Ça ira.

A Novel

William Dugas Trammell

Ça ira.
A Novel

ISBN/EAN: 9783337001315

Printed in Europe, USA, Canada, Australia, Japan

Cover: Foto ©Andreas Hilbeck / pixelio.de

More available books at **www.hansebooks.com**

ÇA IRA.

A NOVEL.

BY

WM. DUGAS TRAMMELL.

———◆———

NEW YORK:
UNITED STATES PUBLISHING COMPANY,
13 UNIVERSITY PLACE.
1874.

JOHN F. TROW & SON,
PRINTERS AND BOOKBINDERS,
205-213 *East 12th St.*
NEW YORK.

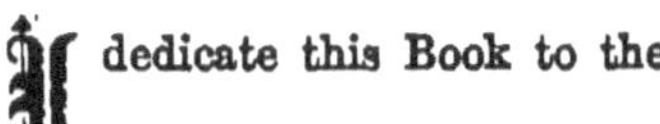 dedicate this Book to the

WORKINGMEN,

and to the memory of all who have ever suffered in their Cause, hoping that the energies of the living, and the inspiration of the dead, may unite to peacefully accomplish that Great Revolution to which all Humanitarians must look with the greatest concern,

The Emancipation of Labor.

THE AUTHOR.

Waverly Hall, Georgia,
March, 1874.

Book 1.

ELKTON.

CHAPTER I.

"Thee thy handmaid Necessity ever precedes."
—HORACE.

The beggars—Tiers-état—Tennis-Court—The pikes—Tocsin—Alarm gun—Phrygian cap—Forward march—Robespierre—Level—Ça Ira!—And has the world got so far?—Doubtless—Even to Ça Ira—But it was not done in a day—Some say it required six thousand years—Others, as many millions—No matter—It required a long time to get there—So it may, doubtless will, require the people of this book some time to get there—Nineteenth century is inquisitive—Must know the whys and wherefores—Must know *how* as well as why things happen—Nor is this a bad thing for the nineteenth century; rather, quite a good thing—It indicates progress; that the nineteenth century wants to get more knowledge into its head—Have not the Democrats of the State of Alabama lately made a law to tax each dog twenty-five cents for school purposes?—And *that* is not a bad thing either, one thinks—Alabama will not rest here—Believes in "march of mind"—Must get herself educated, at all costs!—Has it ever been said, "As goes Alabama, so goes the Union?"—If not, let it be said now; at least as concerns progress and education—Manifestly, among such a people, it would not be wise to omit the whys and wherefores—Allons!

MIRABEAU HOLMES was captain of a company. It was in time of the great war between the States, in which the Southerners lost their negroes and jewelry. Mirabeau was

1*

not captain of a company in the war, but of a company of
boys at the old country school. The boys wore white pants
with red stripes, and they were armed with whistles—
whistles that boys make in spring-time out of bits of chestnut by slipping the bark off when the sap is up—and wooden
pikes, somewhat like the pikes afterwards invented by the
famous war-governor of Georgia. But the captain wore a
genuine dress-sword, of which he was very proud, because it
came from a revolutionary ancestor. Mirabeau looked as
well as he could, for Kate Fletcher was there among the girls
looking on, delighted with the drill. He was in love with
Kate, a pretty girl, some years older than himself.

Mirabeau's father, Dr. Holmes, was a country physician,
a man of intelligence and much reading. In spite of their
pronounced atheism, he could not help admiring the great
men of the French Revolution. Mirabeau he hated especially,
because he was not only an atheist but a sad dog, vastly immoral, always given up to debauchery, running away with
Sophie de Ruffey, in the night, to Holland, getting himself
into Castles of Vincennes, and endless scrapes. But Dr.
Holmes had a passionate admiration for great orators. Lamartine said that Mirabeau was the greatest of modern orators. Cousin affirmed that he was the greatest of all orators;
and so thought Dr. Holmes. And so it came to pass that, in
spite of atheism, Castles of Joux, and Sophie de Ruffeys, the
first-born of Dr. Holmes was duly sent forth upon society
with so big a name as Mirabeau.

The boy was baptized at home. I have heard him speak of
it often in after years. He said he was quite young, just able
to stand alone. His father had fetched a " big preacher " a
long way to perform the important ceremony. He said he
had a distinct recollection that he was stripped entirely naked,
stood upon top of the dining-room table, and then the pious

man blessed him and poured a pitcher full of cool water—
just brought from the spring by Harry—upon his head. It
was on a hot day in August, "And," added he, with a sigh,
"I can almost feel the thrill of it now, as it trickled over my
shoulders, back, and belly, even down to my heels, in a perfect network of streams, settling about, here and there, into
ponds, coves, ports, and armlets." But this was long, long
afterwards. He would not have spoken so irreverently on
that day we have seen him at school commanding a company
of boys armed with whistles and "pikes." These two incidents—the baptizing and commanding the company—in the
very early life of Mirabeau, I have taken as representative.
His religion was put upon him by circumstances over which
he had no control. His intellect and his ambition were his
own. No matter what he went into, he was sure to be a
leader. If he joined a debating society at school, he was
made chairman; if he joined a drill company, he was elected
captain. If there was an honor to be competed for, and the
school was divided, he was sure to be the candidate of his
party.

Before the war the chief occupations of our young men in
the country were fast reducing themselves to this: to go to
camp-meetings, barbecues, associations, the "springs," protracted meetings, and to "ride around." As to what might
have been the history of this Mirabeau, if that of the country had taken a different course, concerns us not to speculate; but the probability is that, in spite of his intellect, in
spite of his ambition, he would have been held firmly but
unconsciously down by that atmosphere of do-nothingness and
know-nothingness which was settling like a pall upon the
South. But, happily for Mirabeau Holmes, happily for his
people, and thrice happily for humanity, this pestilential atmosphere—with the negroes and jewelry—was swept from

the face of the earth.   And at the close of the war he found
himself, though without money, and in the midst of ruin and
chaos, young and strong and hopeful; a very king in the
empire of his own mind, and glowing with ambition to extend his dominions.

.Some years after we have seen Mirabeau captain of a company, if you had been standing one September morning on
the Common of the University, by the terrace just in front of
the "Ivy Building," you might have heard the following
conversation:

"Have you seen this new man?"

"Yes; saw him in the library this morning.   How he
got up there though is the question."

"Why so?"

"Consider his legs."

"What of his legs?"

"Do you know anything of winding blades?"

"No."

"Have you heard of pipe-stems?"

"Yes."

"His legs are like 'em."

"But what do you know of him, in fact, Fred?"

"Why, I have just been telling you what I know of certain
systems of matter, which, according to Bishop Butler, he is
'very nearly related to and interested in.'"

"There you are again.   But come now, as to those 'large
masses of extraneous or adventitious matter distending the
several parts of his solid body,'"——

"Hold there!   'Large masses!' Did I not tell you they
were pipe-stems? And being pipe-stems, how can you call
them large masses?"

"Take a cigar."

"Thank you.   As for this man, seeing that his legs, according to Butler, are no part of himself—and truly they would be a very small part, if they were not stretched out to the crack of doom—he came up to see Hall last night."

" What does Hall know of him ? "

" Used to go to school with him somewhere. Says he is a cat of a fellow. But that's like Fullerton's hog. Do you know Captain Pinter's story of Fullerton's hog ? "

" No. What is it ? "

" Well, you know old Fullerton that lives up here in Cobham—the grand-daddy of Charles Augustus. He used to live in one of the eastern counties. He was poor then ; and stole a hog. He came here and got to be mighty rich. He was just the kind of a man for the Democrats to run for the Legislature ; so they put him up. Now the other candidate was old man Pinter, Captain Pinter's parent. Fullerton thought that nobody here knew of the hog-stealing—you see it was not kleptomania then, Fullerton being poor, but plain theft—or if anybody did know of it, he would not dare to mention it. But old man Pinter knew all about it, and thought he would fix the old chap. So he waited till the crowd had gathered on election-day, and then, mounting upon a goods-box, he called out : ' Oh yes ! Oh yes ! Fullerton, back where he came from, stole a hog ! ' Everybody looked at Fullerton. He was not fat from good living yet, and so he jumped upon a barrel, and called out in turn : ' Oh yes ! Oh yes ! That's a long time ago.' But the Democrats sent him to the Legislature though."

" And so it's been ' a long time ago ' since Hall and this man were in school."

" *Si.* But in fact Hall says he's a cat."

" Yes, but you know how it is with these village heroes : they stand at the head of the class, not because they are sharper than others, but because their mothers have more vanity than most children's mothers—which is saying a good deal. The village hero's mother wants to see him stand first at the 'examination,' so she bribes him to study just enough to get there, and it generally takes precious little. When he comes here, where he finds the very best men in the State, and many of the best from other States, what has he to distinguish him from the second and third rate men? Nothing but the swell-head."

"And what has he to distinguish him from the first-rate men? Swell-head will not answer for that."

The force of this last remark will be observed when it is understood that it was made to an 'honor man.' The 'honor man' proceeded to the library. 'Fred' was Fred Van Comer. The 'new man' was a student who had just entered the University; and as he was said to be a 'cat of a fellow;' and as there was much rivalry among the 'secret societies,' which in this University only 'took in' the 'best men;' and as he came out of the regular time, he naturally attract- ed some attention. He was Mirabeau Holmes.

And as we have not seen him since he was a boy, and only got a glimpse of him then; and as we shall have much to say of him hereafter—that is, unless he dies, marries, gets himself into the State prison, or Noodledom—it may be well enough to take his picture now. He wore a pair of pants thirty-six in the leg and twenty-eight in the waist. In other words, he was six feet two, and his legs entirely too small to think of tights. Fred Van Comer was wrong to speak of his legs, as the politicians say, in connection with winding blades. Still he *was* slightly gangling. But as for this gangling business, I suppose he thought of it pretty much as Captain Pinter thought of his turned-up nose: Captain Pinter's nose turned up 'just about as much as a gentleman's nose ought to turn up.' He had black hair, a long, angular, nervous face, uncertain chin, and cold, gray eye. It may as well be stated here, for the benefit of all who at this moment are mentally making comparisons, and trying if they cannot find something in themselves more remarkable than anything in this Mirabeau, that there was nothing very striking about his appearance at all. He was *not* one of those men, who, as novelists tell us, seem in nothing remarkable at first sight, but who, if you look at them the second time, and closely, gradually impress you as being somewhat out of the ordinary way, something strange, rather fascinating, not to say positively wonderful. I rather think you might have looked into this man's face several times without discovering anything greatly wonderful. Maybe the reader expects to hear that he at least had " an enormous head "—possibly so large and so irregularly shaped that he never thought of finding a hat to fit it in an ordinary store; but always had to have them made to order by Messrs. Blinkum, Slick & Co., New York. Nothing of the sort; he wore a number seven. But his head was all forehead—like Plato's and Ben Hill's. For the rest, he held himself as erect as Jeff Davis; and there was a very perceptible dash of scorn in his face. When he saw another do any work he was a shade disappointed, especially when he had expected something particularly good; when he heard another speak he thought he could have done it better. He had a comfortable opinion of himself; even thought himself good-looking, which is scarcely to be wondered at, seeing that he was very far from good-looking. But he also had a good opinion of his intellectual qualifications, which is rather to be wondered at; for in this he was, in truth, not wide of the mark.

When Mirabeau met in the library the venerable Chancellor of the University, he recognized at once his ideal of a man. His long silvery hair, his noble head, his large, dark eyes beaming with the subdued fire of eloquence and poetry, his thoughtful and reverent brow, his whole face lit up with the largest and rarest human sympathy,—in all this Mirabeau thought he saw the stamp of the loftiest character. And Mirabeau was not at all mistaken. The venerable Chancellor was a man of the broadest and most catholic culture, of liberal opinions, and boundless benevolence. But what do words signify? Scattered over this broad land there are many young men, and this book will come into their hands, aided in their first struggles in life's battle by this noble man, who are already pressing forward to wield the energies and mould the civilization of our people, who can testify that the "old doctor's" benevolence was not an empty sentiment. He was a man of the most exalted piety and an universal sympathy: his sympathy knew no limit whatever; from the tiniest flower to the towering Alps, from the lowest child of darkness to the highest seraph of light; in all things, like the Psalmist, whom he loved, he saw reflected the image of the Creator. The "old doctor" at once took the student by the hand, called him "my son," and exhibited such an interest in him as made this man his fast friend forever after.

"I have always loved to know," says M. Lamartine, "the home and the domestic circumstances of those with whom I have had anything to do in the world. It is a part of themselves—it is a second external physiognomy, which gives the key to their disposition and their destiny." Mirabeau Holmes was a religious man; I may say even deeply religious. Not that he had ever passed through that great conflict between Reason and Belief which every deep and skeptical mind—and all deep minds are skeptical—must, at some time or other, pass through. But he was religious because his parents were pious people, and got him baptized in time.

Moreover, before he was thirteen he had read the whole of the six enormous volumes of Clarke's " Commentary." No wonder he never doubted any portion of Scripture—it was all made so plain to him. Then, again, his father died about this time; his father, whom he had greatly loved. Indeed, everybody loved the good, always gentle, always sympathetic Dr. Holmes. Especially was he beloved by the poor people, and by the slaves upon the neighboring plantations, whom he attended in their sickness. And I lay this down here as the best test of gentleness and generosity of character: To be beloved by your inferiors. Would you, sir, forfeit the love of your faithful dog for the good-will of an emperor ? You would ? " Oh that the sexton were here to write you down—an ass." Pass on—to the Penitentiary. Dr. Holmes and Elizabeth Barclay had married quite young, as was then the custom ; and until the Dr.'s death had never been less than lovers, which was *not* then the custom. They had three children, two of whom died in infancy, leaving only Mirabeau. Dr. Holmes was buried, according to his own request, in the burying-ground of his own church, " Olivet ; " and every morning you might see upon his grave a wreath of rare flowers. For the mistress of " Ashton " had the most beautiful flower gardens in all the country, and she loved them now more than ever. On summer evenings, when Mirabeau was a boy, and when he would be at home on " vacation," she would take him by the hand and walk across the fields to " Olivet." Many years afterwards, when his dear mother was sleeping happily in the little churchyard, by the good Doctor's side ; when storms had swept over the land, and others were threatening; when " Ashton " had fallen into the hands of strangers, and not a vestige was left of the beautiful gardens ; when he himself had passed through more than one of the crises of life, he sometimes looked back

to these walks across the fields with his mother. Who shall
say how much they had to do in the shaping of this man's
life-history ?

And this is a most important fact in the life of this man :
not that he believed in a particular church, or even a particular religion, for that is a matter of but little consequence,
but that his religious feelings were deep. Had he been conventionally religious, the probability is that he would have
lived and died a conventional man, rising, perhaps, to that
"mediocrity of respectability," which, according to the prince
of modern philosophers, "is becoming a marked characteristic of modern times." He believed in the Christian religion
because he had been so taught.

Mirabeau Holmes was a representative man of the most
intellectual and best-educated class of young men of the
"New South," and as such I shall trace his history. Of
what impression, if any, he made upon the world, or even a
small portion of the world; of the stand-point from which he,
at different periods, regarded Humanity, what he considered
his relations thereto, and the consequent resolves as to how
he should conduct himself so as not only to pay in full Humanity's account against him, but to leave a large balance in
his favor; of what he resolved to do, and, which is of far
more importance, of what he did, and how: on the other
hand, of what effect the world had upon himself; of how his
resolves, his aspirings, and his work, were in any manner
modified by the atmosphere of that portion of the world immediately around him, with its conflict of old and new ideas,
prejudices, stupidities, reforms longed for and worked for by
the few, and bigoted "conservatisms," ignorantly, blindly
clung to by the many; in a word, of what this man did in
the world, and what the world did in him, we shall see somewhat in the course of this history.

CHAPTER II.

"Yond' Cassius has a lean and hungry look.
.   .   .   .   .
Seldom he smiles, and smiles in such a sort,
As if he mock'd himself, and scorn'd his spirit
That could be mov'd to smile at anything."

—*Julius Cæsar.*

IN the city of Nashville, in a room of the Capitol, one night in the year 186–, was held a convention of young men. As you entered the room and glanced around, you perceived that here were men from different parts of the country. Here was the polished, aristocratic Virginian; the well-made, healthy-looking, brusque Kentuckian; the nervous, fiery South Carolinian; the intellectual, energetic, wide-awake Georgian; the sallow, silent Floridian; the self-asserting Texan—in short, men from every Southern State were here. But different in everything else, all were alike in this, that they seemed earnest and thoughtful. These men were not only representative of the people of the different States—they were representative of the highest educated thought and feeling of the South. This was a convention of a college "secret society," the largest and most powerful in the South; indeed, it was the largest and oldest in the United States; but the Northern and Southern wings, separated by the war, had not resumed friendly relations. No one could be a member unless he was distinguished for scholarship or oratory, and social excellence. It was made up of the best material; of men likely to wield a large influence, not only in colleges and universities, but in the general civilization of the country. In this convention every college and university of any importance in the South was represented, and ably represented.

Mirabeau Holmes was chairman of the convention. This was the second night of the convention. One of the members rose, approached the rostrum, and whispered something in the president's ear. The president handed him a slip of paper; and when he returned to his place he said : "Mr. President, I propose the following amendments to the Constitution : 1st. The separation of the Southern from the Northern wing of the society shall be final ; and no chapter shall ever be established north of Mason and Dixon's line. 2dly. It shall be the sacred and paramount duty of this society, and of every member of it, to oppose, by all possible means and measures, the Federal Government ; looking always to the reasserting of the independence of the Confederate States." And this wild scheme was born of the brain of Mirabeau Holmes ; he was its father and champion. Here was a very great change ; for the "objects of the society," heretofore, had been solely to cultivate the intellectual and social qualities of its members. It was here proposed, by a sweep of the pen, to change the society from this to a secret political revolutionary power. Some thought of the "Mary Anne," some of Danton, Robespierre, the clubs of Paris, and seemed to hear the "Ça Ira" of those terrible revolutionary times. The member had taken his seat. According to the arrangement, the president was to have called some member to the chair, and made a speech in favor of the amendments. But seeing no signs of opposition, he put the questions promptly, and both were carried unanimously. And thus by a small body of young men—the oldest not over thirty, the youngest probably under twenty, who had met quietly in this city of Nashville, unheralded, save by a short notice in the daily papers—was passed a measure of more significance, destined to have a greater effect upon the thought, feeling, and action of the country, than any number of pompous acts of the Congress of the United States. It might be that on this very day it was enacted by the Congress of the United States of America "that three hundred and fifty dollars be appropriated for the improvement of the harbor at Savannah, in the State of Georgia;" or "four millions and five hundred thousand dollars for the erection of Government buildings at Duluth—such as should be worthy of that metropolis, and commensurate with the dignity of the United States and the financial aspirations of the stockholders of the Northern Pacific Railroad." And if so, possibly at this very hour a thousand wires were spreading the important news through every state and city on the continent; and old Ocean himself kept respectful silence for a moment while the great words, Congress of the United States, flashed along the cable. And next morning ten thousand newspapers, some of them in barbarous and guttural type, repeated the wondrous tale. But this measure of which I am speaking was not telegraphed to any kingdoms, principalities, or newspapers; to certain powers, however, it was mentioned, though in a very quiet way. Late in the night two of the members walked to the telegraph office, and sent the following message to every chapter in the society : " Rejoice ! The great measure passed unanimously." Almost simultaneously this message was received by a small knot of the most influential men in every college and university South. And they all rejoiced.. Acts of Congress, lawyers' parchments, indeed. Bah !

" Strange they don't come on. It's almost ten o'clock."

" I reckon they'll come. The secretary counts on 'em ; and you know he don't make wrong calculations. He says the main man among them will be sure to be here; but he don't look for them before ten."

“ I reckon there must be some understanding, else the captain would have reported before now.”

“ Curious man, the secretary is. I wish I knew all about his life. Never sleeps with anybody; won’t even sleep with anybody in the room with him. The other night at Jackson the hotel was crowded—some railroad meeting there. They had to put him and old ‘ Cassius ’ and me all in one room. He stayed up all night. He told us he had a good deal of writing to do, and if he got through he would come to bed. But he didn’t come.”

“ What did old ‘ Cassius,’ as they call him, say ? ”

“ Nothing. He’s about as strange a one as the other. Never has anything to say. Does anybody know anything about him ? ”

“ I don’t. What do they call him ‘ Cassius ’ for ? They say that’s not his name.”

“ You are a pluperfect heathen, you are. Where’s your Shakespeare ? They call him ‘ Cassius,’ because he’s so lean and hungry-looking. And, hang me, if he don’t look like he could eat a *punkin* through the crack of a lawful fence. I wish I knew all about both of them.”

“ For the secretary, no matter about his life. He knows everything; all our men believe in him; he’s the very man for us. And I tell you, they call him the secretary, but it’s my opinion that *he’s* running this machine.”

“ You are right there, else, as old Veller says, you are one Dutchman, and I’m another; that’s all.”

“ Where is General Cyclops ? ”

“ In Tennessee.”

“ Ever see him ? ”

“ Once.”

“ At a meeting ? ”

“ No.”

"Well, it don't matter. I reckon Arnot knows about as much what to do as Cyclops does. Look at his face—the devil couldn't tell what he's thinking about."

"If he was to hear a toot of Gabriel's horn right now, you couldn't tell any more from his face than if it was a piece of white putty."

"He seems to know all about this fellow that's coming here to-night."

"And, by the way, I've been thinking about it, and I tell you this is the biggest kind of a thing we are getting into. You fellows had no idea of its getting to be such a huge concern when you started it up there in Tennessee." '

"No, *sir*."

"I wish they would come on. Cassius over there seems to be getting restless."

The individual spoken of got up, and came across the room to where the two speakers were.

"What time? Ten? Arnot's just got some news from your State," said he, addressing one of the speakers, who was from South Carolina. "Rapid times—Savannah river lively; your people want a meeting called over there right away. Some rough work 'll have to be done, I *guess*." And the lean and hungry-looking Cassius moved on. This was more than he had ever been known to say before at one time.

Some telegraphic knocks were heard at the door. Almost instantly all the lights in the hall were lowered; and the door-keeper, after a short colloquy with the operator outside, half opened the door. Two men entered, locked arms. One of them, a small, dark man, who would be taken for a Creole; the other, our friend, the chairman of the Nashville Convention. The two men proceeded to the opposite end of the hall, and Mirabeau had time to look around him. The hall was long, narrow, and low, with a row of seats on each side, and with something like a speaker's stand at the furthest end. In an uninhabited old street of the great city, silence without, silence within, save the measured foot-falls of the two men as they proceeded from one end to the other of the hall; all the lamps turned down to a graveyard twilight, save that on the table in front of the chairman, which, suddenly elevated, threw a defiant glare upon the bare walls; all combined to add to the deep, silent sombreness of the place. Here were about a score of men. But Mirabeau, after the first moment, scarcely looked to the right or left, his attention being caught and held by the person they were approaching. It was a face calculated to arrest the attention, especially as it was now glared upon by the single light, which seemed half surprised at the intrusion of the stranger. The small dark man, when they met the chairman, who had risen and advanced a few paces towards them, simply bowed, without saying a word, and went to a seat. The chairman introduced himself as "James Arnot," of South Carolina, and when he shook Mirabeau's hand, the latter started in surprise, but instantly recovered himself.

" Ἐσμεν "——

" Ἀδελφῶν."

" Κύχλος ! Where have we met ? "

" In the Temple."

These enigmatical expressions passed between them in a low voice, and quickly. And then they seated themselves.

" I knew of the meeting in Nashville," said Arnot; "knew what you intended to do there. I wanted to be with you; but looking to the work before us to-night, I concluded it best for me not to be there. You can readily see that it will not do for our men to know that I am a member of the society. Seeing that very few of them could become members, for them to know that some of us were, might create jealousy, insubordination, and lead to the ruin of everything."

During this speech Mirabeau had a moment for observation. He saw that his new acquaintance was almost as youthful as himself, certainly under thirty, of small figure, and features almost as delicate as a woman; of pale face, and rich black hair, which was combed back without parting; the face was immobile, and, in spite of the intellectual brow and deep eye, seemed utterly expressionless. But it did not require an acute physiognomist to tell that these features were immobile not from any lack of activity of intellect and feeling, but from the most perfect and absolute self-control. It might be that this man had given years to the accomplishment of this purpose, that his features should never be surprised or provoked in any way to give the slightest clue to what was passing within. When he had finished, Mirabeau replied:

"I agree with you perfectly."

"And so I telegraphed you to get the convention to send one or more members here to consult with our people if some agreement could not be entered into which might be serviceable to both of us."

"Our people" was the "K. K. K.," and this was a meeting of some of their chiefs. When Mirabeau had been introduced to all present, Arnot explained to them what was proposed to be done, and suggested that one or more members be appointed to confer with Mr. Holmes, and report to the meeting on the following night; meanwhile he hoped not one of them would leave the city. Arnot knew well enough that it would be the wish of all that he himself should undertake this business with Mirabeau Holmes.

When the meeting broke up they went to their hotel—

these two men—conspirators, if you will—and talked long of the business that had brought them together. Mirabeau had heard a good deal of late of a certain secret organization known by the mystical title of "Klu Klux Klan." The papers of the North were full of accounts of their horrible doings. It was charged that this was an extensive organization; that a large number of the most prominent Confederate chiefs belonged to it; that it was purely political; that its object was the destruction of the Union; finally, that every member took a most solemn oath never to scruple at anything, however criminal, that would forward the interest of the Klan, or of the party whose servant the Klan was; all obstacles must be removed without counting the cost; in a word, that they looked to the end, not to the means, and pursued it with the disciplined zeal of a Jesuit. They charged that it was dangerous for a Northern man to go South. (And as for this, there is abundant evidence that it was dangerous enough —to the State treasuries.) It was said that the highways were nightly traversed by armed bands, moving noiselessly about, dressed in long black gowns, their faces fantastically painted, and carrying crosses, miniature coffins, curiously worked banners, skull-bones, and other things symbolical of their business. All of which was indignantly denied by the Southern papers; and they retorted too—with more reason— that the Southern people, though hounded, persecuted, and oppressed with an energy of vindictive malice sufficient among any people less loyal to raise the stones to mutiny, were the most peaceable, law-abiding, and long-suffering people in the universe. Still Mirabeau had regarded the whole matter as little more than newspaper warfare, gotten up for political party purposes. Nothing, therefore, could have been more genuine than his surprise when the whole scheme was unfolded to him.

"The Klan," said Arnot, "originated in Tennessee, and its object was to protect the people against old Brownlow. But it was soon found that our people in every State were almost in as much need of protection as the people of Tennessee."

"And does your object still extend no further than that?"

"That is understood to be our object; still there are a few of us who look a great deal further—to independence!"

"In that I will be with you. But you say some of you look to this; is there not danger, then, of disagreement among yourselves?"

"We are too well organized for that. Officers and men are sworn to obey the orders of their superiors without question. We have a General Council which meets once a year in the capital of your own State. Theoretically this Council is supreme; but practically all power is in the hands of a very few men—I may almost say one person."

Mirabeau found that, nominally, the supreme chief of the Klan was a distinguished general; and that Arnot was, nominally, only secretary. But he had soon seen enough to convince him that, however it might be nominally, the real power was in the hands of the calm, intensely pale-faced individual before him. Mirabeau was shown letters and despatches from many leading generals and politicians. Arnot was an individual who seemed to know precisely what to say, and when. And so here, the moment Mirabeau seemed to miss something, he remarked:

"I suppose you are looking for something from our brave old chief; that is the only thing we have ever failed in. We know his heart is with us; for he has frequently said that 'the principles for which we contended will reassert themselves, though it may be in a different form, and at a

different time.' And I suppose that for this very reason,
probably, he has not consented to join us. We mean to
make another effort to get him, and think we have hit upon
a plan that will succeed."

And thus these two conspirators, having authority, that
night, in the name and on the part of their respective organ-
izations, entered into a firm alliance for the accomplishment
of a certain definite object of the greatest significance.
Here, then, was a combination between the men of thought
and the men of action; always a most powerful combination,
and here a most dangerous.

It was nearly morning when the conference between these
two persons broke up. Mirabeau was much interested in
James Arnot. He, too, would have liked to know his history.
But Arnot let no word drop likely to give any idea at all of
his life. When they went down from Arnot's room, Mirabeau asked him to take a glass of wine. "He never took anything." Wouldn't he take a cigar? "He never smoked."

The next day, and the day after, as Mirabeau rode over the
splendid fields of Louisiana and Mississippi, the coal regions
of Alabama, and the magnificent scenery of North Alabama
and Georgia, he reflected upon what a grand country we
should have when free of the Puritan Yankees! We should
not want any written constitution then; no "checks and bal-
ances;" our interests would be identical; in thought, feeling,
education, sympathy, purpose, blood—our people should be
one; then there could be a real, not a bungling, mechanical
Union, as we now have!

CHAPTER III.

"Where Yonah lifts his bald and reverend head
The humbler Alleghany peaks above,
Beneath its shadows pleasantly is spread
Nacoòche's vale—sweet as a dream of love."

. . . . . .

"'Tis a valley of peace, rich in every soft feature,
In sunshine or shade, in its own verdant green,
'Tis Georgia's Egeria, most lovely by nature,
Carved out of a chaos of wild mountain scene."
—HENRY R. JACKSON.

"WE are going to have a friend of mine with us to-night, Marian; guess who?"

"A friend of yours—can anything be more indefinite than that?"

"More indefinite than that friend? Nothing that I know of."

"See, now, how you are caught! If you don't tell me without guessing, I mean to tell him what you said about him."

"A college chum. You might know now, by just a slight reference to that wonderful process of 'putting two and two together.'"

"A most indefinite college friend—it must be Fred Van Comer."

"A decimal fraction to a theory in metaphysics! But you will be glad to see him—Mirabeau Holmes."

"Mirabeau Holmes! I *am* glad he is coming. You have told me so much about him. But I never heard you say before that he was the most indefinite of men."

"I will not insist on it, then, but leave you to judge."

"Where did you see him?"

"In town, yesterday. He had either been, or was going, to the Falls. I would have brought him with me last night, but he had some business there with a friend of his who would not come. I wish I could have got *him* to come. He made me think of a grown-up page in some old play. You know Sophie Montcalm? Well, this man is just like her."

"What is his name?"

"Arnot."

"A pretty name. And he must be good-looking himself if he is like Sophie Montcalm."

"So he is; but here comes Pompey with my horse. Holmes is going to stay with us to-morrow. I am going to ride a little way to meet him."

Mirabeau was delighted with the unceremonious, cordial manner of his reception by the ladies at "Elkton." And when Mrs. Malcomb remarked that they had heard Robert and his friend Henry Broughton speak of him so often that they had almost come to regard him as a friend of the family before they had ever seen him, that young gentleman immediately felt comfortable. Mr. Malcomb soon came and joined the party on the veranda. And there, for a while, we shall leave them to interest themselves as best they may. Meanwhile, I shall proceed to talk about Mr. Malcomb, hoping to make him at least as well known to the reader as he was to many who had voted for him to fill the highest offices.

Mr. Malcomb could smile from ear to ear without a moment's notice. He had been for many years an eminent lawyer and political leader. Before the great war—in which the people of New Orleans lost their silver spoons—he had been a politician. After said war he had risen to the dignity of statesman. He was also now deeply engaged in the profession of money-getting. He was not an aristocrat—in truth there were not half so many aristocrats in this part of the world as some people seem to imagine. Mr. Malcomb was the representative native Southern statesman of the new order of things. He wore rusty alpaca pants, a black coat that reached to his heels, and upon his head he carried, slightly pitched forward, the tallest and roundest beaver-hat in this or any other State, with the same precision that a darkey carries a pail of water. In religion he was a strict Baptist; and when he walked he jerked himself along as if bound to a twisted board up and down his back. He was a leading man in his church; and indeed many people said that he had, on many occasions, led his whole church to vote for him for high political offices, and thought his great success mainly attributable to this fact. Be that as it may, he never failed to give liberally to any institution of his church —occasionally, indeed, he would give considerable sums to institutions, especially educational institutions, of other churches. And here again it was charged that he never did anything but from the very deepest policy—that for whatever he gave he was absolutely sure of a return vastly larger than ordinary money-lenders could reasonably hope ever to get. In short, it was said that this man never made a miscalculation—that he never failed to put his money, "where it would do the most good."

It was also said that this man could beat any man in Georgia, or elsewhere, at " covering up his tracks." It was currently believed, by some, that he was always engaged with governors, legislatures, city councils, railroad officials, and great speculators, in certain mysteries; and many people seemed to have a vague feeling—some of them expressed it with great clearness and unction—that these mysterious transactions, if the truth was known, were of the very dark-

est character, enormously swindling at all points; and that
if the mask could only be torn off, this saint of the church,
this man who was always ready to give more than anybody
else to all religious, educational, and charitable institutions—
this man, with his honeyed words and gracious smile blandly
spreading from shore to shore, would be found to be the
wiliest hypocrite, the most hardened, skilful, practised, un-
conscionable knave on the face of the earth. Others, mystical and literally, affirmed, "I know not well what he is;
but a precise villain he is—that I am sure of." If he was
on speaking terms with the Governor, some people were duly
qualified to swear that, according to the best of their knowledge and belief, *he* was the real Governor; that *he* was "running the government;" that the man in the Executive man-
sion was a mere puppet in his hands; nay, that in all probability said puppet was put where he was by the influence of
this man himself, in order that he might with greater secrecy
and safety make his "raids upon the treasury." If his carriage was seen in front of a printing-office, it was positively
asserted that that paper had been paid a round sum to publish two columns of lies, editorially, for him at an early day;
for which he was sure, somewhere, at some time, to receive
at least ten times what he paid the paper. If he was seen to
whisper in the ear of a member of the legislature, the member was bribed beyond the shadow of a doubt; if he took
him by the hand—*if you were sharp enough*—you could get
the glimpse of a greenback sticking to the clumsy legislator's
hand when he withdrew it. If the City Council had a contract to let out, or city property to sell, and his name appeared anywhere in the transaction, said council was denounced for having "sold out" to him. If a newspaper
said a good word for him, no doubt it was paid to say it;
but if it was consistently friendly towards him, manifestly

he either owned the whole thing or a large interest in it. Finally, when he deemed it necessary to reply, through the public print, to his accusers, and did so, to all appearances positively unanswerably, this was only another evidence of his wonderful astuteness in "covering up his tracks." He was said to have the advantage of everybody else in this; that he kept a stenographer constantly on hand to take down everything you said; all of which could be so artfully manipulated as always to make for himself a clear case. But the clearer his case the worse it was for him—clearly there was something dark behind; nay, for that matter, he could make black white, or white black, with the utmost precision and despatch. The man was fearfully and wonderfully made ! .

But these were simply the assertions of this man's enemies; and it may be laid down as a rule not to be lost sight of, that it will never do to trust what one's enemies say. Meanwhile Mr. Malcomb's friends remained silent, not deeming it necessary to say anything. Not that these enemies were all persons to be despised; indeed, some of them were individuals of the largest pretentions. Notably, one of them declared, heroically, that he could trace his blood back through four centuries of ancestors, upon whose escutcheon there was never a stain ! for which, probably, he deserved the greatest credit. But Mr. Malcomb remarked, with characteristic pungency, that he had known many better men, possibly a few worse men, perhaps some as vain upstarts, who traced their ancestry back six thousand years; the question of this gentleman's ancestry therefore was peculiarly a question for the pithachologist.

But the case was this : Mr. Malcomb wanted money; so he worked hard to make it. He worked with great skill and energy ; so he made money rapidly. He was deeply religious,

believed strongly in education, and he was wealthy; so he
gave liberally to all religious and educational institutions.
In a word, he was eminently successful; therefore not without enemies. They said to themselves : This man has no better business capacity than I have ; he does not work as hard
as I do; he has no more energy—not so much—and I know
he has no more sense than I have ; and yet he makes ten times
'as much as I do! How is this? Why, I, like a fool, have
been honest all my life ! He is dishonest. But Mr. Malcomb was chiefly assailed as a public man. He had the rare
sagacity to perceive at the close of the war that the civilization peculiar to the South had passed away, and forever. He
advised the people to accept the terms offered them ; they
might consider them hard, but if they did not accept them
they would surely go further and fare worse. But this man
was not only a most sagacious observer of events ; he was
also a most acute and just judge of character. He saw in
General Grant in the beginning what he has since abundantly
proved himself to be : a most generous man, and friendly towards the South. Also he saw that General Grant was not
only the most powerful, by the course of events, but the
coolest and clearest-headed man in the Republic ; that he
was probably the only man who could bring the country out
of the chaos in which it then was. So he advised the people
to accept him. What an Iliad of woes might thus have been
escaped ! The bitterness of those times will long be remembered. One may as well attempt to bottle up the force of
gravity in glass jars, as to estimate the fierceness of this bitterness. Upon this man it spent its utmost fury. But what,
in such circumstances, is the greatest consolation ? It is
even this : to know that what you are denounced for is solely
the good that is in you. What, in such circumstance, is
the greatest solace to human pride? It is even this: to

know that time will not fail to furnish you a sure vindication. And both of these Mr. Malcomb had. He knew that he was right; he knew that time would prove it.

Mrs. Malcomb was universally beloved. As if to make up for the many bad things said about her husband, everybody lavished upon her their praises. She had a certain independence and originality of thought rarely seen in a woman. It seemed to be the object of her existence to make all about her happy. An earnest, common-sense, practical, pure, high-minded woman; a woman who had comprehended this important truth, that she had a work to do; who saw clearly what it was, and went straight forward to its accomplishment. No sham, no semblance, no make-believe, no falsity, but a really true woman, who felt that she was what she was by the grace of God, and that she should do the work well appointed her to do. She called her husband " Mr. Malcomb." Why did she not call him, especially when in presence of strangers, by some of his titles? For Mr. Malcomb had filled more, than one of the highest offices. But she called him " Mr. Malcomb." Could anything be prettier? Many years before, these two had begun life, as the saying goes, at the foot of the ladder, as plain Mr. and Mrs. Malcomb. She called him Mr. Malcomb then, and she called him so yet. Mirabeau Holmes was particularly struck with this. He thought it had a bearing not only upon the character of the wife, but also upon that of the husband. Ten to one, if both had not been made of the best material, she would have called him by his most distinguished title.

To be sure Mirabeau was not prepared to think the best in the world of Robert's father. But his sister—ah! that was different. He had heard much of her. She was not reputed beautiful; but she was universally beloved, even by her own sex, and said to possess every amiable quality. She was said to be a second edition of her mother, which was thought to be the highest praise.

The day after Mirabeau's arrival Henry Broughton came by in the afternoon, and left his sister at "Elkton." That night, after Betty Broughton had gone, they were all seated out on the veranda, in the moonlight and breeze, when Mr. Malcomb said :

"So you have had Betty Broughton with you this afternoon. How did Mr. Holmes like our mountain beauty? Carried his heart away with her, I doubt not."

"From circumstances over which I had no control, but which Robert can probably explain, I saw very little of her. As for carrying away with her the article you have mentioned, why that had just been disposed of," said Mirabeau.

"But if you say you did not wish the title-deeds cancelled when you saw Betty Broughton, I think it will require at least two witnesses to establish a fact so unlikely," said Mr. Malcomb.

"If one would be sufficient, I think possibly the old oak out there might be made to answer," suggested Robert.

"If it had not been too well taught to think of ever telling secrets," said Marian.

"Fortunate training, Marian, or else I think it might refresh the recollection of a very near relative of ours," said Mrs. Malcomb, glancing towards Robert.

"Well then," said Mr. Malcomb, "the case is clear that we have not even one trustworthy witness. So Mr. Holmes must remain at 'Elkton' until events furnish circumstantial evidence. And to-morrow morning, while Robert is gone to town, I will show him the 'Evening Star.'"

"But you must not show him the 'River,' father; you must leave that to me; I must take Mr. Holmes there · we shall be there just at sunset," said Marian.

"How could I have hoped for so much pleasure in one day!" exclaimed Mirabeau.

"What," said Robert, "that I have to ride nearly a half-day's journey, among other things! But I hope you may be as well entertained as you seemed to be this afternoon."

"As if he had any time to observe whether others were well or ill entertained," observed his mother.

"He was willing to trust that to his sister, mother," said Marian.

"What time does the moon rise?" asked Robert, gravely.

"About an hour after dark," answered his mother, who noticed everything.

"Why, what can you want to know that for?" asked Marian.

"Because you will stay at the 'River' to see the sun set; and I thought if the moon, or even any particular star, should rise in a couple of hours, you would stay to see that. And I tell you, Holmes, it is poetical to see from the River the moon rise over the Blue Ridge. It will inspire you to write some verses," said Robert.

"I can answer for not needing that inspiration," said Mirabeau.

"Clearly I shall find you at the River, if I am till ten o'clock getting back," added Robert.

The morrow came, and the people of "Elkton" were up early. They were not what are called "fashionable people." The case is that there are very few, if any, of what are conventionally known—that is in novels—as "fashionable people" in this country. And this was what Mirabeau thought next morning, when, pretty soon after sunrise, he was called to breakfast. He remembered that this had always been the case with him in his ramblings through this and neighboring States. And it struck him more forcibly this morning than ever before, that it would be well enough to have it at once and clearly understood, that when the honest people of this country speak of "breakfast" they mean a meal generally taken at any hour from day-break to eight o'clock in the morning, the main stake of said meal usually being beefsteak —when comeatible—with biscuits, butter, and coffee. He was also of opinion that it was a safe thing to remember that "dinner" with this people always means such soups, bread, vegetables, bacon, roast-beef, pork, chickens, sour-krout, cakes, custards, puddings, pies, tarts, jellies, what not, all or any as the case may be, even down to pea-soup, with or without a napkin, as it is their custom to eat at any time from half after eleven to two o'clock in the day. He also considered that there was a third meal known as "supper," sometimes taken before sunset—that is, by people who go to bed by dark to save candles, but usually from seven to eight P.M., devoted mainly to such mutton-chops, waffles, butter, coffee, and tea as one may be able to afford. In short, by the time he had got to the end of buttoning up his vest he had come to the conclusion that one of the commandments in this country was this: If thou art an honest, working man, and canst by any means contrive to keep thyself clear of the State prison, thou shalt have three meals per day—breakfast, dinner, and supper; besides these three thou shalt have no other meal before thee. As for "luncheon" though, there was no such institution at "Elkton;" neither had he come across it in his travels. To be sure, when he was a boy, his mother had been constantly engaged in giving him something cold out of the safe "between meals." If *that* was "luncheon," why, "luncheon" was well enough; nay, if *that* was "luncheon," "luncheon" was a good thing; peace be with "luncheon!" But as for "luncheon" in the English sense of the word, away with it! We have none of it in this country; neither are we likely to have. As for John Bull—that is, the John Bull of English novels, especially Mr. Disraeli's—all his time, like Gaul, is divided into three parts: dancing, four hours; sleeping, nine; eating, eleven! And may the Lord have mercy upon his soul.

CHAPTER IV.

"Do you think," said Mirabeau to Mr. Malcomb next day
as they rode over his splendid farm, "do you think the
negroes are much worse off now than when they had masters
to provide for and protect them ? "

"On the contrary, my judgment is that they are much
better off now than then. I think the next census will demonstrate that they are growing both in population and in
the comforts of life."

"What of their future ? "

"That is a very large question. In fact, of all the great
questions before us, in my judgment, that is the most important. But, like all other great questions, it can best be dealt
with by the very simple plan of 'accepting the situation,'
making the very best of it you can, looking to the future and
not to the past. It seems to me that it needs no great
amount of wisdom to teach us that in all the affairs of life,
public or private, to accept the inevitable as inevitable, and
strive for the best that is before you, ought to be admitted
on all hands to be the true policy."

" But there might be a difference of opinion as to what is
the inevitable, as to what are accomplished facts."

" I see the drift of your remark. There have been the
greatest and most unfortunate differences of opinion among
our people on this subject. But they will not last very long;
in a little while the hottest Bourbons among us will accept

the situation. They will get up many excuses, and try hard, perhaps not without success with some, to make people believe they are consistent. But the core of the matter will be the same. Your question about the future of the black race, which we are about to get away from, I can only answer in a general way. I do not believe they are going gradually to die out, or go back into barbarism and idolatry, as some seem to think. On the contrary, my judgment is that they will grow more and more prosperous, and make as good free laborers as any country has. But we must treat them kindly, deal honestly with them, and do all we can in our present impoverished condition to educate and elevate them."

" What of miscegenation in the distant future ? "

" I have not much fear of that. The antagonism between the white and black races is too great. But if there should come in a third race, that would act as a kind of middle ground, I would not answer for the consequences. We might then, in the distant future, go the way of Mexico and South America. But I have little fear of that."

" Upon the whole, I see you are hopeful of our future."

" Yes; we have a great future, if our people will only rise to meet it. But they must learn several things. They must learn to look at things as they are, and try to make the best of them. Why should we look back ? We have neither time nor strength to waste in defence of theories and systems that have been forever swept away by the progress of actual events. They must learn that we cannot live by the defeated past. They must learn that we cannot possibly gain anything either by declaiming against or mourning over the past; but that is precisely what most of our leading men are doing, instead of striving to arouse in the people an ambition to bring their country forward, even after all its misfortunes, to be the peer of the greatest and foremost in civilization,

Two things we must have before we can hope to do much, skilled labor and popular education. These are the springs of power and wealth in modern civilization. I have no laments to make over the past. My religion teaches me that whatever is in history is there under Providence, and must be for good."

They were riding over the finest farm of the most beautiful valley in the world. Here were fields of hundreds of acres, level as a floor, square, and with rows running clear across, straight as a " bee-line," and regular as to width. In slavery times the chief end of a ploughboy's existence was to get the overseer to put him to laying off rows ! It was striven for as a post of honor, and they had the best mules. When learning the art they kept at each end of the row a measure for making all the same width, and a slender staff with a tuft of cotton on the end. They drove the staff down at the proper place, and when driving towards it kept the tuft of cotton steadily in view, looking between the ears of the mule. After a while they dispensed with the measure, and for the staff substituted any object which happened to be in the right place.

They rode through sweet meadow-lands and great fields of grain and cotton. The cotton-plants, with their dark, rich leaves, were as high as the horses ; here and there was a full white blossom on the very summit of the stalk, and the long limbs, reaching from row to row, bent to the earth with great speckled bolls. Here and there, say four or five in a field of an hundred acres, were great shady oaks. On a hot summer day nothing could look more cool and watery. These splendid shade-trees were doubtless left for the convenience of overseers and masters. For, manifestly, Providence never intended shade-trees for ' niggers and mules.' Nay, is was for this that they had been placed in Africa instead of a cold country : that they might have the benefit of some thousands of years' training under tropical suns, the better to fit them for the fulfilment of the designs of Providence ; that they should, in due time, be exalted from their heathen barbarism, and brought over here to be taught the wondrous story of the cross ; made happy and sleek upon the fat of the land—a peck of potatoes, or three pounds of bacon and a peck of meal per week, according as the master happened to be saint or sinner—and industrious by being often reminded of the divine injunction, "Whatsoever thy hands find to do, do it with all thy might." All of which was duly considered and ordered by Providence some years before the foundation of the world.

As for mules ! Talk about harmony of design in giving cranes long necks, and ducks and geese web-feet. Cranes and geese, indeed ! They were nothing to 'niggers and mules.' Suppose we had got all these negroes over here and had no mules. Cotton would have been impossible, and the world would have gone naked. (Oh that we had never seen a mule !) Horses ? Horses, indeed ! The whole breed would have been killed out in ten years. Horses were made for white folks ; white folks were not made for cotton-fields ; therefore, horses were not made for cotton-fields ! Mules were made for negroes ; negroes were made for cotton-fields ; *ergo*, design, design—nothing like design !

" We follow this path now," said Marian that afternoon as she and Mirabeau were going to the ' River,' "and at the gate, where you see the large oak, we go out into the woodland. Father said he would make a wide walk all the way to the ' River,' with shade and grass and hedges, but to humor a whim of mine he left it as it is. See what a hard path it is ; it is an old Indian trail. Should you not have left it so ? "

"I think I should like a compromise between yours and your father's plans; that is, I wish the Indians had made the path wide enough for two people to walk in. See! look back over your shoulder; there is your mother looking at us; laughing, I reckon. How absurd we must look, walking along here single-file like the Indians."

"Isn't that pretty enough? Sautee and Nacoochee may have walked along this very path, like we are now."

"Shouldn't you think the young chief must have carried the 'Evening Star' upon his back that night?"

"Tradition has it that she herself was as fleet as the antelope."

"Still he might have carried her, to make sure of her and to show his love."

"In that case I think he would have taken her in his arms."

"How stupid in me not to have thought of that. Sautee himself might have known that much."

"I suspect Sautee could have taught you more lessons than one."

"If he could teach me how to win the 'Queen of the Valley,' I wish he might be induced to visit his old hunting-grounds again."

"Oh, he would not come to the hunting-grounds to teach you that lesson."

"Where would he come?"

"Why, to that pretty grotto in the side of old Yonah there."

"That was their bridal chamber. He would come right down here on the river, where they gathered muscadines together."

"They never gathered muscadines together. The old chief kept strict watch over his daughter. He wouldn't let them go off together."

" I don't remember the legend.   Will you tell it me ? "

" To-morrow, when we go to Yonah and see their ' bridal chamber,' I will see what you know about it."

They had now reached the " River."   It was a spot to linger in.   Doubtless many a Cherokee youth had told his tale of love beneath these very shades.   Nacoochee and her maidens have bathed in these waters, plucked the jessamine flowers that grow upon the banks, and mingled their evening songs with the lays of the zephyr and murmuring Chattahoochee.   The breeze which springs up about noon had died away to a soft zephyr, as if weary of its burden of sweets from the meadows.   And the splendid October sun lingered a moment upon the western hills for a last look upon this loveliest spot in all his dominions, and then, gathering about him his curtains of russet and gold, sank to rest.   They were seated upon the river-bank.

" Do you not like the setting better than the rising sun ? " asked Marian.

" That is as much as to ask me if I like subdued sentiment better than display and triumph."

" To me there always seemed something bizarre about the rising sun ; not only a kind of pompous pride, a haughty insolence, but even a certain amount of vanity, rejoicing in fine speeches and compliments."

" But suppose the sun had consciousness, what a grand life it would live !   Just think ; we have only now witnessed a gorgeous setting : to think that every hour of the twenty-four, and every minute of each hour, repeats the phenomenon.   What a succession of grandeurs !   Or rather what a continued double glory.   Ever rising and ever setting.   If we had been in Japan just now, which God forbid we should have been, we had seen the rising sun."

" Provided we had been up."

"Yes, provided we had been up, which we would have been if ' Elkton ' had been there."

" Or ' Ashton' either? "

" Yes; or any other sensible place. But not being in Japan, but here in America, at ' Elkton' (for which exalted be the name Allah !), we have seen the mellowest sunset I have ever witnessed."

" The rising sun the world flies to meet, and when it gets near enough it falls down and cries, All hail ! The setting sun the world turns its back upon and hurries from."

" Pity to spoil such a pretty sentiment, but this is a scientific age. , The king of day comes rejoicing to fill the earth with warmth, and clothe it in beauty; and so nature welcomes him with music, and scatters flowers before him. But the setting sun deserts the world, leaving it to shiver in the cold and darkness; why should not nature turn its back upon such a monster? "

" Oh, you have not spoilt the sentiment."

" The more disgraceful, then, the attempt."

" The sun does not desert the earth, but the earth the sun; that is, unless you have a new astronomy since I went to school, which indeed you might have, for that was a long time ago."

" What a pity the setting sun cannot express its gratitude to you for your championship! Are there not some inanimate objects that you wish were possessed of consciousness and a language? "

" Yes; this river, for instance, which I love dearly."

" What a pretty story it could tell of its own life and wanderings ! "

" Yes, it rises away up among the mountains. What a little history it has by the time it gets to the sea ! Nacoochee, Indian hunting-grounds, wheat fields of Cherokee, ' Lovers' leap,' cotton plantations, magnolia and orange groves—wouldn't it be pretty? But then the river of yesterday is not the river of to-day. The river we see here now is leaving us—going on to the sea."

"Oh, no. You might as well say that we ourselves are not the same beings we were some years ago, because the bones, muscles, and tissues are continually wearing out, the atoms giving place to new ones."

"I had not thought of it in that way."

"But you asked just now," said Marian, after a moment's silence, "if I did not wish some inanimate objects had feeling, and language to express it. Might they not have a language and ourselves not be able to understand it?"

"Yes, look at the river here. See how gently the little waves rise and fall, and listen to the low rhythmic hum. Certainly there is music—maybe a language. It reminds one of that pleasurable subdued content with which the mind contemplates the conflicts and crises of life which lie back behind, fought and won."

"Just above here is the great gorge where the river had to cut its way through the mountain—that was one of its great conflicts. But some encounter a great many more, and harder obstacles than others."

"So it is with men and women."

"Some are muddy and some clear; but so it is in human character. Let me see. But rivers cannot change their course; many are compelled to lose themselves in wastes and horrible marshes." And her great dark eyes showed that she was curious to know what he would say to this.

"I am not sure but the analogy may go on. The dogma of necessity, in its theological sense, may or may not be true. I rather think we are under the special dominion of geography."

"Do you believe in ' necessity?'"

"Not much since I read Bledsoe's 'Theodicy.' But how do you prove that the will is free?"

"Oh, I don't prove it. But "——

"Well—'as old Dr. Johnson said'"——

"Yes; as old Dr. Johnson said: 'We know our will is free, and there's an end on't.'"

"Ay. You know it because you feel it; but if some one should tell you that he knew just the opposite, and from the same reason?"

"I should not believe it."

"Well, sure enough, there's an end on't."

"But suppose all plants had feeling?"

"The most beautiful, the most highly organized, would have the most delicate feeling."

"Then I should not pluck any more flowers, I could not make any more bouquets."

"I was only supposing a case. Will you make me a bouquet in the morning?"

"Yes; and we will talk about it afterwards—whether it was wrong or no."

"As the French do in their Revolutions, when they try men for their lives."

"I think we had better return, if only to meet Robert before he gets here. See! the stars have been out a long time."

"Why, they are just coming out. I fear the air feels too cold to you."

"No, it does not. But suppose it did, what could you do?"

"I could wish it felt warmer."

"If that would do any good you might wish we had returned half an hour ago."

"Never. I should ask you to stay till the moon is up, if I was not afraid you might take the croup."

" Croup indeed ! Children have croup. I have been out of danger from that many, many years. You would feel shocked if I should tell you how many."

" Not at all. The greater the number the greater the safety. I should only feel glad."

Mirabeau Holmes had no notion of marrying. He did not dream of finding himself in love with any woman. Possibly, to be scrupulously exact, I ought to qualify this by saying that he had certainly dreamed no such dream for some years, up to the evening we have just seen him at the river with Marian Malcomb. Once in his life—but it was like Captain Pinter's story—he had thought of marrying early. Indeed, he had been heard more than once to maintain with much warmth that men ought to marry, ordinarily, at eighteen. Let no one suppose that he had come to this conclusion because he was, or thought he was, in love with Kate Fletcher, a pretty girl in the neighborhood of " Ashton " that he used to " pull candy " with. Kate was some years his senior in years, but he was confident that they should marry on his eighteenth birthday. Not that he was seeking a theory whereby to justify his own intended acts.

But as to this notion of his, that men ought to marry at eighteen, and girls, generally—Kate being the only exception he knew—not more than three years later than the tender age fixed for them by the great Roman lawgiver (in order, said the good Numa, that the Roman citizen might train up to his liking a docile and obedient wife), this notion was honestly come at, and held, as he thought, for the best of good and sufficient reasons. From eighteen to twenty-five, he thought, is the great period of temptation. Very few boys are tempted to ruin before they are eighteen; therefore,
3

if they should marry at that age, the probability is that they would turn out to be industrious men, with temperate habits, comfortable homes, and a plurality of children. Moreover, marriages between youthful persons are almost sure to be happy. Their characters being in the milk, so to speak, easily run into each other and assimilate. But there are cases where, from strong differences of character, if parents are determined quite, it might be advisable to get the matter done with, say, at twelve and fourteen. In this case, failing to assimilate, Pumpkin would still have time, before getting palsied, to arrest the attention of the cook ; and poor Mrs. Pumpkin, after some years of hard but unsuccessful work at assimilating herself to Pumpkin, would still—in a temperate zone—be the possessor of enough lingering charms to justify a feeble hope of eloping with the Methodist preacher. Of course, Mirabeau did not push the argument to the wall this way. " But," he went on, " if men live to be twenty-five without marrying, the probability is that their case is hopeless. They have got themselves into bad habits, drinking, smoking, billiard-playing, what not. Moreover, their plans have probably become unfixed, and their character itself fitful and uncertain. The brain gets crowded with notions, and by the time one is about to be fashioned into practice another pops in, and then another, and another, until he wakes up some fine morning and finds himself a loafer and a vagabond at thirty. Then, seeing that he has passed the age of sentiment, if he marries at all he must make it a matter of convenience—and ten to one it will make itself a matter of inconvenience.

But by and by there came along a certain wheezy Baptist preacher, by the name of Squalls—Rev. John Ebenezer Squalls. People had singings in this country then, and " candy pullings ;" and for that matter I think they have them now.

Rev. Squalls was also a singing-master. His *sol, fa, la* was too much for Kate Fletcher. She sloped with him, and became the mother of his children—counting the eleven by his first spouse, twenty-one in all—and at last accounts the cry was, *Still they come.* All the Squalls children were girls. They had white tow-heads, pinched voices, celestial noses, gander eyes, little hard legs—that is, when they were quite small, I know nothing of them after they were seventeen— little round legs, shiny, long, and of the same size for an indefinite distance—northward. They always wore faded calico frocks, of the bed-curtain variety, the backs being for the most part generally open to conviction. Invariably they outgrew their pantlets the first week. Squalls was said to be an excellent preacher.

But Mirabeau had not thought of these things lately. Probably he could not now tell whether his philosophy had greatly changed or not. Besides, it mattered little to him personally any way, because he was a man with a *purpose.* He had an idea in his head, and was greatly enamoured of it. He had read Carlyle. He had his part to play in life. Behold! even he had a work appointed him to do. He had no time to be thinking of love, marriage, what not. It had never occurred to Mirabeau Holmes that a man of talent and purpose might be so stimulated, encouraged, and aided by a wife worthy of him, as to be able to declare, when he had finished a great undertaking, that whatever was greatest and best in his work, as in himself, he owed to his wife. He had never read Mill's splendid tribute to the memory of his wife. He had a notion, as I have said, that even if his wife should happen to be a woman of real worth, he would still be cramped and fettered. He would not be so free to expose himself to risks—either risks of personal danger, or, which is of much more consequence, risks of poverty. For while he himself might be willing to endure any hardship in the pursuit of a great object; while he might even be willing, like poor Jean Jacques, to sit on a billet of wood, write on a three-legged table, and dine off three onions, if thereby he might only leave some record of the truth; yet, even if the woman he married should not only be willing but glad to share such fortune with him, he could never consent to it on her account. He would sooner renounce his own ambition and devote himself to getting the ordinary comforts of life, hoping, the while, like so many before him, that his son might live to fulfil the destiny of which adverse fate had thwarted him. Then there was the question of children. And while it might be very well for him to burn his last chair and sit on a billet of wood —though why Jean Jacques should burn the chair and sit on the billet of wood, rather than burn the billet of wood and sit on the chair, always has been a mystery to me; but I reckon it was because the chair had three legs broken off and the bottom out—it would not be so well for Miss Holmes to ask her company into a parlor with only a billet of wood for furniture, even though there should be scattered about here and there some manuscript pages of a *Contrat Social*. Better even a cottage piano, a couple of divans, and cane-bottom chairs.

Such were the extreme cases that now occurred to him. As for the ten thousand petty annoyances much more likely to occur in practice, he never thought of them at all. Mirabeau was reasoning about marriage in the abstract, trying not to think of any particular woman at all. He was trying to recall to-night all the philosophy upon this subject he had ever learned. He thought that marriage was a thing that could not well be undone; for even if he had by any possibility ever been willing to think of availing himself of its provisions, he was entirely ignorant of an elegant law they have in the State of Tennessee, to wit: "If any married man, not a citizen of Tennessee, shall wish to remove into said State, and his wife shall treasonably, fraudulently, viciously, and feloniously refuse to cleave unto him and follow him even into said State, then, and in that case, said married man may come, proceed, march, locomote, or otherwise get himself into said State anyhow, and the refusal of the wife to cleave unto him and follow him into said State shall be good and sufficient ground for divorce." This is the standing bid which that noble State offers for immigration; only requiring that the immigrant shall be shrewd enough—and one would think it took precious little shrewdness—to conceal himself for a season among the fastnesses of her mountains and country newspapers.

This was the first night in many that Mirabeau had lain awake thinking of anything but his political projects. But he lay awake a long time to-night. And when he went to sleep his thoughts, like the violet of the spectrum, gliding into the invisible lavender rays, only faded away into dreams of a little brown woman with a pair of great dark eyes, the like of which he had not met with before. But what did the little brown woman with the deep eyes think? There was just a perceptible wish on her part that the morrow, when they would go upon Mount Yonah together, would come on. First thing in the morning, though, Mirabeau was to ride with Robert up the valley towards the headwaters of the river.

CHAPTER V.

" Black eyes you have left, you say;
Blue eyes fail to draw you;
Yet you seem more rapt to-day
Than of old we saw you."

THE next day they went to Mount Yonah. It is the testimony of travellers that the grandest views in the world are to be had from the top of this famous mountain. The views from the high mountains of Europe and the North are generally obstructed by mists or cloud. But from Yonah, which stands like a solemn sentinel at the entrance to Georgia's Egeria, the atmosphere is clear, and soft as the air of Italy. The mountain is of granite, and stands in solitary grandeur, as if scorning the companionship of the baser earth. Over about one-fourth of the horizon you see a vast plain, stretching away across Carolina and a part of Georgia to the Atlantic ocean. Over the remaining three-quarters is a perfect world of mountains. Towards the north the view is grand in the extreme. You may count as many as a score of ranges of mountains, rising one above another, until the last seems to fade away into an unbroken line of cloud. One can imagine with what wonder and awe De Soto and his followers must have witnessed this scene. Every vestige of Nacoochee Town, save a mound here and there, is gone. Nacoochee, queen of the valley, has vanished with her maidens.

" The mountain echoes catch no more the strain
  Of their wild Indian lays at evening's wane:
  No more, where rustling branches intertwine,
  They pluck the jasmine flowers, or break the cane

> Beside the marshy stream, or from the vine
> Shake down, in purple showers, the luscious muscadine."

The El Dorado of the Indian has become the Eden of the white man. But looking beyond the valley, the view is just the same as beheld by the Spaniard near three centuries ago. In all the world of mountains there is not a single evidence of habitation that meets the vision. No spire gleams in the sun above, nor castle or ancient tower peeps from among the giant oaks. There is nothing to remind you that human hearts are throbbing in the thousand valleys below. Nothing can be more impressive than the silence which reigns over these mountains when the shadow of the evening twilight drops suddenly upon the scene.

"I love to come to this mountain," said Marian to Mirabeau, while Robert and Betty Broughton had gone on before to the liberty-pole, planted many years ago on a Fourth of July celebration; "I love to come to this mountain, because it seems so solitary and lonely."

"I wish it would teach me to look so solitary and lonely."

"That would be too bad, unless we had a perpetual leap-year."

"No; for in this case the mountain would be glad to go to Mahomet."

"Well, only wait, say a score or two of years, and you may not need to be taught to look as solitary and lonely as old Yonah."

"That is precisely what I am beginning to fear."

"*Beginning* to fear! Let me see. One takes you to be about the meridian, and just now beginning to fear?"

"Yes; since the last rays of sunset played upon this mountain. One does not fear anything and wish to avoid it until one sees something better."

"What a beautiful lake this must have been before the
waters cut their way through, the mountains yonder."

"Your father says he is thinking of putting a dam across
where the river breaks through, so as to irrigate the whole
valley.   You may then restore the lake at pleasure."

"We should have a little woodland Venice, away over
here among the mountains of Georgia."

They lunched in the bridal chamber of the Indian lovers,
and drank from the spring of pure crystal water that gushes
from a fissure in the granite floor.   They visited the precipice, a thousand feet high, over which the daring Indian
lover was hurled, and from which Nacoochee, breaking from
the arms of her old father, hurled herself after him, into the
gorge beneath.   And then they went upon the mound built
by the broken-hearted father over their grave.   The mound
is now covered with ivy, rhododendrons, and wild-flowers.   A
solitary pine grew from the summit of the mound, and from
its top, during the war, was displayed a Confederate flag.
The pine is now blasted and dead.   It went out with the
Confederacy.

They were driving slowly up the splendid avenue of pines
which leads to Mr. Malcomb's residence, when Marian, taking up a remark of Mirabeau's about the power of the secret
societies, said :

"I heard Robert say you were going to Europe soon."

"Yes ; I am going to found some chapters of our secret
society over there."

"Shall you be gone long ? "

"I hope not longer than five months."

"Then we shall not see you again at Elkton.   But I hope
we shall see you at our house in the city, where we are going
soon.   How long before you go ? "

"In two weeks—if at all."

"Why do you say, if at all?"

"Because you hope to see me at your home in the city."

"I mean when you return."

"Then I shall try to make the five months three."

"Then you will not go to Athens and the East?"

"No; I shall only go to Paris, Berlin, St. Petersburg, and London. I shall not have time to go even to Rome. I do not care especially to go there either. A good many years ago, when I read Lamartine's Pilgrimage, I thought I should wish to go over the same ground with the poet. And I do not say that I should not like greatly to do so now; only there is too much to be done here in our own country. All that such a pilgrimage could do would be to afford myself pleasure. I think it would be wrong to spend months, perhaps years, wandering over the East, gazing and wondering at the ancient ruins, simply for one's own gratification."

"But why need you gaze and wonder, as you say, simply for your own gratification?"

"What else should I do?"

"Write a book."

"Nobody would read it."

"I would."

"You would read it out of sympathy, because nobody else read it."

"What impudence! You think I like you already better than I should like your book?"

"I shall be very miserable if you don't like me better than any book written upon this subject ought to be liked. But I am going to write a book when I get back that I hope you will like, not better than its author, though."

"I don't promise, because it might be a very good book."

"I shall make it as poor as can be."

"If you do, it will give me a poor opinion of the author."

"How shall I make it?"

"As you like it. But what is to be the name of it?"

"'Jefferson Davis and His Friends.'"

"An historical novel. That is a magnificent subject. Are you not afraid somebody will steal the subject from you."

"Yes; I shall begin it as soon as I get back."

"I am impatient to read it."

"I will begin it to-night."

"Are you two ever going to get to the gate?" said Robert, who had been to carry Betty Broughton home, and came up at this moment.

This was Mirabeau's last night at "Elkton." His thoughts had become sadly deranged and perplexed since he came here only a few days ago. And the disturbing element was, of course, Marian Malcomb. As we have seen, he had no notion of finding himself in love. If he ever married at all, it must be several, nay, it must be, probably, many years hence. He was young, poor, and ambitious. He was bent on making a name for himself that the world should learn to pronounce. He believed in the maxim that "A man can do whatever he wills to do." And he often thought of what the "old doctor" said to him one day: "Make yourself, my son, indispensable to the world; and the world will find you, and honor you too." Afterwards, when he had made his name and fortune, it might do to think about getting a wife; but not now.

Still, even in thinking negatively of the subject, Mirabeau Holmes had almost unconsciously set up in his mind an image of the woman he thought he could love, and even worship, if some time in the distant future he should come up with her. But how were the stars that presided over his destiny to know whitherward to guide him? How were they

to know that he had made up his mind never to come across
this ideal woman before he was thirty-five, or perhaps forty ?
But they knew that Marian Malcomb was at " Elkton ; " for
many a time they had danced in at her vine-latticed window ;
or struggled through the high overarching branches to fro-
lic in her loosened hair as she walked in the great avenue of
pines. And they knew that this was the very woman. And
lo ! Mirabeau believed as much himself. The ideal was em-
bodied before him. The vision had become a living, moving
reality. He said to himself, this is the woman I would have
chosen if I had intended to marry ; this is the woman that
would thoroughly sympathize with me, and I with her ; this
is the woman that I could love, even worship. And when
a man has said this much, it is observed, his remaining single
will usually depend upon her resolution rather than his.

But then a new idea occurred to Mirabeau this last night
of his at " Elkton : " his poverty. He could not take a wife
even if he would. But the woman—Mirabeau had already
learned to use the word woman often, as preferable to *lady*,
which latter always reminded him of copper-plate pictures in
old magazines—who had called forth these reflections, and
who was at this very moment viewing the same subject from
quite a different angle, was, fortunately for herself maybe, maybe unfortunately for this Mirabeau, wealthy. But
whether this circumstance of poverty on one side, and wealth
on the other, was fortunate or unfortunate for one or for
both of these two people, whose lives inevitable fate had
now brought within the sphere of mutual effect, where each
should exert an influence over the other for good or for ill,
is a matter purely of opinion, on which I shall leave the
reader to form, after reading their history, his own conclu-
sions. But whatever the reader may think, it was all settled
with this Mirabeau. He closed his eyes to go to sleep ; he

saw clearly—maybe he only thought he saw clearly—the end
of the whole business. He had not thought of this subject
for a long time; he would not think of it again. And if
there was a perceptible tinge of regret in this last thought,
it only shows that this man was getting upon exceedingly dangerous ground. It indicated a conflict between feeling and
purpose. Who can tell where it will end? Manifestly, the
man was not out of danger here. For then he thought
again, Am I to go to work to make a fortune for this special
purpose? By that time the best part of my life may be
gone. Besides,—and he was surprised, even indignant, at
himself,—this would thwart the whole scheme of my life.
If we could just reverse things—and here he turned himself
over in bed, as if to give fortune some feeble notion of how
easy a matter it was to reverse things. One thing is settled:
I will leave this place in the morning, and hereafter keep
clear of it.

Meanwhile Marian Malcomb, too, was spinning away from
her own consciousness upon the web of the future. Mirabeau Holmes was one of the very few men whose University
reputation had extended over the whole State. In fact he
was well known as a young man of the finest abilities, and a
brilliant future was already predicted for him. And women
are observed to have a rare intuitive, perceptive power, especially in matters of love. It would have been curious to
observe the thoughts of these two that night as they went
scampering forth out of their windows, each troup invisible
to the other, to be jotted down on opposite pages by Destiny,
standing by. It reminds one of a game they have, called
Vexation, in which one writes a question or a sentiment on a
slip of paper, and another, without seeing what is written,
writes an answer on the opposite side; while still a third
reads them both.

"Now that you have seen him, what do you think of Holmes?" said Robert Malcomb to his sister the afternoon after Mirabeau left "Elkton." Now, if Marian Malcomb had been the "average young lady," she would, beyond all doubt, have made one of these two answers: "Oh, I'm sure I don't know; I haven't thought of him at all. I guess he is like other young men—a little more vain, perhaps;" or, "He's nice! Do you know, I think he has an air quite *distingué*." But, not to complicate matters, seeing that it was just as it was, and could not have been any other way, that Marian Malcomb was just herself, and could not have been any other girl, even if it had been desirable, which it was not, it may be well enough to let her answer for herself, touching a matter, of which however ignorant she might be at the time, was likely not to be without an influence upon her own life.

"I rather like him, I believe; or maybe it would be better to say, he interests me."

"Why does he interest you? You know you often ask me for the reasons of things."

"But I don't know that I am as clear as I expect you to be. I suppose it is because he talks upon interesting subjects, and has his own way of looking at things."

"Just so. He saw you were better than most women, flattered you accordingly, and you give him credit for it. He talked about art and metaphysics; but he never talks about much else to people he cares for, unless he gets off upon his political hobby."

"Then he was not so complimentary. He said very little about books; I wish he had said more. He reminds me of one of those men that the 'old doctor' used to tell you all were the most interesting: you are certain they keep back a great deal more than they tell. Mr. Holmes talks about things of interest, such as I would talk to you about."

"Himself, for example ? That is what you are talking to me about now."

"I am not talking to you; you are talking to me. I am only answering your questions."

"Well, Holmes *is* an interesting fellow. But I fear—mind you, I am not certain—that he appears much more so than he really deserves, because he has a way of putting things."

"What is he going to do ? "

"That's the question. His course is more difficult to calculate than was that of a comet to our forefathers. For they might calculate with certainty that the comet would not go outside of the universe; but I should not say so much of Mirabeau Holmes. In college he had stronger friends and bitterer enemies than any man there. He never would be neutral. He was sure to be the leader of his party. Some thought him a genius; others thought, or pretended to think, him a vagarist. Still, while he embraced 'an idea' with ardor, he treated people with cold reserve. When asked by his friends why he did not cultivate the acquaintance of such a man, he would say: 'I have not the slightest notion he has anything to say I want to hear;' or, 'What does he know that will be worth my while to be bored two hours to hear ? ' As for what he intends to do, that is as uncertain now as then. Once, I think, he intended to be a philosopher: he read everything from Plato down. Then he thought of studying law, but the 'old doctor,' who knew him better than anybody else, advised him so strongly against it that he gave it up. The 'old doctor' looks to his future with much interest, and, I think, has great hopes of him. Just now he is entirely carried away with this political hobby of his. I

have not a doubt but he firmly believes in the resurrection
of the Confederacy, and himself expects some day to be
president of it. But if Jeff' Davis was living, and was not
made first president, he would not consider it more than
half a triumph. But there is no telling what he will think
when he gets back from Europe. He despises the very word
' consistency.' He would not surprise me by going off after
woman's rights, socialism, and even atheism. Did he tell
you about that wild scheme of his for making-cotton king,
and bankrupting the government ? "

" No ; what is it ? "

" Why, he wants all the cotton planters to enter into a
great corporation. They are to have a bank, and issue bills of
credit. They are to build warehouses at the great southern
seaports, in which the cotton is to be stored until the foreign
vessels come after it, and pay the price in gold fixed by the
authorities of the corporation. The Agricultural Congress
meets and fixes the price of the several grades of cotton
beforehand. The planter sends a bale of cotton to one of the
warehouses ; they receive it, grade it, and send him the
money for it—one of their bank-bills, payable in gold at the
bank. The English merchant comes, buys a cargo of cotton,
and pays the gold for it, which is sent to the vaults of the
bank. He says he could stop all the spindles in New England, and bankrupt the Government in two years."

" That is a very large scheme."

" Yes ; and as wild as it is large."

Robert Malcomb, like his father, was cool, calculating, and
clear-headed. He was a good worker ; patient, energetic,
but not likely to waste his energies. He was a man of purpose, too, and he had a clear perception of what it was. He
had calculated the distance of the object to be attained, and
knew the number of horse-power necessary to remove the

obstacles and carry him to it. He divided lawyers into petti-foggers, common, good, fine, and great. His purpose was to be a great lawyer. He looked upon the profession itself as the greatest of all professions. He regarded it as the guardian of the liberties bequeathed to us by our fathers—the great " conservative " power in the state. It had not occurred to him how little there was in the " institutions of the fathers " at all worth " conserving." He was a man of purpose; but there was nothing vague and indefinite about his purpose, as about that of Mirabeau Holmes. It does not follow, though, that he was more likely to accomplish great things; far from it. He was much more sure to succeed; but what great thing was there within the limits he had set? What does the great-est lawyer, only a lawyer when he dies, leave to humanity? Nothing.

But as for this Mirabeau, ten to one the man would make a miserable failure at all points; get himself into the State prison perhaps, or maybe die in the poorhouse. But then there was the one other chance, and it was worth much more than many smaller certainties. He would do something great, or fail completely and miserably. I think there was small danger of this man getting himself mixed up with Sophie De Ruffeys, absolutely none of your Beatrices and Lauras. No danger here for him. But it was not impossible that he should some day, somewhere, write a *Contrat Social* or stir up a revolution. He had about a ton of explosive radicalism in him. There was also a question of castles of Ham, conciergeries, guillotines, patent improved drops, and what not, strangely mixed up with arches, columns, mauso-leums, even Pantheons. You might catch the outlines of these looming up darkly, and scowling at you from among the restless shadows of this man's horoscope.

Robert Malcomb, clear-headed as he was, had not seen thus

far into Mirabeau's character. He hoped that he might settle down to some profession and become eminent in it. Or
failing in this, that he might turn out to be a sort of Sir
James Mackintosh, a man fitful and uncertain, able to dazzle
but not to illumine; a man of large capacity but small ability;
of much learning and brilliant parts, but of so many notions
that they interfered with and neutralized the force of each
other. Robert's private opinion was that he ought to marry.
He thought that would, so to speak, exert a certain cooling
influence upon him. But he would not have liked very well
for the second person in this transaction to be very near to
him. For he was not quite sure but what Mirabeau would
be capable of quitting his wife without a moment's notice,
either for the cloister, the Oneida community, or the State of
Tennessee, which latter offers a standing reward to all discontented husbands.

"Well met," said Fred Van Comer, as he shook the hand
of Mirabeau Holmes at the Kimball, in Atlanta, the day after
the latter left Elkton; "I was just wishing I could see you.
You must come here to live."

"Why must I come here?"

"Because everybody else is coming. Clarence Hall is here,
and Bramlette, and Van Epps, and Otis Jones, and Burgess
Smith—oh my! everybody is already here but you."

"I intend to come when I get back from Europe."

"Do you? We must go in and drink a cocktail on that;
and I will even let you beat me a game of ivory."

They played the game, and were sitting comfortably puffing
their cigars, when Mirabeau said:

"Fred, what do you think of marriage?"

"I think it is the chief end of life."

"Explain."

"Explain! Now, by the rood, Master Slender, you are

dull. You must be in love. Marriage is the chief end of life because it is the point where most lives chiefly end."

"Well, I grant you, according to our notions of marriage, it ought to lessen the *number* of lives by half; seeing that two lives are made one."

"Oh, in that sense, if we only had a few Solomons now, getting nine hundred into one in no time, the population of the globe would soon be reduced to unity."

"Well, Pascal says that 'plurality which does not reduce itself to unity is confusion.'"

"In that case I suppose Brigham Young, though only a feeble imitator of the illustrious king of the chosen people, is a benefactor of the human race."

"I was serious."

"Were you? It was not I that said Solomon got nine hundred into one. I rather think he got one into nine hundred—if there was any blending of lives at all. But you are serious; so will I be, too. Answer me this, then: Why is marriage like Signor Launce's sweetheart?"

"Because it 'hath many nameless virtues.'"

"Indeed, you are stuck in love; you make poetic answers. Now listen to me. Marriage is like Launce's milkmaid, because it hath more qualities than a water-spaniel, 'which is much in a bare Christian.' Now, why is it unlike the milkmaid?"

"Because the milkmaid was not to be kissed; and the married maid is to be kissed."

"Good. But an institution with so many qualities hath more reasons than one. Look you, here are two more. They are not alike because the milkmaid's vices followed close at the heels of her virtues, while in marriage the virtues follow close at the heels of the vices, where they are in continual danger of being trod on. Again, the milkmaid had no teeth; but I can tell you marriage hath teeth; and, for that matter, nails too; and, for that matter, sometimes a full head of hair too—in the beginning; and "——

"Stop there; I'll not have anything to do with it."

Mirabeau had not been away from "Elkton" two days before he repented of his resolution "to keep clear of that place hereafter." In less than two weeks he was there again, fully determined to declare his love to Marian, whatever might happen in the future. And this resolution he carried out in the most calm and deliberate manner—a manner which he had for some time been trying to school himself into. He simply declared his love to her, and his intention to ask her to marry him when she knew him better. And thus he committed a grievous mistake. This was the second time he had ever seen Marian Malcomb; and yet here he was declaring to her a deliberate intention to court her some time in the future! That will not do for this country. For here, as in England, before one marries, it is necessary, as M. Taine says, "to feel a passion." Marian Malcomb had already begun to like this man; but now, she was not at all certain that he was not a heartless hypocrite. Possibly he had sat in his office and cast his eye deliberately about among the women he considered worthy of his notice, and after weighing many in the balance had concluded that she was the best match he knew, and had come straight to her, without having seen her before, predetermined to declare his love and ask her to marry him. Her higher feelings were outraged, and she was dissatisfied with herself not only for allowing herself to be deceived in her estimate of his character, but because she was conscious of already liking him better than any man she knew. And here she placed a very dangerous barrier between herself and him. See what it is a woman must do, after this, before the man can hope to be successful in his suit: she must confess to herself not only that she has deceived herself in a matter of judgment, but that she has greatly wronged another, and that other the very last man she ought to have wronged, namely, the man that loved her. It needs no very great knowledge of the human mind, I think, to appreciate how difficult a matter it is for a woman to do this. Moreover, a woman, coming to this conclusion, deals most unjustly with herself; for being already decided to be distrustful, she sees through a false medium, and may even degrade the highest expression of sentiment into acting able to be detected by a girl of eighteen.

With Mirabeau Holmes the case was this: he did not feel that Marian Malcomb was a stranger to him. He simply transferred his acquaintance from the ideal he had set up in his own mind to the reality before him. And so, instead of regarding her as a woman whom he had met only yesterday, he saw in her the woman he had loved, but hardly thought to find. We are all observed to carry about with us a large amount of disposable passion; and when this passion happens to be in an ozonic state its possessor is apt to fall down and worship the first object which his fancy can fashion into an idol. But as for Mirabeau, while he had a great amount of love and worship to bestow upon some woman, he had a clear perception of his ideal, and was so enamoured of it that he would have regarded himself as no better than a heathen and an infidel if he had thought it possible for him to bestow it upon any other than the embodiment of this same ideal. Altogether, courtship between these two persons, for the future, had become needlessly complicated, and for Mirabeau the case was manifestly dangerous.

Mirabeau returned to the city the night before he was to leave for Europe. James Arnot, surrounded by some two dozen officers, on the second floor of an old brick building in the western portion of the city, was listening to some reports.

If Mirabeau had only heard some of these reports, he would have deferred his trip to Europe. I think many a swamp and forest would have stood aghast at the recital of deeds which had been enacted in their very midst. But when Mirabeau entered, the meeting was at once adjourned, and these two walked to the Kimball together, but they did not walk arm in arm. It was late that night when they retired. Mirabeau, who was much interested in his companion, proposed that they should occupy the same room; but Arnot was confused, blushed, and made some excuse. They bade each other good-bye that night.

"Some years ago," said Arnot, "I travelled over portions of Europe myself; and I almost wish it was so now that I could be your companion." This was said in a tone so low, and so full of sadness, with just a shade of mockery, that Mirabeau was startled. He looked quickly and searchingly into Arnot's face, and saw the same blush that he had noticed some moments before. He afterwards remembered that tone so full of sadness and self-mockery. In a moment Arnot's face had resumed its frozen stillness.

Mirabeau did not start to Europe next morning. He had not left his room when he was brought a telegram summoning him to his home at "Ashton."

Book 2.

DAUGHTER AND SON.

———◆———

CHAPTER VI.

"The night shall be filled with music,
  And the cares that infest the day
  Shall fold up their tents like the Arabs,
  And silently steal away.

"Forgive me, my child! Reproach not thy unhappy father, whose fondest hopes have proved visionary."

—SCHILLER, *The Robbers.*

IF the reader is of an inquiring turn of mind, which surely I have no reason to doubt, except the very general one that this Republic, counting all, without distinction of race, color, previous or present condition of servitude—previous condition of servitude referring to such Africans and mongrels as the general march of events, slightly aided by Lincoln's Proclamation, set free, and present condition of servitude referring to the female half of the American people, also soon destined to be set free by the general march of events, somewhat hastened, I hope, by Henry Wilson and others—has six millions of inhabitants who can neither read nor write, and thirty odd millions more who are but little better off, he will doubtless inquire why I have written the title of this book " Daughter and Son," instead of " Son and

Daughter." Surely the latter is the orthodox arrangement. I defy any man—except, indeed, one profoundly versed in typology, with whom all things are possible—to point to a single place where it is ever hinted that Abraham, Isaac, Jacob—who cheated his brother out of his birthright in order to be made head of the chosen people—or any patriarch or prophet whatever, ever " begat daughters and sons." They " begat sons and daughters—sons and daughters begat they them." And this is what proves the humanity of that race, that they invariably " begat sons and daughters," just like other people. But I think we shall not find even in profane history any precedent whatever to warrant the conferring of such distinction upon women as giving more prominence to the daughter than to the son. It is almost as bad as if one had said " wife and husband." Doubtless the whole race of forked radishes with breeches on will feel highly indignant. Manifestly the publisher of this book, if he love himself, had best look to his ears. For is it not written that man is the " head of the woman "? And is it not plainly declared in the law-books, with pains and penalties duly announced, that " the woman shall be subject to the man "? Clearly there must be some reason for this kind of proceeding, right in the face, as it were, of the law and gospel. But however it may have been among the patriarchs, or among the Greeks, where, we are casually informed by the historian, " women were regarded simply as furniture ; " or among the Romans, where they were so clearly reckoned as personal property that the use and possession of them for one year gave the possessor a good title to them ; in this book it may be that the daughter is to play a more important part than the son. But however that may be, it is not important that I should give any reason but this, that the last shall be first, and the first last.

There was a ball at Mrs. Walton's. Stop a moment, dear reader. Do not skip ten pages just here. I am not going to treat you to a description of "a girl's first ball." All balls are some girl's "first ball." I doubt not you have read many descriptions of "a girl's first ball." They are all alike. If you have nothing else to do for half an hour but to read a description of a ball, pray go into the garden and hoe a couple of rows of potatoes or cabbages. Or, if you have absolutely nothing to do, why then, though few things could be more unprofitable, just close the book, ditto your eyes, and reflect for a few moments upon the mutability of all human affairs—except "a girl's first ball." Technically speaking, this was not "a girl's first ball;" it was a ball given young George Walton on the eve of his departure for a foreign university. George Walton was the youngest child of Mr. Walton. Mrs. Walton was, in terms of the statute, the mother of him. In him had already happened that oft-repeated phenomenon, the centering of a father's hopes. Not that Mr. Walton had no other children; he had three others, two sons and a daughter. The oldest son was living, and was here to-night; the other son was dead; and the daughter was also—dead. Mr. Walton's hopes now rested in his youngest child, George, a youth of some nineteen years, of great promise and expectations. Mr. Walton, like many men before him and after him, had set out in life with an ambition to do great things. And he had been more successful than most men in this, that he had learned earlier than most men to accept the inevitable. He remembered the Spanish proverb, "Since we cannot get what we like, we must try to like what we can get." His ambition was not lost, but only transferred. He could make money; and he determined to make more than anybody else. His ambition for fame he had hoped to see realized in his oldest son. Any one who

4

chooses, provided he has some little knowledge of human nature, may learn from the census reports of that year that there was something over a million of parents in this Republic who comforted themselves with similar hopes. But even here Mr. Walton again saw that he was disappointed. It is said that hope springs eternal in the human breast. Like most sayings with which Humanity has either flattered or comforted itself, this also is false. There are many men, and women too, and you may meet some of them on the street, in whom, if you could ever achieve that utter impossibility of knowing their inmost being, the springs of hope are long since dried up ; from which even the tears that were wept in their places are gone, leaving nothing but a hardened crust of bitter and salt. But it was not yet quite so with this man. His oldest son, Alf, had turned out badly. Of good mind, good looks, not without ambition, and having all the advantages of wealth, it seemed not unreasonable to indulge the highest hopes of his future. He was sent to a German university, and then travelled extensively. All of which, to be sure, was a magnificent preparation for the part already assigned him in the programme of Destiny—that he should be an accomplished gambler and debauchee. Mr. Walton had given up all hope of him long since. His next son was dead. His only daughter—who ever expected anything of a daughter ?—was also dead, or sunk out of sight.

Mr. Walton was not happy to-night. Once during the evening, as he walked down the great hall alone, he chanced to meet his wife coming from her own room. He saw in an instant that she had been weeping, and he knew that at that moment they were thinking of the same thing. Neither dared to speak to the other. She returned to the saloon. He passed on, out of the door, out of the gate, and on, he knew not whither. Mr. Walton was thinking of another scene. It

was in a distant State; but what mattered that? It was years
ago; but what mattered that? What mattered it whether
it was yesterday or an eternity ago? It was there, in himself. It was a scene on one of those pretty little woodland lakes, children of the great Mississippi, which seem to
have rambled too far in their chase after the butterflies among
the flowers, and got hemmed and caught among the hills.
There was a ball upon the lake that night. A great gondola
rested in the centre, and numbers of tiny shell-shaped boats
glided hither and thither, or rested under the shade of the
great forest trees that threw their shadows far out upon the
silvery waters. The dance went on, and the soft strains of
music rose and floated away in the moonlight. Mr. Walton
sat down in the shade of a great oak. It was on such a night
as this; and now he remembered that this was the anniversary of the very night. He bent his head upon his knees.
The sad night-wind moaned as the spirit of the music, and he
fell into a stupor such as sometimes comes over us when, in
the presence of a great past sorrow, we feel an utter, despair-
ing helplessness.

Then there came and stood before him three figures : one,
a beautiful woman, her long black hair falling loosely to her
waist, and a star upon her forehead—his own daughter; another, a young man, almost a boy, tall and slender—his silk-
en-haired Raffaelle; and then a dark-faced foreigner, that
gazed steadily upon him with a look so burning that he involuntarily shaded his eyes with his hand. The group came
towards him; and the beautiful girl seemed to kneel before
him and take his hand; he withdrew it, and motioned them
away. The scene changed, and he saw dragged from a river
and laid upon the bank the inanimate form of a woman.
A baby was clasped in her arms, bound to her bosom with
ribbons and plaits of hair. Her rich, black tresses were

fallen upon the ground, and the dripping water ran down the bank in small streams to the river. From her neck was taken a small, curiously-wrought locket, in which was found crumpled up a tiny note. The words seemed to burn into his brain: "Alone, alone. Alone in this great city, in the wide world. God himself has forsaken me. I have no friend but my misery; that alone has remained with me and my child. Without friends—without money—without bread. My God! Can it be wrong to die when I can do nothing else? For the sake of my child, my sweet, innocent child, last night I tried to beg. They said she was a rich, Christian woman. She made the servants drive me away. What I am about to do, for myself, is no crime; but my child—God forgive me! I cannot leave it in the world without a friend—I cannot go into another world without taking it with me—I would be alone there. Father in heaven, if it be a crime that I am now going to commit, let the suffering of myself and my innocent child plead with Thee for forgiveness. Of you, my father and mother, I ask forgiveness for all the trouble I have given you; and I thank my God that you are ignorant of the depths of your child's suffering. To that other, if he still lives, I would that the sweet night-wind might bear him my message—that I love him to-night as when he pressed the first kiss of love upon my forehead. One more prayer: as to-night my little Alberta shall go to sleep in my arms, so may we both awake in the morning."

The scene changed again, and he saw the dark-faced foreigner and another, in a wildwood, standing face to face, a few paces apart. He heard the words, "ready," "one," "two," "fire," and two sharp reports, almost simultaneous, rang upon the air. The dark man stood still; from the breast of the other he saw a little whiff of smoke curl slowly upward, and as the man fell forward, recognizing his own son, he attempted

to rush forward with a cry, and the cry awoke him. Mr.
Walton looked around to see if anybody was near. One man
was passing by at a little distance; it was James Arnot. Mr.
Walton had been dreaming a dream that was not all a dream.
He looked at his watch; he had not been here long. When
he returned to the house, he passed a couple of young men
walking in the yard smoking, and heard snatches of their conversation.

"Rich! No name for it. They say he's worth over a
million."

"And no children but boys. If the old cit just had a gal
now, some happy nob might make his jack there."

"But they say he did have a gal; a stunner—like that
hell-bound brother in the house. Got topped though by some
black-eyed foreigner—Italian, I believe—had a baby, run
away, and got to be—what the deuce is it the French say?"

"Fille de joie?"

"No; not that."

"Nymph du pavé?"

"That's it—nymph du pavé. No wonder she got to be a
nymph du pavé, if she was any kin to that child of Satan in the
house there. By the way, they say he's engaged to Ella Leit-
ner. What per cent. would you insure her for, for six months?"

"Not under a hundred, if that's true, with commissions
extra. I reckon it's not true, though. I don't see how a
respectable woman could like Alf Walton."

"The deuce you don't! You know none of us stand any
show with him at all. What if he has brought about a ton of
them to a melancholy end, as the parson says; that's just
what they like. I move we take a few lessons from him.
He'll give 'em if we let him win a score or two of williams."

What principally struck you on entering the saloon was
this, that here was a Democratic ball of the first water. Here

were numerous young men, and not a few old ones, and probably not three in the room who did not *do* something for a
living.   Here were clerks, young merchants, lawyers, doctors,
newspaper reporters, editors, politicians, and even two or
three "nobs."   There was no exclusiveness.   Not that Mr.
and Mrs. Walton deserve any particular credit for it; for
this was the rule in this Democratic city.   'This was a new
city/without landmarks, and made up of all kinds of people
—all kinds of good people, like the people under tombstones.
Even the streets here were Democratic.   You could never tell
from the direction they started in whither they were going, or
where they might end; they went in all directions except
right lines.   But let us enter the saloon.   Here are some
people we must know.   There on the right, in a group of
half a dozen, is Bramlette, a poet; and that superb, brown-
eyed woman is Mrs. Sutherland, known in these parts as a
magazine writer of some repute, but better as a charming
amateur composer and performer of music, and best as leader
of fashion and queen of society.   One should not describe
the dress of a beautiful woman ; it looks like sacrilege.   Therefore all women ought to be well dressed; what an amount of
sacrilege it would save !   And men ought, if possible, to be
well dressed too.   There, for instance, is poor Bramlette,
with a dozen of the largest-sized rice-buttons in his shirt-
front, and pants a foot too short.   Everything is political in
this country.   Bramlette's pants were political;   the knees
were radical, and the bottom of the legs conservative ; that
is to say, the knees pushed forward energetically, and the
bottoms hung back doggedly, giving to the legs a curve not.
mentioned by Hogarth.   There, sitting apart, is Clarence
Hall, a fair-haired young man of twenty-eight or thirty, a
University man, hazel-eyed.   The young lady he is talking to
is Annie Dearing, of ruddy face and dark eyebrows, daughter

of an old-time aristocrat, thought to be wealthy, and known to be pretty. Mr. Hall seems as much alone with the lady he is talking to as if they were in Mrs. Dearing's parlor, with the rich, dark curtains down, at that delightful hour when, the rosy twilight gradually deepening into violet, a richly furnished parlor has an air of repose not to be enjoyed elsewhere or at any other hour. There in the dance is one we have met before, Fred Van Comer, who dances and laughs like a boy; a small man, slightly built, with a great head—the top being much too large for the lower portion—thick, curly, blonde hair, and steel-gray eyes.

The message Mirabeau Holmes received from "Ashton" called him to the death-bed of his mother. When one witnesses the last scene in the life of a beautiful, religious woman, sees her conscious to the last, dispensing a parting blessing and bidding a kindly adieu to friends, calm in the ineffable hope of immortality, divinely trustful of meeting in the future life loved ones gone before and to come after, one sees that Death may not only be disrobed of his terrors but even clad in habiliments of beauty. Such a death was that of Mrs. Holmes. And now, on this night of the ball at Mr. Walton's, she had been sleeping for some weeks quietly at "Olivet." Mirabeau had loved his mother with a love that elevated itself to fervor. But it was only of late that he had learned how much she had done for him; how she had entirely forgotten herself and looked only to him; how, in order that he might have means to continue his studies, she had worked and even endured the pinch of poverty without letting him know—for he would have on no account submitted to it if he had known it. And when he did know, he fervently hoped that she might live to see the day when he could lay at her feet a wealth of fame. But with her the haven was gained, and the vessel's voyage over. On the very day she died she said to him,

" My son, you will show your love to me by not giving way
to sorrow. Remember, I bid you, when you leave me at
' Olivet,' think not of the past, but look only to the future;
from that moment go forward to do and to win. I have
never for a moment doubted that you would be great and
good; and, God willing, I shall still be with you to protect
you with my prayers and love, and to rejoice over all that is
good and great in your future." It took Mirabeau but a short
while to arrange his business after his mother's death, and
leaving " Ashton " in charge of his mother's man of business,
he was soon in the city again, where he determined to make
his future home. He must defer his trip to Europe, as it
was necessary he should be at " Ashton" in the winter. But
learning that George Walton was going, he transferred his
commissions to him, promising to be with him in the spring.

That night, after the ball, Bramlette went to Fred Van
Comer's room. Mirabeau was already there. Fred got there
before Bramlette.

" I wish Bramlette would wear better clothes," said Fred.

" Are not his clothes good enough ? "

" No; they are bad at all points. I mean to give him a
slight hint when he comes here. He said he would come
directly; but talk of a man with breeches a foot too short—
Comment allez-vous, Monsieur Bram*lette*. Look in that box
there, and get a mild cigar, and light it, and sit down, and
improvise us some poetry."

" An ode to your cigar; it will crown you with wreaths
of smoke," said Mirabeau.

" We will weave you a triple crown," said Fred.

" Will not some one throw in some flowers ? What say
you, Fred, to that bunch of geraniums ? " said Bramlette.

" Capital," said Mirabeau. " Maybe we should then have
two poems—an ode from you and a wail from Fred."

"Wail, indeed! I should not survive to write mine epitaph—I should not live to see whether I was dead or no. These flowers! I would not give them to crown Corinna herself with! I would not contribute them to the corner-stone of St. Peter's! Know, O miserable man, that they were given mo by Marian Malcomb," said Fred.

"Marian Malcomb!" involuntarily exclaimed Mirabeau.

"Ah! whitherward listeth the breeze now?" said Bramlette.

"Humph," said Fred; "this thing is getting complicated. I move we resolve ourselves into a committee of the whole on poetry, and sing by turns."

"If we proceed now," said Mirabeau, "both of you will have the advantage of me; for see there, Bramlette has flowers too."

"Good! You play critic then—sing us a Dunciad," said Fred.

"Only a small bachelor-button I have," said Bramlette.

"Who gave it to you?"

"Mrs. Sutherland."

"Oh!"

"Ah!"

"Why not put it on your shirt-bosom?" asked Mirabeau.

"I think he has plenty of them there now," said Fred. "Valley of Jehoshaphat! Bramlette, what do you want with fifteen buttons of that size in your bosom? Do you propose to keep the women out, as it were?"

"Maybe he only means to keep his own heart in," suggested Mirabeau.

"It will go down through his breeches' legs," said Fred.

"Mercy!" cried Bramlette, "or you will send my wits after it."

"Never overtake it—the legs are too short," said Fred.

" What else did Mrs. Sutherland give you ? " asked Bramlette.

" A piece of advice—to let everything else go, and write poetry," said Bramlette.

" She deserves no credit for that," said Fred, " except for agreeing with me.   I had just said it to her."

" Let me do myself the credit to agree with both of you," said Mirabeau.

" But what did she say to you, Fred ?   I saw you talking," asked Bramlette.

" She said if she was queen of some favored region—as if any region would not be a favored region that she was queen of—all the people should go elegantly dressed," said Fred, returning to his gentle hint.

" To say nothing of political economy," said Mirabeau, " looking at the matter from an art stand-point, I think it would require even a longer time to train her people for this promised land than Moses required for the training of Fred's ancestors."

" Yes," said Fred, " even though she should occasionally resort to a trifling miracle."

" What do you mean by a ' trifling miracle,' Fred ? " asked Bramlette."

" Oh, no harm, no irreverence," said Fred. " A trifling miracle is not a miracle like what my old ancestors used to work, with the utmost comfort and despatch—such as stopping the sun, moon, and all the planets, in their circuits around the earth ; or even the crossing of the Red Sea, which, you remember, was miraculously allowed to be repeated by Napoleon and his staff, some three or four thousand years afterwards, lest in so long a time there might have grown up some doubt about the possibility of performing such a feat," said Fred.

"That is what you do not mean by a 'trifling miracle'; but tell us what you do mean?" said Mirabeau.

"Oh, Babylon! A Scotch miracle, a Scotch miracle," said Fred; "only a Scotch miracle; such as John Knox and the other Presbyterian preachers used to work—raising the dead, for example, which seems to have been rather common among the most eminent divines. But speaking of Presbyterian preachers, I wonder where Mr. Brooke was to-night?"

"I reckon he was at Mrs. Harlan's; I saw him there when I passed," said Bramlette. And then he explained to Mirabeau that Mr. Brooke was pastor of the Presbyterian charge of which Mr. Walton was an eminent member. Mr. Brooke was much thought of in the city, not only as a learned and eloquent preacher, but as an accomplished member of society.

Mrs. Sutherland was a woman deserving more than a passing notice. A little more than half a score of years ago, you might have seen her a tall, graceful, brown-eyed girl of seventeen. Even then she had probably felt more of what it is to be alive in the world than most women ever have cause or power to feel at all. She was then an orphan. Her father was one of the old-time aristocrats—a rare specimen. There was, in truth, but one Warren Mason. His great weakness was vanity of hereditary rank. He was proud, exclusive, narrow-minded, imperious, reckless. Undoubtedly of great personal honor, still his weakness was stronger than his honor. He would close his doors to intellect, talent, genius, unless accompanied, as is seldom the case, by certain stars, quarterings, azures, gules, and other trumperies of heraldry. He plunged recklessly into debt, without the least thought of how he was to get out. Mrs. Mason was a noble, true woman; but she had been taught in the old school—not actively to keep trouble off, but to help her husband to endure it when it came. As was sure to be the case, the time came when the magnificent estate of Warren Mason was sold under the sheriff's hammer. Then came family troubles, tragedy, a part of that world of tragedy which is enacting daily around us, but concealed from the world, through all of which the noble devotion of the wife and mother shone with a celestial power and pathos. Mr. Mason soon died. His wife followed him. It is not to be supposed that one of so deep and sympathetic a nature as the daughter, Margaret, passed through all this without being deeply impressed. This experience of her early life gave coloring to her future. It was necessary that this woman should live; and that she should be what she was, this, and no other, training was necessary. Thus it is that the universal law is ever compensatory; also looking ever to Humanity, and never to the individual; caring not whether the individual be great or small, happy or miserable, but ever glorifying Humanity, and looking onward to the time when the happiness of the whole shall secure the happiness of every one. Let no one say I am making too much of the early life of this woman. Consider the future; and let no one say this shall lead to great things, that to small, and this other to none at all. For verily, with our poor understanding of it, this is a wonderful world we have all somehow been got into; and I for one, on this rainy morning in July, an east wind blowing the while, am right truly glad that among "the more than billion of human players now playing each his allotted part in this wonderful play, coming in and going out, waking and sleeping, eating, drinking, hungering and thirsting, resting and toiling, loving and hating, worshipping and cursing, even I am one, and have that within me which shall carry me on and on, it may be through future lives, in future worlds and systems. My dear reader, maybe you have a shilling in your pocket, and intend to go into the next show that comes along to see what you can see. Maybe you have enough to take you to New York, and mean to see Barnum's Museum. Or, maybe you have thought of going to the Old World to see the wonders there—museums, Louvres, zoölogical gardens, ruins of ancient barbarisms, what not. Or, perhaps, though I hope for the best, you have not any shilling at all in your pocket, nor even a solitary nickel, to take you into the side-show to see the big snake and the monkeys. Nay, it may even come to this, though I see not any hope of this book ever coming into the hands of one so poorly off, that you never heard of a show in all your life, nor ever saw anything that you thought more wonderful than a betsy-bug or a snapjack. But to all, and every one, shilling or no shilling, nickel or no nickel, whether you have seen all the wonders of the East or only a poor snapjack, I say, there is a great show for you in the future; truly a most wonderful show; it will not cost you as much to see it when you have got there as you have to pay to see a poor old monkey, so old that he has worn himself bald-headed behind. Bless you, no! Kings, princes, aristocracies, parliaments, congresses, all combined, shall not be able to prevent you. As sure as you have lived, no matter how, so sure shall you see this wonderful show of the future. Verily, yes! you shall see it with eyes. Tune up your viol, reader; or, if you have none, then bones must even answer in its place, and dance for joy that you, too, are alive in the world!

But to return to Mrs. Sutherland. And right here I may say that there was not a woman in any area of country you might mention that one would like better to return to and remain with. Margaret Mason, as we have seen, was left an orphan, and what property had been saved to her from the

wreck of her father's estate, her guardian, according to the
custom, proceeded to convert to his own proper use, benefit,
and behoof. She soon married Dr. Sutherland, at the time
of which we write a most genial man, an eminent physician·
and professor, and devoted to his wife. She now had several
children, of whom, however, it is not my intention to write,
save to wish them all manner of happiness, especially one of
them, a brown-eyed girl, much like her mother, whom some
of our people—none more than the author—will, doubtless,
be glad to meet again before the close of this history. Mrs.
Sutherland was now devoting herself mainly to music.

In the course of these few pages I have several times mentioned a pair of brown eyes; too often, maybe the reader
thinks. Better to be thankful that it is no worse than what
it is; for if I had mentioned them as often as I have thought
of them, there would be nothing else on the last ten pages.
Maybe you have no belief in glorious brown eyes? You
never saw a pair in your life outside of novels. You have
no faith in their existence. Go straight to Mrs. Sutherland,
but expect not to come away whole. *Allons!*

CHAPTER VII.

"He is the half part of a blessed man,
Left to be finished by such a she ;
And she a fair divided excellence,
Whose fulness of perfection lies in him."
—K. John.

"How goes the world, and all the courts thereof, with thee, Clarence Hall, this night of our Lord ? I hope the said world hath this day well and truly paid, or caused to be paid, at least one hundred dollars of what it justly owes you," said Fred, taking a seat by a bright coal-fire in Clarence Hall's office, having already taken a cigar out of the box on the mantle, and lit it.

"As to what the world has paid me, I can speak very positively about that—not a shilling. As to what the world owes me, I am getting doubtful on that point."

"Uneasy on that point are you ? as the fly said when he lit on the point of a needle. Better get off of it, then."

"I was just thinking, as you came in, of what the old ' doctor ' used to say to us sometimes ; you have heard him say it : ' You will be valued, my boys, just like a horse, for the work that can be got out of you.' "

"How else should he be valued ? For what he *is* indeed? There might be much difference of opinion as to what he *is* —endless disputes. But disputes : that word in the ears of your profession is like all the words of Beatrice—tuneful, sweet."

"Are you ever serious upon any subject ? "

"Not if I can help it. But I am serious sometimes, be-

cause of circumstances over which I have no control. For
example, I am particularly serious to-night about two things
at the very least."

"Proceed."

"Well, I must get something to do by the end of this
week, or I shall have to call upon you, for the sake of that
which suffereth long and is kind, which believeth all things,
endureth all things, and is not puffed up, to get me out of a
debtor's prison."

"They might send you to the chain-gang for cheating and
swindling, or obtaining goods on false pretences; but we have
no imprisonment for debt in this State."

"What's done with it?"

"Abolished."

"When?"

"By the new constitution."

"Do you mean to say that the Rads did it."

"Yes; that is one good thing they did."

"Umph! I suppose it was a matter of self-defence; abolished it to keep themselves out."

"What else are you serious about?"

"Yes, yes, I have seen a woman, and what must be her
daughter. But the beauty of that girl! It is like the beauty
of a flower in the garden of Kaïpha! The wind of the si-
moom sweeps off all other perfumes from the clothing of the
traveller, but it can never sweep off from the heart the odor
of this flower. If the pavement was a bed of flowers, her
fairy feet would not bruise the tiniest violet. Her form is
like a branch of the oriental willow. Her cheek is rich and
full as the dark muscadine. Her bosom is like the snow-
flake that rests upon the highest mountain, above the atmosphere of earth, before it is caressed by the zephyr or blushes
at the kiss of the morning sun.

"And her waist is as slender as the letter Alif, her breath sweeter than the breeze that blows over the Spice Islands; and her voice resembles the voice of the harp of David. Extolled be the perfection of Him who created and finished such beauty and loveliness!

"Henceforth I am out of danger of atheism. I shall believe in design, and an omnipotent designer evermore. I can account for watches on a desert island; I can account for the cedars of Lebanon, the bay of Naples, the Alps, the valley of Yosemite, the volcanoes in the moon, the spots upon the sun, the sun itself, and all the stars, without an omnipotent Creator. But here is perfect perfection; nothing but omnipotent perfection could have designed and finished it.

"If a mere mortal may look upon such beauty and live, where shall be our Nebo?"

"Nebo! No Jordan's waves shall fright me from the shore. I have come to ask you. You know her mother. She lives in the little brick house, with the vine-covered veranda, just around the corner and up the street a little way."

"I know of no Juvenile soon; so you must wait till Sunday, and see her at church."

"Church—church. *I will go.* I have not been in two years, but I will go Sunday. Just the sacrifice I would like to make for her."

"We must go early—to Sunday-school."

"To Sunday-school! Yes; I will learn all the catechisms by heart. Under other circumstances this would be the death of me. But I am like old Luther now; I would go if I knew every tile upon the top of that church was a devil. Good-night!"

Clarence Hall was a lawyer—had studied at the University—had ideas, you know—wanted to raise the profession, as 'Mr. Brooke' would say. He felt that the profession in

Georgia was sadly in need of elevation. And he thought, who should elevate it but the better class of young men who were just then entering it? men who, having graduated at the University, and taken their degree at the University Law School, could not fail to bring into the profession that dignity, scholarship, and legal learning of which it stood in imminent need. Clarence Hall occupied the highest round among this class of young men in his profession. If Clarence Hall's idea of " elevating " the profession, of " reforming " it in some sense, was rather vague, he was clear enough as to what he should do for himself in the profession. He was determined to become a great lawyer. Moreover, he would not be so long reaching the upper story as most who get there. He would not depend solely upon plodding and rising gradually; but, as he would doubtless have some time to spare, say for three or four years, he would write a law-book which should go far at a bound to make his reputation. The result of this would be that he would find himself elevated to such height as to be able to step right off upon the balcony of the upper story of the temple, thus finding his way into said upper story by a new route. This, then, could not fail to attract attention; and a large practice follow as a matter of course. And then—and then—why, yes. And then—O stars, shine out your brightest! Sing sweet, ye nightingales! And then he would—marry—Annie—Dearing. Then he would grow great.

Clarence Hall believed in a " female soul," and he believed, too, that the female soul was the " complement" of the male soul. No wonder, then, he should begin to grow great in earnest as soon as he was married. One would think he might widen out; might spread; might grow deeper; might also be purified and elevated by woman's love and trust. Verily, there was no end to what he might do; for he should then and there become a complete man—a man at all points! Of course Clarence Hall did not express the idea in such style as this; but the core of the thing was all the same. Clarence Hall was a man of far better intellect, far more learning and culture, more generous ambition, in a word, was a far better man at all points than many who have looked forward, not altogether without reason, to a seat on the Supreme Bench of the United States. And although he was not getting on as briskly as he had hoped—for he had hoped that by this time his practice would at least amount to two thousand a year, while in fact it had not yet gone beyond four hundred—he had still not lost a particle of his hope and energy. Still he was not getting on as well as he thought he ought. His book, which he thought ought to have been finished by this time, was not more than half completed. And he had begun to see that it is a difficult matter to write a book, even a law-book, which one would think any clod-head might write. But if Clarence Hall had only looked around him, he might have seen that he was doing well, all things considered. To say nothing of the score of young attorneys around him, who by regular attendance upon all justice-courts, and by dint of "copying," barely managed to get some five dollars per week to pay their board-bills, but whom he, not without reason, considered below his own standard, there was Van Comer and Bramlette, neither of whom was supposed to be doing as well as himself. Fred Van Comer we have seen something of; he was determined after a while to try the uncertain field of literature, but was now employed as reporter for one of the city papers. Of Bramlette we have also seen somewhat—his short trousers mainly; but now it is necessary to look beyond the man's trousers—not that we are to look especially, or even at all, to that eighteen inches of leg and foot which protruded from the bottom of his trousers' legs, nor that we are to strip him, inversely as a prize-fighter, in order to look beyond the trousers. What we are now to look to is the man's inner self, his heart—not his mere flesh-and-blood heart, for that we should never get to through the dozen rice-buttons on his shirt-front, six times as many as there ought to have been if he had been a girl, and no better looking than he was.

Bramlette was a poet. Do poets wear trousers a foot too short? Poets wear what they can get. Besides, nobody that knew this man would have been at all surprised to see him attired in a solitary toga. He was not like the conventional poet—long, thin, silky hair, smooth face, delicate features, slight figure, and tuneful voice. His voice was deep and harsh, his frame angular, his face rough and uneven. And what a jaw he did have! Beyond all doubt it was as large and strong as that sacred bone which, in the hand of Samson, a judge in Israel and a mighty man of valor—according to the decision of the priests at Nice—is reported to have been the death of vast quantities of Philistines. But as to how a man, as big as Samson must have been, could find enough water to drink, and that too when he was very thirsty, in the bone aforesaid, I leave that to the theologians—Rev. John E. Squalls included—feeling satisfied that they will "reconcile" it with every word in the English language ending in *ology*, including typology. But here is some of Bramlette's poetry:

OVER THE WALL.

Lo! upon a garden fencing
   Hung a vine, with pendent bough,
Wooing, then, the sunlight glancing
   From its purple leaflets' glow.

And the winds one day came o'er it,
  Sweeping down through brake and vale ·
Lifted up the vine, and bore it
  Out beyond the garden's pale.
Hidden then, the truant cluster,
  From the gardener's watchful thrall,
Bloomed in all the rich sun-lustre,
  Just beyond the garden wall.
And the gardener ne'er had known it,
  But that he, one summer day,
Crossing where the breeze had blown it,
  Came to where its branches lay.
And he found it here all laden
  With a rich and luscious crown,
Precious fruitage—only hidden
  Till the harvest breeze had blown.
Mourner! o'er life's garden railing
  God hath borne your dearest love ;
Lifted it to bloom unfading,
  'Neath the amber skies above.
You shall find it there before you,
  When you leave your earthly thrall,
Ripened into perfect glory,
  Just beyond the garden wall.

Prove all things. I very much doubt if the reader, in spite of the most positive assertions, nay, in spite of affidavits, could have been made to believe, without these verses, that Bramlette was any poet at all. While in the University, Bramlette had made a prodigious reputation. Would anybody believe it, statesmen and scholars actually contended as to who should be the fortunate individual that should supply him with means! for he was very poor. And when he set out in the world he found, to his amazement, that he was already well known far and wide, and that great things were expected of him. Poor Bramlette! Ten to one this will be the ruin of him. What right had his friends to believe that he could escape the ten thousand cares and mishaps that contend with, and, ten to one, overcome the stoutest hearts and clearest heads? That this man, in a fortnight's time, should rise to such height of successful eminence as that they all might join in chorus, Behold what genius can do!—each one the while thinking how much credit himself deserved for his part in the transaction? Here is what a better than common judge of character might have written of Bramlette about the time he left the University: Nervous, wayward genius, vertiginous from very weight of brow! Uncertain only of thyself, while true to principles, to foemen, and to friends, what shall we say of thee? For thy orbit gyrates in cycloidal curves beyond the ken of soothsayers' view, or telescope of astrologers; nor will calculus, sines, cosines, tangents, nor radii weave out thy thread of destiny. Where look for the threatened force, the positive or negative attractions foreboding evil to those gyrating sweeps in thine now uncertain orbit? But lo! the inspiration comes—hark the whiffling wings—swoop lower, ye whispering mystic nymphs, and tell us! Aha! look—yonder! yonder! yonder! See? Ay! There; we see in each cycloidal centre a polished shaft of Parian rock—the caps, the pedestals of the matchless forms of winged cherubs, each armed with quivers full, and bows sprung to the ear. Each shoots as the body sweeps along, and shot after shot tells upon the riven heart: bleeding, quivering, dying. Ah! yet still the impulsive force of beauty lures along the cycloidal curve—and on, and on, and onward sweeps. It is gone! Alas! This is all we see! The questions, At which shaft will you fall? and when fallen will you stick? Yet, when the threatening force is repelled or absorbed, and the broad and sturdy pinions sweep into their annual course, its flight will be upward, soaring steadily amidst the galaxies of orators and poets, theologians or statesmen—carving a name on the highest and most spotless shield of all. *Vincit qui se vincit!*

The same might also, at one time, have been written of Schiller, who abandoned law and became the Teneriffe of German poets—Goethe always being the Orizaba among them. Also, it might at one time have been written of poor Burns, who was at length " patronized " by the great, gauged whiskey-barrels, and ended one of the mournfulest tragedies Humanity has ever been called upon to weep or witness ; of Dickens, too, and god-like Rousseau. Shall I add, that if you will take your position in front of the post-office you will probably see a score of men of whom also these words might once have been written ? Forty years old, and unknown to their next-door neighbors—unless they happen to have vicious wives or sickly children !

The next Sunday came, and Fred, duly armed with catechisms, went with Clarence Hall to church. They got a seat where Fred could have a full view of Olive Sutherland—she of the voice of the harp of David, and form of the oriental willow. Fred wanted to talk, but Hall would not " talk in church."

" Who is that sitting by her, Hall ? "

" That is Emma Harlan ; very pretty ; but I will tell you more of her after church ! "

Emma Harlan was much like Olive Sutherland ; perhaps slightly more infantine in appearance. But her cheek was browner, and resembled a luscious ripe peach—the sunny side of it. The class to which the two girls belonged was a favorite of the pastor's—for Mr. Brooke was a gentleman of taste, with an ardent admiration for the beautiful—and he often conducted it himself, as he did to-day. Rev. Melancthon Brooke was universally honored, not less for high Christian piety than for social virtues. He was a man of fine culture, and, for a Presbyterian preacher, had liberal opinions. He had the rare good fortune—the result of talent, culture, good manners, and genial disposition—to be liberal and good-humored without subjecting himself to the imputation of " worldliness." Mr. Brooke was not considered a whit less strict in all essentials than the most fervent follower of John Knox. If any member of Mr. Brooke's flock had set out to find a man who, if necessary, would even die at the stake for his religion—a most difficult undertaking then, as now—Mr. Brooke would have been the man selected for such martyrdom.

Alf Walton—a dark-visaged man, probably the most distinguished-looking man in the house except possibly the preacher himself—sat just in front of Mr. Brooke, and scarcely took his eye off him while he was hearing the class. Alf Walton had been here for several Sundays past, and Mr. Brooke had observed more than once his eye fixed keenly upon himself. And Mr. Brooke, though a man of easy grace, and utmost self-control, grew a little nervous under the scowling gaze. Alf Walton thought that Mr. Brooke was his rival. Not only so, but in his own mind he accused Mr. Brooke of having no purer motive in seeking to gain the favor of Emma Harlan than himself. Forgetting all about, or paying no attention to, Mr. Brooke's high character as a clergyman and Christian gentleman, he placed him on a level with, and as no better than, himself—an epicurean debauchee—and saw that here was a rare case for scandal. It was not a difficult matter, he thought, to find a clergyman engaged in the devilish work of seeking the ruin of the innocent lambs of his flock. Pray do not put down Mr. Brooke—a very bad man, full of the blackest plots, murders, arsons, thefts, seductions, and all the catalogue of crimes, because Alf Walton thought so. Mr.

Brooke was a man of splendid physique, of high and noble forehead, intellectual brow, and full, open, gray eye, beaming with culture, good-humor, and benevolence. Alf Walton thought he had one advantage over Mr. Brooke, even if he had not the livery of heaven in which to serve the devil. Mr. Brooke was a married man. He well knew that vice, to approach innocence with any hope of finding favor, must be carefully hid beneath the spotless robes of virtue, or obscured by the very glow of love. Moreover, he had one other great advantage, or what might be so, gold—yellow, glittering, precious gold; " the yellow slave that can knit and break religions; " gold—" the ever young, fresh, lov'd, and delicate wooer, whose blush doth thaw the consecrated snow that lies on Dian's lap ! " But it was for the former rather than the latter purpose that Alf Walton hoped he might use this yellow slave, that will "lug your priests from your side." How shall this simple girl escape this accomplished villain ? And if Alf Walton's conjecture was true, would there be any hope for her at all ? Would not her greatest security against the one be her greatest danger from the other ? There was one hope—she might marry ; but this was away out in the lavender; because she was very young, very poor, and yet of an intelligence and culture that raised her up into the circle where men make money a consideration.

Mrs. Harlan, Emma's mother, was a widow, and an invalid. She lived in a neat little cottage on Ivy street. She had been left a widow about the beginning of the great war between the States—in which we all lost our negroes and trinkets—with five children, Emma and four brothers. One by one the four manly boys had all fallen upon the battle-scarred hills of Virginia. She was left destitute, and came to this city with her little girl. She received assistance from the Freemasons. At first she was able to do needlework,

5

but soon her health gave way, and she was a confirmed invalid.   She was a good woman, and bore her hard lot with such
unmurmuring resignation as touched the hearts of all who
had any to be touched.   She was not sick enough to be in
bed ; and Emma, according to her earnest wish, was kept in
school by her friends.   It was not far to school, and so
Emma came home every day ; and afternoons, when returned
from school, she sang to her mother, and frequently brought
her pretty bouquets and flowers ; for Emma was a favorite of
the girls, and they knew of her sick mother at home, and
how glad she was for Emma to bring her flowers.   They
lived alone ; but there never passed a day but some one
called.   Besides, Mrs. Harlan could always find company in
the little library of books she had collected.   Mr. Brooke
was her pastor, and always came twice or three times a
week.   Dr. Sutherland came every few days, and sometimes his noble wife, who, I doubt not, if by her viva-
city and sympathy she helped to lighten the weight of sorrow that pressed heavily upon this poor widow, felt better
than when she received the highest praises of her admirers.
If there was a children's party at Mrs. Sutherland's, she
was sure to have Emma there ; and as far as was in her
power, which we have seen was considerable, she saw to
it that in society Emma was treated with the consideration due to herself, without regard to the accident of her
surroundings.

But the friend whom Mrs. Harlan always welcomed most
gladly was the Christian soldier and minister, General
Clement.   Alas, alas ! that language, even the best, is so
trite, and the noblest epithets so often applied to the commonest men, there are none left worthy to apply to this one.
There was a tie between them which the reader will understand.   All four of Mrs. Harlan's sons had gone out to the

war in General Clement's old company. Ever in front of the battle, he had seen them all die faithfully at their posts. Every one of them he himself had promoted for gallantry upon the field. The last that died was on the final, fatal day at Petersburg, and the brave General felt his heart wrung as it had seldom been before. This was the youngest. The General came up with him while his life was leaping away. Is it strange, O reader, that in this last supreme moment he thought of his home instead of glory and successful war? He had scarcely breath to speak.

"Dear General, you know I am the last of us—you will see my poor mother, and little sister—say a word of comfort to them. I had hoped to live; but "— The young soldier had passed over the river to join his great Captain. The noble General Clement never forgot the words of the dying soldier. And not many days now passed that he did not call in to "say a word of comfort to the mother and sister."

In the afternoon of the Sunday we have been speaking of, Mr. Brooke called at the cottage on Ivy street. Bramlette was there. In the course of conversation Mr. Brooke found that his new acquaintance had a head on his shoulders much better filled than his breeches' legs were; and that he was also a man of much better taste than one would think from a superficial view of his shirt-bosom. As to how Bramlette came there, why, he just happened to stop there a few minutes one afternoon with General Clement, and Emma came in while he was there. This explains why he had been there several times since. The next day an elegant phæton stopped before the little cottage on Ivy street, from which a distinguished-looking gentleman emerged and entered the house. He introduced himself, and begged to leave a large, richly bound Bible, on the fly-leaf of which were these words: "To the best student of the Bible-class, from one who has watched her course with interest." And on a slip of paper between the pages, " For Miss Emma Harlan." With the utmost grace the gentleman begged Mrs. Harlan would not mention his name.

CHAPTER VIII.

"There was a time when I could not have slept, had I forgotten my evening prayers. . . . . There was a time when my tears flowed so freely—oh, those days of peace !—Dear home of my fathers—ye verdant, halcyon vales !—O, all ye Elysian scenes of my childhood !—will you never return ?—Will your delicious breezes never cool my burning bosom ?—Mourn with me, Nature, mourn !—They will never return ! never will their delicious breezes cool my burning bosom !—They are gone !—gone !—irrevocably gone ! "—SCHILLER, *The Robbers*.

JAMES ARNOT lived in the wildest and most solitary region of the Blue Ridge mountains. The square, old-fashioned, wooden house was built upon the summit of what had been a towering conical peak ; but the top of the cone was cut off, as if by the levelling sword of some plebeian god, for its haughty insolence, and had rolled down the side of the mountain, and dashing itself across the small stream which flowed between the adjacent hills, formed a small but beautiful mountain-lake. From the truncated summit there had sprung, as if before held down by the superincumbent pressure, a great forest of pine and chestnut. There was now no road leading to the summit of the hill. The house had been built many years before by a family in the South, intending to spend part of the summer in these wilds. But it was scarcely finished when one of those " accidents " came along which stand for nothing in our calculations, but for much in the book of fate. So the house had never before been inhabited by human beings. There had been a road leading up to the house. Beginning at the base, it wound spirally around the mountain, and came to the summit on the side from which it started. You might see traces of it now ; and on the esplanade, which was perfectly level, containing some five or six acres, without shrub or flower except native ones, and without a sign of fence or garden, might still be seen remains of a circular drive.

There was not another house in ten miles of this place. Not an echo of civilization was heard here. But you might hear the dismal howl of the wolf upon the neighboring hills; and on a still night you might catch a few notes of the wild chorus from Indian Swamp, where the treble of the eagle and the nighthawk mingled with the wailing of the panther, and the low bass of the deep-hooting owl. This fearful swamp was some miles distant, and was so called from a wild Indian legend connected with it. Arnot lived here without any servant, and with no companion but the old man we have seen with him. The walls of the rooms were curiously painted; the rough pictures corresponding with the wildness of the surroundings. There were some pictures of the most splendid natural scenery. Here was a chaos of mountain-scene; as of mountains of all sizes, and all shapes, from the polished cone to the most jagged bear, hurled pellmell at each other by contending giants, and left just as they had fallen or rolled against each other, crushing and tearing themselves into the most grotesque shapes. Here were also mountain-lakes, and waterfalls, and streams with banks covered with water-oaks and stunted cottonwood, matted with vines of grape and muscadine. On the walls of one room were pictures of rare birds of the American forests, and wild animals; while on the walls of another were representations of various Indian rites and ceremonies—the green-corn dance, war-dance, council of peace, courts of justice, games, and marriage ceremonies. Arnot's sleeping-room was on the second floor; and here were representations of several Indian legends. On one side, at the head of his bed, the well-known legend of "The Evening Star," than which not the mystic fancy of the

North, nor the gorgeous imagery of the Southern Orient, has furnished any legend more beautiful. The scene upon Yonah was given just at the moment when, the death-dance ended and the daring young lover hurled over the precipice, Nacoochee breaks from the arms of her old father and leaps from the height. Sublime love! Heroic death! This is the grandeur of humanity. And it may glow in the breasts of Indians. Verily, there is a common brotherhood of spiritual, as well as animal, humanity!

On the wall opposite was a representation of the legend of Indian Swamp. Scene, a wild wilderness: a beautiful young white man, apparently a Spaniard, stands upon a round pole, which is supported at one end by the fork of a tree, and at the other by a stake about which a fire has been kindled. The young man stands erect, and part of his rich, black hair, which seems to have been tucked under, has come down, and falls over his shoulder almost to his waist. He has a cord about his neck, which is fastened to a limb overhead; and a circle of Indians, who seem to have been dancing around him, are just in the act of running away. A great hawk rests upon a broken branch of a dead tree; and an eagle is poised for flight from his perch upon the top. The head of a wolf was seen through a neighboring thicket.

It was one night soon after his return from Georgia; and James Arnot was alone in his room. Without, the night was dark; and the fitful wailing of the wind about the eaves and corners of the house, and through the low branches of the great chestnuts, mingled strangely with the monotonous, solemn, dirge-like notes of the lofty pines. Above all was heard the impatient roar of winds lost among the chaos of hills and valleys around. Arnot sat in a large arm-chair before the fire. The logs had burned down to a great bed of coals, which sent forth that fierce, red glare that reminds one of a dying Indian. Why is it that people in trouble will think aloud?

"I said I would reach the bottom—I have done it. But I wish there was more to do—or else—yes—or else—I had not begun. Suppose—but why suppose? Can the numbered years be called back? Can mortals pluck leaves from the book of Fate? or can I unwrite even one little chapter? And yet, I will suppose—speculate upon what good was present to Jehovah's eye, and dismissed for the present ill. See—yes—that night and the consequent years. Could not disgrace and scorn of fortune be endured for one little life? I would accept it now, though it should last a thousand years. Failures, poverty, death of relatives, desertion of friends, buffetings of fortune—all that many fret and magnify their poor lives with—ye are less than trifles, scarce worth a thought in the endurance. Misfortune is but counterfeit, and puts on the royal robes of suffering. But shall a few years stand against eternity? Only three years—or has the past been at all? Maybe it is only in the mind itself. We cheat ourselves with fear of this phantasm memory, as by hopes of what, like fools, we call the future we prick ourselves on. No! memory is a lie—there is no past —there is no future. And yet—I fear. There. I will write it down, that I will not fear. But there's a pen can only write in blood—ha! and a dagger too, could tell a tale would freeze living coals to arctic adamant."

Then he closed his eyes, and his thoughts went far out upon the other side of silence. So he sat for an hour. Then he got up, went to a trunk, and brought out a small volume. He turned to the fly-leaf—"'My mother'—yes, 'from mother to' me.. I will fancy myself a child again—I will read a chapter—then I will say the old prayer we used to say at home—and go to bed." He read the chapter, and

in a few moments the silent figures upon the walls looked
upon a scene they had never witnessed before. James
Arnot was kneeling at his bedside, and his head rested upon
the little book sanctified by a mother's prayer. He meant
to repeat the simple prayer, which, as children, they used to
repeat at home long ago. But when he came to the words,
"God bless father and mother," he thought of his own child,
and there went forth from the abyss of his soul a wail that
might have made the dead pictures shudder. "Lost—lost—
lost." The cry came from the last depth of agony. Blasted
and riven, this human soul had clung to one hope. It felt
within itself a spark of the everlasting—it could not be
destroyed—it was beyond the power of fate; somewhere in
the infinite world of spirit there was one soul with which
this could claim, and from which it could receive, sympathy;
there was but one—there never would be another; but there
was one—and that too was indestructible by God or fate:
it was James Arnot's child. Here was a human soul without hope in time, and with but one in eternity, looking forward to the time when it should meet its own child, and receive that sympathy without which, it seems, the immortal
spirit itself would die. How true it is that things the most
palpable will frequently not occur to the mind when contrary to its strongest hope. It was only now that it occurred
to Arnot that this meeting might never be—that they might
be in worlds apart.

It is only the sense of companionship that makes life at all
endurable. Were there but one man on the earth, he would
be a terror to himself. Were there but one spirit in heaven,
heaven itself would be a dismal solitude. And what solitude
more solitary than the solitude of the utterly unsympathizing
crowd? What then must be the supreme agony of the soul
that suddenly feels itself utterly alone forever! No wonder

5*

Arnot rose almost mad with terror and despair. He looked down at himself as he would upon some strange animal, and started; he saw his shadow upon the wall, and started again. Then he walked across the room, and sat down before the fire. "Lost—lost—lost; alone—alone—alone. My sweet baby, I will never see thee more." And then, after a silence:

"But the soul—it is immortal—and they say the mind can never lose anything. The thoughts and feelings that enter it are not coloring-matter to be bleached out by the dews of time, but the very threads—woof and warp—the mind itself. And death cannot destroy it—cannot change it—not one memory can it touch, or one feeling. I will not forget thee there, my pretty child—my own sweet baby-girl. And that thou art happy I will be glad, though I never see thee more."

How is it, O reader, that a strong man should thus be overcome—thus mourn the inevitable? James Arnot was not a strong man. Arnot laid another log on the fire and went to bed.

While the scene I have been describing was enacting in the room, there was quite as strange a one going on outside. A window on the north side of Arnot's room opened upon the roof of a back porch. The blinds of this window had been securely nailed, but by accident they had been left so they could be sprung, so that if there was a light in the room one from without might see what was doing within, without being himself visible. Growing here by this porch was a great spreading chestnut, and some of the branches reached over upon the roof, so that nothing was easier than to go from them upon the roof, and to Arnot's window. It seems strange that Arnot, so cautious, had not seen this, and cut the limbs off. But if Dr. Webster had only broken the leg-bone of his victim, making it impossible to identify the height, he could not have been convicted of murder. In nothing does fate mock endeavor more than in this, that, do all we can, study and calculate as we will, something so plain as to be staring us in the face will be left unobserved. So it was with Arnot. Not for the half of his fortune would he have left his room so that he could be watched from without. And yet here was the tree, with branches almost like a flight of steps, from which you might step upon the roof, and to the window. And the blinds were left so that they might be sprung; and, as if to make everything perfectly secure against himself, the blinds were shut and nailed, so that one on the outside would not be in any danger of discovery from having the blinds suddenly opened from within.

The old man stood at the window, and watched the scene I have been describing. He heard what Arnot was saying, and followed him thus: "'No memory'—ha! I would you had a thousand; for that ever you did one good thing I will not believe. 'Suppose it had not been'—why, then, I had not been here—I had been at home, my children with me—and you been hung for some lesser crime than that you'll shortly die for. 'Three years'—ha! I think it's three times three—three years, sayest thou?—bring it nearer—make it three months—three days. 'Misfortune only counterfeit of suffering'—good, my Lord. 'Who hath seen the past?' —two of us here, my Lord, I think have seen something of it. 'There is no future'—ay, my Lord, there by chance you have once hit upon the truth, for I think there is little left for thee. There. You will sleep, will you? I will watch thee—for this have I followed thee. I would thou hadst ten thousand lives, that thou mightst thus be forever living and dying. But my soul so thirsts for thee, it will not be delayed. No! Though a legion of hissing adders pursued thee, thou shouldst not live another day. Now he wakes. 'Fancy thyself a child'—will you? Why, so thou canst—but not a devil—for that thou art already. 'Prayer!'—now thank thee, my Lord, for this. We'll mock thee. 'Lost—lost'—nay, thou shalt not be so lost but what the hawks and wolves will find thee. 'Alone—in eternity'—oh, be not troubled, the devil will provide thee company. 'But the soul's immortal'—why, so it is—but the body's mortal—and that thou shalt know before another moon shall rise and set. 'What is death?' Ay—ay—I think you can answer that better when the moon shall hang over Indian Swamp, and thou under it. 'My child'—what's here?—I would I had not lost that —I would I had heard it. 'My pretty child!'—will you say that again? No—he is going to bed."

"I'll not forget thee there, my pretty child—my own sweet baby-girl." This was what Arnot said. But the latter part of the sentence was not heard by the old man. Why? Only a gust of wind. Was this gust of wind, then, a special providence? Not at all. Or was it—which some will doubtless think more likely—a special interference of the devil? No more than the other. And yet these words— "My own sweet baby-girl"—were most important to be heard. They were the very words, of all that was said by James Arnot that night, that ought to have been heard, one would think, for more lives than one depended upon them; and but for that vicious gust of wind the next chapter, and all the succeeding chapters of the lives of these people, had been wholly different. Thus do we often come near to our better destiny, and then are whirled forever away by things as light as a gust of wind. But think not that this was special providence or devil's trick. The wind would have blown just the same if Arnot had said anything else, just the same as if he had made any common observation, or the kitten mewed. The old man descended from the roof. Two dusky figures from the thick shade of a great oak hard by approached him. The three walked off together some hundred yards, and sat down in a thick clump of undergrowth.

CHAPTER IX.

"For my part, I am certain that God hath given us our reason to discern between truth and falsehood; and he that makes not this use of it, but believes things he knows not why, I say it is by chance that he believes the truth, and not by choice; and I cannot but fear that God will not accept of this sacrifice of fools."—CHILLINGWORTH.

"And thus the whole world forms a necessary chain, in which indeed each man may play his part, but can by no means determine what that part shall be."—BUCKLE.

"I FEAR you have been reading infidel works too much," said Clarence Hall to Mirabeau Holmes, taking up the remark of the latter that he found himself involved in an "involuntary skepticism."

"The truth is, Hall, and I cannot shut my eyes to it, that religion with individuals is a matter of geography, and with nations a matter of civilization."

"You must admit, though, that there is some one religion which is true, and being true, agreeable to God."

"If there is such religion it must follow that God has so distinguished it, by signs and tokens, from all other religions, as to be recognized by the commonest minds."

"So He has manifested it, by miracles that can only be attributed to the Author of Nature."

"Yes; but these manifestations ought to be equally obvious to all mankind, and common to all times and places. As for miracles—alas, alas! I never saw a miracle in my life; and I never saw anybody that ever saw one."

"But others have seen them; there are crowds of witnesses. These facts are as well attested as any historical facts whatever."

"Pardon me; I have not found them so well attested. All religions have rested their credibility upon miracles, and their most learned followers at least believe that they rest firmly; for they say there can be no doubt about the authenticity of the miracles. But then suppose they did occur, how are we to know whether they are from God or from the devil? for the Bible itself tells us that they may be performed also by the latter. You tell me that God hath spoken. He hath not spoken to me. You say He hath appointed others to teach me His word. How am I to know that they are not impostors? You say that I am secured from that by His manifesting the mission of His messengers by miracles and prophecies. But those who claim to be such messengers do not work miracles. If one of them should come and harangue us in the following manner: ' I come, ye mortals, to announce to you the will of the Most High; acknowledge in my voice that of Him who sent me. I command the sun to move backwards, the stars to change their places, the mountains to disappear, the waves to remain fixed on high, and the earth to wear a different aspect!' Who would not believe this man to be a messenger of God if he should work such miracles? As for prophecies: how am I to know they were not written after the events prophesied? Or how am I to know that, even if the event did happen as prophesied, there was not an accidental concurrence? to say nothing of the fact that if the prophecies in the Bible have any meaning at all, it is so vague as to escape anybody but a most profound typologian. But all these things are related in books. Who wrote these books? Men. But many others, besides those we have, claim to be genuine; who decided which were genuine and which not? Men. They are written in languages that are dead, nowhere understood. Who translated them? Men. Always human testimony! It is always men that tell me what other men told them! What a number of these are always between me and the Deity! We are always reduced to the necessity of examining, comparing, and verifying such evidence. I tell you, Hall, I have almost said with the Savoyard, 'Oh, that God had deigned to have saved me all this trouble! Should I have served Him with a less willing heart?' I scarcely know what I believe; but I know one thing that I do not believe. I cannot believe that the dark, vindictive, partial, jealous, angry, bloody God of the old Hebrews is the all-wise and all-benevolent God of the universe. I cannot believe in Judaism; every God-implanted principle of my being revolts at it. I wish that Jesus had cut loose from it entirely; the problem would have been easier. There, I have said more to you on this subject than I ever have said to anybody else. God knows how I long to know the truth; and He knows, too, that I have sought it earnestly, and shall continue to. Will He condemn me if I fail to find it?"

Hall was just going to answer this long speech, when Fred Van Comer entered with—

" I heard you say something about ' my old ancestors' as I came up the steps. No remarks. Remember, as Disraeli says, ' Mine were princes in the temple, when yours were naked savages on the British Islands.' But I am thinking now more about posterity than ancestry. I think I shall marry."

" Ah! I think you said some time ago that marriage was the chief end of life," said Mirabeau.

" Yes; but to change one's opinions is generally to correct one's errors. After consulting my attorney I say that marriage ought to be, according to the statute, the chief beginning of life. I have been thinking if ever any bachelors became great. How is it, Hall?"

" Well, there is your great exemplar and apostle, Buckle, who is a bachelor."

"So he is. But one must look to the French Revolution for great men. Let me see. There was Mirabeau. He had to make temporary arrangements with Sophie De Ruffey, and others too numerous to mention. I reckon he was never outdone by anybody but Solomon. Voltaire tried bacheloring, I believe; but he had to take up, in a more quiet way, though, than the man of the Tennis Court, with that old countess. And look there at Jean Jacques. If he had not had any children to send into the street maybe he would not have written the *Contrat Sociale ;* and one cannot see how a man so simple as never to be able to tell the difference between the price of three onions and a leg of mutton, was ever to get any at all, without some sort of a wife to help him. But I just came in here to tell you, Holmes, that I have made an engagement for us to go to Mrs. Malcomb's to-night."

"The mischief you have ! Why, I have an engagement myself to go to General Clement's."

. "Nobody going with you ? "

"No."

"You must break it. Of two evils choose the lesser. I signed your name to the note, and mine too. If you break the engagement you made, there will be but one word broken ; but if you break the one both of us made, there will be two lies told."

"What are you going to do when you get back from Europe ? " said Fred, as he and Mirabeau walked home from Mr. Malcomb's next evening.

"That depends. What do you think of journalism ? "

"That is going to be the biggest thing in this country. The orator's occupation's gone. The newspaper press will make presidents and congresses from this on."

"But you have some experience as an editor; why did you come back here from Etowah ? "

"You see they got it out up there that I did not believe in the Trinity, and they ruined my business. That village has two thousand inhabitants—mostly Methodist preachers. Now it so happened that I had three partners, and all three of them Methodist preachers. They pretended to think I was about to be lost; they prayed for me in public and cheated me out of my part of the profits in private. One of them, old Watt, would never let an advertisement of a liquor-house go in the paper, while he was a regular red-nosed toper. They never had any amusements up there; they said first-class people didn't dance. They had what they called sanctification meetings. And because I would not go to them they considered me as good as damned already. But one of them bought two large lexicons from me, Greek and Latin, worth, you know, about twelve dollars apiece. I told him to take them on with him to college, and some time he might pay me what they were worth. He said they were worth two dollars apiece down there, and cheated me out of my. books accordingly. He was one of the sanctification leaders. One Sunday the preacher preached a sermon at my partners from the text, 'Be ye not unequally yoked with unbelievers,' calling us by name all the way through. One day I loaned one of my books—it was Buckle's Essays—to a young fellow there, and it was all over town in no time that John Moon was reading Van Comer's infidel books. That night he was seized upon by half a dozen—the fellow that cheated me out of my books among them—and carried by prayers and a sufficient amount of main force—as Voltaire said of the incantations, administered with arsenic, destroying a flock of sheep—to a 'sanctification' meeting. But when I went to Washington, and wrote back to my paper that I had called upon President Grant, and intimated my belief that he was a gentleman, that was the feather that broke the camel's back. They wanted to tar and feather me for it. In short, that little ville is like the prince of the Spanish breed, devout, orthodox, and ignorant.

"But surely, they did not carry all their sectarian zeal into business?"

"I reckon they did. Not that they were also ignorant in business—they were shrewd enough; they prayed with one eye open. I heard a lawyer say that he had to go up to be prayed for at every 'protracted' meeting, else his practice would be broken down. Bless you! they sing sol fa la and shout up there yet!"

"Have you ever been up there since you left?"

"Bless my soul! I haven't told you about it. Yes; I just got back from up there this morning. I went there to write up a scandal case—the local paper would not publish it because a preacher was into it—the worst case you ever heard of. You will see it in the morning. I put it in great black letters this way : 'In the lurch'—'A preacher trapped'— 'Beautiful maiden seduced by a Rev. brother-in-law'—'A case of eight years' standing'—'Begun when the girl was only fourteen'—'Moonlight rides to night-meetings'—'The scoundrel fled'—'The girl arrested and bound over to Court'—'Two of the best families plunged in grief'—'&c., &c.' The mischief! I wish I had shown it to you before it was put in. I have not told you half of the heading even."

"You have an awful array of it. But who on earth can they be?"

"The man's name is Squalls, and "——

"Stop! Squalls—Squalls—did you say?"

"Yes; Squalls—John E. Squalls, I believe."

"Well, well! Who would have thought it of that little, tallow-faced, wheezy scamp?"

"What! did you know him?"

"I have seen him. His present wife was Kate Fletcher,

one of the prettiest girls I ever saw. I went to school with her once. She was my sweetheart when I was a boy. I would like to see her now. I am so sorry for her. How does she look?"

There is something inexpressibly tender about a school-boy's love. It is the purest, most ethereal, most utterly un-selfish feeling ever experienced by the human heart. And when the remembrance of it comes back to us, hallowed by time, nothing can be more beautiful or more touching. Like the most distant star, its light will struggle, it may be, for scores of years through the gloomiest voids, the rays never wandering to mar its beauty, and come straight to us, beaming upon the heart with ineffable tenderness. It may be, dear reader, that you have already gone far into the winter months of life. But that matters nothing. Look back to your school-boy days, and for a moment you may be a boy again. Think of your school-girl sweetheart. It may be fifty winters since you have seen her. She may be old, and wrinkled, and gray. Suppose you met her on the street to-morrow? You would not see the age, nor the wrinkles, nor the gray. For you have loved her once; and you would see the pretty girl on the old playground. Let me tell you —I hope you know it already—if your heart did not throb with a feeling it has not known for all these years, you are yet a stranger to the rarest flower that ever bloomed in the garden of the heart, the sweetest notes that ever melted from its tenderest chords. . . .

Arnot went to bed, and was soon in a troubled sleep. And now we may look around us. The door was strongly bolted and double-barred. Under his pillow Arnot had placed an unsheathed dagger-and a large pistol, the mate to which was laid on the bed within reach of his right hand. A repeating-gun rested against the head of the bed, and on the table were two other large army-pistols. On the mantel was a looking-glass and a pair of vases full of wild-flowers gathered that morning from some nooks and coves in the hills where they had been protected from the cold winds. There were also upon the table a small escritoire and the Bible we have seen. A couple of chairs, an old wardrobe, a trunk, and some pieces of carpet, completed the furniture of the room.

When Arnot waked he was shaking with cold and fright. He sat upon the side of the bed. He looked at the pistol which he had tightly grasped in his hand, and found that he had broken off the trigger. It was this that had waked him. He had dreamed a horrible, fearful dream. He tried to recall it: a band of armed negroes seemed to enter his room from the north window. He saw them plainly; saw them hoisting the window, entering, and approaching, and yet he could not stir in his bed. It seemed that there was one old friend among them; one that mocked and jeered him bitterly. It was a clear, bright night. They carried him, with a cord about his neck, to Indian Swamp. They placed him upon a cross-piece supported by forks, and tied the cord to a high limb overhead. There was a great crowd of them. They had pans and bones, and they danced and sang around him. Suddenly he seemed to think of his power of ventriloquism. He made a noise as of some one approaching; repeated it—louder and louder—and from different quarters, till fear seized upon the negroes, and they fled in all directions. What then? His arms were bound tightly at his back. To die—to die—to die—alone in that dreadful swamp! Days and nights passed. He was perishing of hunger. He grew fainter and fainter. His eyes grew dim. He was blind. He felt the flapping of the wings of the night-birds. He heard the chilling scream of the eagle overhead —the cries of the hawk and panther—the growling, barking,

and fighting of a thousand wolves, all around and under
him; he felt them clawing and gnawing at the stakes which
supported him.   Then there came a lull—dimness and
silence.   He fell—and the darkness rolled over him.

Arnot knew not how long he had slept.   The gusty wind
had sunk into a monotonous dirge.   The moon rested in the
fringe of the western mountains.   The log he had lain upon
the fire when he went to bed had burnt down, and there was
no light in the room except the red glare of the dying coals.
The moon shone in through the blinds of the western windows; and its shadows, mingling and contending with the
deeper ones of the coals in the hearth, formed many a weird,
fantastic figure upon the walls and floor.   Arnot looked
around the room; his eyes fell upon the picture on the opposite wall, and almost started from their sockets.   Horror of
horrors!   He seemed to see among the fantastic shadows his
own name.   It was plain, perfectly plain, for an instant, and
then vanished.   It was directly under the young Spaniard
with the long hair, in the picture.   Then he saw his whole
dream in the picture.   He was transfixed with dread.   There
was the very pole he had stood upon; it was full of small
knots that hurt his feet.   The negroes had run away, just as
the Indians were in the act of doing here.   The very eagle on
top of the dead tree seemed to scream.   And there was a flapping of wings among the trees.   He got off the bed.   He was
numb and cold.   He went and sat down before the fire.   Why
did he not make a light?   Only because he never thought of
it.   And yet it would have altered things strangely if he had.
He put his feet to the coals, and tried to think over all that
had happened that night.   He went over his dream again
and again; and now for the first time their coming in at the
north window impressed itself upon his mind.   Why at the
window?   Why at the north window?   And then, quick as

thought, he was at the window examining. He seemed to take in the whole situation at a glance. The chestnut tree; the limbs reaching upon the roof; the blinds sprung, so that one from without could observe all that was going on within; the blinds nailed, so that there was no danger of being suddenly opened from within. Moreover, nothing would be easier than to come upon this roof, draw out the two poor little nails, and rush or slip in and murder him in his bed. What a fool he had been! All his precautions had gone for nothing. He put on his clothes; went to get one of the pistols from the table to put in his belt, in place of the one he had broken in his dream, and his eye fell upon the Bible he had left there. He picked it up, muttering to himself, "The first time I have read a word of it in years, and see what a night it has brought me." · Then he thought to throw it in the fire. He stopped.

"But my mother gave it me. She would not have had me pass a night like this, for she always loved me—and—God knows—she may even be thinking of me to-night, somewhere. Her name is in it—I cannot burn that."

Then Arnot quickly turned to the fly-leaf; he tore it out, folded it neatly, kissed it, and put it into his pocket-book. The rest he threw into the fire, where it began to smoulder among the coals and ashes. But he could not but think of the window. And thinking how easy it was to draw the nails and open it, it occurred to him to examine it again. He did examine it; and he not only found that the nails were already loosened, but he thought he detected that they had been tampered with from the inside instead of the out. He thought of the old man in his dream, and the whole truth seemed to flash into his mind. Quick, quick! There was not a moment to be lost. They might even now be in sight. Arnot glided quickly down-stairs. He looked cautiously around him, and not seeing or hearing anything, he went to the old man's door and knocked. Getting no answer, he turned the bolt and entered. The bed had not been slept upon. His suspicions were now confirmed. He believed there was a plot on foot to murder him, and that the old man was at the head of it. And now he remembered a fierce, half-hungry, half-mocking gleam he had sometimes seen in the old man's eye, at times when he thought himself unobserved. He believed that the work was to be done this very night, for he had never known the old man to leave his room before at night. He looked to where his pistols were accustomed to hang at the head of his bed, and they were not in their place. He was quite sure that if they came at all they would come to his window.

The moon had now gone down behind the mountains, whose vast shadow rested upon the lower hills and valleys. Arnot came out of the old man's room, and keeping as much as possible in the deeper shade of the trees, moved off some distance and lay flat upon the ground. He watched, and listened. He would have gone to a clump of trees further off and directly in front of his window, but his quick perception told him that that would probably be the very covert from which they would come. It was, in fact, just where the three men had gone. Suddenly there was a light in Arnot's room; and one of the three men, coming out of the thicket to see what it meant, was himself seen by Arnot. The light soon went out. It was probably only a leaf from the book Arnot had thrown into the fire. Arnot's heart thumped against his ribs as he saw three men emerge from the thicket and advance towards the house. They walked slowly. They were talking low; but Arnot heard them. Two of them were negroes.

"They ought to have been here to-night. This delay may ruin everything. I only loosened the window this morning—

while he was off down there under the hill after flowers. He goes down there every morning when he is here. If I had known they were not coming, I would have waited till to-morrow. He sees everything, and may look to the window before to-morrow night."

"S'pose we git him when he goes down thar?"

"That will not do, for two reasons: in the first place, we might miss him; and if we did, I can tell you he would not miss us. In the next place, we want to take him to the Swamp."

They now came to the great chestnut, and stopped. The old man then pointed out to them how they were to go upon the roof, and in at the window. The night was still, and Arnot could hear every word they said.

"Remember—just at twelve. The moon, from that chestnut by the thicket, will be just in the top of yonder pine. I will be there with the shadow from that tree. Don't bring more than six with you. Any number may meet us at the Swamp —but don't bring more than six here."

"But dat devil—shore yer got der winder loosen?"

"Yes. He will not have time to turn in his bed. I have not followed him this long for nothing; and many a one of you has he sent home."

"He won't send no mo'. What we guine do wid him when he dead?"

"Leave him to the hawks and wolves, as the fortune-teller said must be done."

Arnot placed himself behind the tree from them, and bounded forward, swift as the wind, sure as the spring of the panther, and noiseless as a tiger on carpet of felt. Quick and clear the shots rang upon the midnight air. Two of the men fell upon the spot. One negro fled, crying, "Murder, murder!" Another shot—he seemed to spring into the air, and fell heavily upon his face—and James Arnot knew well its meaning. He went to see, and he was not mistaken. When he returned, the old man was sitting bolt upright against the tree. Arnot approached him. He was stone dead. As to what led the old man to this fifth act in his life-tragedy, Arnot could not conjecture. The truth never occurred to him—that it was all a *mistake*. So it is, in deepest tragedy, and in lightest comedy; the parts we play are our own by necessity.

CHAPTER X.

"Seek a good wife of thy God, for she is the best *gift* of his providence."

"Oh, two such silver currents, when they join,
Do glorify the banks that bound them in."
—K. John.

I AM going to relate, perhaps, the most important event since Adam. If men were prophets, such as many of the old Hebrews are reported to have been, or if they could take any ordinary act whatever and trace it out to its remotest consequences, would it afford them more matter for thought and wonderment than they now find in tracing backwards? or even than the taking of any small historical fact and tracing it to its known consequences? Take the marriage of two German peasants, Luther's parents. Could anything be more in the ordinary way? And yet see the consequences! Not, to be sure, but what the Reformation would have been, even if Luther had never been born; for it would. But not like it was. It is quite certain that if Martin Luther's parents had never been married; or, considering the laxity of the times, if they had never seen each other; or, to make the matter perfectly safe, remembering that some people prefer darkness to light, because, etc., if they had never come within ten statute miles of each other, Martin Luther never would have been the head of the Reformation. Consider for a moment—it is worth your while—the extraordinary state of the case. The father would probably have married some other woman; the mother some other man. Or, failing in this, they would naturally have adopted a policy as nearly like it as the circumstances would admit. In either case it is easy to perceive that it would have been with the child, Martin, at a somewhat earlier period though, pretty much as King Solomon proposed to do with that one for which the women contended. But in such case, as to which half, upper or lower, would have gone this way, and which that, I leave to be speculated upon by the curious reader; being myself only certain of this, that if the common people of Germany of that day were no better off than the people of this Republic at this—six millions of whom can neither read nor write, and twice that number having no more notion of the multiplication table than an infant clam has of the binomial theorem—there was not much choice either way, head or heels.

The capital of Georgia, at that notable period of its history of which I am now writing, had twenty thousand inhabitants, counting the women, and one hundred and twenty lawyers; that is, six lawyers to every thousand people. Now, take out the women, and you have six lawyers to every five hundred people. Take out the four children which statisticians allow to each family, and you have six lawyers to every one hundred people; that is, three lawyers to every fifty people; that is, one lawyer to every sixteen and two-thirds people—but as this fraction of a man was likely to be hung where there were so many lawyers, he may be left out of the calculation altogether. One hundred and twenty thousand dollars, divided variously, from boring expenses, up to ten thousand dollars, among the one hundred and twenty lawyers, was what it annually cost this devoted little city to get its disputes settled, hang two-thirds of a man, and set free several whole ones who deserved hanging. Annually, then, it was necessary for this democratic, whirligig little city to put its hand into its small breeches' pocket—but here I beg pardon; it becomes necessary to explain. They never did do things here as they did anywhere else. The rule is for cities to grow too big for their leg-apparel; but here it was just the other way. It happened in this wise. The Council, having their own patriotic ends in view—but as to what their patriotic ends were, neither grammarians nor rhetoricians have provided any decent way of expressing; but it can be abundantly proven that the Council had no more patriotism in their heads than a Pennsylvania Legislature—the Council, having their own patriotic ends in view, took a pair of large, second-hand pants, cut the legs off to make them short enough, put the pieces where they would do the most good—after the manner of economical housewives—and thrust into them the tiny legs of this infant committed to their charge. But the Fathers believed in the eternal fitness of things. And so they immediately formed several small *crédit mobiliers* for stuffing these empty legs with bran; for the trousers hung shabbily about the infant's legs, presenting a disgraceful appearance. The legs were duly stuffed with bran; that is, the Fathers pretended to each other that it was bran, but in fact it was nothing but shavings and sawdust. But as for the part above the confluence of the legs, that fell to Mr. Keener, a drygoods merchant. Now this Keener had a certain piece of damaged checks; so instead of stuffing the part in question, he simply made a blouse that should reach below it; and for raw and gusty days the pieces cut off the legs had already been put where they did the most good. And so it happened that this city was duly dressed out in a truly picturesque, independent, democratic fashion. And so it happened that this capital had to put its hand, not into its small, but into its large, and, as it were, empty pocket, and take out one hundred and twenty thousand dollars for its lawyers, out of which sum Clarence Hall received about five hundred. This was not enough for Clarence Hall to marry on. But it has been observed that where there's a will there's a way. It was so here, at any rate. And it all happened in manner and form following:

Among all the scores of washerwomen about town, who should Clarence Hall have but Betsy Wiley? Betsy Wiley looked up to Clarence Hall as the very highest development of the man and lawyer, for Hall had learned this lesson, that if you wish to be popular with your inferiors you must make them believe that you consider them of some importance. Betsy's husband was a well-to-do mechanic, and lived down in Oak street. It so happened, one Monday morning, that Betsy was unwell, though such a thing had not happened, so far as anybody outside the family knew, since the birth of her last baby; and her lord and master thought himself not too good—a thing which cannot be said of many of his betters—to do for one morning what his wife had done for scores. So, taking her large basket, he went forth to gather together the soiled garments of the young gentlemen who weekly trusted their fortunes to Betsy. That was a fatal day for Dick Wiley. He was caught among the numerous railroads which infest the central portion of this city, and was killed. Luckily, he was killed while returning home; after he had been seen by respectable witnesses who could testify that he was not drunk. Now if Betsy had only gone after the goods that morning, which she would have done if, of all the mornings of the year, she had not been sick on that identical morning, the whole matter would have turned out just as differently as could be conceived even by the imagination of a Hindu or a Typologian.

Not many days after the event just recorded, Van Comer was in Hall's office.

"I believe, Hall," said Fred, "you are glad the poor negro got killed."

"Not at all. But as he did get killed, I am glad his wife was my washerwoman, and knew me well enough to employ me against the road. It is a good case, and if they do not compromise with me at three thousand dollars, I will sue them for ten, and eventually get half of it."

"Why then should you be willing to take three now?"

"Because of the delay, and some uncertainty. Besides, I am needing money, and I get half of what I recover."

"Needing money! Why, I hear everywhere how prodigiously you are doing. Some say you are making money like a mint; others, more definite in their knowledge perhaps, say you are making six thousand a year."

"I am making some money; I am saving a little, but not six thousand a year."

Fred could have gone on and told his friend that it was not only occasionally to be heard on the street, but that it was even believed, and probably acted upon, by some friends, in whom he, Hall, was much interested. Fred knew that the Dearings themselves entertained the most extravagant notions of Hall's progress in getting both reputation and money. Manifestly this was a thing vastly important for Hall to know. But one never sees things but from one's own standpoint. How was Fred to know anything of the importance of this matter to his friend? In the first place, he did not know the difference between Hall's reported and his actual income; he did not dream, however, that it was so great as to be almost ludicrous. As for Hall himself, how was he, being in love with Annie Dearing, and looking at things from a high moral standpoint, to know that the Dearings ever even so much as thought of what his income might be? Here then was something of the last importance for Clarence Hall to know, and his friend could make him know it; but the one, from his standpoint, seeing not its significance, and the other, from his, not even knowing of its existence, it was passed by. Fred supposed, rightly, that any information Hall wanted to give, he would volunteer, and so said nothing more on the subject.

"In such cases as this, can you sue the road for as much as you like?"

"Yes; and the jury determines how much the man was worth to his family, and assesses the damage accordingly."

"Some lives, according to that rule, would bankrupt the Erie. There is Mrs. Sutherland"—

"When will you cease to be extravagent in your praises?"

"When I cease to find objects deserving more than I can imagine."

"But in your high estimate upon your chief of women, the law would come in as a great gulf between you and the jury."

"Not, I hope, like that between Dives and my old grandfather Abraham's bosom is reported to have been. But that was an ignorant and barbarous age; we have had progress since then—development—march of mind. If poor Dives had only put off being born, say three or four thousand years—provided, you know, as Sterne says, it could have been done with any convenience to his father and mother—if he was as well off as he is reported to have been, some enterprising engineer would have bridged that gulf for him in no time. But why should there be any such gulf between me and a sensible jury?"

"Because under the law a husband cannot recover for the killing of his wife."

"Do you mean to say that under the laws of this country, if a woman's husband is killed by a railroad she can make the company pay; but if a man's wife is killed by the same railroad, under the same circumstances, there is no harm, no damage done at all?"

"In law, none. And not only under the laws of this country, but of England also. But you must hear the reason of it."

"Oh, hang the reason of it! Any reason for injustice must be absurd. Once I thought there was reason in all things outside of a Theological Institute, except a Scotch miracle. But I am beginning to think I shall have to make another exception against the law of the land. Look, for instance, at Bramlette's case. Do you know how that was?"

"No; how was it?"

"Why, Bramlette's father was wealthy, and had but two children. But as nearly all of his property had come by his wife, it was a whim of his to leave everything to his wife, and trust her to provide for their two children. Bramlette's mother married again—Judge Yelverton, a widower, who had not a dollar. By fair promises he prevailed on her to put off signing the marriage contract until after they were married. Well, you know when they were married the law made all her property his. Then he refused to make any settlement. He soon died, leaving all of Bramlette's and his mother's property to some of his own children by a former marriage. Of course, she could dower the property; but she soon died; and Bramlette, the only one of the children living, was turned out of his own home without a penny. The law handed all of his property over to strangers.

"That was very hard. But the law is altered now."

"Yes; I suppose it is. And it was done by that same radical convention that abolished imprisonment for debt, was it not?"

"No; but it was done by a radical legislature."

"What is Bramlette doing now? I scarcely ever see him," continued Hall.

"I don't know what he has been doing. I see him in the library every night. But he is going up on the State road soon, he told me, to edit a country newspaper."

"I am beginning to fear for Bramlette. The more I observe, the more strongly am I convinced that for a man to do anything great it is first necessary for him fully to believe that the world has a special use for him, that there is some one work which he must do with all his might, and purely for its own sake. Without that conviction, and the energy to put it to practice, he may become the pleasantest of friends, and a most learned man; but while he may *be* much, he will certainly not *do* any great work."

"Yes, he may, if he has genius, even become a Hamilton or a Mackintosh. In any case, such a man as Bramlette ought to trust to literature; he might do something, might even do much for the world, comparatively, in literature; but he would do nothing at anything else."

"Suppose we go to supper? It is just eight."

"Let us wait a few minutes, by all means. Have you not learned yet that all the clerks are there until five minutes past eight?"

"No; but what if they are?"

"Why—here comes Holmes. See here, Holmes, I was just telling Hall always to wait till after eight o'clock to go to supper, when all the clerks have left. If we go before, we shall have to hear all twenty of them ask every other 'How's biz?' I had rather eat thistles. I tell you how we will fix them to-morrow night. We must get there first; and when they all come in, we must start up a clattering conversation in French; we will talk about them, of course—call them names. They will not say a word; but I fear they will giggle. When they giggle they mean, 'biz is biz;' only the letters all get tangled in their throats and noses."

"But, now I think of it, I am a little skittish of my French; suppose we break down?" said Mirabeau.

"Ah, now that gives me a new idea. We must do like they did with that scamp Parolles—you know Parolles, in All's Well that Ends Well—speak what terrible language you will, no matter what, or whether it has any meaning or not. Let us have it that way part of the time anyhow, so we may laugh at ourselves too. I say : *Throca mouvousus, cargo cargo, cargo.* Holmes says: *Boscus thromuldo boscus.* Then Hall puts in, with great dignity and gravity: *Kerclebonto blonederdonedergewdenstronke.* Then we laugh at ourselves; and they laugh, too; and we proceed to make fun of them for laughing at what they know nothing about."

When Clarence Hall informed the railroad company that he would accept three thousand dollars, as damage for the killing of Dick Wiley, and let the matter drop, they expressed the greatest surprise that he should think of even finally getting so much for the life of a mere negro, even though an honest and thrifty mechanic. Hall said nothing to this, but quietly intimated that if his demand was not acceded to he should not only pursue them by the ordinary methods of the law, but that he should also bring suit for damages against the City Council, because they allowed so many tracks and cross-tracks to be run through the heart of the city. The railroad men began to think seriously of the offer to compromise; for they feared that such a suit might have the effect of calling forth an ordinance prohibiting the running of freight-trains up to the car-shed. The railroad men asked time to consider. He could only give them till next day. The next day Hall was informed that his proposition was accepted, and that the three thousand dollars awaited his order.

Clarence Hall was one of those men who seem to be inspired in early life with the belief that the world has some special use for them; that there is some particular work for them to do. Clarence Hall believed this even when a boy; and by the time he had left the University, and set out in life, the belief was almost raised to fervor.

"The crises of life," said the "old doctor" to us once at the University, "are very silent." And most men of eminence will agree that the whole bent of their lives was determined by something seemingly of the smallest importance: a book, a word, a look, may have been sufficient. When Clarence Hall was a boy, he read the "Lives of the Lord Chancellors." Endless vistas of greatness opened up before him. From that day he determined to be a great lawyer. Is it strange that a young man of rare intellect and daring ambition should almost worship this profession? If Hall had seen the profession in its true light, as only a mass of preposterous quibbles and barbarous conservatisms, of course he would not have thought it possible for it to furnish meat for greatness to feed upon. But we must view the subject from his standpoint. With him it was the noblest of all professions. The mission of the true lawyer was "to vindicate the truth— to maintain justice—to assail wrong—to defend right—to detect fraud—expose crime—protect virtue, and shield innocence." Clarence Hall saw that in his own country the legal profession was most powerful. And he saw that, being so powerful, itself ought to be elevated to the highest standard of Christian morals. It was the mission of this profession to preserve civil liberty. It was the mission of this profession to lead the people into paths of honor, integrity, virtue, prosperity. It had been confided to this profession

to mould the institutions of the country for good or ill.
And Clarence Hall wished to rise to the head of this profession in his country. Was it not a worthy and a generous
ambition ?

When Hall got the three thousand dollars he felt better than
he had thought it possible for money ever to make him feel.
He now had about two thousand dollars. Moreover, he got
the credit of managing the affair with the railroad with ability
and tact; and his practice received a considerable impetus.
The negroes were especially well pleased, and brought him
most of their business. Hall had now learned to discard
fancy figures; and so, in estimating his next year's practice
he did not put it at five thousand dollars, but thought he
might calculate upon one-fifth of that sum. Clarence Hall
had long had a settled determination to marry as soon as his
income would permit. He thought the time had now come.
He had two thousand in cash; he could calculate upon an
income of one thousand the next year; and there was his
book besides. To be sure, his book was not much, if any, more
than half done. But he would complete it now ! We have
seen that Hall believed that there was such a thing as a "female
soul," and that the male and female were "complements"
of each other. What might not a man do under the inspiration of such companionship as he should have ? He should
have somebody to work for, making every labor a labor
of love. He would have somebody to love, trust, and
lean upon him. All that was highest and best in him
would be called forth. He felt that he should be a better
man, a better Christian, a better lawyer; that his sympathies should be enlarged and deepened, his ambition elevated and purified. He would finish his book immediately;
maybe he might write two or three others. In the fervor of the moment he thought he should then be equal

to any work whatever, from plodding energy to soaring
genius.   Let not the reader suppose that Clarence Hall
was deceived in himself, for he was not.   You might have
searched any area of territory and not found any man on
whom the shrewdest observers of human lots would sooner
have risked a favorable prophecy.

Nor was Hall likely to be deceived in his ordinary calculations.   He was not one of those visionaries whose eyes are so
fearfully and wonderfully made as to see only phantasms and
figments, and never objects of denser stuff at all.   This was
not among his faults.   Besides his intense orthodoxy—which
some indeed will consider a virtue, but others a fault—his
chief fault has already been indicated: a most refined, yet
strong, selfishness ; and yet I dare say it may be a question
whether this refined selfishness be not the inevitable result
of such speculative belief, when the speculative belief itself
is refined.   Clarence Hall was not vulgarly selfish, but rather
generous and liberal.   His selfishness was of a very high order, it was beautified by the poetry of his nature, and sanctified by the religion of his geographical situation.   He believed
that woman was in deed and in truth, as well as in poetry,
Heaven's last, best *gift* to man.   And he believed fervently,
religiously, and particularly, that Annie Dearing was made
especially for him, Clarence Hall.   He decked out this essentially low idea—though perhaps unconsciously to himself—in
such garb of poetic imagery that it seemed to rise before him
as a beautiful ideal reality.   Such was the magic lantern with
which this man deceived himself.   He believed that he also
was created for her.   But her sphere was an entirely subordinate one.   She must lean upon him wholly, and in perfect
trust.   She must draw her life from him as the earth does
from the sun ; and, like the earth, she must strew his path-
way with flowers and enliven it with music.   The will and

purpose, the responsibility, the work and grand ambition of life, were all his.

Clarence Hall *and* Annie Dearing were married. He did not "take her to wife," as our worthy ancestors used to do in their day and generation. "Nous avons changé toute cela." That is, we have changed all the form of announcement. Meanwhile, the thing itself remains pretty much as it was. We go on "taking to wife" just as ever—only we do not take so many, according to the statute, as first-class people are reported to have done in the fervid era of King Solomon. Clarence Hall and Annie Dearing were married! Said I not that I was going to relate perhaps the most important event since Adam? Who shall say that it was not? Think of Luther's parents! The world, at the time of which I write, was certainly in as great need of a reformer as it was in the day of Luther, and is still so. A world reformer, Humanity may scarcely look for from the legal profession. But then such reformer might owe his paternity even to a lawyer. Clearly, Hall stands a better chance than did old Luther. The trouble is, they might all be girls! Still, let no one affirm yet that this was not the most important event since Adam.

Mirabeau Holmes was already in Europe, and was writing back to Marian Malcomb. When he was in London he went to see Carlyle. Carlyle's Essays had been to him what the "Lives of the Lord Chancellors" had been to Clarence Hall. It was these "Essays" that first inspired him with a restless ambition to "do somewhat" in the world. They opened up to him a whole universe, but full of mist and dream and shadow. And these two books were fit types of the destinies as well as the ambitions of these two men.

Bramlette was going to try his hand a while at editing a country newspaper, and correspond with Emma Harlan the while. She might look for many a true poetic gem from this man of rough exterior.

Fred was going to Sunday-school, and everywhere else that he thought he should see the flower of the garden of Kaipha; carrying always with him one of the liveliest, jolliest, and best-filled heads you might meet with in any scope of country.

Mr. Malcomb had been prevailed upon to become mayor of the city ; and, with the assistance of Mr. Walton and Dr. Sutherland, who were councilmen, and one or two other men of influence, was just beginning a crusade against conservatism, to establish in the city a complete system of free, public schools, and to build a hospital.

Mr. Alf Walton continued his machinations, and Mr. Brooke his fine sermons and visits to the little cottage on Ivy street.

James Arnot left his wild home in the mountains, and went —— ?   Allons !

Book 3.

ST. ANTOINE.

CHAPTER XI.

" Which is the true culprit, the Assembly or the Commune? History will tell. I accept the principle of the Commune. If any one comes to my house to take a fugitive of the Commune, they will take me also. If he is given up, I will follow him. I will share his seat. And for the defence of right, by the side of the man of the Commune, vanquished by the Assembly of Versailles, will be seen the man of the Republic, proscribed by Bonaparte." —Victor Hugo.

There is a place in Paris which I love above all others. No other spot on the globe is so able to excite the highest emotions. Is it, perhaps, that Democratic Paradise—the Champs des Elysées? No! Nor the Tuileries, nor the Louvre, nor the Luxembourg, nor the Jardin des Plantes, nor even the Hôtel des Invalides. It is the old Faubourg St. Antoine. Gamins, sans-culottes, proletaires, dwell here. Here is the hotbed of insurrection. At certain periods aristocrats and tyrants may lose their heads here without a moment's notice. The tocsin of war will sound here when the substratum will no longer be crushed. *Ça ira* has been chanted here, and will be again. The cry of *Vive la Révolution!* has been heard in these parts; also, *Vive l'Humanité!*

Gamins and sans-culottes. *Vive l'Humanité* indeed!

Had you not better cry *à bas l'Humanité?* Or had you not better hurrah for the Flood and pray for another! *Vive l'Humanité?* Wherefore? What has Humanité done for you? Made you miserable. Answer this: How much of life have you enjoyed? Have you, or your ancestors for a thousand years, ever known exactly what it is to be entirely clear of hunger? Do you expect your children ever to know? Better to hurrah for the Flood! But there also is the Place Bastile, and beyond, Père la Chaise. Still, let Humanity be thankful to the Poor Quarter of Paris. Thankful for the Revolution. Thankful for the Commune. If the time ever comes when it can no longer be said that, in the midst of all manner of wealth and plenty, by far the greater portion of the human race are still condemned to the lowest battle of animal life—the battle with hunger—much will be due to the Poor Quarter of Paris. Which, think you, will stand for most on the balance-sheets of Humanity —Arc de Triomphe or Belleville, Tuileries or Montmartre? I think there can no longer be any doubt upon this point. I reckon this also to be settled, that civilization owes more to the proletaires of Faubourg St. Antoine than to all priests, lawyers, and politicians together. So of Humanity; for Humanity owes everything to Civilization. Not that Humanity owes anything to the priests, lawyers, and politicians. On the contrary, I am much disposed to put them along with princes, of whom the Commune said: "Society has only one duty towards princes—death. It is only bound to observe one formality—proof of identity."

It was late in the afternoon of 17th March, the eve of a day that will be remembered in history. Three persons, one at least of whom we have seen before, were walking slowly through the Faubourg towards Place Bastile. They turned up the broad Boulevard Richard Lenoir, and went across to

Place Royale, where they sat down to rest. One of them was Mirabeau Holmes. Another was an Italian, young, of coal-black eye, and singular beauty both of feature and figure; his name was Simona. The third was a small man, not above middle age; his face exhibited a calmness upon the surface, but below you might recognize evidences of strong feeling: this man was Cluseret, afterwards Delegate of War, and almost Dictator of Paris. Cluseret was a naturalized American. He came to the Confederate States on the breaking out of the war between the States, and fought under General Lee in Virginia. It was this that furnished the basis of the friendship between him and Mirabeau. They had been together several times since Mirabeau had been in Europe. A few days before they had met, in London, Simona and Assi—a name already famous throughout Europe—whither they had gone from the chiefs in Paris to consult with the General Council of the Internationale upon the present grave state of affairs in the French capital. Mirabeau, for what at least appeared to him to be good and sufficient reasons, had already joined the Internationale. They had all just this day returned to Paris. They had been sitting here but a short time when they were approached by one whom they all seemed to recognize; they all rose to meet him.

There are some faces which, like a great work of nature or art, fill one with emotions of the sublime. One feels oneself in the presence of something great and good; one is elevated, and feels a lofty pride. If Robert E. Lee had lived among the ancients they would have deified him. Whoever has stood in his presence has felt himself thrilled and elevated with grand emotions. One felt oneself in presence of the highest humanity; bordering upon the divine. And here was a face strikingly like that of the great

Southern hero.   It was the citizen Delescluze, Tancred of
the Commune.   A meeting of the chiefs was to be held that
night to learn more fully the result of the late conference in
London, to decide upon some course of action, and to organize
for the immediate execution of whatever should be determined upon.   The meeting was held in No. 6 of the Rue
des Rosiers, the same in which the Central Committee of
Montmartre was holding its sittings.   It was necessary to
be in close communication with the Committee, for this Committee had now assumed control of the National Guard.
And although the chiefs could, if it became necessary, even
crush the authority of the Committee, from the threatening
aspect of affairs it judged best, indeed of the utmost importance, that all the leaders should act in concert.   Some of the
most influential of the chiefs were also members of the Central Committee, notably Assi, Jourde, Lullier, Billioray, and
Babick.

Mirabeau Holmes was present at this meeting, of such infinite significance to Paris and to the cause of Humanity.
Flourens, Delescluze, Assi, Cluseret, Dombrowski, Rigault,
Gambon, all the leaders were there.   Outside circumstances
now furnished the immediate cause, or occasion, of an insurrection.   The question was, whether the times were propitious for launching the country into that great Revolution,
to which the brave and enlightened friends of Humanity have
long been looking as the fearful but necessary remedy for
those evils which civilization thus far, instead of destroying,
seems only to have made more unendurable, and more appalling in their now almost cosmic magnitude.   It was decided here to-night, as it had already been by the General
Council, that the times were not yet ripe.   But this conclusion was not reached without much sadness.   Most of these
chiefs were young.   Some, however, were not.   There was

the virtuous and upright Gambon. He had labored for a generation in the cause of Humanity. He had learned the completest self-abnegation. During the whole course of his life he had been altogether occupied in the cause of the poor and suffering. Totally forgetful of self, disdaining honors, fame, wealth, and fearless of poverty, imprisonment, death, he had been all his life looking forward to the time when he might lay down his always devoted life in the cause of the people. Here evidently was an opportunity, even if not the most propitious. Possibly he might not live to see another. But once more the promptings of self were put aside. So be it!

And there too was the stoical Delescluze, heart and head of the Commune; Flourens, the ardent, universal democrat; Felix Pyat, the friend of Garibaldi; and Dombrowski, exiled to Siberia by the Russian government because he dared to be the friend of the people and the enemy of tyrants. The leaders decided that, as matters now stood, Paris should not rise. The committee, however, to which was now added several others of the leaders, was to sit all night, for there was no telling what unexpected emergency might arise. Paris was full of rumors that a gigantic conspiracy had been formed at Versailles for the overthrow of the Republic and establishment of the monarchy. Many were confident that the rumors were true. And some, even among those who had the best right to know, believed that this *coup d'état* might be looked for at any moment. One thing, though, was pretty certain: the conspirators would not attempt this without first disarming the National Guard. On the other hand, any forcible attempt to disarm the Guard would be considered proof of the conspiracy, and the first act of the dreaded *coup d'état*. In this case Paris would rise; but in any case the times were not ripe for the great Revolution. On the signing of the treaty of peace by the National Assembly of Versailles, fifty thousand National Guards had been allowed to retain their organization and their arms. Not because the Assembly wished it—far from it; but because it feared the Nationals, and knew that they would even refuse to be disbanded or to give up their arms. But why should the Assembly fear them? Were they not Frenchmen? Were they not fellow-citizens? Both. But they were also ardent republicans, and under the influence of the most vigilant and active democratic leaders. These leaders had not yet forgiven the conspirators of 4th September. Delescluze had declared publicly that he only took his seat in the Assembly to impeach them. But why should the Nationals refuse to disband or to be disarmed? Because they distrusted the Government of Versailles. They believed that the conspirators of 4th September meant to overthrow the Republic and bring back the monarchy. They had since been confirmed in this belief. Several plans had been proposed at Versailles for disarming them. But the Assembly had not yet dared to try to execute any of them. For a few days past, especially, the excitement in Paris had been high. The Nationals claimed the right to elect their own officers. The Government attempted to force upon them a commander appointed by the Executive. The Nationals refused to recognize him. Matters were getting dangerous. The atmosphere was ominous of insurrection and war. The leaders were in hourly communication with Versailles.

On the 16th a great meeting of the Nationals had been held at Montmartre in the open air. They protested against the appointment of a commander over them by the Executive. They unanimously elected Garibaldi commander-in-chief of the Guard. They elected members of the Central Committee, and pledged themselves to obey it till Garibaldi could be heard from. They declared that the National Guard would not surrender its arms; that it would defend the Republic. Meanwhile the Internationals throughout the world were in constant communication—for what purpose, and with what result, we have already seen. It was far in the night when the conference of leaders at No. 6 Rue des Rosiers broke up. The committee was to sit all night. Couriers were constantly coming in from Belleville, La Villette, Montmartre, Faubourg St. Antoine, and other quarters. If the Nationals were attacked during the night they were to give the signal—three guns.

The meeting at No. 6 Rue des Rosiers was not the only one held in Paris that night. The Mayors of Paris met at the Mairie of the second arrondissement to discuss the situation. All of the members of the Assembly from Paris were also in council. And the Republican clubs had met in every quarter of the city; some counselling moderation, others cursing the Assembly, and demanding the Revolution; but all agreed in this—that the Central Committee would not betray them, and that it should have their utmost obedience. It was quite late when the clubs and other meetings broke up. The city was quiet. The chiefs, however, at No. 6, did not go home. Of those who were not upon the Committee, some went to Belleville, some to La Villette, others to Montmartre and Place Bastile; Delescluze remained with the Committee. It was three o'clock in the morning. Hark! Boom! A single gun, in the direction of Belleville. Half a minute—boom! in the direction of La Villette. Boom! from Place Bastile. And then all three in concert—Boom! Boom! Boom! It seemed to wind and tremble and growl, every street, wall, and cellar sending forth a roar, and to roll grandly forth over the fields and hills of France, waking the sleepers. A rattle of musketry in the direction of Montmartre. A rocket rose high in the air from the neighboring Buttes de Chaumont, stood still for a moment, glaring with its blue flame upon the frightened air, then burst, the varicolored sparks flying in all directions. Montmartre was attacked. Fifty National Guards had been stationed there to guard the artillery. There were more than a hundred pieces, and it was this that the Versailles Government especially dreaded, and determined to capture at all costs. M. Thiers and his associates and the generals commanding the department had been in consultation all the day before to decide how these guns were to be secured, and with the guns the Heights of Montmartre, which overlooked the whole city.

A band of picked men, soldiers of the line, was placed under the command of a trusty officer, fearless, quick, and cunning. The men were ordered to disperse themselves through the city, and exactly at half-past three to take positions already assigned them, as sentinels, guarding every approach to the Buttes. Gen. Susbielle then quietly advanced and placed seven-pounder guns in every avenue leading to the Heights. At a given signal the first band rushed upon the fifty Nationals who were guarding the Heights. And so cautiously had the attack been arranged, and so promptly and silently was it executed, that the Nationals were seized and disarmed before they dreamed of the presence of an enemy. They had no time to give the signal agreed upon—three guns—if any quarter should be attacked. At this moment all seemed lost to the Nationals. The Heights, their main stronghold, was taken. This position commanded all others. But the chiefs were active and vigilant. Couriers were continually passing and repassing. At this very moment one was approaching the Heights. He saw what had been done; flew to the neighboring Heights, still in possession of the Nationals, and sent a rocket hissing into the air. Boom! replied Belleville; and Boom! Boom! answered Villette and Faubourg St. Antoine.

It was now four o'clock. Alarm bells were ringing. Drums were beating. People rushed into the streets, and instinctively cried, *Vive la République! Vive la Liberté!* A heavy force of Nationals from Belleville now came thundering along Boulevard Rochechouart, crying, *Vive la République!* Nationals now began to arrive from all directions. They seemed to come forth from every corner; nay, to rise out of the earth. The General, seeing that it would be impossible to hold the position, now determined to abandon it and to remove the guns with him. But there were now great crowds in the streets, and the troops were surrounded by the Nationals. The troops started. The crowd refused to give way, and some of them cut the horses' traces. The intrepid officer, with the select band of *Chasseurs d'Afrique,* ordered his men to advance and open a way for the guns. He commanded them to draw. A hundred sabres leaped from their scabbards. " *En avant,*" shouted the officer. The Chasseurs hesitated. The crowd shouted, *Vive la Ligne!* and *Vive la Garde Nationale!* The troops of the line now began generally to fraternize with the Nationals. The excitement was supreme. " *En avant!* " again shouted the officer, and single and alone he dashed into the seething crowd. Some were crushed beneath the hoofs of his frightened horse, and many fell beneath the rapid blows of his sabre. Cries of terror were heard in the crowd. The daring officer fell, riddled by a score of bullets. The infuriated crowd now fell upon him and rent him limb from limb.

At this moment General Lecomte appeared upon the scene. The Central Committee had also sent orders to the Nationals to retake the guns at all costs. General Lecomte placed himself at the head of a regiment of the line and ordered them to advance upon the crowd. The crowd cried, *Vive la Ligne!* and the troops elevated the but-ends of their muskets in the air, and cried, *Vive la Garde Nationale!* But the troops having possession of the guns had not yet fraternized with the Nationals. General Lecomte ordered them to forward, and if the crowd did not make way, to fire upon them. The troops advanced. The crowd shouted, *Vive la République! Vive la Ligne!* The troops moved, arms at " charge bayonets." The Nationals were fired upon. The firing became general, and many were killed and wounded. General Lecomte was killed. The troops abandoned the guns, and retreated in the direction of Place de Clinchy. Suddenly a terrific roar was heard in the direction of Place Pigalle. Boom! Boom! Boom! A score of cannon were pouring forth fire and death. Shot and shell came whizzing and shrieking up the Boulevard. The Nationals at Place Pigalle, seeing the retreating troops coming briskly towards them, thought themselves attacked, and fired upon them. The mistake was soon discovered, and the troops continued their retreat towards Place de Clinchy.

.It was now nine o'clock. The last of the troops of the line were gone. Montmartre, the intrenched camp, and all the guns, were in the hands of the Nationals. The troops had also left their artillery in the hands of the Nationals. But one of the most fearful incidents of the day has not been mentioned. General Thomas, formerly commander of the Guard, was recognized by some of the crowd. He was approaching the scene of action. It was just at that unfortunate moment when the troops had fired into the dense mass of people. Many, including some women and children, were killed, and the wounded and dying filled the air with fearful cries. The crowd was frenzied. General Thomas approached. They recognized him. They fell upon him. He was hurried against a wall and shot. It was not done by the National Guards. There was not a National among them. It was done by the infuriate mob. General Thomas was said to be a good officer

How much was his life worth ? Say ten thousand of the lives of the *canaille*. Let us hope that *Satory* furnished an altar large enough for the expiatory sacrifice. Fearful enough, too, one would think. Still, being, I hope, a better man than the traitors at Versailles, let us mourn over the fate of General Thomas. Not because he was General Thomas. No! But because he was a man, like the rest of us—a man of flesh and blood. The killing of General Thomas was a crime. It was murder, perhaps. But consider the circumstances. Above all, remember it was done by the mob, not by the Nationals. Remember, especially, that it was not by order of the "Central Committee." The Committee knew nothing of it. Not one of the leaders knew anything of it, officially or otherwise. It was done by the mob—the raging, frenzied, mad mob—in the midst of terror, revenge, shrieking, wounds, and death.

Two other officers came near suffering the same fate. It was afterwards announced that they were saved by " a young man not more than seventeen." This " young man " was an American. It was James Arnot ; for he too was here, and happened to be looking upon this tragedy. " Good Heaven ! Shall the men be killed without a hearing ? " This was said too low to attract attention. He made his way through the crowd to where the self-appointed executioners were. He resolved to make an effort to save them at the risk of his own life. " Hold ! " he cried, " the Committee orders that these men be brought before them. Here is the order. Quick ! I have other orders to carry." Quick as thought he took out a paper from among several others, thrust it into the hand of one of the men, and darted through the crowd. He calculated that the men, on seeing that the paper was no order from the Committee, would suppose that he had simply made a mistake, that he had given them the wrong paper. But the man was not able to read. So he merely pretended to read the paper, and then stuck it in his pocket. He had no doubt but it was all right. "These men are to be carried before the committee," said he; and off they marched with them. Arrived at No. 6, the man handed the paper to a stern-looking young man who was standing in the door. It was Simona. He read the paper, and turned pale as death. It was the fly-leaf that we have seen James Arnot, on a memorable night, tear from his mother's Bible.

"Who gave you this?"

"A young man with orders from the Committee."

"Would you know him if you were to see him again?"

"No. I hardly saw him at all."

Then, to himself, "Impossible—impossible."

A guard was called. The men with their prisoners were taken before the Committee. The prisoners were aides-de-camp of General Lecomte. By order of the Committee they were immediately set at liberty.

By the middle of the day the Central Committee had assumed complete control not only of the National Guard, but of Paris. The red flag of the Commune floated from Montmartre, from the column of Place Bastile, and numerous other points. A committee of barricades had been appointed early in the morning. Many had been erected. They had gone up as if by magic. There were several in Faubourg St. Antoine; an almost impregnable one in Place Bastile; another at Rue de la Roquette; another at the junction of Boulevards Voltaire and Richard Lenoir; another near the Chateau d'Eau; and several in the quarter of Montmartre. The excitement seemed to increase instead of wane as the day advanced. Early in the afternoon five thousand Nationals formed in the Montmartre quarter, and from then till midway the afternoon they traversed the principal thoroughfares of the city. By four o'clock they were probably ten thousand strong. They carried red flags and beating drums. Alternately they muttered "treason," "conspirators," and cried, "*Vive la République!*" They were followed by vast crowds of men, women, and children. Some of the men had on red caps; and the women and children chanted snatches of the Marseillaise Hymn, Ça Ira, and other revolutionary songs. At four o'clock the vast procession turned down the Rue de la Paix, and, after a slight show of resistance from the commandant, took possession of Place Vendome. Thence they proceeded to the Hôtel de Ville. They at once took possession of it, and the Central Committee installed themselves therein. The Ministry of Justice was also taken possession of, and everywhere the tri-color flags were hauled down and the red hoisted.

Late in the day all the Mayors of Paris (Paris is divided into twenty arrondissements, each having a Mayor) and all the Deputies of Paris present in the city, met at the Mairie of the second arrondissement to discuss the situation. They first waited upon Ernest Picard, Minister of the Interior, and submitted a plan of settlement. But nothing came of it. Then they waited upon the General commanding the Department, De Paladines. The General declared he could do nothing. Finally they went to Jules Favre. The basis of settlement proposed by the Mayors and Deputies was simple enough, and furnished an easy solution of the difficulty between Paris and the Versailles Government. This was what they proposed: (1.) The nomination of M. Langlois as the Commander-in-Chief of the National Guards. (2.) M. Edmond Adam as Prefect of Police. (3.) M. Dorian as Mayor of Paris. (4.) The Deputy, M. Billot, as Commander of the Army of Paris. In a word, they wanted to name their own officers. They demanded officers whom they could trust; officers who would not betray Paris into the hands of the Government of Versailles, which, they were now firmly satisfied, was plotting the overthrow of the Republic and the return of the monarchy. It was well known the world over that if such a *coup d'état* was contemplated—and it is certain that it was—Paris was the only obstacle in the way of the conspirators. And though the chiefs have been killed—murdered in cold blood upon the order of any petty officer into whose hands they happened to fall; though the poor people, prisoners—men, women, and children—have been mowed down by the thousand on the plain of Satory, as a huge offering for the *crimes* of the Commune; and though the very name has been branded with every epithet of infamy that ingenuity could devise, the truth is, that even the Republic of to-day owes its existence to the Commune! It may be—who can tell? —that it was this very consideration, as much as any other, that swelled the sickening sacrifice into such barbarous proportions.

Think you, perhaps, that it is strange that I, an American and a Southerner, should say so much for the Commune? Know, then, of a certainty, that I would go farther to grasp the hand of a poor exiled Communist, than of all the kings in or out of Christendom. I would rather place a wreath of flowers upon the grave of Delescluze than any in France! If the propositions submitted by the Mayors and Deputies of Paris had been accepted—and they ought to have been, of right, independent of the great issues which were immediately involved—the Republic would not have suffered; there would have been no "War of the Commune;" there would have been no triumphs for the Republic on the field of Satory! M. Jules Favre submitted them to his colleagues. They accepted the propositions. They sent them to the *Journal Officiel* for publication. The war was over.

Paris was saved. The Republic was saved. But there was more consultation. M. Thiers and his associates reconsidered their previous action. They undid what they had done; sent to the office of the *Journal Officiel;* countermanded the order to publish the basis of settlement; plunged Paris in blood and civil war. For this crime they are responsible. They pretended that they did this on hearing of the death of Generals Thomas and Lecomte. But this could not be; for this was in the afternoon, and all Paris had heard of the death of the Generals early in the morning. But even supposing they told the truth—which they did not—who is such an idiot as to say that this was sufficient reason for plunging the country in civil war?

CHAPTER XII.

"Qui meurt pour le peuple a vécu."
LE CHANT DU DEPART.

ON the morning of the 19th, instead of publishing the
basis of settlement agreed upon, the Government posted on
the walls of Paris a proclamation calling upon Paris to lay
down its arms, and surrender unconditionally to the Assembly! The last of the troops of the line had quitted
Paris, and were on the road to Versailles. The red flag of
the Commune had everywhere taken the place of the tri-
color. The members of the Government present in Paris
also left for Versailles. If the Central Committee was a
band of outlaws and assassins, if their only object was bloodshed and pillage, as was charged by the traitors at Versailles,
and spread over the world by tyrants and their dupes; why,
in the name of reason, why were these men, against whose
traitorous machinations Paris had taken up arms, suffered to
remain in Paris, not only after the terrible events of the
18th, but until noon of the 20th—a whole day after the last
of their soldiers had quitted Paris? Why were they then
suffered peaceably to depart? Why did not the populace
rend them in pieces? Nay, why did not the Committee—
incendiaries and assassins (!)—have them arrested and brought
before their bloody tribunal, and shot without ceremony, as
was the custom with themselves?

Let any man say what would have been the course taken
by the great Republicans of '92. All the army of Versailles
could not have protected them; every man of them would

have been taken, and summarily shot. But the great men of '89 and '92 were successful, and have been deified. Justly too. This would have been their course. They would have done well. That this course was not taken by the men of '71 must ever be regarded as a strong proof of their moderation; nay, perhaps, of their too great consideration for tyrants when the cause of the people was in danger. The Central Committee issued the following:

"HÔTEL DE VILLE, March 19th.

"CITIZENS: You had charged us with organizing the defence of Paris and of its rights, and we are convinced that we have fulfilled this mission. Aided by your generous courage, we have expelled the Government which was betraying us. At this moment our mandate has expired, and we again deliver it up to you, as we do not pretend to take the place of those whom the popular breath has just overthrown. Prepare yourselves, and immediately hold your communal elections, and give us for recompense the only one we ever hoped for—the true Republic. In the meantime we retain, in the name of the people, the Hôtel de Ville."

And to show that this was no make-believe, intended simply for effect, another decree was immediately issued that the elections for the communal council should be held on the following Wednesday, March 22d, and the municipalities of the several arrondissements were charged with the execution of the decree. It was said afterwards that this was only a pretence of surrendering power on the part of the Committee, as two-thirds of the members got themselves elected members of the Commune. But this saying itself is a mere pretence, a most intense pretence. It lies very near to the supreme black in the spectrum of truth. The Committee anticipated this; and so they decreed that the elections should be held by the various municipalities. That most of themselves were elected only shows that they had hitherto done their duty faithfully, and that they retained the confidence of the people. But the elections were not held on the 22d. The Mayors and Deputies objected. They wished to make one more effort to save the Republic, and at the same time prevent civil war. The elections were postponed until the 26th.

Mirabeau Holmes found himself treated with the most distinguished consideration by the members of the Committee and all the Republican leaders. The simple fact that he was an American had much to do with that, of course. An ardent democrat, and a member of the Internationale, he was little like the Mirabeau Holmes of a few years ago, except in the passion for finding out the cause of right and justice and enlisting fully and for life on its side. But even his enthusiasm had grown larger and solider. He had not been in Europe all this while a mere looker-on. He had read much, and had been studying civilization in its native soil. He felt as one feels when one visits those places which are the birthplaces of events which have shaken ancient systems and created new ones. If one desires to study civilization, one must go to the Old World. Mirabeau Holmes had also seen much. He had little conception before of the prodigious amount of human suffering even in the midst of the highest civilizations. If Professor Huxley had declared "that even in the city of Liverpool there were forty thousand savage men and women, and that they were more savage than the savages of India," he was inclined to think the dark picture borrowed unreal blackness by being placed alongside of the light of English civilization. But he found that the half had not been told. It was not long before he came to the conclusion that there must be something wrong in the civilization which produced side by side such astonishing and various luxury, and such infinite depths of wide-spread suffering and despair. Then he inquired if there might not be something wrong even with the *first principles* of that civilization. He joined the Internationale. That he was an American, an ardent democrat, and a member of the Internationale; that he was already the friend of Cluseret and Delescluze, could not fail to give him a warm welcome among the chiefs at Paris. They proposed that he should allow himself to be chosen a member of the Commune. This he declined; but lest it should be thought that it was for lack of sympathy, he signified his readiness to accept any suitable position that might be tendered him after the election of members of the Commune. He had already conceived a high admiration for the character of Delescluze, a brave, virtuous, unselfish man, wholly given to the cause of the people. Moreover, Delescluze was a man of the noblest intellect, and the most generous culture. Nor have the most reckless defamers of the Commune been able to deny that he was a thinker of a high order. His stoical enthusiasm and purity is acknowledged by the strongest enemies of the cause for which he laid down his life.

It was the day before the Mayors and Deputies of Paris went to Versailles to make one more effort for peace and the Republic, and on the very day that the Versailles people had succeeded in getting up a small procession of "respectables" to march up and down the principal streets and cry, *Vive l'ordre! Vive l'Assemblée Nationale!* that Delescluze said:

"The people at Versailles do not want peace. What they do want is the monarchy. Until the 18th they were still uncertain of the means to be employed. They knew that Paris was in their way. They knew that Paris was watchful

What they did not know was, whether Paris would succumb to treachery. They now know that Paris cannot be betrayed for the monarchy. Paris must be crushed. To-morrow the Mayors and Deputies go to Versailles to try to avert civil war. See what reception they will meet with. They will not be tolerated except by a few Deputies of the Left. They will be insulted. Possibly they will be driven from the chamber. What is certain is, they will not be allowed to speak, because they would speak not only to the Assembly, but to France and the world. The Assembly will not have peace."

On the following day the "respectables," the party of "order," again paraded the streets. They carried a tri-color flag with the inscription, " *Union of the Men of Order ; Vive la République !*" They promenaded the principal streets on both sides of the river, crying *Vive l'ordre ! Vive l'Assemblée Nationale !* Early in the afternoon the crowd, which now amounted to about a thousand, marched down the Rue de la Paix, giving evidences that it was their intention to occupy Place Vendome, which was guarded by a battalion of National Guards. The Nationals guarding the entrance were formed in three ranks, and expressly ordered not to fire on the crowd. . The first line had orders to raise the but-ends of their muskets in the air (a token of peace), and if broken by the crowd to retire behind the third line. The second line had received the same orders. The third line was to cross bayonets and remain firm ; but they were not to fire. The crowd advanced. The first line raised the but-ends of their muskets and gave way. The crowd continued to press upon the Guards. The second line followed the example of the first. The third now stood at "charge bayonets," and refused to give way. The crowd shouted *Vive l'ordre ! Vive l'Assemblée Nationale !* and continued to press forward. Seeing the Nationals would not give way, they became violent, swaying to and fro, and redoubling their cries. They raised the cry of *A bas les Assassins! A bas le Comité!* Several individuals seized the muskets and attempted to wrench them from the hands of the Guards. One of the crowd recognized Maljournal, an officer of the Guards and a member of the Central Committee. He seized a revolver, fired upon him, and Maljournal fell, seriously wounded. General Bergeret, commandant, now ordered the great drum of the Place to be beat. For several minutes it rolled, mingling with the furious cries of the crowd. Again and again they were ordered to retire. An individual in the crowd fired upon an officer. He was cut down by a sabre in the hands of a lieutenant of the Guard. At this moment several shots were heard from the neighboring houses, which had been occupied by the crowd, and several of the Nationals fell wounded. Everything was now uproar and confusion. The Nationals advanced slowly, fixed bayonets. The crowd now rushed upon them and attempted to disarm them. The firing from the rear was repeated. Two of the Guards were killed, and the firing from both sides became general. To disperse the crowd was but the work of a few seconds; but many of them were killed and wounded. It was afterwards pretended that the Guards fired first, and then wantonly slaughtered a great number of peaceful and orderly citizens; that the Rue de la Paix was filled with blood and carnage.

There were but two Americans present—General Phil. Sheridan and Mirabeau Holmes—one from the North, one from the South; of course they would have disagreed if possible. They saw the whole affair from the Westminster Hotel, Rue de la Paix. Both affirm that the account here given is positively the true one. It may be objected that

Mirabeau Holmes was, or afterwards became, an interested party; but General Sheridan was not likely to make it light on the Nationals from any misgivings as to the *possibility* of an armed soldiery wantonly firing upon and slaughtering a crowd of unarmed, peaceable citizens. At least one would judge so from the record he made during tho great "war between the States," in which the Southerners were unfortunate enough to lose their negroes and silver spoons. General Bergeret—whose sayings deserve consideration, not only because he was Commandant of the Place and afterwards a prominent member of the Commune, but because also of his known uprightness of character—gave, in effect, the same account of the affair. In concluding his report, General Bergeret used the following language: "We do not want war, nor do we want to kill each other, for our enemies are scarcely out of the city. What can we do? The Government attempted to take our cannon and to prepare for a monarchy. The Assembly has a fixed determination to force a king upon us. Let us avoid further bloodshed."

Meanwhile, the Mayors and Deputies had gone to Versailles; and there was enacted such a comedy as France herself has seldom been called upon to witness. It was disgraceful. It was criminal.

In the great wars of the Fronde, which for years desolated France, the questions at issue were mainly these three: Who should sit, and who should stand, in the presence of Royalty? Who should hand the king his napkin to wipe his fingers with? (for kings have fingers too, just like other people, and get them greased if they eat chicken-wings). Was it lawful for anybody but a princess of the blood to help the queen on with her shift? Not that this last is such an insignificant question either—provided the queen be young and good-looking. In this case I **am** clearly of opinion that it would be extremely lawful, in fact highly proper, for somebody other than a princess of the blood to help the queen on with her shift, or off with it either. As for my part, being an American and a Georgian, I would scorn to live in a country where it was not lawful for a gentleman to be a gentleman at all points. But can the mind of mortal man conceive of questions more ridiculous than the first two given above; or more absurd than the last—after the queen has lost her teeth? But it was reserved for the National Assembly to decide that it was strictly lawful and imperatively necessary to plunge the country in civil war, because the Mayors of Paris on entering the chamber responded with similar exclamations to *Vive la France! Vive la République!* from the Deputies. If it had been proposed by a Deputy that the Mayors should be allowed to say *Vive la République* in the chamber, the case would be vastly different. In the case supposed no one who knows the Assembly would be at all surprised that the Deputies should denounce each other with the utmost éclat, break up in the wildest confusion, and proceed to declare several Republics, Empires, Monarchies, and *Provisaires*, one and indivisible. But here it is entirely different. The Mayors had already said their *Vive la République!* and all the gods of the Panthéon could not unsay it. The case was this: M. Arnaud, a Mayor and a Deputy, said that " he, in common with his colleagues, Mayors of Paris, in view of the gravity of the situation, had come to Versailles to place himself in communication with the Assembly. He knew that none but members had the right to a seat on the floor, but asked that, under existing circumstances, an exception be made in favor of the Mayors. (Violent protests on the Right.) It would be sufficient that one of them, who was also a Deputy, should make the communication, so as to prevent any idea of disorder. He merely wished to observe that, as they had all come together, and been jointly delegated—

On the Right: "By whom?" (Great noise.)

Voices from Right: "Was it by the existing Executive?"

M. Flouquet (Republican)—"You desire, then, civil war?" (Renewed and continued uproar.)

Finally, after much disturbance, it was decided by the President, who had more sense than most of the Deputies, that a tribune should be placed at the disposal of the Mayors, and that their communication could be read by some one of them, who was also a Deputy. He observed that this could be done without infringing upon their rights, prerogatives, and interests—a thing that must not be thought of—implying that civil war was far preferable. The Mayors then entered, each wearing a tricolored scarf, the insignia of their office. The whole Assembly rose and welcomed them with cries of *Vive la République!* from the Left, and *Vive la France!* from the Right. But when the Mayors responded with similar exclamations, immediately there arose a great tumult. The Right: "Order! Order! They do not respect the Assembly! They have no right to speak! Treason! Invasion! Out! Out! Clear the hall!"

M. Flouquet and several on the Left: "Hear us, we implore you! You are plunging France in civil war!"

But the Right only redoubled their cries. Many of them put on their hats. And finally the Assembly broke up in the midst of the greatest confusion and tumultuous uproar. The Mayors immediately returned to Paris, and agreed with the Central Committee that the elections should be held on the 26th. The next day Louis Blanc made a final effort to avoid civil war. He stated that the Mayors had determined, under the exigencies of the times, to hold the elections on the 26th; and he asked, in the name of the Deputies of the capital, the Assembly to declare that the Mayors had acted like good citizens in consenting to that course. M. Blanc added that he himself thought there was great danger in postponing the elections. The proposition was rejected by a large majority, only a few members on the Left voting in the affirmative.

The Communal Council was elected on the 26th. It was composed of one hundred and six members. Those principally known to fame were Assi, Blanqui, Delescluze, Flourens, Felix Pyat, and Gambon; also Generals Bergeret and Cluseret, and afterwards Dombrowski. Cluseret was made delegate of war, and Bergeret commander-in-chief of the forces in the field, with Flourens second in command. Forts Issy and Vanves, and all on the south, were in the hands of the Commune. Mont Valérien on the west, which was finally the ruin of the Commune, was in the possession of the enemy. The Commune had now organized an army of a hundred thousand men. The war between the people of Paris and the conspiring monarchists at Versailles had begun in earnest. The red flag floated from the palace of the Tuileries. The Government at Versailles issued a decree that all prisoners falling into their hands should be immediately shot. This was the beginning; Satory was the end. And these are the men who call the Communists assassins! The Commune, hoping to prevent such murder, decreed that for every prisoner thus assassinated, *four* of the Versaillese should be shot.

On the afternoon of Sunday, the second of April, a splendid body of fifty thousand soldiers set out towards Versailles. Drums were beating. The people were singing and shouting. The army was reviewed by General Bergeret before it set out. It was here that Mirabeau Holmes, being at the side of the General, witnessed one of those stirring scenes never seen save among the French or Italian people. A most beautiful woman, mounted upon a superb white charger, and displaying the red flag of the Commune, advanced into the midst of the soldiers. Her hair, that would shame a raven's wing, bound loosely at the back with a fillet, fell to her waist, and from her forehead glittered a diamond star. She waved her banner, and sang the Marseillaise. She sang as she had sung once before to the heroes of Garibaldi. When she ceased, the very air seemed to glow and tremble with the energy of inspired fervor. For a moment there was silence; and then the vast multitude sent their caps into the air, and the heavens and earth seemed frenzied with enthusiasm. Full of the most active sympathy, Mirabeau Holmes was already seized with the ardor of the French people. Here a most happy thought struck him, and from this moment his place in the heart of Paris was secured. He proposed that the whole people, citizens and soldiers, vote the beautiful woman a crown; and the proposition was adopted amid a perfect fury of applause. The beautiful woman was Alberta Simona, sister of the Italian patriot. Having signified her wish, Mirabeau was immediately presented to her, by her brother, the Colonel.

The column moved forward. Some were shouting "*A Versailles!*" "*A Versailles!*" while others were chanting snatches of their wonderful hymn:

> Allons, enfants de la patrie,
> Le jour de gloire est arrivé ;
> Contre nous de la tyrannie
> L'étendard sanglant est levé.
> Aux armes, citoyens ! etc.

Tremblez, tyrans, et vous, perfides,
  L'approbe de tous les partis.
Tremblez ! vos projets parricides
  Vont enfin recevoir leur prix.
    Aux armes, citoyens ! etc.

Amour sacré de la patrie,
  Conduis, soutiens, nos bras vengeurs !
Liberté, liberté chérie,
  Combats avec tes défenseurs !
    Aux armes, citoyens ! etc.

The army was divided into three corps, commanded by Generals Duval, Eudes, and Gustave Flourens—General Bergeret commander-in-chief. The main body of the enemy, in all some fifty thousand, was strongly intrenched upon the heights of Meudon. The Nationals attacked them. Again and again the Nationals charged ; again and again they were forced back by the storm of bullets and grape and canister from the heights. Five thousand picked men were gathering for a final charge. Alberta Simona had been watching the battle ; but now she would stay no longer. She advanced, standard displayed, to where the General and some officers were standing, in a perfect shower of balls, in front of where the column was forming. She was in a few paces of them when she was struck, and fell from her horse. The whole army uttered a cry of pain. Officers and soldiers gathered for a moment around her. The General was wounded and was bleeding profusely. Mirabeau's hand was shattered, and he was also bleeding from a sabre-cut. Alberta begged her brother to go, and leave her with the General and Mirabeau, both of whom had to be borne from the field.

Simona placed himself at the head of the five thousand men. There was no yelling, no shouting. Not a sound broke the roar of cannon and musketry. " En avant ! "

And this splendid column swept swiftly across the plain and up the heights, to do or to die. In the trenches. Hand to hand, and steel to steel. A shout of victory rends the air. The red flag floats from the battlements! But the Nationals are almost spent with fatigue. Half their number lie dead upon the plain and in the trenches. The enemy is reinforced. The red flag is torn from its place. And the Nationals are again forced back down the hill and across the plain.

General Flourens was also defeated at Rueil. That brave man was surrounded, and compelled to surrender himself a prisoner. When asked who he was, he replied: "One who has spent his life in the service of the people. I am Gustave Flourens." He had already thrown down his arms. The gallant officer, Captain Desmere, to whom he had surrendered, rushed upon him, and cut him over the head with his sabre. Then all fell upon him, and the brave old man was riddled with balls. His body was taken to Versailles and placed on exhibition. "Qui meurt pour le peuple a vécu!" A place in the Panthéon awaits it!

The more one reflects the more one wonders at the extraordinary moderation of the Commune under the most trying circumstances. It was decreed that the public treasures of the Paris churches should be seized. Concerning this seizure the *Mot d' Ordre*—Henri Rochefort's paper—said: "As for the sacred vases studded with emeralds, or the emeralds enriched with finely-chased vessels, we do not hesitate to declare them public property, from the simple reason that they are derived from the generosity of those to whom the Church promised Paradise; and that an assurance of imaginary blessings, given to extort money or articles of value, is designated in all codes as swindling. We cannot say how the first Christians understood religion; it has since been strangely revised, corrected, and augmented; but at this hour, and for many centuries past, it has become the pretext for all sorts of extortions and intimidations. For this reason we infinitely prefer seeing the Commune make requisitions on the churches rather than on merchants and manufacturers." Of course, M. Rochefort was speaking of the Catholic Church, which never fails by all sorts of threats and death-bed terrors to extort money or other valuables from its blind and ignorant devotees. Still, an intimate acquaintance with New England witcheries and "Scotch miracles"—as Fred Van Comer termed them—would not probably have softened his judgment. But M. Rochefort was not the Commune, not even a member of it. The Commune seized the *public* treasures of the churches, because it was that, or let the people starve! Was not that sufficient reason? The only wonder is, that *all* the treasures were not seized. There was a proof of its moderation. From the great Bank of France, with its two thousand millions of dollars, it only demanded the pitiful sum of twenty odd millions! They only wanted enough to keep the brave defenders of Paris from starving. They themselves were serving without pay. The following decree was also issued:

" Paris, April 12, 1871.

"THE COMMUNE OF PARIS—Considering that the Imperial Column in the Place Vendôme is a monument of barbarism, a symbol of brute force and false glory, an affirmation of militarism, a negation of international law, a permanent insult cast by the victors upon the vanquished, a perpetual attack upon one of the great principles of the French Revolution, Fraternity—decrees the Column of the Place Vendôme shall be demolished."

It was right and proper. I appeal to any man not a Frenchman, at all capable of exalted hopes for the future of

Humanity, if the logic of the Commune is not unanswerable. I say "any man not a Frenchman." For even Victor Hugo —of whom it has been truly said, "In a better world than this Victor Hugo would be a grand man "—has been so far blinded by the National vanity as to declare—"The Column destroyed was a sad hour for France." But let Victor Hugo be forgiven; for he also said—"I was not with them (the men of the Commune). But I accept the principle of the Commune." The Column was overthrown on the 16th May. The following description may be interesting to my readers.

"In 1806 Napoleon had this monument erected in honor of the victories of the Imperial armies. The column was of Tuscan order, copied after Trajan's pillar. Height 135 feet, circumference at the base 35 feet, base 21 feet high and 20 square. The column was covered with bas-reliefs in bronze, composed of 276 plates made out of cannon taken from the Russians and Austrians in the Imperial campaign of 1805. The bas-reliefs were three feet eight inches high and circled the column 22 times, making a spiral 840 feet long. They were a series of tableaux, 76 in number, having for their subjects the principal incidents of the Austerlitz campaign. The bas-reliefs begin with the breaking up of the camp de Boulogne. The first represents the troops in review and the Havre flotilla rounding Cape d'Alpreck. The commentator construes the appearance of the ships while Napoleon was inspecting his army into a desire on the part of Ocean to pay also its tribute to the emperor. Then we have the departure of the various corps from Boulogne, Brest, Utrecht, and Hanover, on the great converging march, which, until last year, was perhaps the finest campaign opening ever planned. The troops are represented as taking farewell of the sailors, who were to have ferried them over to the battle of Dorking; we see them on the march, crossing rivers, entering towns, and in their various arms of artillery, cavalry, and infantry. In the sixth tableau the Emperor appears before his servile Senators at Paris, and informs them that the war against the third coalition has begun. The will of the eternal enemies of Europe is accomplished (said the Emperor on that occasion), the peace I hoped would continue is broken, blood will flow, but the French name will win a new lustre. A few words like these were quite sufficient to cover the demand for 80,000 men of the next year's conscription. The tableaux continue; the soldiers are still on their road, crossing the Rhine at Mayence, Manheim, Spires, Dourlach, and Strasburg. Then comes the Emperor himself, riding over the bridge of Kehl, with his headquarter staff, on the 1st October, exactly one month after the breaking up of the camp. The submissive Electors of Baden and Wurtemberg, who are rewarded with crowns after Austerlitz, receive their benefactor; and in the 15th tableau the first blow is struck at Donowerth by the 4th corps, thirty-six days from Boulogne. Then we have Murat clearing the road to Augsburg and Ulm by the combat at Wertingen, and the passage of the Danube at Newburgh by the 2d and 3d corps. The plot thickens. Augsburg is entered, and the Emperor harangues the troops, 'after the manner of the Roman Emperors' upon the imminence of a great battle. The 24th tableau depicts Soult's success at Meningen; a spirited relief and a long inscription tell how Ney forced the bridge at Elchingen, which gave him his title of Duc. The enemy are driven back upon their intrenchments before Ulm, and the Emperor arrives at headquarters on the 15th October. Two days afterwards—31st tableau—Berthier, surrounded by his staff, receives the capitulation of General Mack. The panorama continues; the garrison of Ulm file out and lay down their arms. The Emperor receives General Mack in tableau 33, and then

comes what the legend calls 'a superb and ingenious allegory,
dedicated to the glory of the Emperor Napoleon.' The allegory is as simple as superb, being nothing more nor less than
Victory writing on a shield the words, 'Capitulation d'Ulm.'
A few more scenes, among which is the desperate fight at
Krems, where Frenchmen met Russians in a narrow defile,
and were so crowded together that they could not use their
muskets, and fought with unfixed bayonets—brings the spec-
tator to the quarters at Schönbrunn, the entry into Vienna,
and the surrender of the keys of the capital. A deputation
from Paris arrive with felicitations, and then the Emperor is
seen quitting Vienna with many of his Generals for Braun.
The great blow is impending; a reconnaissance is pushed on as
far as Olmutz; Presburg is entered; the heights of Santon are
occupied by the artillery. On the night of the 1st December
the Emperor, wrapped in his cloak, visits the advanced posts;
it is the anniversary of his coronation [A BAS LA RÉPUBLIQUE?]
and the soldiers light pine torches till the whole camp is
illuminated. High up the column began the series of bas-
reliefs in which its climbing glories culminated. The Sun of
Austerlitz rises, and the Emperor was to be seen on horse-
back, giving orders to the Marshals and Generals. A furious
cavalry charge breaks a column of the enemy's infantry, cap-
tive Generals surrender their swords, and Oudinot's foot-
guards drive a body of Russians into the icy lake of Augerd.
[Poor devils! was it for this they were born? For this, in part,
that the Column was erected by the victors?] In the next
scene the battle is won, the Emperor of Austria has craved
an interview, and is asking his *bon frère* to grant an armistice.
Further on still, French soldiers carry off cannon and other
arms from the Vienna Arsenal. Talleyrand arrives at Presburg to negotiate the treaty, which is signed by Napoleon the
day after Christmas-day [*and by which some considerable area*

of territory, and goods and chattels—such as horses, sheep, men, cattle, women, hogs, furniture, children, etc., were disposed of? Down with the Column!] St. Mark's Lion and some richly decorated gondolas denote the cession of the Venetian States, the Electors of Bavaria and Wurtemberg receive their crowns, the Imperial Guard enters France bearing captured standards, the Emperor returns to Paris, and passes under the Arc de Triomphe, a car laden with spoils of war follows, and last of all, hundred-voiced Fame proclaims the high deeds of the campaign of 1805, while old Seine, reclining on his flood, listens to the story of so many glorious battles."

Just so! "The Electors of Bavaria and Wurtemberg receive their CROWNS." What do the people receive? Death, for the most part. Some receive the loss of one or more limbs. Others, various glorious wounds. As for the rest, why, one half of them receive each a knapsack full of "spoils of war." Where do these spoils of war come from? Well, from certain poor, miserable, oppressed devils, pretty much like the victors. But there is one glorious consideration both for the living and the dead among the victors—it is OFFICIALLY declared that they " deserve well of the country." Ought not that to be enough to satisfy reasonable men, not to say patriots, for the loss of legs or heads? Ungrateful dogs! To your holes! in the Faubourg St. Antoine. But whenever you get a chance, remember to tear down the Imperial Column, and all else like it. The Column was demolished on the 16th May.

Meanwhile several changes had taken place. Dombrowski had succeeded Bergeret as Commandant of Paris. Citizen Mirabeau Holmes had become a member of the Commune. Rossel had succeeded Cluseret as Delegate of War. Forts Vanves and Issy were demolished, and the Versailles army was gradually closing in upon Paris. Deputations from all

8

the principal cities of France had gone to Versailles to intercede for Paris; but the invariable reply was: "Some more houses will be shelled, and more men will be killed; but Paris must be crushed."

On the 9th May, Rossel, Delegate of War, resigned. He was arrested next day, and escaped—to be afterwards ignominiously shot at Versailles. Poor Rossel! He presents the most pitiful figure in all the history of the Commune. One day Colonel Lepreche, commanding the trenches, summoned Rossel to surrender Fort Issy " within the space of one quarter of an hour," else " the whole garrison shall be put to the sword." Rossel sent the following reply:

"PARIS, May 1, 1871.

"To Citizen Lepreche, major of the trenches before Fort Issy:

"MY DEAR COMRADE: The next time you venture to send us so insolent a communication as your letter of yesterday, I will have your messenger shot, in conformity with the usages of war.

"Your devoted comrade,

"ROSSEL,

"Delegate of the Commune."

Citizen Delescluze succeeded Rossel as Delegate of War.

On the 29th April there was a grand demonstration of all the Freemasons of Paris. The grand procession, with music and flags, entered the Hôtel de Ville about noon, which had been decorated for the occasion. All the members of the Commune, wearing their red scarfs, were present. The walls were adorned with devices of flowers and olive branches. Upon the floor of the Court of Honor, and upon the stairways, were carpets of crimson. When the court was full, Felix Pyat rose to pronounce an address. Shouts arose from every side: *Vive la franc-Maçonnerie! Vive la Commune! Vive la République Universelle!* "Brothers, citizens of the great country—of the universal country," said Felix Pyat, "faithful to our common principles, Liberty, Equality, and Fraternity, having posted your manifesto—manifesto of the heart—on the walls of Paris, you go now to plant your banner of humanity on the ramparts of our besieged and bombarded city. You go to protest thus against homicidal balls, in the name of right and universal peace. (Shouts of *Vive la République! Vive la Commune!*) You go to stretch out to the men of Versailles a disarmed hand—disarmed, but only for the moment—and we, the *mandataires* of the people and defenders of its rights; we, the elected by vote—we wish to join ourselves with you—the elected by ordeal—in this fraternal act. Five favored names —members of the Commune—have been designated by lot to accompany you in this glorious, victorious act. (Renewed shouts of *Vive la Commune! Vive la franc-Maçonnerie!*) Your act, citizens, will remain in the history of France and of Humanity. Long live the Universal Republic!" (Loud and continued shouts of *Vive la Commune! Vive la République Universelle!*)

Citizen Beslay, member of the Commune: "Citizens, the whole Commune of Paris wish to take part with you in this great manifestation. I was not one of the fortunate five yesterday; but I asked, nevertheless, to go before you as senior of the Commune of Paris, and also of the Freemasonry of France, of which I have been a member during fifty-six years. What can I say to you after the eloquent words of Felix Pyat? Citizens, Brothers: Permit me to give to one of you the fraternal embrace." (Citizen Beslay embraces one of the Freemasons. Great applause— *Vive la République!*)

A Freemason, banner in hand: "I claim the honor of planting the first banner on the ramparts of Paris—the banner of *Perseverance*, which has existed since 1790." (Applause.)

The Band played *La Marseillaise*.

Citizen Leo Meillet, member of the Commune: "It is the flag of the Commune of Paris which the Commune is about to confide to the Freemasons. This flag should accompany your pacific banners; it is the flag of universal peace, of our federative rights. It will be placed in front of your banners, and before the homicidal balls of Versailles." (Citizen Terifocq, Freemason, takes the flag from the hands of Citizen Leo Meillet.)

Citizen Terifocq: "Citizens, Brothers: I see at our head the white banner of the Lodge of Vincennes, on which are inscribed these words: 'Let us love one another.' We will go and present first this banner to our enemies' ranks; we will stretch our hands to them, since Versailles will not hear us ! Yes, Citizens, Brothers, we will address ourselves to the soldiers, and we will say : 'Soldiers of the same country, come and fraternize with us; we will have no bullets for you so long as you send us none of yours. Come and embrace us, and let peace be made.' (Prolonged applause.) And if this peace is accomplished, we will return to Paris convinced that we have gained the most glorious victory—that of humanity ! If, on the contrary, we are not heard, but fired upon, we will call every vengeance to our aid. We are certain that we shall be heard, and that the Masonry of all the provinces of France will follow our example. If we fail in our attempt for peace, and if Versailles gives the order not to fire upon us, but to kill only our brothers of the ramparts, then we will mingle with them—we, who until now have taken service in the National Guard, only as a service of order, those who have hitherto not belonged to it, as well as those already in its ranks—and all together we will join the companies of war, to take part in the battle, and to encourage by our example the brave and glorious soldiers—defenders of our city." (General applause, and prolonged shouts of *Vive la Commune ! Vive la franc-Maçonnerie !*) Citizen Terifocq waved the flag of the Commune and cried, "Now, Citizens, no more words—to action ! "

The Band struck up *La Marseillaise*, and the procession of Masons, accompanied by the delegation of the Commune, filed out of the Hôtel de Ville. The flags were planted upon the ramparts at Porte Maillot. When the Masonic banners were seen, General Montaudon, commander at that point, and himself a mason, ordered the firing to cease for a short time. Meanwhile a deputation was sent to Versailles. They received from the Versailles lambs only the stereotyped answer: " More houses will be shelled and more men killed, but Paris must submit to the Assembly." The firing recommenced. The masonic banners were riddled. The cannonade was now fearful in the extreme, far more terrible than the Prussian bombardment. Many of the shells, passing over the Arc de Triomphe, went crashing and screaming along Avenue Champs Elysées.

The following was published by Delescluze, the Delegate of War: " We point out to public indignation the conduct of the Colonel commanding the 39th of the line. When the Versailles troops took possession of the Park of Neuilly, that infamous butcher ordered eighteen prisoners to be shot, swearing that he would do the same with every man from Paris that fell into his hands. Let him beware on his side of falling into theirs." The following was also published by the Commune:

                                          " Paris, May 27.

"The Government of Versailles has just disgraced itself
with a fresh crime, the most frightful and most dastardly of
all. Its agents set fire to the cartridge manufactory on the
Avenue Rapp, and produced a frightful catastrophe. The
number of victims is estimated at more than a hundred.
Women were blown to pieces, as well as a child at the breast.
Four of the criminals are in custody."

This was indeed a fearful crime. What object could there
be in blowing up this factory? Paris had more arms and
munitions of war than there was any need for. The blowing
up of this large manufactory could accomplish nothing but
the fearful death of some hundreds, perhaps, of women and
children. I say, "perhaps some hundreds," for there were
ordinarily about one thousand women employed in the establishment; and from some apparently mere accidental circumstance nearly all of them had left the establishment at five
instead of seven o'clock, their usual hour. The enormity of
the crime must still be measured by the intention. The Versailles lammies! The Commune demolishes the Column.
The lamblings of Versailles blow up, a house containing a
thousand women, and many children: *à bas les assassins!*

In a dark, still room, in the beautiful Rue de la Paix, a
beautiful girl lay wounded and dying. It was the Italian
patriot girl, Alberta Simona. Her brother was not there.
There were only two or three attendants in the room, besides
two visitors; the visitors were the Citizen Delescluze and
Mirabeau Holmes. The terrible roar of artillery shook the
house. Simona had been sent for; he was defending the Porte
Maillot; he could not leave his post. His beautiful sister,
whom he loved with a passionate devotion worthy of himself
and of her, must even die without a parting adieu, without a

last sweet kiss from the brother she idolized. Such sacrifices the cause of liberty demands. For once, the stoical face of Delescluze was wet with tears. What did he see before him? A beautiful young girl, who had left her own country and come, in obedience to a divine sentiment, to offer up her pure young life upon the altar of liberty. As for Mirabeau, he had from the very first been attracted to this girl. So much beauty, such sweetness, such inspired sentiment had awakened in him the highest feelings of devotion and love. And no wonder. Even that is the beauty of life. That it is that makes life divine. And there was something divine, too, in the feeling with which she inspired him. There was nothing selfish in it. Indeed, he could not have defined his own feeling; it was too ethereal. Language expresses the thoughts and feelings of common Humanity. And Humanity has scarcely yet had need of language to express the most exalted and ethereal sentiments. It was now several days since she had received the fatal wound; and more than once had Mirabeau been at her bedside. He was here to-day for the last time. She wished for her brother. They had made a promise to each other in Italy, when they were with the patriot army of Garibaldi, that when either of them came to die it should be, if possible, in the arms of the other. But even this sweet consolation was denied them. Bien!

The Commune of Paris, with uncovered heads, followed the sacred dust of this girl to Père-la-Chaise. And that dust, too, when the great time comes, shall receive a sacred niche in the Panthéon. Meanwhile, let a shaft of polished marble, pure and white, rise high in the air; and let a golden railing enclose the spot where she fell. Carve Excelsior upon the marble; but plant no weeping willow there!

CHAPTER XIII.

"Serrez vos rangs, qu'on se soutienne!
Marchons! chaque enfant de Paris,
De sa cartouche citoyenne
Fait une offrande a son pays."

THE most trying times had now come upon Paris. All hope was gone of succor from the other large cities. Faithful to their traditions, Lyons, Marseilles, and one or two others had displayed the red flag, and demanded to be led to the rescue of Paris, the Republic, and the principles of '89. But the Assembly, having the name of the Republic on its side, and having the confidence of the rural districts, to say nothing of armed forces at every point, the risings in the cities were speedily put down. Paris was left to its fate. The cities had also sent deputations to Versailles. "Some more houses will be shelled, and some more men killed, but Paris must submit," was the answer they received. Bien! So also say we. There may be, doubtless will be, some more triumphs for oppression and injustice yet. Some more cities may be shelled, doubtless will be; some millions more of unfortunates will be slain in the field or starved in the cellar; there may even be a few more Satorys yet, but the grand time will come! Humanity will triumph at last! Close up the ranks! Destiny approaches, and victory sits upon her banners!

Delescluze received the following:—

"PARIS, *May* 16, 1871 (*Tuesday*, 7 P. M.).

"CITIZEN DELESCLUZE:—A citoyenne who is entirely devoted to you has a most serious communication to make you; only as she wishes to make it to you alone, she begs you to keep absolutely secret the reception of these lines, and also to find yourself to-morrow (Wednesday, 17th) in the Rue Neuve-des-Petits-Champs, at No. 48, under the entrance to the Ventadour Baths. You must appear to be strolling, and no one will pay you any attention. Be there at four o'clock. You may have to wait five or six minutes at the most. A carriage will stop before you, and you must enter. Be without fear; the person who wishes to speak to you will be alone. Put a flower of some kind in your left button-hole, so that the coachman may distinguish you at once. Above all, discretion. Not a word of this to those surrounding you.

"Yours, with all my heart,

"JEANNE LACASSIÈRE.

"P.S.—Burn this."

Delescluze was "without fear." He met the citoyenne at No. 48, and had disclosed to him a dark conspiracy of four members of the Commune for delivering up the city to Versailles. One of the conspirators was Cerisier, a weak, timid man. Delescluze immediately went to Cerisier, and got from him knowledge of the whole affair. They were to open the gates at one o'clock at night. When the troops appeared that night, expecting to meet the conspirators, and to have the gates opened, they were fired upon, and most of them killed. These were the darkest days of the Commune, and through them the character of Delescluze shone with the noblest and most conspicuous lustre. Now in the War Office, issuing orders; now upon the battlements, in the midst of iron and blood, and pointing the cannon with the utmost coolness and precision of aim; and now assisting and encouraging at the barricades;

everywhere showing a stoical grandeur of character worthy of an acient hero. He knew that the decree had gone forth —Paris must fall! And he knew, too, that, whatever others might do, there was one man in Paris that should be faithful to his promises. And that man was himself. If he had been less unselfish, not wholly devoted to the cause of Humanity; if he had found pleasure even in his own glory, he might have looked beyond the din and smoke of the final struggle, and found cause to rejoice. For fate had already unrolled the long list of Humanity's martyrs, and there, high up on the sacred scroll, might be seen the name of "DELESCLUZE" in a coronal of glory.

On the night of Sunday, the 21st of May, the gates having been opened by treachery—not, however, by any member of the Commune, but by one Monsieur Ducatel—the Versailles army entered Paris. In consequence of the conspiracies and defections, and the changes of officers resulting therefrom, there seems to have been such confusion that there was a considerable portion of the army within the walls before it was known even at the War Office. Indeed, it was not till Monday morning, late, that it was generally known in the city. By this time the enemy had penetrated as far as the Arc de Triomphe, and the tricolor floated from the summit of that monument. And now came the times of terror and death. The Committee of Public Safety issued the following:

"PARIS, May 22.

"Rise up, patriotic citizens! To the barricades! The enemy is within our walls! No hesitation! Forward for the Republic, the Commune, and Liberty! To arms!"

They also published an appeal to the Versailles troops. "Like us," said the appeal, "you are proletaires, and like us, you have an interest in not allowing to the conspiring monarchists the right to drink your blood, as they profit by the sweat of your brow." They were appealed to to imitate the course they pursued on the 18th of March, to come and fraternize with the people. But the assailants showed themselves only too ready to carry out the bloody programme of Versailles. There is but one recorded instance where the men refused to obey their brutal officers. It deserves to be recorded. In the Rue du Temple a barricade, after repeated charges and a most heroic defence, was finally taken. The brave defenders fought to the last, and several hundred were taken prisoners with arms in their hand. This circumstance, instead of arousing the admiration of the officer, determined him to have them all murdered on the spot. There were several women among them, and one child, a boy about twelve years old. They were all turned over to a captain, with a corps of execution, with orders that they should all be immediately shot—child, women, and all. The turn of the child came. He was pushed against the wall to be shot. He asked to be allowed to speak to the captain. The captain advances, and asks what he wants.

"I should like," said the child, drawing a watch from his pocket, "to carry this to the concierge who lives opposite; he would know to whom to give it."

The captain looked at the men; for he was only executing orders, and it was necessary that he be careful lest he be placed against the wall himself for disobeying orders. They all seemed to understand that the child only wished to make his escape. "Let him go," said the men with one voice.

"Well, go! and hurry yourself!" said the captain.

What was their amazement, when, suddenly, running as for life, and almost breathless, the child reappeared, and placing himself with his back to the wall, exclaimed "*Me*

voilà!" This was too much for them. Some of the men
threw down their muskets; some looked to the captain, and
then at the boy, lost in admiration. The captain seized the
boy by the shoulders, gave him a furious kick, saying, "Get
out of the way, you wretched little imp!" But the several
hundred men, and the women too, whose heroic bravery
ought only to have called forth admiration, were all shot, and
their bodies, some of them still quivering and writhing in
death, thrown into a heap. The following was issued from
the War Department:

"PARIS, *May 22d.*

"The citizen Jacquet is authorized to requisition all inhabitants, and all objects necessary to him, in the construc-
tion of the barricades in the Rue du Château d'Eau and of
the Rue Alhouy.

"Wine and whiskey alone are and remain excepted.

"All citizens, men or women, who refuse their aid, shall
be immediately shot.

"DELESCLUZE,

"Delegate of War."

Orders were issued to erect barricades everywhere. The
Faubourg St. Antoine bristled with them. Several were
erected in the Rue de Rivoli, Rue St. Honoré, and on the
Quai. They were also numerous in the neighborhood of
Père-la-Chaise, Château d'Eau and Montmartre, in the north
and east, and at Pont Neuf, Place St. Michel, and in the
Boulevard St. Germain, in the south and west. And they
were not such either as usually spring up in a single night.
They were constructed mainly of paving stones and sacks of
sand, and were very strong. "Ah! ça ira, ça ira, ça ira,"
was not heard in the streets. All—men, women, and children—went silently, swiftly, desperately to work to build bar-

ricades and die behind them. At one time thirty women appeared at the War Office, and demanded guns to arm a barricade in the Place du Palace Royale. They were all in mourning. Each one of them had lost a husband, lover, son, or brother. There were no horses to drag the guns. The women hitched themselves to the guns and dragged them to the barricade. They carried displayed the red flag of the Commune. Citizen Jules Vallés delivered them the guns, the flag, and an order from Delescluze commissioning them to aid in the defence of Paris. One of them also received the embrace of citizen Vallés in the name of all, and they departed to the barricade.

Then came the mistresses of the primary schools—established by the Commune. They desired to employ the children under their charge in making bags to be filled with sand and used in constructing barricades. Thus it was that everybody—soldiers, citizens, masons, women, boys, and little girls—wanted a part in the defence of their city. I, for one, wish the name of every one was preserved. I think I could read the bare record of their names with as much interest, and with as sacred a fervor, as the grand deeds of any patriot that has shed his blood for the Right, that has died in the cause of Humanity. Verily, verily, I wish the dust of every one of them, whether they died behind the barricades; whether they were hurried against the wall and shot; whether they were slaughtered at Satory; or whether they survived the conflict and shall die hereafter at home, or in exile, no matter how nor where, I wish the dust of them all might be gathered into some Panthéon of the world!

On Tuesday afternoon there were five men met together in the War Office of the Commune. I think you might take any known area of country, through any number of recorded centuries, and you would not find a company more venerable than that. Five men embodying so much exalted heroism, so much fidelity, so much stoical yet enthusiastic emotion, coming from countries so far removed from each other, of lives and fortunes so different in everything but in laboring and hoping for the same grand result; five such men as these in the War Office, I reckon, had never before come together. I wish the group was put upon canvas and placed in some Louvre of all nations. These five men were Gambon, Delescluze, Mirabeau Holmes, Dombrowski, and Simona. Gambon and Delescluze were both Frenchmen. Gambon, upright, pure, ardent, wholly devoted; Delescluze, simple, stoical, and grand as a Doric column. Mirabeau was the only native American of any prominence in the Commune. He was representative of his countrymen; fervid, free, generous, ambitious, always ready to sacrifice himself in a just cause. Dombrowski was a Pole. He had served with great distinction in the Russian army; but that Despotism, dreading his liberal opinions and his fiery patriotism, had exiled him to Siberia. Simona was an Italian patriot and scholar, a friend of Mazzini, an officer in the army of Garibaldi, and had surrendered himself to the royalists with that great man.

It was of no use now for the leaders to try to deceive themselves. They had met here for half an hour's consultation. What else could they do but fight to the last? If they surrendered, they would all be shot forthwith, without trial or ceremony. Not only the leaders—that, to them, was matter of the smallest consideration—but, judging from the past, all of the National Guards, besides thousands of citizens—men, women, and children—would be shot also. No! They would all die at their posts. They would leave such a heritage of triumphant devotion as Humanity had not seen before. They would astonish the world by their resistance.

The defenders of every barricade would die with arms in their hands.

"And yet," said Delescluze, "it is necessary we look only to the good of the cause. It may be that it does not demand this sacrifice of every one. It may even demand that some shall save themselves. You, citizen (turning to Mirabeau), I think are one of them. Yours is a great country; in fact (mournfully), it seems our greatest hopes for the future rest with you. I see, too, that the Commune will stand in need of friends—strong friends, able to assail as well as defend. The cause for which it dies, though it be the grand cause of human freedom, of universal fraternity, will be covered with every infamy. For the rest, calumny will be heaped upon us individually too. Allons. That matters nothing. We must look to America. We can hope for justice only from the Republic of Washington; and in that Republic, too, rests our hope of the future. We must have champions there. You can save yourself easily with the assistance of your Minister. You have proven your devotion. The cause will need you at another time, and, maybe, on another theatre. For you, citizens (to Dombrowski and Simona), you who have so often drawn your swords for the good cause, you both have countries that have struggled, and will struggle again, for liberty. They will need your swords and your counsels. Humanity will accord to you that you did all here but make the final sacrifice, and that you denied yourselves that for a greater, perhaps, hereafter. As for us two, my comrade (to Gambon), *our* way is clear. I only wish that Delescluze may be as faithful to his promises as Gambon will be to his."

"Yes;" said Gambon, "*our* way is clear. Let the records of the past indicate the future. If Gambon is the last to survive, then will Gambon carry the last Red flag that floats in Paris."

"The dust of an Italian patriot," said Simona, "can ask no more than to mingle in the same soil with that of the heroes of '89 and of the Commune."

"As for me," said the brave Dombrowski, "I have no country. I spoke for liberty once; I found a home in Siberia. I have fought for liberty; I shall find a home in France. Moreover, I have a special reason. I hasten to the barricades."

"I will go with you," said Mirabeau. "Shall not my country have one representative, however unworthy, among the Immortals?"

They all, but the Delegate of War, rose to go.

"Comrades," said Gambon, "we shall not all be together again. Give me the embrace." And these five strong men, gathered here from the four quarters of the globe, for a common struggle and a common sacrifice, silently embraced, and departed in different directions for the barricades, Delescluze remaining a short while to finish some orders. Dombrowski's "special reason" was, that for some hours, the day before, he had been deprived of the command of the army.

Four strong barricades had been erected in the Boulevard Magenta: one at its junction with the Boulevard Rochechouart; another at Château d'Eau; and two others at about equal distances from these severally.

Through the influence, or perhaps by the authority, of Delescluze, the order to arrest Dombrowski was quickly countermanded, and that brave man, who at the daily and hourly risk of his life had traversed alone and on foot the whole length of frozen Siberia and Russia, that in a foreign country he might aid in the work denied him in his own, without a murmur resumed his post of honor and danger. Montmartre had been taken about noon. Its courageous defenders had fought to the last, and died with their arms in their hands. Only a few prisoners were taken; these were overpowered and their arms wrested from them. They were hurried against a wall. *Vive la Commune!* The prisoners were dead! "*A mort les incendiaires!*" one of the bloodthirsty butchers had cried as they were pushing the prisoners against the wall. "Liars and assassins!" said a National Guard, "had we wanted to destroy Paris, could we not any day, for the last two months, have done it by turning our guns upon it? Cowards! Cowards!" Montmartre, Place Pigalle, Places Clinchy and Europe, and all west were now in the hands of the Versailles troops; and they had already begun a fierce attack upon the strong barricade at the northern terminus of the Boulevard Magenta. It was necessary to take this barricade, because it was heavily armed with cannon, and in the hands of the Versaillese these guns might be turned upon the other barricades to the south. Boulevard Magenta being a broad open avenue, and the other barricades armed with cannon, it would be almost impossible to dislodge them, especially from the immense barricade at Château d'Eau, unless this first one was captured. It was to this barricade that Dombrowski, Mirabeau Holmes, and several members of the General's staff hastened from the Hôtel de Ville—alas! to which one of them was to return only too soon for the hopes of friends, but not too soon for the full measure of his glory. When they reached the barricade it was in the midst of a furious attack. The assailants, by crawling along the sidewalks and dodging into the doors and recesses of the walls, had occupied the neighboring houses, and from the doors and windows of the upper stories were pouring a destructive fire over the barricade. The General saw that the position would not long be tenable. He immediately sent off the members of his staff present with orders to the commandants of the other positions to mass as many men as possible to be used effectively, behind the works, and to occupy with small bodies of resolute men the houses for some hundred yards in front. He then mounted upon the barricade, in the midst of a shower of balls, and lowered and pointed several of the guns, so as, in case of assault, to rake the street even from the very foot of the works. This was hardly finished when the quick eye of the General detected the heads of lines of assailants gathering in the cross-streets, as if simultaneously to debouch in the main street and assault the works. Dombrowski seized the red flag, and displaying it from the summit of the barricade, called out: "Soldiers, you are about to be assaulted. They are already forming for the charge in yonder streets. Let us all swear to die here rather than surrender!" At this very instant the assailants dashed into the street, and came forward with a yell. "We swear!" "We swear!" "Vive la Commune!" was heard on every side amidst the roar and rattle. The flag was torn from the General's hand. Mirabeau seized it and remounted to his side. A ball struck his left arm, by which he held it, firing with his right; another ball grazed his forehead and he fell to the ground. Only stunned by the blow, he was on his feet again in an instant. "Vive la Commune!" shouted the gallant General as a bullet pierced his body, and he also fell to the earth still grasping the flag. Amid the din and smoke his fall was not immediately noticed. Mirabeau called to a litter near by. The General was placed upon it, and Mirabeau, with three National Guards, carried him to the neighboring hospital of Lariboisière. As they were moving off with him the General was recognized, and many came and covered him with kisses. They found Dr. Cusco, chief surgeon, at the hospital. He asked how long he should live: he was in great pain. "Not longer than two hours," replied the surgeon. "Then give me a piece of paper," said the General, and the following order was sent to his chief of staff:

"SOLDIERS! CITIZENS! Hold the barricades! Let not a man leave his post! Let not a man surrender!

"DOMBROWSKI."

This was Dombrowski's last order. In one hour, between seven and eight, Dombrowski was dead. At half-past eight the General's chief of staff, Brioncel, came to the hospital, followed by the escort of the General.

"Where is the General?" he asked.

"He is dead," replied the attendant.

"Then give me his body."

When the body of the General had been delivered to his staff, and placed in a cab, the Director of the hospital arrived, and asked, "Why they were taking away the body." "It is our General's," replied Brioncel; "we don't wish the Versaillese to have his body." As the carriage was about to start to the Hôtel de Ville, several soldiers kissed him on the forehead, with many expressions of endearment. About midnight the body of Dombrowski was taken from the Hôtel de Ville to the cemetery of Père-la-Chaise. The body was dressed in a Polish jacket, and wrapped in a red flag, the same that the General had displayed from the barricade, and fallen with in his hand. The body was for some time exposed on a litter. Colonel Dombrowski, brother of the General, was present; Mirabeau, Vermorel, several other officers and chiefs, and the commandant of the place, Bruneseau, were also present. The commandant then called in the soldiers who were on guard in the cemetery, and each in turn kissed the General on the forehead. The body was then placed in an oaken coffin. Some words were written upon the lid by the General's brother. The coffin was then closed and placed in a vault.

One more final attempt was made to influence the Versailles soldiers. The following was posted on the walls:

"COMMUNE OF PARIS.

"*Federation of the National Guard.*

"SOLDIERS OF THE ARMY OF VERSAILLES:—We are fathers of families. We are fighting to prevent our children from being, one day, under a military despotism. You will be, one day, fathers of families. If you draw on the people to-day, your sons will curse you, as we curse the soldiers who tore the entrails of the people in June, 1848, and in December, 1851. Two months ago, on the 18th of March, your brothers of the army of Paris, their hearts infuriated against the cowards who had sold France, fraternized with the people. Imitate them. Soldiers, our children and our brothers, listen well to this, and let your consciences decide. *When the watchword is infamous, disobedience is a duty!*

"THE CENTRAL COMMITTEE."

On the morning of the 24th, thirteen women were shot in Place Vendôme. They were assisting in defending the barricade. It was *afterwards* pretended—the crime was so horrible that some pretence was necessary—that petroleum was found upon their persons. Ten women and children, some of the children only ten years old, were also arrested near the New Opera. They were murdered on the spot. There were many such instances. In no case was there pretence of trial or investigation. While these butcheries were enacting in Paris, the gentle Assembly of Versailles, reprosentatives of the people, were engaged in passing the following :

"The Expiatory Monument, raised to the memory of Louis XVI., shall be immediately repaired." (*Loud applause on the Right*). Bah !

CHAPTER XIV.

> "———— This is the very top,
> The height, the crest, or crest unto the crest
> Of murder's arms : this is the bloodiest shame,
> The wildest savagery, the vilest stroke,
> That ever wall-eyed wrath, or staring rage,
> Presented to the tears of soft remorse."
>
> —*King John.*

On the 24th, Wednesday, Raoul Rigault, the famous Prefect of Police, and Procurator of the Commune, was shot. Rigault was an atheist, without pity, and entirely dominated by passion. But there was not a man in France so competent as he to fill the office of Prefect of the Paris Police. So swift and accurate was his knowledge, and so firm his rule, that during the whole reign of the Commune there was not a single insurrrection, or even conspiracy, among the adherents of Versailles. If anybody was hostile to the Commune, Rigault knew it almost before he had spoken it to himself; and he was immediately arrested. Rigault wanted to create a "reign of terror," but the Commune would not hear of it. When he was captured he was just entering his hotel in the Rue Gay-Lussac. His captors were proceeding with him toward the Luxembourg, when they were met by a petty officer. He halted them, and asked Rigault his name. Rigault replied with a shout of "Vive la Commune !" "À bas les assassins !" He was placed against a wall and shot. His head and face were horribly mutilated, and the body left in the street. All day Wednesday was one continued roar of cannon and mitrailleuse. Place Vendôme, Place Concorde, and the Tuileries were now in the hands of the enemy. The strongholds still in possession of the people were the Buttes Chaumonte, Belville Heights, Château d' Eau, Place Bastile, and the heights of Menilmontant.

It was not till night came, and darkness enveloped the city, that the fearful extent of the conflagrations raging in different quarters was fully apprehended. The palace of the Tuileries presented the appearance of the crater of an enormous volcano in action; while ranged about it were conflagrations of the Palace Royale, Ministry of Finance, Palace of Justice, Central Markets, Hôtel de Ville, Conseil d'État, and Palace of the Legion of Honor, like great irregular jets of flame leaping and whirling from the sides of the riven mountain. Meanwhile the terrible roar of cannon continued, and shells were hissing, screaming, and crashing in every direction. The cannonade was kept up all night. The people were compelled to abandon the central portion of the city, and fall back on the Château d'Eau and strongholds throughout that quarter. The outer Boulevards were in possession of the enemy. There was no escape.

It had also been proclaimed that no mercy would be shown them. The people saw almost hourly evidences sufficient to convince them that this was no idle threat. Men, women, girls, and boys—all, when they fell into the hands of the enemy—were immediately shot. They were thrown into heaps about the corners of the streets. Some of them, not dead, were smothered and crushed beneath the bloody and frequently mangled bodies. There was nothing left but to fight with the energy of despair. Is it wonderful that they sometimes also fought, and even retaliated, with the fury of despair? For all of which the conspirators and assassins of Versailles are alone responsible. And it was not only privates, and such petty officers as that which had Rigault shot, that were guilty of these cold-blooded murders. . On Thursday

Millière was taken by a sergeant and several private soldiers in the Rue d'Ulm. This sergeant was a better man
than most of his brother officers. He did not feel that he
had the right to shoot down a disarmed prisoner, though a
member of the Commune, as if he were no more than a beast
of prey. The sergeant felt that such a proceeding would be
very much like murder. Would it not have been murder
itself? Can even the most dimly lighted conscience give
but one answer? Millière was taken before General de
Cissey. It may be that this gallant General was already
looking forward to preferment. He was afterwards made
Minister of War, possibly for this and many other similar
feats. General de Cissey, of his own royal pleasure, ordered
Millière to be taken to the Panthéon and shot. Arrived at
the Panthéon, Millière was made to stand upon the top step.
One officer forced him to turn his face to the wall, another
ordered him to face his executioners, and the two fell to
violent quarrelling. At last the murdered man faced his
executioners. He uncovered his breast. " *Vive la Repu-
blique! Vive la Peuple! Vive la Commune! Vive
————*" Millière was dead; and the body rolled down the
steps.

Jules Vallés was taken prisoner early on Thursday morning. He was immediately led out to be shot. His ferocious
murderers could not restrain themselves till they reached the
place they had fixed upon as the place of execution. One
of them struck him on the back of the head. M. Vallés
turned upon him, exclaiming, " *A l'assassin!* " Another
then struck him a violent blow on the back with his musket.
His spine was broken by the blow; and the poor man fell to
the ground, fixing upon his murderers a look of the greatest
horror. All now fell upon him; some firing upon him, and
some thrusting their bayonets through his hands, neck, and

face. Still he was not dead, when one soldier, perhaps better than the rest, shot him through the head. *Vive l'Assemblée Nationale ?*

M. Varlin, Delegate of Finances, was taken prisoner and shot at Montmartre. Johannard, member of the Commune, was taken and shot at Vincennes. General Eudes, member of the Commune and of the Committee of Public Safety, was taken at Vincennes, and, as was the custom, immediately shot. Lefrançois, member of the Commune, was taken prisoner at Rue de la Banque, and, with lawful haste, immediately shot. M. Jules Miot was taken on Monday, the 29th, at La Muette, and, for the sake of consistency, immediately shot. In the Rue du Temple five hundred of the people—many women and a few children among them—were taken while bravely defending a barricade. They were immediately shot, and thrown into a heap, there to remain till they could be carted away. And yet, on Sunday morning, after all this, and ten thousand times more like it, the Government of Versailles OFFICIALLY declares, " *These expiations do not console us.*" Bien! Of course it was highly proper that the poor lamblings should be " consoled." But where shall one find perfect " consolation " ? Let us hope that the gentle Government came as near it at Satory as is consistent with the limited resources of poor humanity.

Poor France! In the conflagration of the Hôtel de Ville the busts of all the monarchs of Europe were lost! The busts of Queen Victoria, Prince Albert, the King and Queen of Portugal, the Kings of Prussia, Belgium, and Italy, the Czar of Russia, the Sultan of Turkey, and many others were destroyed! No wonder " these expiations do not console us." But let not the good Government despair; for I have an abiding hope, and I trust a well-founded hope, that they, the members of the Versailles Government, may some day be allowed to gaze upon the originals of these busts in that country where go "all that ever reigned."

It was not until Friday that the Versailles troops began to take many prisoners. And then you might see great droves of them driven along the streets towards Satory. In one body there were as many as five thousand—men, women, and children. For the most part they were bareheaded, and many of them were without shoes. Some had on blouses, and some no coats at all. Most of them were ragged and dirty, and many of them were covered with dust and blood. The women were in tatters, with dishevelled hair, and occasionally uttered a wild cry of pain and anguish as they were pricked by the swords of the Guards to hurry them along. The drove was several deep, and more than a mile long. They were driven along between two rows of cavalry. The dust and smoke was so thick that one could scarcely breathe. Many of them were wounded, and the wounds were still bleeding; the blood dripping along the street, or oozing out and saturating their clothes. Some were exhausted from loss of blood, and some—the old and feeble—were exhausted from fatigue and the thick dust. They fell prostrate in the street, and were either trampled to death or left to die in the heat and dirt. Blinded by the dust and smoke, the unhappy creatures would frequently get out of line, which was not allowed. They were shot down, or thrust through, or whacked to death with swords. And then they were either thrown out upon the sidewalk or left to be trampled into the earth by the horses of the Guards. Oh! that the Versailles Government might be "consoled!"

The members of the Commune—those who had not been killed or were not at the barricades—when the Hôtel de Ville was abandoned, retreated to the Mairie of the Eleventh Arrondissement.

It was on Friday, about noon, that Citizen Delescluze, the Delegate of War, embraced his colleagues, who were still with him, and quietly set out toward the Château d'Eau. At the Château d'Eau seven enormous barricades had been erected. For two days a perfect storm of balls and shells had been hurled against this stronghold from the batteries in the Rue de Turbigo and Boulevard Magenta, and for thirteen hours it had sustained a most terrible attack from every direction. But one street opening upon the place was now in the hands of the people—Boulevard Prince Eugène. The people, profiting by the lessons of the previous days, had taken possession of the houses in front of the works; but the soldiers climbed upon the roofs of the houses, advanced from one to another, and poured a destructive fire into the ranks of the people behind the works. Delescluze proceeded silently along the Boulevard Prince Eugène, with the calm indifference of a stoic philosopher. Shells and bullets were falling and whizzing in every direction. He was deep in thought, thinking not of himself, but of the great cause that now, after so much sacrifice, was lost again. He met Gambon and Mirabeau Holmes; Gambon was going to Belleville; Mirabeau to a barricade farther down the street, to bring up about a hundred men that had been stationed there. Delescluze only said: " Lost again. Humanity will look to another time, and, maybe, another place, but the final triumph cannot now be far off. It will be sufficient reward if we have hastened it." Several officers and citizens gathered around him and entreated him to turn back. He only pressed their hands and kept on his way. Delescluze had probably done more than any other man to incite the people to resist their oppressors, the conspirators of Versailles. And when they rose, he promised to remain with them to the last. He would lead them to success or he would die in their midst. The cause was now lost. Delescluze was going to prove his fidelity. He was in citizen's dress, and carried in his hand a cane that he had carried constantly for many years. When he reached the barricade the battle was at its height, raging with inconceivable fury. But the people died as resolutely as they fought. There were no cries of pain or terror. The wounded died without groans. There was no sound but the roar, the crash, and the shouting of the assailants. The air was thick with smoke; it was stifling. The people had been at their posts in the midst of this terrible scene, without intermission, for thirteen hours, many of them for two days. They were covered with sweat, many with blood, and blackened with powder. The ground was strewn with splinters, balls, and fragments of shells. The gutters were flowing with blood. Broken guns, paving-stones, and pieces of furniture were also scattered around. When Delescluze reached the barricade he was recognized by many of the people, and they greeted him with a shout of *Vive la Commune!* Delescluze responded with a single shout of *Vive l'Humanité!* took his place at the barricade and began to fire with his revolver.

The carnage was now fearful. The walls were battered almost down, and the people were falling thick under the fire of the chassepots. About two o'clock the works were fiercely assaulted at every point. Exhausted by fatigue, more than half of them dead upon the ground, and overpowered on every side, the brave people, though they fought with the fury of despair, were all either killed or disarmed. Not a man, not a woman, not a child surrendered. Every one fought to the last; till the soldiers, sick of carnage, wrested their arms from them.

Late in the afternoon the body of Delescluze was found, riddled with balls and surrounded by the corpses of twenty-eight soldiers. And the next day it was officially announced by the Versailles Government that "the too guilty Deles-cluze has been picked up dead by the troops of General Clinchant." If the reader would elevate himself to the last height of moral sublimity possible for him to reach, let him contemplate, for a while, Citizen Delescluze on his way to the barricade to redeem his pledge to the people. In such men rest the best hopes of Humanity. They may be "picked up dead by the soldiers of General Clinchant," or the soldiers of any general, butcher, or tyrant whatever; yea, their bodies may be burned to ashes, and the ashes given to the winds; their pure, heroic deeds may all be falsified; their very names be made the synonyme of every infamy. They may find no place in the Panthéon, and no monument may rise to their memory. Nay, no monument will rise; for the people for whom such heroes live, and for whom they die, are all poor, condemned to battle with famine, unable to raise monuments in brass, or marble, or stone. But will they die? Will they be consigned to ignominy, even though historians add their little mite to the combined powers of ignorance and tyranny? Verily, no! Human feeling is a wonderful preserver; immortal as eternity, and more subtle than the planetary ether, surviving alike the shock of em-pires and successive systems of thought and religion. Nor can tyranny, with all its manifold appliances, any more ex-tract this subtle and powerful essence from human history, than can science extract the electric fluid from the globe itself. No! only the evil dies; the good never dies. Have you ever done one good thing; one thing for Humanity, completely forgetting your poor self? Thou art not less than immortal. The heroism of the Gracchi, branded as sedition, and charged with every infamy, still lives to warm the great heart of Humanity. And so with this Delescluze. Forgetful of self, he lived a life entirely devoted to the cause of the poor and oppressed; and when the hour came he embraced death, as he had devoted his life, without a murmur and without a regret. He, too, has taken his place in the constellation of Humanity's gods, enveloped in the glory of Humanity's love and blessings. And his heroism will ever live, in spite of all princes and politicians and priesthoods, to elevate the affections, clear the vision, and strengthen the arms of heroes that shall come after.

Gambon had said that, unless sooner overtaken by death, he would carry the last red flag that floated in Paris. He was faithful to his promise. It was on Sunday morning, about eleven o'clock, that Belleville, the last stronghold of the people, was taken. Gambon and several other members of the Commune, escorted by fifteen boys, foundlings from the hospital, who had formed themselves into a company and joined the forces of the Commune, established themselves in the Mairie of the Twentieth Arrondissement. Perceiving this to be untenable, they retreated to the Rue Fontan-au-Roi. They carried the flag of the Commune. They stopped at a restaurant and ordered a frugal breakfast, leaving the foundlings to stand guard, with a bugle, to give the signal if the enemy approached. When they had finished their breakfast they began erecting a barricade. Gambon was the only one who wore in his button-hole the badge of the Commune. He wore also on his lappel a head of Liberty fixed in a silver triangle, on the three sides of which were the words "*Liberty, Equality, Fraternity*, Commune of Paris." The barricade was scarcely half finished, when, suddenly, the enemy was upon them. Gambon seized the flag and mounted upon the barricade. He was alone upon the barricade. All the others had taken to flight. He fired his last charge. The enemy rushed upon him and secured him. What sort of man was this Gambon? and how should he be treated? He ought to have been given a palace. He ought to have been placed in a triumphal car, and drawn through the streets to the sound of music. He ought to have seen his portrait in the Louvre of nations, among the heroes of all ages. His ears ought to have been greeted with plaudits. Poets ought to have composed hymns in his praise, and children ought to have chanted them in the streets. Why? Because for thirty years he had been sacrificing himself for the Republic and Liberty. He was taken to the Rue de la Banque and shot. Let him rest with his compatriots and the heroes of '89, till Fame, from the Panthéon's summit, shall welcome his dust to its rightful home!

It was Sunday morning, the 28th of May, that the sun in heaven—"Liberty's darling"—struggled through the clouds and smoke that enveloped the heights of Belleville, to shed for the last time his sympathetic beams upon a people who, in all their lives, had found nothing else to rejoice at. They had not felt, and could not possibly feel, any other sympathy, nor see any other smile. With the springs of immortality within, and longing for the unseen, almost unhoped for, Better, they were still condemned, as their fathers had been, by a civilization based upon poverty, ignorance, and fear, to live without comfort and die without hope.

In a small back room of one of the houses in front of the barricade a young soldier—a citizen-soldier—lay in the agonies of death. A few minutes before he had fallen, while defending the door against the assailants. The young man was George Walton. He was too near gone to recognize one of his attendants. In a few moments he was dead. The battle was raging furiously; the enemy seemed determined to occupy this house at all hazards. At this moment an officer entered, and said the house must be abandoned in half an hour, as it was necessary to fire it. There were two attendants in the room where lay the body of George Walton: one, an old woman; the other, a slight figure, dressed in black, bent over the body, kissing the fair forehead, and seemed in the greatest grief. When the courier informed them that the house would be fired in half an hour, the figure kneeling over the body rose and said to the woman:

"Madame, this young man is a near relative whom I have not seen in many years. I wish to save the body. I have money enough to make you and your daughter comfortable, and I will give it you if you will assist me."

"Bien. But what is one to do?"

"In the first place, give me, quick, some of your daughter's clothing."

In a few moments James Arnot was dressed in a plain but neat suit of female apparel; a light, airy muslin dress, with lace collar, and belt of black ribbon, contrasting strangely with the roar of death and the enveloping pall of smoke. The hair which had seemed to be turned under heretofore, was loosened and fell in rich tresses upon the shoulders. And even in the midst of that scene, when James Arnot looked down upon his graceful and symmetrical figure, he was startled to see how nearly it was still like it was in a far country, on the bank of a great river, long ago, when he was last dressed in similar apparel. He went to the dead body, took off the watch, and the diamond pin from the bosom. Then he examined the pockets and found a diary and several letters, two in a large, commercial hand, and one in an anxious, rather trembling female hand, both of which he knew full well. Just at this moment an officer entered— a tall, dark-faced man, of high forehead and steady gaze. And when he ordered the house immediately cleared, and fired, one saw that his words were low and tuneful, more like the voice of a poet or artist than soldier. He walked on into the back room; but when he got to the door and saw the figure at the side of the dead man, he suddenly stopped, and seemed as one transfixed to the spot. He leaned against the door-facing, and drew from his pocket a slip of paper: "To Viola Walton, by her loving mother." The words were pronounced aloud, but as if to himself. James Arnot started, looked at the officer, and the steady light of his eye became wild and shifting. But the heart of a woman does not need any proof. She rushed forward, exclaiming, "Alberto! Alberto!" and fell upon the Italian's bosom. Then she drew back, and gazed into his face, fearfully, almost timidly.

"My own! My long lost! My little violet of the Mississippi!" and he kissed her forehead again and again, with the eloquent fervor of Italy. Their voices were dumb, but their hearts were active, and, through their own mysterious medium, soon made themselves known to each other. Flowing out like the aroma from the uncased perfume, the life of each mingled with the other, and they became one. If there had been any need of it, there was no time to tell of mistakes and disappointments, and the consequent long, long years of anguish and suffering that had divided them, and that each had borne alone. No! The remorseless, unhasting, but unresting march of fate, stops not for individuals, however high or low they may be. The building was on fire, and the flames were rapidly approaching.

The body of George Walton was placed upon a blanket and borne out, through the back door, into a neighboring building. In an inside vest-pocket they found a little trinket which Viola Walton immediately recognized; a tiny golden necklace which she herself had worn when a child. This little necklace was fastened by a small, richly studded locket. She opened one side of it and found the well-known picture of her mother, and a cloud seemed to pass over her features, and she hesitated before opening the other side, for she remembered now that her own picture had been there, and she was fearful that her brother, too, had abandoned her, and taken out the picture, ashamed to wear it. But no! The boy had trusted to his own feelings; this was his own sister—if lost, still his sister. Sometimes he had dreamed that she was not dead, but still living, somewhere on the broad earth, may be in poverty and shame. But still she was one of God's poor suffering creatures, and his own sister. Many and many a time had he passionately kissed this little picture, and vowed within himself that if he should ever find her, though in the lowest den of shame, not all the hideous social laws framed to disgrace and damn the weak and unfortunate should prevent him from rescuing her and acknowledging her as his own sister; for something vaguely told him that the misfortune was hers, the fault not her own. But misfortune or fault, his course would be the same. The picture was there: the bare, white arms, the childish face, the short little curls about the forehead. Again she knelt and covered the face of the noble boy with kisses. And then she rested her head upon the Italian's bosom, telling him of this other joy.

But let no mortal think to escape the iron hand of fate. A squad of soldiers entered, and Alberto Simona and Viola Walton were arrested. Bribes were offered in vain; in vain Viola, whose face was now again lit up with a parting gleam of that marvellous beauty whose morning light had waked to music the hearts of her worshippers, softened by the halo of a divine pathos, knelt at the captain's feet. He would not allow them time to bury their dead brother. No! These two people were necessary to make up the forty thousand people; the number which the assassins of Versailles had determined to shoot at Satory. The captain, for a large bribe, could only be induced to allow them fifteen minutes. There was another woman now present, besides the one that had come with them from the burning house. They were both mothers, and had both lost sons, fighting for the Commune. Here, then, was common ground, as misfortune ever is. A sum of money was placed in their hands, and they agreed to take the body, place it in a metal coffin, and bury it neatly. The body was to be wrapped in a red flag and buried, dressed just as it now was, in order that it might the more certainly be identified. The Italian then clasped the necklace around the right arm, after taking out one of the pictures—that of Viola—from the locket and putting a little lock of his own, Viola's, and their brother's hair in its place. The tiny picture, with a lock of hair as before, was then placed in an envelope, with a letter, which was read to the women, and from which they learned that they would receive a double reward if they were faithful to their promises, and the envelope was backed to Mr. Walton, at Atlanta, in Georgia. At the suggestion of Simona, this was placed in another envelope, addressed to the American Minister, with a short note that it came from an unfortunate countrywoman, and the women were charged to deliver it. Then they gave them a slip of paper on which was written these words, to which they both signed their names: "George Walton fell on the 28th of May, 1871, fighting for the liberties of that people of Paris who also, in perilous times, came to the rescue of his own people in their struggle for Independence."

Their time was now out. Each one knelt down and kissed their brother a final adieu. Then they embraced the two women, and marched out among the crowd of prisoners at the door. They were then marched towards the Château d'Eau, where a column of eight thousand prisoners from Belleville had halted for a few moments to wait for numerous squads, some of more than a hundred, and some of only two or three, coming in from all directions. When the vast drove moved off down the Boulevard St. Martin, it numbered between nine and ten thousand. When the head of the column had reached the Arc de Triomphe, prisoners were still defiling upon the Place Concorde, the rear of the column reaching as far back as the Madeleine. There were many old men in this drove of human beings, so old and feeble, indeed, that few of them ever reached their destination. There were also many children, some under ten years old. Also more than two hundred women. When the column reached the gate of Satory there were not nine thousand. The brutal guards were often heard to boast that many *accidents* happened on the way.   When an *accident* happened, the poor man or woman who had fallen, either from exhaustion or loss of blood, was simply whacked th rough the head and thrown upon the sidewalk. *Bien !*

CHAPTER XV.

"——— Formez une sainte alliance,
Et donnez-vous la main ! "—BÉRANGER.

THE largest butcher-pen of modern times is Satory.   It is
in the form of a parallelogram, and contains several acres.
It was once used as an artillery park, and there still remain
the stables used for the horses; but this was before it had
occurred to the Government that they would serve the cause
of justice and Humanity by transporting hither forty thousand people—exclusive of those who fell on the way by
" accident "—to be shot.   It is said that these forty thousand
were the poorest animals ever slaughtered in Paris; which,
indeed, is not wonderful, seeing that in the case of human
animals the ordinary process must be reversed—from fatten-
ing to starving.   It is stated that the Government would
have kept these forty thousand penned longer—at least
through the heats of summer—but for two reasons.   They
were afraid that natural death from starvation and bad
treatment—which was at least natural for these poor devils—
might rob the muskets of some of their lawful victims.
For one, I give little credit to this, as I cannot imagine the
Government was so short-sighted as not to see that they
could send back to Paris any morning or evening for a couple
of thousands to supply any deficiency or supposed meagreness
of the offering.   The controlling reason seems to have been
this, that the Government was in hot pursuit of " consolation," and eager for the *dénouement.*   Of course, if tho
victims had been kept penned they would all have died of

starvation and fevers after a while.   But this *diablement* snail-paced " consolation " was as good as no " consolation " at all !   So it was decided that the " expiation " should, if possible, be huge enough and brisk enough to " console " themselves and satisfy all reasonable demands of tyranny and injustice the world over.

The butcher-pen of Satory is surrounded by walls, and when the great drove of nine thousand victims, less what had fallen on the way by_ *accident,* entered it, there were numerous holes in the walls through which ferocious cannons scowled ominously.   When the vast drove arrived, the old stables had already been filled to suffocation, and many thousands were huddled together, here and there, and enclosed by ropes.   The drove was marched in a short distance from the gate, and being huddled close together, a rope, tied at conve- nient distances to stakes, was drawn around them, and a strong guard with chassepots put over them.   They were directly in front of several large guns charged with grape and canister, which were ordered to fire into the crowd upon the slightest manifestation of disorder.   All the pre- vious night the rain had been falling almost constantly, and the wheels of artillery and ambulance wagons, together with the trampling of horses, men, women, and children, had con- verted the pen into a horrible quagmire.   One sank over one's shoes in the mud and water.   The rain had now also commenced to pour again, and beat upon the poor shivering wretches pitilessly.   Many, as I have said, had been wounded ; some of the wounds were sore, and some still fresh and bleeding ; so that when a squad was moved from one place to another for any cause, to be_ shot mainly, one might see stains of blood here and there and little pools of bloody water. Some of these wounded had their friends with them, who did all they could for them, which was very little.   Others were neglected. Many were very old, some very young; most of them were fainting from fatigue, and all of them were hungry. They were too tired to stand. They threw themselves upon the ground, and the water settled around them, sometimes several inches deep. Guards were posted thickly everywhere; they were for the most part savage, mad, covered with wet and mud; their faces were begrimed with smoke and powder, which, mingling with the rain that beat in their faces, presented a frightful appearance. The wretched prisoners were nearly all bareheaded, many barefooted, and the great majority scantily dressed or in dirty tatters. They were shivering, their lips pale and bloodless, and their teeth chattering in the cold, drifting rain. Simona pulled off his coat and put it around Viola's shoulders, and bribed one of the guards to throw him a miserable piece of puncheon to stand upon. This was not allowable, and so they resorted to the following stratagem: Simona advanced towards the rope with an air of insolence; the guard, who already had the puncheon in his hand as if to place it for his own feet, hurled it violently at Simona as if he meant to knock him down. Thus was Viola kept out of the mud, which was more than ankle-deep. But this proceeding came near costing the Italian his life; for when the guard threw the puncheon at him another near by exclaimed, " Shoot the wretch!" and he was just about to do it himself, when the guard, with an oath, informed him that he could take care of his own beat.

Simona regretted that they could not be lodged in one of the stables, but in truth it was better to be out in the rain than to be inside of one of these places and have to breathe the disgusting atmosphere. The atmosphere was noisome in the last degree; it seemed impossible to breathe it an hour and live. To the natural stench of the stable was added the bad odors exhaled from many bodies crowded together, all dirty, and some sick and dying, and the foul breaths, many doubly so from most nauseous whiskey which had been swallowed by the miserable wretches in hopes of deadening their fearful sufferings. Here were many disgusting, or rather say pitiful faces, and they scowled at you sullenly, silently, as you passed along. Now and then you found one that tried to smile; but it was a disheartened, sickly, hopeless smile. "It was wonderful," says an observer, "to see such a number of ignoble faces, and with such a vile expression, brought together." Considering the previous history of the Versailles Government, I think it not wonderful at all that—Paris conquered—they should be "brought *together*," and that, too, just as they were—in these identical horrible pens and stables.

That there should *exist* "such a number of ignoble faces, and with such a vile expression;" nay, that there should exist even in a single city twenty times "such a number of ignoble faces, and with such a vile expression," cannot be wonderful to any man at all acquainted either with the cruel history of Humanity, or with the present sickening condition of the human race even in the most civilized countries. Wonderful? Just .God! The only wonder is that the vast majority of the race in civilized countries have not sunk into savages and brutes. Condemn a family, or a colony, to a thousand dismal years of grossest ignorance and darkest superstition; sickness without relief, and hunger without the hope of bread; winter without fire or clothing, and con- -tinued toil without hope of bettering their condition; surround them with every misery,—and deny them every comfort; heap upon them every ill, and shut out from them every hope save that which gleams once in a century through the fierce but fitful fires of revolution; place them, moreover, in contact with those whom they regard as their oppressors, and in the midst of boundless but unlawful plenty and luxury, and how should they have any other than "ignoble faces, with such a vile expression?" One thing was observable on all hands: there were no repentings of what they had done, no curses, no revilings, no reproaches against their chiefs; but when they were shot they unanimously shouted, *Vive la Commune!* Every man and woman and child of them went to heaven for it.

If our friends were sorry that they had not been lodged in one of the houses, they were glad when they found that the women's stable was already crowded, and consequently they would not be separated, at least for the night. And knowing this, they rightly judged that they would probably not be separated at all; for it was certain that a large number of them would be picked out to be shot next morning; and Simona, having been an officer and well known, could hardly hope to escape. Towards night the rain had ceased, the moon was up and occasionally shone through rifts in the white clouds scudding away to the west. There was nothing to disturb the solemn, prison-like silence, save the monotonous slush, slush, of the guards, and the occasional sharp "*qui vive*" of the sentries outside the gates. Soon the clouds cleared away, the stars shone out, and a gentle wind began to blow. The two lovers, long separated, and made acquainted with every grief, thought not of rest, even if rest had been possible. Simona now learned for the first time that their child was dead, or supposed to be, long since. He did not even know the child's name; and when she said " Alberta Simonetta," he covered her with kisses.

" My angel," said he, " we shall be separated in the morning; I shall be taken away; I shall be killed; and you will be left alone."

She said nothing, but she had resolved that this should not be. He continued—"And I am troubled that we have never yet been united according to the forms of law."

"Trouble not yourself about that, my love; it will all be one when we have passed over and met on the other side. Think you not, dear Alberto, that after all the highest law is the law of the heart?"

"Heaven bless you for that, my sweet! Yes; and that has been my sole comfort through all these miserable years. Thank you, thank you, my sweet, my precious flower!" Then, after a moment, he continued—"But it has occurred to me—suppose, my love, my life, that we here to-night, in sight of Heaven, solemnly join our hands, as our hearts already are, and make our sacred vows? We are already in the midst of the great Temple of God; his throne shall be our altar, the silent stars shall be our witnesses, and our ceremony shall be the sacred vows of our own hearts to each other."

"Yes," answered Viola, filled with the light of poetry and love, "for see! the beautiful full moon hath shone out to weave for us our bridal wreaths, and the sweet night-wind shall be our marriage hymn."

And there, before the altar of the Great Unseen, in the midst of his holy Temple, and crowned with a coronal of silvery light, these two joined their hands together, and repeated the vows making them one in life and in death, in body and in spirit, in time and in eternity. And they felt, rightly too, the ceremony more sacred than if it had been performed by priest or magistrate. And then he kissed her on the forehead, and she leaned her head—alas! how much suffering had it endured—upon his bosom. Alas, alas! how pitiful and mean are all our shams and make-believes, "legal arrangements," when measured by the grand reality! When Simona spoke again he said :

"When you said, just now, my Violet, that the sweet night-wind should be our marriage hymn, did it occur to you that it might also be something else?"

"What else, my Alberto?"

"Might it not also be our parting hymn?"

"Yes; our requiem too. But consider, this sweet wind is also the requiem of departing winter, and the herald of approaching summer. This is the last; the dark days are past, and the joyous are come. So let it be with us, my Alberto; our stormy days are past, and we enter the fields of sweet-scented summer."

Next morning's sun rose clear and beautiful; and the birds were out, singing, in strange contrast with the surrounding waste of mud and water. Some of the people were trying to dry by the sun; many were coughing and wheezing from colds they had taken; some were dying, and a few were dead. Early in the morning, as had been expected, a body of three hundred gendarmes marched in, and their officers immediately began to pick out from among those last brought in, all the regular soldiers—of which there were few —officers and chiefs of the Commune, and the *pétroleuses*, for immediate execution.

They had already called out more than a hundred, and Simona had begun to think that maybe he would not be taken, when an officer came up to him and said, " You are Simona, the Colonel of staff to La Cecillia "—half assertingly, half inquiringly.

" Yes," replied the Italian, " I am Alberto Simona, Colonel of staff to the patriot-general La Cecillia; I have fought for liberty with Garibaldi in Italy, with Jefferson Davis in America, and with the Commune in Paris. If that be enough to entitle one to die for it, then am I ready."

"And you?" said the officer to Viola—"are a *pétro-leuse?*" Viola answered by shouting defiantly, "*Vive la Commune!*" Simona was thunderstruck. Viola was no *pétroleuse;* she told him she was not. But what was done could not be undone; and they marched out with the hundred and fifty victims.

But just as they were leaving the crowd a strange event happened, which caused the Italian to tremble, and Viola almost to sink to the earth. A small, dark man, of lean face and burning black eye, stepped up beside them and said in a hurried but revengeful tone:

"Ha! Italian, and your Mississippi flower! I come to redeem my pledge; your lives have been miserable; I will make your death so. Did you think to die content? Bah! I tell you a secret. Your child still lives—' Alberta Simonetta'—(and he called the name with suppressed rage)—she is in a work-shop, one step from the concert room. If you could only live you could save her. Adieu." He darted quickly back into the crowd, and they two were hurried along. Now indeed it was hard to die. These two had suffered much in their lives; but the hardest blow, it seemed, had been reserved for the last. But something must be done, and that speedily. It occurred to them to write a note to their father, Mr. Walton, and trust to one of the soldiers to deliver it to the American Minister.

"My poor, poor father!" cried Viola in anguish; "he will not know where to go; he will die of grief."

"Yes, your father is old—will be borne down with grief—will not know where to seek. I know one of your countrymen; I saved his life once in Italy, and he made me promise him faithfully if he could ever serve me, at any cost, to call upon him. Strange that I should meet him here in Paris and save his life the second time. He was a member of the Commune; but he escaped. Let us write to him—to be given to your father in case it does not come into his hands. I have his address here—'Mirabeau Holmes, Atlanta, Ga., U. S. A.'" These words were spoken half aloud, half to himself apparently. But it was agreed that this was the course to be adopted. As they approached the ground where was drawn up the corps of execution, they observed a knot of individuals in plain citizen's dress, and with note-books in their hands, whom they at once took to be report-ers for the great newspaper press. There were several Englishmen, and evidently one American, a tall, spare man, who seemed restless. Simona called out to know if there was an American on the ground. The tall, restless man immediately held up his hand, and obtaining permission from the officer, advanced. They spoke a few words; the tall man asked, as a favor to the paper he represented, to be allowed fifteen minutes to converse with the prisoners, one of whom was his country-woman; and what would probably have been denied to any dictate of humanity, was readily accorded to the representative of the great New York newspaper. An American is almost sure to be good at heart. The tall man was much affected at the brief recital of the sad story of the Italian patriot and his unfortunate, still beautiful country-woman. He pledged them the honor of himself, of his paper, and of his country, to execute their wishes to the utmost of his power. He bade them adieu. The command was given. "VIVE LA COMMUNE!" The hundred and fifty were dead.

Book 4.

PEACH-TREE.

———◆———

CHAPTER XVI.

"———   he seemed
For dignity composed, and high exploit:
But all was false and hollow; though his tongue
Dropp'd manna, and could make the worse appear
The better reason, to perplex and dash
Maturest counsels; ——— "
                                        PARADISE LOST.

MEANWHILE several things have come to pass in America; notably, in the hub of Georgia. In at least one of these events Clarence Hall was doubly interested. They were both girls, nice little wee things. Their beauty was not like that of the full moon in a dark sky; they were much too small for that. They rather resembled little twin twinkling stars. But what man was ever satisfied with a girl-baby? Have not the Spaniards this proverb, "Guays padre, que otra hija os nace?" And have not we found it necessary to translate it into English, thus—Alas, father! another misfortune (daughter) is born to you? Manifestly, this must be done to meet the exigencies of the times. Clarence Hall was very glad; but he was a shade disappointed. In fact, upon reflection, he was to a small extent doubly disappointed. Here was a clear loss; it might ruin everything. Why might

not Clarence Hall some day be President of the United States?
And why might not his son be, after him?   He had had better
opportunities than Puritan John Adams, and was a much
better man.   His son would be equal to John Quincy, if
metaphysicians tell the truth, at the tender age of one second.
Might not education do the rest?   But this unfortunate delay might spoil everything!   Clarence Hall and his pretty
wife and babies lived in a nice little house out on Peach-tree
street.   To be sure, they did not live in grand style, or anything approaching to it.   But still they lived rather expen-
sively, considering they only had about two thousand dollars
to begin with, that Clarence was only a poor Attorney with
an income not exceeding five hundred dollars, and that Mr.
Dearing, for all his grand pedigree, could do nothing for
them.   Clarence Hall was not without common sense, and,
in higher matters than every-day affairs are supposed to be,
he had also considerable practical sagacity.   So that when he
was married he knew that he ought to take a comfortable
little house in some other part of the city than on aristocratic
Peach-tree.   There was a neat little brick house with flowers
and terraced yard covered with a mat of rich green grass, on
Marietta, which suited his taste exactly; and as for the loca-
tion, why it was enough that Mrs. Sutherland was almost
next-door neighbor.   Before speaking to Annie, Clarence
wished to know what Mr. Dearing would say to the place as
a home for them.   Mr. Dearing was not pleased with it.   Then
Clarence mentioned a pretty little place with shady walks in
a different quarter of the city; this was out on Mt. Vernon
street, where the Malcombs lived.   But this was entirely
too far from Mr. Dearing's.   And then it occurred to him
for the first time that perhaps almost anything would be ob-
jectionable but a somewhat pretentious establishment on
Peach-tree.   Of course, under all the circumstances, in spite

of his good sense, nothing was more natural than that Mr.
Hall's notions and prospects should expand to meet the occasion. And so the house on Peach-tree, which cost more
than the whole of his *present* income—the word *present* being
always italicized when he thought of his condition and prospects—was taken, and of course must be furnished with some
degree of correspondence.

The consequence of all this was, when they were married
and at home Mr. Hall was already in debt several hundred
dollars, and, besides, immediately began to live beyond his
income—his *present* income. The careful observer of human
destinies needs not another word to help him to the conclusion that, whatever his natural talents—and they were of a
high order—whatever his attainments—and they were in
keeping with his talents—whatever his ambitious hopes—
and they were large and generous—the scales were now
turned against him. But not irretrievably so. What! will
not genius rise superior to fate? Will not perseverance
remove every difficulty, surmount every obstacle, and at
last attain the hoped-for eminence? Yes, if Humanity have
pressing need of it. Does not such need always exist?
Allons! But come; whatever may be our differences concerning providence, foreknowledge, will, and fate, here is a platform broad enough for all of us to stand upon: perseverance, with help enough, can surround itself with difficulties
which itself may not remove. How shall genius soar if its
wing be clipped? Shall the eagle ascend, though chained to
an anvil? Plainly, I think, there is such a thing as gravita-
tion in the world.

But speaking of Clarence Hall's babies (in terms of the
law), he half-way ventured to express to his better half just
a slight regret that it had not seemed good to providence to
send them at least one boy. "Oh, Clarence!" exclaimed his

10

wife, "how can you say that? Are not you afraid God will
send a judgment upon you for talking so?" Alas, alas!
The judgment soon came, sure enough: one of the babies
died. Of course, he had better understanding than to suppose this to be a judgment sent upon him; but his wife had
not. He was both surprised and hurt: surprised that his
wife should entertain a notion so narrow, and, as he thought,
so unworthy of her; and hurt that she should mention it on
such an occasion, even if she believed it. The first shocked
his reason, and could not but give him at least an intimation of
how far intellectually his wife was below himself; for though a
sincere Christian, he thought he could easily separate the truth
from superstition; forgetting entirely that, however easy it
might have seemed in his case, still it was an undertaking
in which the greatest minds, to say nothing of his pretty
little wife, have almost universally failed. But his sensibili-
ties were also hurt. And it was this probably that concern-
ed him even more than the other, for he too was still the
unconscious slave of the past in so far as to believe that
woman's only business here was to love some particular man
with all her might, and to furnish him an object upon which
to bestow his surplus affection, and particularly his protect-
ive aspirations. A woman should love her husband, look
up to him in the coarse affairs of will and intellect, anticipate
if possible all his wishes; in a word, envelope him, transport
him, in a whole flood of affection. People were, and are to
this day mostly, especially in the Empire State, so simple as
to consider marriage an institution—they object to the word
partnership—in which the husband was bound to furnish the
brains and the wife the heart._ Well, had Clarence Hall got
the thing he wanted? No, truly; but he had got the thing
he thought he wanted. Mrs. Hall was as devoted a little
wife as any connoisseur could have wished. She loved her

husband to the last extent of her capacity, almost worshipped him. As for his part, why, he had already begun to feel that he had something to protect and provide for. What he really wanted was a companion; he thought that a woman of certain qualities, which seemed to him altogether adorable, would make the perfect companion. Now, he had been so fortunate as to marry his own incarnate, ideal woman. Still, as we have seen, he had even now begun to feel somewhat disappointed. Alas! Clarence Hall, you had not learned the most important, probably, of all lessons—that the most perfect companionship, the ideal of marriage, can only exist between people equal in intellect and in culture.

The Malcombs lived on Mount Vernon street. Mr. Malcomb was engaged in an extensive business, and was making money rapidly. He had also been prevailed on by all parties —for his splendid executive and financial abilities, and rare judgment in all practical matters, as well as his great influence as a business man, were acknowledged on all hands— to accept the office of Mayor of the city. And this was a good sign, for two reasons: first, it indicated the decay of strong party animosities; for three years before, if any man had dared to suggest Mr. Malcomb as a suitable man for democrats to vote into an office of honor and trust, he would not only have been politically outlawed, but a strong effort, and probably a successful one, would have been made for his social outlawry. Such an effort had in fact been made against Mr. Malcomb himself; but owing to his great influence with his church, with his old party associates, with business men, and, notably, with that very small but powerful class whose independence and elevation of thought and culture raise them above the heavy and noisome atmosphere of ignorance and prejudice, and which in this Empire State probably finds its highest representative in the venerable

Chancellor of the State University, the effort had signally and miserably failed. To be sure, one pompous old aristocratic ass, with the shallowness peculiar to his order, chiefly remarkable for these three things—his relationship to the great statesman of his name, his voluminous, vast, bottomless, and interminable agricultural erudition, and his infinite boring proclivities—did attempt to put the scheme into execution. But this essay awoke in Mr. Malcomb no other feeling than a regret that in a few days he should have to devote the accustomed fifteen hours to the old gold-headed cane, that he might explain away his conduct. And in the second place, this compromise of the two parties was a good sign, because it showed that the business men were taking matters of importance into their own hands; that not party bickerings and word-quibbles, but questions of material wealth and progress, should enter as the important elements into the management of their municipal affairs. And the acceptance of this office also shows to advantage one of the prominent traits of Mr. Malcomb's character—his willingness to serve the people in any capacity in which he could be of benefit to them. There was probably not a man in the State, who, having filled the high offices that Mr. Malcomb had, would have accepted the office of Mayor.

Robert Malcomb married Betty Broughton, and had made a pretty clear start in pursuit of the object which he ever kept steadily in view; he was already receiving at least his proportionable part of the hundred and thirty thousand dollars annually contributed by this little city to the health and comfort of her hundred and odd lawyers. Marian, almost as soon as she was here, had become an universal favorite—at least near enough so to authorize the expression from an American. Still—to be exactly precise, as Captain Pinter would say— she was not quite an universal favorite; she was not adored by that class of young men technically known as *swells*. This class she had the rare good feeling, and, perhaps, among women, the still rarer good sense, to despise, and while she could not, without the greatest provocation, say or do anything liable to give the least pain to any one, however unworthy, still there was felt to be a repellant force between them. As for Alf Walton, who, in spite of his known intrigues and multiplied immoralities, was received with high favor among the belles, who languishingly called him the "King of Hearts," it is superfluous to say that he was not a visitor at Mr. Malcomb's.

"How is it," said Fred Van Comer to Bramlette one day, "that this little brown woman who never sings, never plays, never waltzes, and never flirts, and is not considered beautiful either, is the most popular woman in town?"

"Consider her eyes," said Bramlette.

"Only some of your poetry, my dear fellow; you know she is not considered beautiful."

"But she does sing and play too, sometimes—for her very intimate friends."

"But to come back. What I said, in a general way is true; she neither sings to society, nor plays for society, nor waltzes, nor flirts with the American people, nor is she thought to be beautiful; but still, to the best of my skill and knowledge, she is the greatest favorite in town. Why?"

"One can never tell. We must say, like the French, she has a charm about her."

"Well, Bramlette, you are the honestest man I know, and, *pace*, the best. Now, if I had asked almost anybody but you, especially one of that large class who pride themselves upon 'knowing a thing or two' of human nature, but who in fact never any more get to the bottom of the human heart than those pants get to the bottom of your legs, the answer would have been a shrewd wink and a mysterious whisper of ' money.' "

" Humph! That could never be. Here is myself, already half in love with her, and I never thought of that, I know. I believe you are in love with her too, and I reckon you never thought of it till this moment; and there is Mirabeau Holmes, whom I suspect to be in much deeper water than either of us, and whom all will allow to be as pure of such contaminating thoughts as consecrated snow. And as we are a portion of your American people, and must not consider ourselves better than the rest, there must be some other reason why the little brown woman is so great a favorite."

" I wish the clerks would not go there—at least so many of them, and so often."

" What have you against the clerks ? "

" Oh, ' business,' man, ' business ! ' They talk loud, and laugh horse-laugh. Besides, they worry her, I know they do. I wish they were all in the Gulf. I tell you it would be an act of charity to her for one to put them there."

" I am not so sure that she would consider it a kindness to her to put them all there, if accounts be true."

" What do you mean ? "

" I mean Tom McComb."

" Blast the Scotchman ! As I was going over there the other night I passed him, and I asked him, with the broadest kind of a twang, ' whore are ye gangging till ? ' He paid me for it, though; he sat me out, though he knew I had an engagement. Finally, after eleven, out of pure philanthropy, I proposed to go. Would you believe it ? he would not budge ! "

" Think you she would agree for him to be put into the Gulf ? "

"May be not; but that would be the greatest kindness of all."

"Why so?"

"Because that is a designing man. As far as my observation goes, the average Scotchman has three principles, expressed by the three meanest words in the language—hardness, stinginess, and craftiness. And this fellow means to gain her confidence by playing upon the very highest feelings of her nature; he is greatly interested about all religious matters, goes to Sunday-school, teaches a class, makes addresses, and tries to appear as sanctimonious as an old Covenanter. I tell you what, I feel like I do at a quaker meeting, whenever he is in the room. I am all the while fearful that he will break forth into singing psalms."

"Afraid he will sing psalms, are you? What an idea! What would you do, Fred?"

"Do? Why, I would listen mournfully till he got through; and then, before he had time to invite us all to unite in prayer, I should sing the doxology and pronounce the benediction. Queer, that this man should stand foremost among the rivals of such a man as Mirabeau Holmes."

"I know not whether he loves her or not, but if he does, it will be with a fervor not often seen, I think."

"What! you, a poet, say so much! I think you say rightly, though—'a fervor not often seen.' Still, I am sorry for Holmes; I don't think he stands the best of chances. Don't you think his religious belief will be fatal to him there?"

"Unless he changes it."

"Nonsense! As if a man could change his belief. But suppose he does not 'change it,' or, what is of more consequence to consider, that it does not change itself?"

"Well, then, I think his religious, or rather his *no-reli-*

gious, belief, as indicated in his letters of late would be fatal to him."

" You call a man's belief ' *no-religious* ' because he denies the dogmas of the European Church ? "

" No, but because he denies the truths of our religion."

" Yes ; *your* religion ! As if there were not many other religions, and some, I think, much better. But we will not discuss that. I wish I could have been with you at Hall's the other day."

" I wish you could. Hall has the nicest, sweetest wife, and prettiest babies in the world. He says he is the happiest of men ; and I think he is."

" I reckon it all made you feel sadder than a bachelor-button you got once."

" Far from it. It only made me feel hopeful."

" By showing what a man can do—sometimes."

" Yes."

" I went home to dinner with him some time ago. I was not expected ; and so I could get some idea of their every-day life. The babies were there, dressed just as prettily as if it had been done by Titania and her fairies. They were not sent out into some absurd nursery, but kept in the room with the balance of us. I took them in my arms, rolled them on the carpet, and played with them generally. I got my bellyful of kisses."

" Bellyful of kisses indeed ! Did you get anything else ? "

" Yes ; I got one of the nicest little dinners you ever saw."

" Ah ! That is what I was thinking of. I will hear your report."

" Now that I think of it, I fear I can no more tell you the wherefore than you could explain the attractiveness of the little woman on Mt. Vernon street. But there was a charm about the table. She is the only woman I know who seems to understand the poetry of the table. I have been there several times. Let me see: I noticed that the cloth covering the little round table was white as snow. In the centre was a pretty fruit-basket, with grapes, oranges, and one or two other kinds of fruits, ornamented with leaves and flowers; and there was such a pretty little nosegay on each napkin that one was almost sorry to move it. The butter was moulded into shells and all sorts of pretty shapes, and placed in butter-dishes in the form of leaves, green leaves, contrasting prettily with the rich yellow butter and the snow-white cloth."

"And the dish of salad was ornamented with bright flowers and slices of hard-boiled egg, and orange peel, and the dishes of roast and mutton were trimmed with sprigs of parsley."

"Exactly; I never knew before how simple a matter it was to make a table pretty. Is it not strange that our women know so little about the poetry of the table?"

"One is not ashamed to eat at such a table as that. All the grossness, all the coarse materialism is gone."

"I tell you what, Bramlette, I am beginning to think like you, that Hall has the nicest, sweetest little wife in the world. Unless I can get somebody to give me thirty-nine lashes, I mean to go on a pilgrimage as an act of penance for once thinking ill of her."

"If you can just put it off a while," said Clarence Hall, entering at this moment and hearing only the latter half of the sentence, "I fear I shall be in the mood to give you thirty-nine every morning, if you like."

"How so?"

"I shall want to take spite out of something if I am beat, as I fear I shall be."

"You mean for the office of city attorney? Why, I thought you were sure of it."

"I thought so too. But I find there will be strong opposition."

"Is not Mr. Malcomb for you?"

"Yes; but Mr. Malcomb is not the whole council, or even a majority of it."

"What are they going to oppose you for?"

"Why, because I am in favor of public schools in the city for negroes."

"Why, the question is wholly irrelevant, has nothing to do with the office whatever."

"Exactly. But it is known that Mr. Malcomb is in favor of the schools, and intends to bring the matter in shape before the council. It is also known that Mr. Malcomb favors me for this office; and it was supposed that I, too, approved of his public school plan. When asked about it I could only reply that I did."

"Well, well. We might have known it. They would not have been American people if they had not cut some such caper. Anything in the papers about it?"

"Yes—a communication from 'Cato.'"

"Give it me. I will reply to-morrow to it. We must take a bold stand, and whip them out on that question."

From the day on which we have seen him leave the Sunday-school gift, Alf Walton ceased not his visits to Mrs. Harlan's cottage. That he should triumph, he firmly believed. That it would not be easy work, he knew; but he soon found that he had not counted all the difficulties in his way. He even finally thought to turn respectable, and use, as a last resort, his father's influence. Said he to his father one day, putting on an air of virtuous philosophy—

"Father, you know the life I have lived; I have no desire now to make the story better than it is—a life of recklessness, extravagance, and debauchery. But it was not always so.

When I entered the University my life was smooth behind me, and all was fair ahead. But, trust me, so great a change is not without corresponding cause. My life you know—the reason of it you only know in part. That is away back in the past, and as for what it was, no matter—what's done is done. I despised friendship, believed all women false—loyal only to lust and frippery. And for a score of years I have thought I found it so. You used to say that there are periods in every man's life when he may turn back and seem to reverse the decree of Fate itself. I am come to one, the first one, and I want your help."

Mr. Walton could not have been more amazed. A mother never gives up a child as lost; a father does. Mr. Walton had this one. And that he was any longer acknowledged, not to say supplied with money, he owed entirely to his mother's influence. Mr. Walton said nothing, could say nothing, but looked inquiringly into the face of the tall, handsome, bronzed man before him; and really he thought he had never looked so commanding. The speaker continued:

"If I can win this girl, whose passionate feeling rises so high above the atmosphere I have known, into the upper regions of purest love, I will marry her, live with her and for her, and the future shall only be more bright as the past is dark. But she is clothed in such an armor of friendship, and my character, falsely assumed twenty years ago, is such, that I need your assistance."

He then told his father who the young girl was, how he had happened to observe her, what he had already done, and all he knew about Mrs. Harlan. His father must go to the good General Clement, to Dr. and Mrs. Sutherland, and to Mrs. Harlan herself. Thus did this bad man, in his bad cause, seek to enlist the powers of virtue's self. He did not mention Mr. Brooke, of whom he entertained a profound distrust; for Mr. Brooke, as we have seen, and as Alf Walton well knew, was, notwithstanding his broad and exalted piety, thoroughly versed in the ways of the world. Mr. Walton believed his son, and that evening, when he told his wife, they two, the old father and mother, wept for joy and hope as they had not in many a long year. So there was joy in Mr. Walton's house. The faithful mother's heart was full; God knows how many prayers, how many almost hopeless cries, she had offered in anguish at the throne of Omnipotence; and now they were all answered! Answered at last! Happy, happy, ever happy day! and she tripped lightly along the hall, and sung in her heart for joy, as in the long-ago days of hope and promise.

But a great sorrow was just ahead. And I know there are many who will consider this strengthening hope, coming just at the time it did, as specially sent by a benevolent Providence to sustain these two in the great affliction which was soon to overtake them. It was but a short while after the events just narrated, that the Waltons were all seated at a rather early breakfast, for Mr. Walton was going to leave that morning for a distant city. Strange enough, they had just been looking through the columns of a New York paper, where they found, in an article on the "Commune," a list of the names of all the prominent foreigners killed, and a statement that not a single American had been killed, and only one or two engaged in the war. This, though they could not tell why, nevertheless afforded relief from some vague fears which, somehow, they seemed to inhale with the very atmosphere. They had not heard from George in some time, and they had just been speaking of him uneasily. Mr. Walton was just saying that he knew they would get a letter before he should return, and they must telegraph him at once; when the carrier entered with a message from the telegraph office.

"From the American Minister at Paris," Mr. Walton read aloud. Every one turned pale, the air seemed to leave the room, and there was an ominous stillness. The son took the package from his father's hand, and read, He only said, "George is dead." Mr. Walton's head fell forward upon the table, and he uttered a deep groan; Mrs. Walton was borne to her room by the servants and her son,

The noble women of Paris, whose sons had been faithful to liberty, were also faithful to their promises. These two had also lost sons: one, a mere boy, had died like a hero at the barricade; and the other, a tall, fair-haired youth, had died ringing the defiant shout of *Vive la Commune!* in the very muzzles of his assassins' guns. And all three had been laid away together. And here the body of young George Walton should rest until his father should come to bear it away to its native soil in the West. And shall his grave be less sacred here? Verily, no! I think the clods are sacred here. Every one mingles with the dust of a hero. The American Minister, according to the genius of his people, when the women carried him the letter left with them, did not wait the uncertainty and slowness of the mail, but sent the contents of the whole letter, with a word of condolence from himself, by cable.

It was not until the next day that Mr. Walton read the message. Meanwhile his son had already sent what message was necessary in reply to the Minister.

The next evening but one, Alf Walton was at Mrs. Harlan's. They were sitting in the west window of the little parlor, when he said to Emma—

"This gentle wind brings us the sweet scents from your little garden; they come as if to woo us thither. Let us go;

for I am going off to-morrow on a long journey, and should like to see it to-night; and you must give me a flower, which I will carry with me all the way."

"Oh, I see!   It requires something to remember me."

"Come into the moonlight, and I will show you how far you are mistaken."   The moon shone beautifully, and when they reached the little flower-garden, he said to her:

"Could you think I wanted a flower only to remember you by?   See here what I have!"   And he drew carefully from his breast-pocket a small case, and taking out a tiny picture, held it so the light would shine upon it.   It was a picture of herself.

"Did you think I wanted a flower for that?"

"What betters it that that should stand instead of the flower?"

"This, my timid beauty, is only to feast my eyes, that else would sicken from want of light from what they love; my heart, my soul, your own self doth fill.   Will you not give me the flower too?"

"Where go you to-morrow?"

"To France; we have just received a telegram—my brother is dead—and I go to bring home his remains."

"Your brother George?   I am so sorry.   My brothers all died in the war.   I am so sorry for your mother; but you are left to her.   Poor, poor mother, no one was left to her."

"My precious darling! let me be a son to her and a protector to you.   I must, I must declare to you what I have delayed so long.   Light of my life!   I cannot tell you how long, how patiently, how singly I have loved you; for love cannot be measured by years and months, but by longings, by dreamings, by hopes and fears.   But I have a confession to make, and I make it before my most sacred shrine— your own heart.   I could not offer you a heart, a life, that was unworthy of you. But sorrow is a great purifier, and love is a great elevator. I have known both; and to-night I declare to you, that now for the first time I know that with your confidence and love I could be worthy even of you. I, of my mother's children, am left alone, you of yours; united, we two shall lighten their hearts and comfort them. And for ourselves, let the star that so kindly heralds the roseate morn stand surety for a happy day." He looked earnestly, searchingly, into her face; it was covered with a blush, and, well as he knew the workings of the heart, he mistook the import of that blush. Still the poor girl was standing upon exceedingly treacherous and dangerous ground. For she was reflecting at that moment that maybe, after all, this man before her was in earnest, maybe he spoke the truth, maybe he was an injured man; and she blushed that probably in her own heart she had been unjust to this man; not only unjust to a fellow-being, but to a man who most of all stood in need of simple justice, and, above everything else, the man who was at that very moment elevating and dignifying her with his confidence, and laying at her feet his love and life. He saw not the meaning of this blush; he took it for the glow of love. He seized her hand:

"Only one word, one hope—or better,"—and he quickly folded her in his arms. This time it was the blush of offended innocence; she drew back from him, and said, in a tone that showed she was offended—

"Mr. Walton, I did not come here for this; I must not listen to it;" and then again, fearing she was unkind, she added in a kinder tone, "Mamma is alone; ought not we to return to the house?"

"Yes; but give me one hope, one promise. Say that you will think of me, dream of me, sing of me; that my image shall be constantly in your heart, my name ever on your lips; that you will be wholly mine, as I am yours. Oh, I will turn fire-worshipper! and daily, long before the western lark shall herald the morn, will I greet the rising sun with a prayer for you, and as he sinks to rest I will ask his parting blessing upon all you love. And in that sweet hour when you close your eyes to sleep, and the winged spirits are there to bear heavenward thy latest prayer, wilt thou not then utter my name? and then with sweet good-night kiss the sacred air that presses upon thy lips, and the cords of electric love will bear it to me in the east!" Thus it was that this scamp proposed to kiss by telegraph! They had now reached the steps, and he at once bade her good-night, without giving her time to speak, choosing rather to leave the impression with her that he believed from her silence she had promised him everything. Moreover, he had already decided upon a last, desperate game; he would not leave the city to-morrow, but put it off till the next day. In the meantime this desperate game was to be played.

The next afternoon from the events just narrated, Emma was at Mr. Brooke's. They were in the parlor—Emma, Mr. Brooke, and his daughter Claude, a beautiful and accomplished young lady, about one year Emma's senior. Mrs. Brooke was a beautiful, highly cultured woman, but of exceedingly delicate constitution. She had now for several years been a confirmed invalid; she never left her room, and indeed was understood to be sinking under a sure but quiet disease. Mr. Brooke had only two children—Claude and a younger sister. Emma never knew where she had rather be—at Mr. Brooke's, General Clement's, or Mrs. Sutherland's. Mr. Brooke was as accomplished a man as one might ever meet, at least *prima facie.* Upon entering the parlor you saw that every niche and corner was occupied by some beautiful little statuette; the walls were covered with the

cartoons of Raffaelle, and pictures from other great painters;
and on the tables were several volumes of the great poets,
Shakespeare, Goethe, Dante, Tasso, the French and ancient
dramatists, all in their original languages. Mr. Brooke
was a most excellent reader, and he often read fine passages
from the poets to the girls. Mr. Brooke had just been saying that he never went to theatres except to hear a great
singer.

"No," said Claude, "I thought I should like to go to see
Forrest in Hamlet at least once while he was here; but father
said he would not go."

"Above all things I would not see a great tragedy acted.
I cannot imagine anything more absurd. The high intellectual enjoyment that you get from reading it must give way
to emotions almost entirely animal—a thing of the nerves and
flesh and blood. It is essentially degrading. In a word, it
substitutes for intellectual feeling animal feeling, for the ideal,
the gross material. Comedy may be acted to make people
laugh—that I do not object to; tragedy never! I know the
opinions on this question of the Chancellor of the University,
who is the best authority in such matters I know, and I
agree with him exactly. But we were speaking of Hamlet;
let me read you some passages. I read you that passage in
which Polonius gives some precepts to his son, about to leave
for France." Mr. Brooke read the speech of Polonius, ending
with the ever-great words—

> "This above all: to thine own self be true;
> And it must follow, as the night the day,
> Thou canst not then be false to any man."

"Come now, for a criticism! What say you, Emma, to
this passage?"

"I think he ought to be a very wise and good man who spoke this last precept—such a man as Brutus, or Washington, or Lee. But is this not a great deal better than what goes before it?"

"What say you, Claude?"

"That the last three lines are so much better than those above, that they never could have been spoken by the same person."

"Right, both of you. Polonius is a garrulous, shallow-pated old man, and these three lines ought never to have been put into his mouth at all. As you say, Emma, they would do for Brutus, or Washington, or Lee, but not Polonius. The idea of putting such words into the mouth of a man who has just been advising his son to wear the finest clothes he can buy! The fact is, the poet seems to get impatient with the old man, and lest the son be ruined for the want of wholesome precepts, himself steps in and arms him with this one. But now I will read you what Laertes says to his sister, poor Ophelia, concerning Hamlet, 'and the trifling of his favor.'" And Mr. Brooke read the passage ending with these lines:

> "Then weigh what loss your honor may sustain,
> If with too credent ear you list his songs,
> Or lose your heart; or your chaste treasure open
> To his unmaster'd importunity.
> Fear it, Ophelia, fear it, my dear sister;
> And keep you in the rear of your affection,
> Out of the shot and danger of desire.
> The chariest maid is prodigal enough,
> If she unmask her beauty to the moon:
> Virtue itself 'scapes not calumnious strokes:
> The canker galls the infants of the spring,
> Too oft before their buttons be disclos'd;

> And in the morn and liquid dew of youth
> Contagious blastments are most imminent.
> Be wary, then ; best safety lies in fear ;
> Youth to itself rebels, though none else near."

And Mr. Brooke proceeded to speak, like a wise and pious father and friend, upon the subject of these lines ; for of one of these girls before him he was father, of the other, beloved pastor and friend. Was it Providence, dear reader, or Fate, that of all the splendid passages in Shakespeare, Mr. Brooke selected this particular one, on this particular afternoon, and spoke upon it so wisely, so warningly, and so feelingly? Heaven knows one of them stood at that moment in great enough need of some such warning as this. Special Providence, or inevitable Fate? One would like to believe the former? Say you so? *Allons!* Special providence let it be, then.

Late in the afternoon Miss Brooke went part of the way home with Emma. Something was said about young George Walton, who had been much loved by Mr. Brooke, and of whose death they had just heard that morning ; and then Claude told something of what her father—whom she almost worshipped—had said about how mysterious it appeared that both of Mr. Walton's younger sons, high-minded, generous, and likely to be useful men, should die, leaving only Mr. Alf —a gambler, a debauchee, and a bold, bad, unscrupulous man. And then Miss Brooke said something about a daughter of Mr. Walton's, beautiful as a star, of whom it was whispered she had been led to disgrace and ruin by a young Italian, many years ago. She was thought to be dead ; but it was not known certainly. At any rate, she had sunk out of sight.

When Emma got home she found a beautiful bouquet and note from Mr. Alf Walton, saying that he had postponed his

departure until to-morrow, that he might see her again this
evening. Meanwhile that accomplished gentleman was busily
arranging his plans.

"You will be there promptly," said he to a long, lean,
hungry-looking individual, with whom he had been closeted
for an hour. "We will drive as if to the theatre; we will
alight at the front door, and come straight in; we will not
sit down; you must perform the ceremony promptly; if you
get out, don't stop, say anything; she will not know the difference. You understand now. She will think it simply a
secret marriage. Be on your guard. Meet me at the depot
to-morrow at nine. I will not be baffled. I will succeed at
all costs."

"Have you tried all other plans but this?"

"Yes."

"And failed?"

"Yes."

"That's a new deal in your fortune, far as I know."

"Yes; it's new as far as I know or as far as anybody else
knows, I reckon. All on account of that damn'd eagle-eyed
villain of a parson."

"Suppose you fail to-night?"

"I'll not fail. But if I do, I will come by and let you know."

The false justice went his way. Early in the night Mr.
Walton's splendid phaeton stopped in front of Mrs. Harlan's
cottage. Mr. Alf was in it. Emma met him herself. He
was quick to detect a decided change in her, he thought, since
last night. But he was confident in his art of persuasion.
He contrived dexterously to recall the whole of their conversation of the night before, hoping to place her in the same
state of uncertainty she then was, and then to overpower her
with the rushing madness of his devotion and ardor by proposing that they be married within an hour. He brought

into play ever power and every art he was master of; proceeding all along on the supposed understanding that her silence of the previous night was mutually understood to mean consent. He appealed to her love of adventure even, and endeavored to arouse her ambition by the grandest prospects and most eloquent and burning promises. And then he appealed to her thus:

"My father and mother are both old, weighed down with grief; how it would fill them with joy for you to come to them like sunshine in the midst of their night! Besides, they cannot live long; my father has vast wealth, and no one to give it to; as for me, I want it not; I want nothing without you. And I might die myself, even on this very voyage; think what a consolation then it would be to them that our union had not been put off till my return. And what a consolation it would be to me in such an event—to know that she whom I loved best of all the earth was securely raised above the possibility of want, above the changes of treacherous fortune, the death of relatives, the loss of friends. Think, on the other hand—Good God! I cannot think of it. Consider your mother. Would it be worth nothing to see her raised above the possibility of dependence; to surround her with every comfort, every luxury; to make the balance of her life smooth and happy, and, above all, to let her know that her child was safe in the arms of a husband who would protect and honor her, and lavish upon her all the wealth of his love? Come, my precious! My arms and my heart are open and longing for thee. Your mother knows me not; therefore she gives not her consent. But when I return, and we relate to her this last test of devotion, how happy she will be, and how she will applaud the heavenly impulses of her child. Come! The constant stars look kindly down, and long to bless us!"

CHAPTER XVII.

"Three men are beloved by God: he who is of a sweet temper; he who is moderate
in his habits; and he who does not always obstinately adhere to his first resolves."
                                                    TALMUD.

ONE morning, in the latter part of June, Marian Malcomb
was surprised to receive the following note:

"MISS MARIAN:

"I have just returned to the city. May I call this morning? Truly and faithfully,

"MIRABEAU HOLMES."

To which she immediately sent the following answer:

"MR. HOLMES:

"I will wait to tell you how glad I am that you have
returned. Come at twelve.

"Your friend,

"MARIAN MALCOMB."

Mirabeau had expected his return to be a complete surprise, even to his intimate friends, such as Van Comer, Bramlette, and Hall. But the surprise was with himself when he
found them all awaiting him at the car-shed. Fred was gaily
decorated with a red scarf—the badge of the Commune. He
rushed to Mirabeau, gave him the fraternal embrace, and then
turned on his heel, throwing his head back with the abandon
of a gamin, and sang out jauntily, "Ah! ça ira, ça ira,
ça ira." Then he cried, "Vive la Commune!" and the friends,
with several others in the crowd repeated it. Meanwhile, a

considerable crowd had gathered around them; but as the meaning of the demonstration was known only to some half a dozen friends, and as the object of it was personally unknown to the crowd, they might still have escaped; and this Mirabeau wished to do—not that he objected to standing upon the head of a barrel and addressing a crowd for five or ten minutes—what American ever did? but because he was worn out with travel, covered with dust, and his arm was paining him. But this was exactly what his friends determined he should not do.

No one who has not witnessed it can have any idea of the marvellous rapidity with which a crowd gathers in any American city, even when no one seems to know the exact object of the gathering; there is no parallel save Paris. The reason of it is the quick perception and the lively and exciting sympathy of the people. The throng threw itself across the sidewalk; a whisper had rapidly run through the crowd of what was up; and so, when Fred called out, "Holmes!" the crowd, according to the custom, immediately on all sides raised the cry, "Holmes! Holmes! Holmes!" This is eminently a speechifying people; always—more the pity—they have been wholly swayed by their orators. Plainly there was but one escape. In the hurry and excitement Fred had dexterously transferred his red scarf to Mirabeau, unknown to him, and so, when he stepped upon the platform of a car standing by, he was really a Communist chief, with the insignia of his office. Mirabeau forgot his pain, and he felt for a moment a thrill somewhat like he was wont to feel among the crowds that used to assemble in St. Antoine. In a deep voice, full of emotion, Mirabeau said:

"Citizens! I have fought two months in Paris for what many in this crowd fought four years in Virginia and the West. Here, our heroes were killed and our chief imprisoned; there, chiefs and heroes died behind the barricade, or were brutally murdered by monster assassins. Let this forever be a custom around the camp-fires of Humanity's army: when the sentinels have all answered, 'One o'clock, and all is well,' and the corporal calls out, 'They all answer,' let the captain ask, 'Do the men of the Commune answer?' Citizens, heroes will grasp their swords in their graves when the solemn answer is given, 'No; they all died in the cause of Humanity!' Long live the Universal Republic!"

There is probably no people in the world so like the people of Paris in its impulses and sympathies as the people of the South. The fact is—and it has not been sufficiently observed—our people are much more French than English. Mirabeau, in these few words, from the associations in his mind at the moment, naturally and impulsively adopted the same style that he would have used in speaking to a crowd of proletaires in the Faubourg St. Antoine, and with the happiest effect. A few in the crowd cried, " *Vive la Commune!* " while the mass, knowing nothing of French, shouted, " *Hurrah for the Commune! Long live the Republic!* " When they reached the hotel, Fred seized the pen and wrote on the register, after Mirabeau's name, " Commune of Paris." Mirabeau objected to this, saying that he did not want anything said about his return, and about his being a Communist, as it might appear that he wanted to give himself an air of importance, etc.; whereupon Bramlette handed him one of the morning papers, pointing him to the following: " Mirabeau Holmes, of this State, a member of the Commune of Paris, is expected to reach the city this morning, on the Augusta train," etc., etc. After he got to his room he found out the secret of the whole matter. In Liverpool he had met with General Cluseret, who had made his escape from Paris in the last days of the struggle, and they returned to this country together. Cluseret, although claiming to be a naturalized American, was really a Frenchman. Mirabeau was the only native American who held an office under the government of the Commune; and Cluseret judged that any honors or distinction shown him would be considered as shown the representative of America in the Commune, and would be taken as so much respect shown by his people to the cause he had served. Knowing some of Mirabeau's friends, from having heard him speak of them, he secretly telegraphed them as to the time of his expected arrival. Cluseret himself travelled under an assumed name, wishing to remain for some time unknown in this country. Mirabeau's three friends did not tell Marian Malcomb, or indeed any one else, of his expected return to the city, rightly thinking that as she could not fail to be present in his thoughts, so, if he wished it, he would inform her himself. Of course, however, she, and everybody else—for all the people of this city, to their honor and to the honor of the city be it said, both can and do read—would see the notice in the morning papers. But it so happened—just as everything in the universe happens—that Marian had not seen the papers that morning. This was the way of it: Mr. Malcomb lived on Mt. Vernon street, about a mile from the post-office, near which was also his business office. He always drove down in his carriage very early in the morning, and, partly to enjoy the morning air and partly to see what was doing in the city, his daughter generally accompanied him. They would go to the post-office, from there to Mr. Malcomb's office, and, leaving him there, return home by a different route. This morning Mr. Malcomb's brother had her seat, and so Marian had not taken the grand round, and had not yet seen the morning papers. Mr. Malcomb himself was at that moment jerking himself along Wall street, erect and

11

stiff, as if bound to a board running up and down his back, wearing the highest beaver-hat ever known in this State, which he carried on top of his head, slightly pitched forward, with the same precision as you have seen a darkey carry a pail of water.

Mirabeau found Marian out in the yard among the flowers. She gave him a tiny rose as they walked towards the house, which he placed in his button-hole, saying " he would wear it in place of his red badge."

" Will it live so long ? "

" As long, I hope, as the memory of the other. You can make it immortal."

He found her the same quiet, little, brown woman, with a charm somehow.

" You must tell me now," said she, " how you escaped. We saw something of it in a New York paper, but it was too meagre. Tell me all about it." ·

" Ah, then, must I say so much about myself ? "

" Certainly, if your friends wish it. Come, I will sing you one verse of a song first." And she sang in a low, sweet voice the last stanza of that wonderful song, C'EST NOTRE TOUR."

" *Au Retour.*
" Chants du pays, à notre âme ravie,
   · Vous apportez les accents du bonheur.
Pays, sois fier ! tu nous donnas la vie,
   Nous la dormions pour garder ton honneur.
Côteaux charmants, rive connue,
   Nous revoyons vos bords chéris :
Souhaitez nous la bienvenue,
   Chants du pays, chants du pays."

Then Mirabeau related to her, briefly, how, with the help of the American Minister, he had escaped from Satory.

"And now," said he, "you must tell me what you all have been doing here."

"Oh, I suppose you know everything of importance that has happened; about politics, and all that. Some of our friends are married. I waited on three couples last winter. None of our friends, I am glad to say, have died. Mrs. Sutherland has written a novel, and made herself famous; my Sunday-school class has been going on bravely, and we have the nicest club you ever saw. And to-morrow night is club night; you must join; all our friends belong to it."

"To-morrow night—where? And tell me how I must get there."

"At Mrs. Hall's—Clarence Hall's! Why, that will be nice. You see, we have an equal number of ladies and gentlemen. After each meeting the secretary keeps a list of the ladies' names, and each gentleman writes his name opposite that of the lady he is going with."

"Then I must go alone to-morrow night, evidently."

"No, you can go with me. I say this much because I am president for the next meeting. Mr. McComb was going with me, but he had to leave the city to-day."

"Are you not afraid to tell me so much?"

"Afraid of what?"

"Of turning my head—making me believe I am a favorite of the gods."

"No compliments. Have you seen any of your friends?"

"One—yourself. Several of them did meet me at the car-shed."

"Did they know you were coming?"

"It seems they did, but not from me. But tell me how you have been."

"Oh, as usual. My life, of course, must be without incident. I ride over to town with father every morning, early;

read the papers, and sometimes read some in books ; help
mother with whatever work she has ; dig among the flowers,
and make a great many bouquets—you see I have not learned
yet that plants have feeling ; and generally have callers in
the evening. I go to the club once a week, and once or
twice we have been on an excursion to Stone Mountain ; one
time Mrs. Sutherland went with us. Do you know her ? ”

“ No, but I have long wanted to, and now I must not put
off seeking her acquaintance.”

“ You must read her book first, though.”

“ Have you read it ? ”

“ Yes.”

“ Tell me something about it.”

“ The critics are all down on it, all but Mr. Stephens.
They say it is immoral in its teachings, and it *has* got a great
deal of kissing in it.”

“ What does Mr. Stephens say ? ”

“ He says that it is not immoral, and that it gives evidences of power of a high order, especially dramatic power.”

“ I fear you will agree with Mr. Stephens, out of sympathy, because all the others are against the author.”

“ No ; I think Mr. Stephens is right, though. But there *is*
most too much kissing.”

“ And hugging too ? ”

“ You have read it ? ”

“ Yes, coming home, I found a copy in Washington.”

“ What do you think ? ”

“ Just as you do. Three things struck me particularly : the
wonderful dramatic power, or rather, as Mr. Stephens says, the
evidences of wonderful dramatic power ; the high morality
of the book—too high, I know, for most critics, because most
critics are narrow, ignorant, bigoted, superstitious, dogmatic,
conservative ; but what I like best about this book with such

a detestable name—"*Love-sick*," indeed!—is its manifestly strong tendency towards liberalism. I believe it is the only instance I know of in our Southern literature of anything that looks like a revolt against a miserable 'conservatism.'"

"'Ignorant, bigoted, superstitious, dogmatic!' What fearful adjectives. But I have not heard you speak so of 'conservatism' before."

"No, I have only learned anything of its true import since I saw you, and knowing that, I hate it with all my might. It is the enemy of Humanity."

"But we are told to love our enemies."

"Well, if it must be so, my love for 'conservatism' is boundless; I wish the word, the idea, and all who believe in either, in a better world than this!"

"Well, well, 'times change, and men change with them!'"

"But 'principles never?' I know of no other instance of so much folly compacted into so few words. My belief is that a great portion of the mistakes and consequent woes of Humanity come from what is called 'sticking to principles.' But where is your mother?"

"At my sister's."

"I am sorry, I wanted so much to see her."

"She will not come till late in the afternoon; but will you not come then to tea?"

"I am already promised to Clarence Hall; he wants me to see the baby."

"Yes, one of them died. They were mighty sweet little wee things."

That evening Mirabeau went to take tea with Clarence Hall and his wife and baby. Fred and Bramlette were there; and all three agreed that it was the pleasantest, nicest, *petit souper* they ever saw. Mirabeau fully appreciated what had so struck his two friends—the poetry of Mrs. Hall's table. But, on the other hand, he saw with pain that Mrs. Hall had grown quite pale; and he thought he could detect, in spite of every effort, that Clarence himself was a little restless, as if uneasy about something.

Ours is a wonderfully migratory people. Even at the time of this writing—the 30th day of August, very early in the morning, a mocking-bird singing from the top of yon rich magnolia the while—many of the founders of the club, some of our friends among them, no longer meet with it; some are in the far West, Texas, Salt Lake, and the Golden State, and some have gone to seek their fortunes in the metropolis. It is only safe to say that few, if any, are in the Federal capital. It seems that our people no longer have anything to do or to say there. But' wherever they be, or wherever they may be hereafter, they can never forget those delightful evenings at the club.

The first evening of Mirabeau's attendance was one of the pleasantest. Otis Jones—poor fellow, he has married since —read a curious paper from the *Pall Mall Gazette* on this question: "*Are men and women fond of each other?*" The conclusion was, that the fondness of the two sexes for one another is only pretended; that, in· fact, it is the great fundamental hypocrisy of the race. The pretence that men and women are dying of liking for each other is altogether a fraud. Statistics give no account of any such mortality. Men and women keep aloof from each other; they do not like each other; and their natures must alter greatly, radically, before they ever do like each other, or get along together tolerably. Whenever one gets an insight into the core of things, one sees clearly that men and women are domestic creatures under compulsion. The two sexes do not like each other's society: boys hate girls, and girls return the feeling; men support the costliest clubs, smoke, frequent the billiard-saloon, the card-table, hunt, fish, do anything to get away from women; and all the women have clubs in their drawing-rooms. Old men care nothing for women, except as nurses; old women creep together, and remain together, though it may be they have nothing whatever to say. So strong and so general is the antipathy between the two sexes that it has been considered a work not only of philanthropy, but really a work of genius, to contrive ways and means for keeping men at home with their wives even so long as morality and domestic economy imperatively require. Female writers especially are continually teaching their younger sisters artifices and stratagems for keeping their husbands at home, at least a decent portion of their time; which indeed is only imitating nature—nature having found it necessary to bribe them with children in order to keep them together at all. And just here I desire to make a note, which is this: that whenever this bribe is not given, it may be taken as conclusive evidence that nature does not wish them together at all, but altogether apart. To resume: the truth is, the tastes of the sexes radically differ. No one can doubt that men and women dress, not for the opposite, but each for their own sex; nay, further, men and women always have a contempt for each other's styles. Moreover, that men and women neither like, nor respect, nor even understand, each other, is also evident from their conversation.. Whence else comes that artificial style of talk, the miserable shams and pretences, the absurd and wholly unbelievable compliments, which the sexes indulge in towards each other? Nothing of the kind is seen among men, or women either, who honestly like and respect each other. Plainly, the sexes are strangers to each other, and hence betake themselves to compliments. It is wonderful, and quite as sad as wonderful, how extremely rare it is for husband and wife, even in the course of a long

life, to become really intimate. Considering that the relation
is so close, and the ties so intricate, and especially the many
trials that even the most prosperous must share together, it
is astonishing that it should be so. Nor can it be doubted at
all that the cases are rare indeed where husbands and wives
have not at the bottom of their hearts some sense of griev-
ance against each other. However sad it may be, the fact is
undeniable, that the interest which the sexes have for each
other is confined wholly to one thing—love—and this begins
and ends with the central portion of life. Now, why not say
at once, honestly, that the only interest which the sexes
have for each other depends, in its last analysis, exclusively
upon a low animal propensity? Does not the logic of the
case lead inexorably to such conclusion? Manifestly this
love, which only exists during the central portion of life,
cannot have for its foundation anything in the mind;
for the plain reason that there is nothing in the mind which
exists only during this portion of life. Clearly, according
to the logic of this case, the only interest men and women
have for each other must, in its last analysis, be only the
animal propensity aforesaid; but for that wonderful, though
lowly and simple arrangement, the two sexes are the mortal
natural enemies of each other! Of course, this last idea was
not much talked at the club that night, owing to the exces-
sive modesty of the American people. But the subject
furnished much matter of conversation. Almost every one
present denied the whole thing, from personal experience
mainly, passing such absurd and unbelievable compliments the
while, as went far to prove the very thing they were denying.

That was a pleasant evening at the club. Olive Sutherland
was there, beautiful as the evening star; Fred scarcely left
her side the whole evening. Emma Harlan, too, was there,
her full-rounded beauty as perfect as the dark magnolia-tree,

yet as graceful as the willow of the Orient; Miss Brooke, tall, of classic features and cultured face, cold gray eye like her father's, and royal tread; and Mr. Brooke himself, by special invitation, was there.

"I think," said Mr. Brooke, "that the church is not tolerant enough of innocent pleasures. To be sure, none are proscribed which it defines to be innocent, but the very definition the church gives of innocent enjoyment needs to be vastly more liberal. Once I know, and it was not very long ago, whatever was natural was thought to be, ipso facto, wrong; as if God had not made our natures! But we shall get along. The church, I trust, will not be always learning these two things: first, that in matters of every-day life we are not to be governed by the narrow ideas of the early Reformers and Puritans, who seemed to think long faces, tears, sighs, groans, and a thousand self-imposed afflictions, necessary to a holy life; and secondly, that in matters of doctrine we are not to be confined by the narrow horizon of apostolic times; neither are we to suppose but what there is a wisdom higher even than the wisdom of apostles—the wisdom that controls and directs human events." Manifestly here was no ignorant, narrow, contemptible, bigoted, besotted priest.

"What think you of the paper we heard read to-night?" asked Mirabeau as he and Marian walked home; the Club must walk, it was not allowed to ride.

"The intention seems to be to show that men and women are very different from each other."

"Yes; fundamentally, naturally so."

"Which, I reckon, is meant to lead to the conclusion that their spheres, as they say, must be entirely different from each other, and their education too."

"But this goes a step further, and makes them naturally dislike each other. Do you believe that?"

11*

"It would seem very strange that it should be so; but I don't know what to believe, do you?"

"I know my own belief on the subject. It is true that the sexes do not understand each other; that they do not dress for each other; that, as a rule, they find more pleasure in the company of their own sex than the opposite; in a word, nearly all the facts are true. But the mortal heresy is in making all of this *natural*. In fact, it is altogether unnatural, and due entirely to false ideas and a false system of education. If one studies, *à priori*, the principle which regulates the present relations between the two sexes, one must see that it is monstrous, therefore unnatural; if one studies it historically, one finds everywhere traces of its brutal origin."

"What is this principle?"

"That men are born to will and command; women, to please and obey."

"But do you think that married people so seldom become really intimate?"

"Yes; I fear the case is sadly rare where they ever become companions in the highest, truest sense of that word. Nor can it ever be different until the world learns this, that real intimacy, true companionship, can only exist between equals. This is the ideal of marriage! Think of what it may be between persons of equal intellect, equal rights, equal culture, of similar tastes, and similar aspirations. Let their intellects and culture, then, be of a high order, and their ambition broad and generous; and, finally, let them have for each other that love which is alone worthy of the name of love—love founded upon high esteem and appreciation of character. This is the sacred ideal of marriage."

"I think you right to say that this sort of marriage is very rare. And it must be confessed that the picture we are accustomed to see drawn looks pitiful enough by the side of yours."

"Oh, yes! The ordinary picture, even in its highest estate, what is it? That a man finding a slight deficiency in his own nature must appropriate another small nature in the shape of a wife to supply the deficiency—fortunate, small as the need is, if, haply, he find a complement large enough. He needs something to protect; he must have a wife and children. As for the wife—poor little complement!—she must walk humbly before him, happy, as Pericles says, if not spoken of at all, either for good or ill; she must learn and practice the most perfect self-abnegation, have no will, no opinions of her own; she must learn to anticipate, by the glance of his royal eye, all her husband's wishes; in a word, she must live in the light of his countenance in the same sense that a cabbage lives in the light of the sun."

"Yes; let me you tell what I heard Dr. Williams say the other night in an address to a graduating class of young ladies. He said, the highest and holiest duty of every woman is to love and save some one man!"

"Precisely. But we must have a different class of teachers from Dr. Williams."

"Think you they could accomplish much in this country?"

"Yes; I know there is a fearful mass of darkness, ignorance, miserable conservatism to be got clear of; but people will accept the truth when they get light. The first thing to be done is to get our 'State University' open to our women. Is it not wonderful that our 'State University' should be closed against our women? For the higher education of her sons our State spends many thousands of dollars; for that of her daughters, not one cent! Is it not monstrous?" . . .

Clarence Hall was quite right in saying that Mr. Malcomb was not the Council, or a majority of it. Mr. Malcomb was liberal, the representative man of the new order of things

in the State as well as in the city; but the majority of the
Council were conservative, in sympathy with the great
majority of the controlling classes. The business energy of
the city getting for the time the upper hand of its worn-out
and ridiculous politics, Mr. Malcomb had been prevailed on
to accept his present office; but this action being entirely
abnormal, and things having gone back into their ancient
and time-honored rut, he found it almost impossible to impart any of his own liberal views to his colleagues, or to en-
gage them in any of his progressive plans. That he did anything at all is only due to his marvellous tact and energy.
Still he had done much. Under almost every conceivable
discouragement, the growth of the city in population and
wealth was truly wonderful; within a few years both had
been almost trebled; and with all its braggadocio, quite as
marvellous as anything else about it, it was already the metropolis of the State, and aspiring to be the metropolis of the
Gulf section. Mr. Malcomb, with the aid of a few others,
had also, by consummate management, succeeded in estab-
lishing, for the whites, an excellent and thorough system of
public schools in the city. He was now endeavoring to
make some such provision for the colored population. And
in this, Hall, as was indeed to be expected, seeing that he
was a young man, a University man, of liberal culture and
enlightened understanding, ardently sympathized. But, as
might also have been expected from the prevailing ridiculous
conservatisms, this eminently just and progressive measure
was opposed with much violence by the dominating party—
the "time-honored principles" men. There was to be an election, by the Mayor and Council, of a city attorney, an office
of considerable trust and handsome salary, but usually given
to a young man supposed to possess superior talents; and the
less money the candidate had, the better, for sympathy and

an earnest desire to help along the young and deserving are among the nobler characteristics of this people; but, above all things, he must be "square" in politics. Hall, as we have seen, was a candidate for this office, and had the sympathy of Mr. Malcomb.

On the day before the election was to be, Hall, at the request of Mr. Malcomb, called at his office for a short interview upon the subject.

"I have sent for you," said Mr. Malcomb, going, as was his custom, straight to the subject, "to ask what you wish to be done to-morrow. You know, of course, that if you are a candidate I shall give you my vote; but my judgment is, we shall be defeated; and I think it right to tell you. But for this question of the schools, which certainly ought not to have been brought in at all, being quite foreign, and which is therefore the more unfortunate for you, I think we should not have met with opposition. Still, if you remain a candidate, I shall do all I can for you."

"Whether I am successful or beaten, I am under equal obligations to you. And I will say also, that I would a thousand times rather be beaten for my adherence to a policy so eminently wise and just, than succeed by opposing it. Moreover, though I should be beaten, yet, if you, or this measure which you represent, shall gain any strength by agitating the question, I am content."

"My judgment then is, that I would make the fight; for we can bring such influences to bear that we shall barely be beaten. I think we can so manage as to leave a very small apparent majority against the school measure—much smaller, in fact, than really exists; and in this way the measure will, as you suggested, be strengthened. We should have gotten a small majority but for the Governor's speech the other day."

"I looked upon that simply as an expression of the Governor's individual opinion. But I see now: that agitated the general question, the newspapers took it up, and scattered it among the people."

"Yes; and it may be that some of our electors, or some of the friends of our electors, want some favors from the Governor. Do you remember what he said in his speech?

"He said: 'The negro must not be educated. Teach your bootblack Greek, and he at once either becomes a rascal or is called to preach.' The truth is, our Governor is a partial failure: he began his administration with a declaration, as you know, of his belief in the 'omnipotence of honesty,' and immediately, as all the State knows, united his influence with that of others to prevent the exposure of one of the leaders of his own party. And now he comes forward with a belief in the efficacy of the 'ignorance of the masses.' Such a statement must have sounded strangely enough in the atmosphere of the University."

"I think, though, you do the Governor slight injustice. He did not say he believed in the 'ignorance of the *masses*,' but in the 'ignorance of the *negro*.' I say a slight injustice, because the principle involved is quite the same. But as we have spoken of the Governor, I will not omit to say that, however widely we may differ on many of the greatest questions, I cannot but honor the man who has, in spite of many obstacles, made his way from the anvil to be Governor of the State."

Clarence Hall left Mr. Malcomb's office, feeling much depressed. The truth is, his private affairs were not in the best condition; and he had not till now quite given up the prospect of getting this office. The salary attached to it, though small, had really become an item with him. Mirabeau was quite right when he thought he detected a sort of unrest, a vague uneasiness and restlessness. Clarence Hall was *in debt;* and he did not at all see his way out. He felt dissatisfied, knew that he was testy, and in low spirits. But he did not wish his wife, whom he had left after dinner with a slight headache, to see him so; and when he started home late in the afternoon, he thought to revive his spirits by stepping across the street to the "Turf Exchange" and taking a glass of brandy. He swallowed a good large glassful, and not being at all in the habit of taking it, the effect was greater than he had looked for; besides, it was just the opposite of what he intended: instead of making him feel better, it only made him feel worse, and added also something of a "don't care" feeling. It so happened that he met Mr. Dearing just coming out of his own gate, and stopped to speak a few words with him. He talked rather loud, and his wife, who was lying on the bed, came to the window and looked out to see what was the matter. He thought he made a great noise getting up the steps, and in the hall he stumbled over an unlucky chair and fell with a crash. His wife's headache was worse than it had been at dinner, and the baby was sick and fretful. Clarence Hall was quite wretched.

But let us see what some other of our friends were doing on this identical night. The prevailing opinion was, that the practice of law and the study of literature were quite incompatible occupations. And when it once got to be suspected that a young attorney was running off after literature, the litigating public became shy of him, shook its head, and said he would not stick; wanted to do too many things at once; was theoretical, airy, wouldn't do to tie to; in a word, that man was as utterly lost as tax-money. Bramlette was exactly in this predicament now. He had not paid much attention to this fact, because, being a man of culture and understanding, he must have despised it; and furthermore, the impulse to read and write was to him irresistible. Consequently he frequented daily the Young Men's Library, and was always engaged in taking notes. Of course, the litigating public observed this, and the inevitable result soon followed. But it cannot be denied that Bramlette, though he possessed undoubted genius, was inclined to be vacillating, fitful, and uncertain. His notions seemed to crowd each other out. And, as Brooke of Tipton was at least once known to observe, a man may have any number of notions, and nothing come of them; nothing come of them, you know. So it was with poor Bramlette. Sometimes he thought he would write for magazines; sometimes he thought he would write books; he thought of trying to get a professorship in some college; and then he thought of letting everything else drop, and giving his whole time and attention to his profession. But as for this latter, it had become quite distasteful to him, and he had about given it up. Mirabeau Holmes and Fred went to the Library. Bramlette was not there, as he usually was; and so they went to his room. They found him seated at a rather large round table. He was leaning forward, his head resting upon the table, and did not observe them until they had entered. The table was covered with note-books, straggling sheets of paper, and a great mass of manuscript, all in the greatest confusion.

"What is all this mess you have here?" said Fred, at the same time taking up a piece of the manuscript and beginning to read—"Chapter Second—voyages and discoveries—"

"Take seats, and I will tell you what it is," said Bramlette, picking up a newspaper which had fallen at his side and putting it on the table. "You see," he resumed, "I got a notion into my head to write a School History of the United States. I could not imagine a book that was more needed, especially in the South, or one that would be likely to pay its author more handsomely. In fact, all the school histories of this country we have being Northern books, a correct history written from a Southern standpoint would run the whole of them out of our schools and be used by everybody. That was what I thought, and that is what I think yet. What do you all say?" They both agreed. "Well, I took it into my head to write it; and for two months I have been working upon it with all my might. I have got a third of it done. Now just read that announcement"—handing him the newspaper. Fred took the paper and read the announcement, to the effect that Alexander H. Stephens, Vice-President of the Confederate States, and author of a "History of the War between the States," had completed his "School History of the United States," and that it would appear at an early day.

"So you see," resumed Bramlette, "all the work I have done goes for nothing. To say nothing of the fact that Mr. Stephens's name alone would be sufficient to enable his book to overpower mine, his will be in the hands of everybody long before mine could be finished; and you know one of the universal, standing complaints among our people is, having to buy so many sorts of schoolbooks."

"Yes," observed Fred, "it's about as universal, and more standing, than bowel-complaint in summer."

"What do you propose to do, then?" asked Mirabeau.

"What can I do but stop, short off, and go at something else?"

"Do! Why, go ahead and write your book. Let us think about this a little: if Mr. Stephens had not already, at least to a great extent, appeased the wrath of the country which he brought upon himself by his course during the war, his book would be of advantage to you rather than otherwise; but this he has done by writing the 'History of the War between the States.' I don't know all that this book of his will be, but we all know enough of the author to know that in the book the political portion will overshadow all the rest. It may even be scarcely anything more than a history of the politics of the country."

" I had not thought of it in that light."

" It is strange that you had not."

" No; it is not strange at all," said Fred; " he never read Buckle."

" I have it; I will lend it to you; it is necessary for you to read it at once. But a man might know, I should think, without having read Buckle, that the history of the politics is not the history of the country itself; in point of fact, it is a very small portion of it indeed. We want something like a history of the civilization of this country. We want to know something of the character of our people, and of the forces that have operated to make it what it is; we want these forces arranged into general and local, so as to enable us to account for local characteristics. We want a history of discovery, invention, literature, art, science, education, and all manner of industry; we want a history of the progress of knowledge in all its branches."

" What about Politics, Religion, and War, the trinity of all ancient and modern histories down to Buckle?" asked Fred.

" Of course, a short account must be given of each of them; but it must be entirely subordinate. That is, they must be subordinated in this sense: That they depend absolutely, and necessarily, upon something beyond themselves, to wit: *Knowledge.* Given the amount of knowledge, and the extent of its diffusion, in any country, and if you know its traditions, you may determine with absolute certainty what its politics will be, and what its religion. And as for War, if anybody will point out any good as likely to arise to Humanity from the digestion of any number of tons of war-*fact*, why, I will agree for a portion of our libraries still to be given up to that sort of books. Write your book, my friend, by all means."

"Have you decided, then," said Fred, " to quit law entirely?"

"Yes. I am completely disgusted with it. I wrote to the old Doctor about it the other day. You know he was very much opposed to my studying it at first. He says it would be better for me to quit it even now."

"I am glad," remarked Fred, "that you have quit it. I can abuse it now as much as I please. Old Senator Macon was right when he thought it to be the most contemptible profession extant. He considered it beneath the dignity of a private gentleman, and wanted to hand it over to the government. As for my part, I would rather roll a wheelbarrow or groom a jackass than be a lawyer."

" I have often thought of William Wirt's saying, that he had no title to remembrance but the British Spy. And he was greater than most great lawyers. I think he told the truth," said Bramlette.

· "The law is essentially a profession for only ordinary minds. Its very terms exclude the possibility of high mental effort. The highest mental effort, indeed the only truly high effort of the human mind, is creative effort, and the very terms of the law exclude all idea of creation. The mere politician, low as he is comparatively, is yet one step above the lawyer. The mere lawyer cannot create, he can only interpret; he must confine himself to this subordinate and essentially low office; he can only interpret and arrange; the moment he goes beyond this he is outside of the law," said Mirabeau.

"And all this is true of the upper story; but when you descend to the wrangling lower story! The bare thought of it makes me stop up my ears and hold my nose," said Fred.

"You are both unquestionably right. I know it now; but I did not several years ago. I studied law in obedience to an ambition and design formed when a boy. Then the lawyers and orators—and orators were mostly lawyers—controlled the country; but *nous avons changé tout cela!* " said Bramlette.

Mr. Malcomb thought there was slight difference in believing in the "ignorance of the masses," and believing in the "ignorance of the *negro*." But not so his colleagues of the City Council. Mr. Malcomb endeavored to show them that it was not only the duty of the State, or city, to provide for the education of all, black as well as white, but that it would in this case be immensely to their own advantage. He showed them that the greatest of our needs was *skilled labor*, and this we could not have without educating the laborer. He then placed it upon the low consideration of dollars and cents, showing that it takes more to take care of our criminals than it would to educate all, and that our prisons are mostly filled with the ignorant. This was the argument in reply: If you educate a villain you only increase his capacity for mischief; all negroes are villains; therefore we will not educate the negro!

Clarence Hall was beaten; but, as Mr. Malcomb foretold, only by a very small vote.

CHAPTER XVIII.

"The real temple of the Supreme Being is the universe; his worship, virtue; his festivals, the joy of a great nation assembled in his presence to knit closer the bonds of universal fraternity, and to pay him the homage of intelligent and pure hearts."— ROBESPIERRE.—*Speech in the Convention.*

MIRABEAU HOLMES was now often at Mr. Malcomb's. Marian was always glad to see him. She expected something better from him than from most young men who visited her. She admired him, admired his talents, his ardent sympathy, his lofty aims, and his delicate sense of honor. He recognized all these qualities in her, and he loved her for them, which indeed is the same as saying he loved her for herself; for it was these that made herself. And she felt for him at least that esteem which is the only foundation for love of the highe·t order. I must not omit to mention here one reason why these two liked to be together—a reason quite independent of all higher or deeper considerations : they did not feel obliged to be continually laughing when together. The reader must know. that in this wonderful, ridiculous little democratic city, this was a custom: " Good evening, Miss . Susie." " Good evening, Mr. Jones. I have scarcely had a glimpse of you this evening." (Laughter.) " I have been out on the veranda, and in the other room, looking for you for an hour." (Renewed and continued laughter.) And then Mr. Jones asked : " How have you been enjoying yourself, Miss Susie ? " And Miss Susie answered and said : " Oh ! charmingly." (he he he ! ha ha ha !) And then Miss Susie observed, says she—" How have you enjoyed *yourself*, Mr. Jones ? " And Mr. Jones remarked, says he—" Splendidly !

only I wish I had seen more of you." (he he he! ha ha ha! ha he he, ha ha, he- e-e ee!) In short, dear reader, it was a "he he he," and a "ha ha ha," in great force. Laugh, laugh, laugh! Laugh everywhere; laugh at everything; laugh eternally, till the crack of doom. Custom demanded this. If you failed to observe it, two things followed: your companion voted you stupid, unable to appreciate a good thing, and probably did some original thinking to this effect— "Casting pearls before swine;" and then your companion was also slightly miserable at not being able to *entertain* you, in spite of your horrid stupidity. The fact is, there was so much of this laughter that people of culture above common, and with some just notions of the eternal fitness of things, were bored out of their lives almost. Not that laughter is, *per se*, a bad or improper thing; far from it. A good shaking laugh occasionally is good for the health. Fred Van Comer said once, that it ought to be one of the main duties of the State, coming under the head of "sanitary regulations," to place a copy of Pickwick Papers in the hands of every family, with an injunction to read at least one chapter night and morning. As to that two millions of grown-up men, and four millions of women, among us, who have not learned the art of spelling printed letters, clearly they would have to be supplied with an "Illustrated Pickwick," and look at the pictures with the children.

So in the midst of this universal mania, it was refreshing for two people who appreciated each other, to get together and talk, with a mutual understanding that this ridiculous custom be quietly ignored. The lives of these two people were becoming more and more interwoven day by day. Mirabeau did not feel himself "consumed" by love. He rather thought that this "consuming" sort of love was the Epicurean love, which mainly makes itself known by such exclamations as these : "What an arm ! What a bosom ! What an ankle ! Oh ! she's a rare piece ! " And this, doubtless, is the kind of love that Philosopher Paley deems a most unsafe foundation for marriage.

Many have said, but only Buckle has shown, how impossible it is for any man, however great, to escape the pressure of surrounding opinions. It was known to her friends that Mrs. Sutherland was about to publish another book. Mirabeau Holmes looked for it with special interest; for he had conceived a high admiration for her talents, which was not at all diminished by a contemplation of her surperb personal beauty. Moreover, he said to Fred one day that he believed she would be able to withstand the pressure of conservatism and phariseeism. Fred thought she would not. The book came out—duly embellished with scripture quotations, and "States rights." One evening at a tea-party at Mr. Brooke's, Mr. Brooke, who read everything, introduced the subject of Mrs. Sutherland's last book.

"The French Count," said Miss Brooke, "speaks broken French. And what a ridiculous fellow that Paul is ! When Gertrude tells him there is nothing in her heart but ashes, he meekly asks her to ' give him the ashes ! ' But Marian has just shown me that that comes from Lucile. Can you repeat the lines, Marian ? "

" I don't know that I can ; but I think they are something like this :

> " ' ——though ruin'd it be,
> Since so dear is that ruin, ah, yield it to me. ' "

" It seems to have been written in a great hurry," observed Bramlette.

" It reminds me of ' half-hammer '—a hop, skip, and a jump," said Fred Van Comer.

" But what a statesman is Mr. Hall ! Great, without

doing, saying, or thinking anything above John Smith. But that is not wonderful, seeing that he is a conservative of the Junius ilk," said Mirabeau Holmes.

"But Mr. Stephens says the book is a literary treat," said Mr. Brooke.

."The man that finds it so would dine contentedly off a brick-bat custard," said Fred.

Mirabeau had never been in Mr. Brooke's parlor before; and finding here a fine painting, and learning that it was from a Georgia artist, he expressed his admiration.

"I fear I should not have thought you a great friend of art," said Miss Brooke. .

"Why?" asked Mirabeau, abruptly.

"Did not the Commune pull down the Column? Was it not hostile to art?"

"I doubt not Mr. Holmes can answer that satisfactorily; at least to the 'Left' of any audience," said Mr. Brooke.

"The Commune demolished the Imperial column," said Mirabeau; "I myself voted for its demolition. I think the reasoning of the Commune itself ought to be satisfactory to everybody—except 'divine right and lilies of Bourbon' people. The Commune was not hostile to art. The magnificent portrait of Washington presided over its deliberations, and the walls of the Court of Honor were covered with portraits of other great Republicans. In an art-point of view, the Column was worthless; but if it had been the finest specimen of art on the earth it would have been demolished all the same. The Column represented the glorification of Militarism, and the negation of two of the principles of the Commune—Equality and Fraternity. The Commune was not hostile to art, but it was hostile to Despotism, and to whatever glorified it. The 'Arc de Triomphe' was not demolished. Why? because it represented, though only in part, the triumphs of the Republic and Liberty. It was this that made it sacred. Think you they would have destroyed the Bunker Hill Monument? The last one of them, chiefs and people, would have died in its defence!"

"You speak of two of the principles of the Commune—Equality and Fraternity," said Bramlette; "of course you mean universal equality and fraternity?"

"Yes."

' "But have I not heard you say that this war was not the work of the International Association; that it was not intended to be a universal social and political revolution; but that it was only to protect the Republic and the rights of Paris?"

"Yes."

"Why, then, should you demolish the Column because it represented the negation of universal fraternity?"

"Though the Commune did not pretend to inaugurate the great Revolution of which you speak—for indeed it expressly disclaimed it—yet, the principles of the Commune and the International Association are identical. We look forward to the Universal Republic, which, indeed, seems a dream of enthusiasm and worthy to be laughed at only to tyrants and their either ignorant or designing abettors. Under the Universal Republic wars shall cease; love of country shall give place to love of Humanity; imaginary State lines shall not be sufficient to make people enemies; all shall acknowledge the whole human family to be a Common Brotherhood, having common interests, a common sympathy in a common struggle, a common glory, and a common destiny. This is the ultimate aim of the International Association, with which the Commune was certainly in the warmest sympathy. That the International Association will finally succeed in its mission, I will not suffer myself to

12

doubt for an instant. The time will surely come when all the world shall.unite to raise a monument to its founders."

"If that all be a dream, it is certainly a very grand one," said Marian.

"But," said Miss Brooke, having retired from the room a moment, and reëntering with a book in her hand, " we shall not let you off so easily as that. You have told us the ultimate object of the Internationale; but by what means does it propose to accomplish the end ? This book—History of the Commune—says the programme of the Internationale is this :

"' The abolishment of all religions.

The abolishment of all property.

The abolishment of all family.

The abolishment of all nationality.' "

"The question, then," answered Mirabeau, "is simply this, whether you will believe its own declarations, or the representations of its enemies ? The case is, if the objects of an institution are good, palpably good and pure, they must be misrepresented before the enemies of the institution can hope to assail it successfully."

"To the honor of Humanity be it said," interrupted Mr. Brooke.

"And when I see a man," resumed Mirabeau, " in an attack upon anything, resorting to misrepresentation and falsehood, I at once become suspicious that, for his purposes, that thing is too good to be exhibited in its true colors. So with the author of this programme. The only thing about it which is not false is that concerning the abolition of nationality. But as to the abolishment of nationality, no one can be so simple as to suppose we mean simply and abruptly to wipe out national boundaries; we mean that the spirit of nationality shall give place to the spirit of Humanity ; but we do mean that even now all peoples ought to refuse to go to war with and butcher each other at the command of their tyrants; and we also suggest that they emphasize their refusal by cutting their tyrants' heads off. As for the family, though certainly the institution might be greatly improved, the charge that we mean to abolish it is quite as false as the idea is absurd. As for the 'abolishment of all religions,' this is what we purpose: To fill the whole world with *light*, knowing that all false religions, in other words all forms and systems of superstition, will disappear before it. But if any religion should interfere to prevent this, we should crush such interference at all costs. Nor would we allow priests to extort money from the people for any pretended remission of sins or promises of rewards hereafter; we call that obtaining money or goods under false pretences; it is swindling; we call for its punishment by law."

"Did not the Commune believe in atheism?" asked Miss Brooke.

"No."

"Some of them were atheists."

"Yes; notably, Rigault was an atheist. And some of the fathers of the American Republic were infidels; notably, Jefferson. But the Republic was not therefore unchristian."

"What was the religion of the Commune?"

"One God; the immortality of the soul; and a virtuous life. And the precepts of its religion were these three: Trust in God; love virtue; and do good to one another. Of course, you understand that I speak of the majority; there were many differences of belief among the individuals."

"But what about the abolishment of property?" asked Mr. Brooke.

"That," said Mirabeau, "I believe is what most people call

the practical question. The International Association does not propose to abolish property, but only to hit upon some plan by which its benefits may be more equalized. I need not speak of the enormous wretchedness of at least nine-tenths of the human race, or of the admitted fact that it is increasing instead of diminishing. Not to enter into the whys and wherefores, the *fact* is, that there is enough and more than enough in the world to make the whole human family comfortable. But somehow, through no fault of the nine-tenths, or any merit of the one-tenth, all of it has got into the hands of the one-tenth; the nine-tenths starve, and the one-tenth wastes enough to make them comfortable. Manifestly there is something wrong. We propose to rectify this wrong and provide for the future."

"That is very indefinite. What *is* the Internationale, and *how* does it propose to 'rectify this wrong and provide for the future?'"

"The Internationale is essentially and purely a WORKING-MEN'S Association. It has now more than four millions of active members; but all the working-classes, that is, all the producing classes, of all countries, are, and must be, consciously or unconsciously, with us in sentiment. The French workingmen are only the advanced guard of the modern Proletariate. Class-rule can no longer disguise itself under a *national* uniform. When, after the late great war between France and Prussia, the National Governments of the conqueror and the conquered fraternized for the common massacre of the workingmen, they demonstrated to the whole world what was already clearly understood by the Internationale, namely: *That the-National Governments of all countries are one as against the Proletariate ;* that they are ever ready to ignore for the time their own differences, and to unite in crushing, by wholesale massacre if possible, every effort of the working-class to break the chains of that slavery which has reduced it to starvation and almost to despair. Now, the Internationale is a counter-organization of labor against the cosmopolitan conspiracy of capital. But *how* does the Internationale propose to free society from the confessedly frightful evils of our present system of civilization? The Internationale has seized the idea that that system is *itself* the necessary parent of these evils; the Internationale means to crush it; especially does it mean to destroy it in its economical and political aspects. Does the Internationale mean to abolish property? No; but it *does* mean to abolish that class-property which makes the labor of the many the wealth of the few. The Internationale means to destroy utterly the *wage-system* of labor, for that system is the *immediate* cause of nearly all our woes; this wage-system, I repeat, whose wretched delusions and prostitute realities have long since been unmasked to all who do not wilfully close their eyes to the truth, the Internationale has resolved to abolish from the face of the earth—and it will *do* what it has resolved to do. This wage-system, or capitalist system, the Internationale means to supersede with a system of *co-operative production*, in which every *producer* shall receive the *whole* of what he produces. It means for co-operative societies to take under their own control the producing energies of the country, and thus not only put a stop to those periodic convulsions incident to the capitalist system, but so direct and regulate production as that every producer shall get all that he produces and no more, and so that not a single energy or capacity to work shall ever be involuntarily idle. This is the great work the Internationale has resolved to accomplish. All other issues are subordinate; many of them different in different countries; and they all group themselves about this as a centre. The Internationale does not propose to accomplish its work in a day. Nor has it any ready-made utopias to introduce *par décret du peuple.* But it will accomplish its work, though it may be, doubtless will be, after long and severe struggles, transforming circumstances and men. It is known to all the world, including even conservatives—who always stand with their back to the future—that our present system of civilization is surely doomed. Corruption has seized upon its vitals and riots in all its members. The Internationale has resolved to hasten its collapse, to sweep the rubbish from the face of the earth, and to erect another structure in its stead; not a permanent one, perhaps, or rather, certainly not a permanent one, but one in which every member of the human family shall find a home and the possibility of at least moderate comfort. Meanwhile, in the full consciousness of its historic mission, and with the heroic resolve to accomplish it, the Internationale can well afford to smile at the pitiful slanders and coarse invective of its enemies."

" But what of the strictly political aspect of the question ? " said Mr. Brooke.

" I will answer you in the words of the famous Central Committee : ' The Prolétaires of Paris, amidst the failures and treasons of the ruling classes, have understood that the hour has struck for them to save the situation by taking into their own hands the direction of public affairs. They have understood that it is their imperious duty and their absolute right to render themselves masters of their own destinies, by seizing upon the governmental power.' The Internationale means to establish a government of the people *by* the people. It will not be afraid of giving great power to the government, because the people will be the government itself. The Internationale desires such a government as that of the Commune of Paris—the most perfect that ever existed, the prototype of the ideal government of the future. When the smoke and clouds of prejudice and slander shall be cleared away, then will be seen the *true* Commune of Paris; and coming ages shall vie with each other in erecting monuments to its martyrs. Paris shall be seen as it was: 'working, thinking, fighting, bleeding Paris—almost forgetful, in its incubation of a new society, of the cannibals at its gates—radiant in the enthusiasm of its historic initiative ! ' "

CHAPTER XIX.

"And coming events cast their shadows before."—CAMPBELL.

CLARENCE HALL'S affairs were in a bad way. His wife never inquired concerning his business. She had not the slightest notion whether it was prosperous, or on the brink of ruin. True, he was in great need of sympathy, and once or twice he had ventured to seek it from his wife; but he met with such a resigned and confiding trust in his own omnipotence as at first to startle him, and then set him to thinking whether he had not been mistaken in some of his notions about "complements." At first he tried hard to deceive himself; but no man in such case ever yet succeeded. Their opinions never clashed; they never disagreed about anything. She never said to him, "I would do this," or, "I think I would have done that." Sometimes Hall thought it would be a relief even to hear one poor old "I told you so." He began to feel utterly lonely. No man feels so before he is married. It is only afterwards, and when he is startled to find that between himself and his wife there is no companionship at all. Mrs. Hall was not lonely; her husband kissed her every day when he left home, and when he returned. He allowed her to buy whatever she wished. She had no idea that her husband was miserable. She had not, as he was continually afraid she would do, perceived his restlessness. One night, while sitting at the supper-table, they were startled by the alarm-bell. Hall walked to the door and looked out. There was a great fire, apparently just where his office was. His book, on which he had spent so much labor, and from which he expected money to help him out of his present embarrassments, lacked only a few pages of being finished, and was locked up in a desk in his office. He uttered a cry of pain; and leaping to the ground, fairly flew along the streets in the direction of the fire. He was too late; the building was already completely wrapped in flames. Dumb with despair, he stood with arms folded upon his breast, and the flames glaring upon his face, and saw the whole consumed. Furniture, library, papers, manuscript —all gone! And when he made his way back home and told his wife what had happened, she only asked where he would take another office! He thought that his capacity to be astonished at his wife's indifference was long since exhausted; but now he stared at her a mingled look of curiosity, astonishment, and despair. He turned away, and Mrs. Hall kissed her baby, exclaiming, "Poor baby! papa's office burnt." I cannot give any conversations between Clarence Hall and his wife at this period. There were none. He was now utterly ruined; and his wife knew nothing of it. For some time his creditors had been pressing him; and it was with the greatest difficulty, and by making the most confident promises, that he had succeeded in putting them off so long. Meanwhile he had worked desperately upon his book; always going back to his office after supper, and frequently working all night, and till breakfast next morning. His wife's headaches had also of late grown alarmingly frequent, and she was getting paler and more feeble. Hall was occasionally compelled to stay at home on this account; and sometimes his clients called at his office and found him away. From this cause, as well as from the almost constant attention he gave to his book, his business was sometimes neglected; and his practice, instead of growing, had really diminished. He knew that his creditors would now come down upon him.

12*

Let a man be crippled by misfortune, he thought, and, like a wounded animal, he is fallen upon by the pack and devoured. He knew of no one upon whom he could call for a loan, even if he had had any prospect whatever of soon, or ever, being able to replace it. His father-in-law was quite out of the question. Indeed, Mr. Dearing's business was itself in almost as desperate a condition as his son-in-law's. His elegant residence on Peach-tree had more than once been levied on and advertised for sale. But by shrewd management on the part of his lawyers, by " taking the homestead," transferring, and putting in claims to what the homestead could not be made to cover, his creditors had up to this time been kept at bay. But they continued to worry him ; and it was with the utmost difficulty he could make enough to keep along, and pay his lawyers' fees. Only a short while before the burning of Hall's office Mr. Dearing had been to him and offered to " take all the money he had to spare, at good interest."

" My affairs," said Mr. Dearing, " are temporarily embarrassed ; and as I suppose you have some money to spare, I thought I would propose to take it and pay you the interest that I should otherwise have to pay the bank." His son-in-law assured him that he had no money on hand.

" Ah ! " said Mr. Dearing, " I was not aware that you had made any investment ; I supposed your money was idle in the bank."

" I have not made any investment, nor have I any money idle in the bank either," answered Hall, a little nettled ; not knowing what a complete delusion his father-in-law was under concerning his affairs.

" Oh, it doesn't matter ; it doesn't matter at all," said Mr. Dearing, a little hurt in turn, that his own son-in-law should refuse to lend him money ; " I only thought that as you had it to spare, and as I had to pay the interest anyhow, I might as well pay it to you as anybody."

"You speak, sir, as if you doubted the truth of what I say, when I tell you that I have no money, either in the bank or elsewhere."

"I think, sir, you need scarcely grow angry about the matter. You say you have made no investment; what have you done with your money?" asked Mr. Dearing, bluntly enough.

"What have I done with my money! Why, spent it upon my family—every cent of it, and gone in debt besides."

"Spent it upon your family—spent it upon your family, and in debt," said the father-in-law, now thoroughly astonished and beginning to be frightened as the truth vaguely dawned upon him.

"Yes, spent it upon my family, and in debt."

"I understood—the general impression—can I have been mistaken in supposing—that your practice alone amounted to at least several thousand dollars?"

"Several thousand dollars! Suppose I were to tell you that it scarcely amounted to so many hundreds?"

Mr. Dearing was struck dumb with astonishment and horror. He had supposed that Hall's practice amounted to about six thousand dollars; and when Hall said that he had spent it all on his family, he began to think that possibly he was mistaken, and then to rapidly consider whether it was *possible* for him to have been mistaken by *half*. But an idea struck him.

"Ah, you say, *suppose* you were to say so and so. You don't mean to say that your income actually *is* less than, at least, three thousand?"

"Yes, I do. I mean to say that it is less than a fourth of it."

"Good God! If I had known this—"

"What?· I suppose you will say your daughter should not have married me!"

"You deceived me, sir; you acted dishonorably, sir; you ——." And Mr. Dearing was going on in a loud and angry tone, when he saw Bramlette approaching the door, and ceased; but Bramlette, seeing Hall's father-in-law, and supposing that they·might be on private matters, passed on to another door. Mr. Dearing checked himself instantly; for one of the cardinal rules of good society in those parts was, that family quarrels, of which there were a great many, must be kept inside the family. But when Bramlette had passed on, Mr. Dearing resumed, in a low, sneering tone:

"May I ask how much it is *exactly?*"

"You may, if you wish, ask till doomsday," replied Clarence Hall, with the utmost contempt; and turning on his heel, left the office.

Whence came this quarrel between Clarence Hall and his father-in-law? Was it providence, foreknowledge, will, or fate? The very next day after his great misfortune, the officer came, in the morning, with a summons from one of his creditors, and in the afternoon he returned with two others, for the creditors were watching each other, and each one was afraid that the others would get ahead of him. Clarence Hall had already been forced to give his notes in place of his accounts, and the notes were made small enough to be sued in the justice courts; so that the cases could be tried in ten days, and in ten more the property levied on be exposed to sale. Something must be done, and that without delay. To begin with, the comfortable establishment on Peach-tree must be given up; and afterwards all expenses must be reduced in every possible manner. Clarence Hall resolved upon this course, and he was glad that he could do so without consulting the Dearings. He was even glad that he had quarrelled with

his father-in-law, for had it not been for that quarrel, he
would feel bound to consult him on so important a matter,
and he knew that Mr. Dearing would strongly oppose such a
course. It was against his own judgment that he had at first
taken this establishment, but his wife's family would not
listen to anything else ; and besides, he was not hard to per-
suade to consent to anything then that he thought would
gratify his wife in the smallest particular. That was his day
of high hopes and generous ambition ; the future stretched
out before him like a far-reaching elysian field. The high
and dangerous mountains before him sank in his lofty view
to mere hillocks, and the calcined cliffs that told of upheaval
and ruin were hid beneath the rich foliage of fancy. Rushing and turgid streams became babbling brooks, pleasant to
the ear; and the treacherous marsh was hid beneath the
poetic leaves of Vallombrosa. What mattered a few hundred
dollars ! Was the spirit of love and hope to be bounded in by
the low horizon of dollars and cents ! Suppose he should not
even be as fortunate as he thought he might safely calculate
upon ; nay, suppose, in the inscrutable dealings of Providence,
some slight misfortunes and reverses should overtake him ?
Should he not only strive the harder, and rise superior to fate ?
Was not the accomplishment of any design only the measure of
the effort required ? And who should set limits to the effort
of the human mind ? Was it not the highest glory of god-like
minds to conquer fate itself ? But it was not often in those
days that Clarence Hall found himself in this mood, and
asking these questions. It was only in those moments when
highest enthusiasm succeeds to deepest reflection, as the
loftiest mountains ever rise beside the sublimest depths of the
ocean. It was not often; for, as I have said, Clarence Hall,
from a happy temperament, happy surroundings, and a really
brilliant prospect, could not but dwell mostly upon the more

pleasing, if less elevating picture of life. Many a time he
had thanked God that it was so well with him. He had
started even with the world, free from the depressions of
poverty on the one hand, and from the temptations of indul-
gent riches on the other. If, upon leaving the University,
he found himself thrown wholly upon his own resources, and
had even felt a little pinched for a time, it was just enough
to whet the edge of endeavor, and he could not have wished
it otherwise. If at one time he had thought that he was not
getting along so briskly as he could wish and had hoped; if
indeed he had begun to grow even a little restless, he was
soon brought to acknowledge that it was " all for the best."
But when he had married ! then indeed should his career
truly begin. Clarence Hall was not an enthusiast; he did
not set his mark too high; he did not indulge in any wild
fancies. Still his hopes were high. He knew that Providence had given him the very woman that even his most
sober speculative belief told him ought to be his wife—the
" complement " of his own nature. He was thankful ; he was
hopeful ; his better judgment told him to " keep even with the
world ; " but his wife's family thought he must of course take
a comfortable home, at least in an aristocratic quarter—that
is, the most nearly aristocratic in this essentially tumble-down
democratic capital. A few hundred dollars was not much, to
be sure, and his imagination expanded to meet the occasion.
Thus it was that Clarence Hall had got " behind " in the very
beginning; and, like all other people that ever did start so,
or ever will start so, he got further and further "behind " every
day. Once since they had been married Clarence Hall had
had an opportunity of giving up the house. He had taken
it until October, the month in which real-estate men dis-
pose of property for the year. He determined to leave the
house, and adopt his original plan of taking a neat little cot-

tage elsewhere. But, as we have seen, his wife's babies—or, according to the statute, *his* babies, his poor wife being only their mother—were born on the night of the second of September at nine o'clock, and consequently on the first day of October were less than one month old, and their mother, not being an Irishwoman, was not yet well; all of which, to be sure, was a difficulty which Clarence Hall, if he had only exercised a little foresight some nine months before, could, though perhaps, as it were, with some slight inconvenience to himself and family, have put off at least a month. But we are not here to talk about what might have been ; nothing could be more unprofitable. Far be it from me to quarrel with Clarence Hall, or to make wise observations on what he ought to have done ; the poor man has quite enough to trouble him. And, besides, the President of the United States, or the Emperor of Germany, supposing he could call back a few years, or any other man, would have done just as he did.

When Clarence Hall's office was destroyed by fire he was left without a dollar; and when he was sued next day, he found himself without credit also. He had not a single piece of furniture for fitting up a new office, nor a single book. And yet he must get an office immediately. He had a beautiful and valuable watch; it was a family keepsake, and he would not part with it under any considerations. He tried to borrow a hundred dollars ; but " money was very scarce," and none of his friends had any. There was no other chance; he pawned his watch for a little more than half its value ; of course he would redeem it ; he would not allow his watch to go even if he had to sell anything else he had. He bought a few pieces of ordinary furniture, a few books, and fitted him up another office. But all of his papers had been burned, and this put himself and his clients to much inconvenience ; and though no man was certainly so

big a fool as to suppose that he was at all to blame for the loss
and inconvenience, yet some two or three of his clients were
dissatisfied, and took away their business. He was now also
compelled to be at home frequently; his wife had grown paler,
and kept her bed at least a third of her time. His mother-
in-law came frequently to see them, and when her son-in-law
was present never lost an opportunity of making cutting
remarks. But there was one consolation: he had quarrelled
with his father-in-law, and that obviated the necessity of
consulting him upon the contemplated change. Clarence
Hall almost thought this quarrel a special providence; and I
doubt not the pious reader has also come to the same conclusion. But the first thing to be done was to save his furniture from immediate sale. If he could only get it put off to
the Superior Court, possibly by that time he might be able
to make " some arrangement." But how to put it off—that
was the question. To be sure, he could " take the homestead."
But he shrank from that as being unjust; he even thought it
dishonorable; for these notes on which he was sued were for
the purchase-money of this very furniture; and he thought it
would be little if any better than swindling. So it went on
till the day before the furniture was to be sold.

When Clarence Hall went home that day to dinner, he
found his wife frightened, trembling. Her mother had seen
one of the printed notices of the sale, and had brought it to
her. Her nerves were already weak. She was alarmed,
and took to her bed. What a man will not do on his own
account, he will frequently do for his family. Clarence Hall
felt that he could be sold out, and turned moneyless and
creditless upon the world. But there was his baby; there
was his sick wife. And, after all, it would not always be
thus; his affairs would take a turn for the better some time;
and then he could pay all he owed; and he mentally resolved

to pay a high interest. He applied for " the homestead." But that could not be passed upon immediately. It was necessary that his wife put in a "claim" to the property. He went and brought in an officer; and his wife signed her name to the claim. Then there was cost to pay—several dollars. He had no money for that. He was infinitely troubled. He met Fred Van Comer on the street; he knew that Fred was working for a salary; but he thought he might have as much as he wanted; besides, he only wanted it " for a few days." Yes; Fred had ten dollars; but it was in his room. He had to go by the printing-office first; but he would bring it to Hall's office in the course of an hour. Now that was a pious lie of Fred's. He had not a dollar in the world; not even a' quarter to play a game of billiards with. Although he was not aware of the whole truth, he knew that Hall was hard run, and thought that possibly he might be in urgent need of even a few dollars—as indeed he was. So he told him he had the money in his room; resolving to go to Bramlette, whom he had seen with twenty dollars that very morning. He hastened to Bramlette's room.

" Bramlette, I told a lie just now—I said I had ten dollars in my room. I haven't got a cent; and unless you give it me, I shall tell another; for I promised to have it at a certain place in half an hour."

" Well, well! I havn't got a dollar either."

" The mischief! what did you do with that twenty dollars I saw you with this morning? "

" I had just got it, and have paid my board with it." Fred spun out of the room, with fingers in both ears, and went sailing down the street. He found Mirabeau Holmes, got the money, and carried it to Hall's office.

The quarrel between Hall and his father-in-law had grown worse; and Hall vowed that neither he nor any of his

family should ever go to Mr. Dearing's again. Hall had
fully determined to give up their house on Peach-tree. But
when the time came, his wife, who had continued to grow
feebler, was very weak and nervous. The physician said it
would not be safe to move her so far; her nervous constitution might be dangerously affected by the shock. Alas!
for that quarrel with his father-in-law! She might else be
taken thither, which was just across the street, till everything
was done. Moreover, his wife herself made the first objection she had ever made to anything: she was too weak to
move. There was nothing to do but take the house again,
and it could not be taken for less than a year. Alas, alas!
Clarence Hall! there are no special providences in this world!

"How is it," said Robert Malcomb to Mirabeau one
evening at Mrs. Robert's tea-table, "that your notions have,
in so short a time, been completely revolutionized?"

"Do you remember what Descartes says about his pursuit
of truth? 'When I set forth in the pursuit of truth,' says
he, 'I found it necessary to reject everything that I had
hitherto received, and pluck out all of my old opinions, in
order that I might lay the foundation of them afresh;
believing that by this means I should the more easily accomplish the great scheme of my life, than by building on an
old basis, and supporting myself by principles which I had
learned in my youth, without examining if they were really
true.' It is not presumption in me to say that I have found
it necessary to do exactly what Descartes did; not presumption, because this is the identical course that must be taken
by every mind in the earnest pursuit of the truth; and by the
smallest not less than by the greatest."

"But it does not follow that in this process you must
necessarily find all your old beliefs to have been false,"
said Robert.

"I should rather think that one brought up in a Christian country, with the lights of education and religion before him, would find most of his beliefs to be true," said Mrs. Robert.

"I can answer for myself: to say nothing of the religious dogmas which I had been taught to accept not only without examination but on the vaguest possible hearsay, it might 'be thought that at least one's fundamental political belief, acquired in such a republic as this, should contain a large portion of truth. For one, I found my own to be almost wholly false, warp and woof, with scarcely here and there a thread of truth. Delescluze said to me on that very morning that he went, in obedience to his promises, to seek his death among the people—'Yours is a great country; the grand hope of the world is in your people; Humanity looks to you for the first of its final triumphs,'" said Mirabeau.

"I do not claim," said Robert, "to be up in French politics. Still I have often seen and heard the expression 'triumph of Humanity;' but to me, I must say, it sounds vaguely enough. What did Delescluze mean by it? or what do you mean by it?"

"It is admitted on all hands," answered Mirabeau, "that the great calamity and opprobrium of civilization is, that while countries have advanced in power and wealth, while they have grown rich in all manner of increase, in all manner of comfort and luxury, nine-tenths of the *people* of those countries are still condemned to the lowest battle of animal man—the battle with starvation. Nine-tenths of the human family, in every country but our own—and under the same system the same results must soon follow here—exist in a state of struggle and wretchedness which makes existence, instead of a boon, almost an insupportable burden. And what is most fearful of all is, that this condition is growing worse year by year; it is infinitely worse than it was a century and a half ago, according to the admission even of the highest 'conservative' authorities, such as the writers in the London Quarterly."

"But has not this wretchedness been clearly proved, or at least a large portion of it, to be traceable to their own improvidence, ignorance, insobriety, and unthrift?"

"No, not a large portion of it. A small portion is doubtless traceable hither. But how does this better the case? It reminds one of the absurd old theological dogma of predestination—'you can and you can't; you shall and you shan't.' This very ignorance and unthrift is due to something! What? It is a *necessity* of their condition! In point of fact, though, a very, very small portion of this appalling wretchedness is due to the ignorance and unthrift of the people themselves. True, it may be attributable to their *ignorance*, in a sense; but a very different sense from that understood by tories and conservatives: it is due to their ignorance in this, that being ignorant of their power, they do not rise up and crush the system that necessitates their condition."

"But how," asked Mrs. Robert, with the practicality of the sex, "is all this to be rectified?"

"Yes; how?" added Robert. "I suppose you would call this a 'triumph of Humanity.' But this *how?* is it not one of the 'enigmas of life?'"

"Yes; it is one of the 'enigmas of life' to those who, instead of coming out into the light of reason and truth, grope among the gloomy cells of superstition and barbarism; to those who think it better that millions of human beings should die in wretchedness, in obedience to what a barbarous age may have taught to be an abstract right, than even to inquire whether that abstract right be a right at all or not. As to this *How?* for Europe I know of but one plan; the half-way measures of Mill and Odger will not do—they do not.meet the case; the case is desperate, and the remedy must be deep and comprehensive. Let some prophet rise up and say to the people, and let them be taught to understand and obey him: 'The world has plenty, and to spare. Behold on every side enough for the whole human race! But on every side the people dies of hunger and wretchedness! By an unjust system, all comforts, and all luxuries, have been given to one-tenth of the human race. They cannot consume the comforts. The luxuries waste before their eyes! And yet there is enough for all! enough, and to spare! Let the people rise up and crush the system which oppresses it and reduces it to despair. The people starves! And yet it dare not reach forth its hand for the bread that rots within its grasp! Down with the system! Let.property be universalized.' And this is precisely what will be done, sooner or later. As for me, I have, but one rule of right—the good of the people. When the people starve, and that too from no fault of their own, and when I see plenty and to spare all around them, I confess to you I should not much stop to leisurely read and metaphysically consider charters and lawyers' parchments."

"All this I understand," said Robert, "to apply to Europe. What of our own country?"

"In this country we have no need 'yet of the desperate remedy already necessary for Europe. The end can, I believe, be accomplished without such means. But one thing is certain, if it is to be done, our people must be wiser than they have been in the past. And this is the very first step to be taken: our Universities must be largely endowed and tuition made free in all; the classics must be discarded, and the time and labor hitherto wasted upon them be given to science and industry; they must also be thrown open to all, without distinction of sex or race. We must also have a *national system* of *compulsory* education. No more public lands must be given to railroads; but all the public domain must be immediately divided out among all our people who have no land or other property, *in trust* for themselves and their children for, say, three hundred years. We must have a law prohibiting any man, or set of men, from operating any manufactory except upon the *co-operative plan.* We must have universal suffrage; capital punishment must be abolished by Congress—the States are too slow; and we must have a prohibitory liquor law, making it a penitentiary offence, if need be, to make or sell it. These are some of the things that ought to be done in this country; but the most important of all is to have a *national system* of *compulsory* education. Knowledge, above all things, is what the people need. But I confess to you I have little hope of politicians doing anything. I say candidly that I believe if it were not for one man among us the country would go to pieces; it seems to me that he alone is holding it together; and that man is General Grant. European nations have waged fierce wars because a princess of one declared she could wear a smaller slipper than a princess of the other; but I know of nothing more contemptible than the endless and senseless quibblings and wranglings of our politicians over written constitutions, parchments, and law-books, and almost the whole of it, too, relating to the past. We have such a grand mission—so much to do for ourselves and our children, and, above all, so much to do for Humanity; and yet, instead of coming together and pushing boldly on to a common destiny in a great cause, we are wasting all our energies in wrangling with, defaming, and thwarting each other."

As they left the table and went into the parlor, Robert could not but feel self-complacent that he himself had long ago predicted that Mirabeau would some day go off after Rousseau in politics, and possibly in religion too.

Mr. Brooke was not only pastor of the wealthiest Presbyterian church in the city, but had some property of his own. He kept a carriage and horses. Frequently of afternoons he would drive out with "the girls," as he called Miss Brooke and Emma, and it might have been observed of late that Mr. Brooke, instead of driving first to Mrs. Harlan's cottage and leaving Emma there, now usually returned first to his own home, and, depositing Miss Brooke, rode on with Emma alone to her mother's. Mr. Brooke always went in a moment to say a word with the mother, and then went with the daughter into the flower-garden. In short, Mr. Brooke managed to be with Emma a considerable portion of his spare time. Nor was this wonderful at all. Emma, to be sure, was now really a young lady, but she was never anything to Mr. Brooke but a child. It was not to be wondered at that Mr. Brooke liked her; that he ever found pleasure in her company. She was not only innocent, confiding, and of the most gentle and sweet disposition, but she had naturally a good mind, and that it was well cultured was due in considerable degree to Mr. Brooke himself. It is needless to add that she reposed in Mr. Brooke the fullest trust; that she looked up to him as father, friend, teacher, pastor—indeed, almost as to a divinity. But Mr. Brooke, with all his learning and all his piety, was not by any means exalted above human weaknesses and human passions. His wife, as I have said, was an invalid, and he was a stout, healthy man, with a body full of electricity, and warm, red blood. His wife certainly could not live always, and the probability was that she would not live very long. Was it strange that Mr. Brooke had already looked upon this little girl, sweet and luscious as a perfumed strawberry, with a light in his great gray eyes that would have made her tremble had she known its true meaning? Allons! Maybe Mr. Brooke's invalid wife will die; and if she does! who could blame Mr. Brooke for wanting to bite this berry? Still, Emma dear, thou art not safe from harm. Alf Walton may come back, and even the light in thy pastor's eye may rise to a consuming heat for thy innocence. Yet, one can hardly see what it should profit anything in heaven or earth, that thy poor little life be ruined, and thy heart made to bleed. And yet —— Allons! God protect thee, Emma dear, and all good spirits shield thee with their wings.

Was there ever a man with breeches too short that had a warm, full heart? Yes, indeed! And that man was Nathaniel Bramlette. And of this I will make oath this second day of September, year of the Republic ninety-seven, before any notary in the county. And I would do the very same thing if he had a thousand buttons on his shirt, and though his jaw-bone was as strong as an anchor. Poor Bramlette! he loved Emma Harlan. Accursed poverty! Accursed fate! Sometimes he would go to Mrs. Harlan's and stay for two hours, saying tender, poetic things; and he had already been inspired to write several poems, two of which he published anonymously, and the others he kept in his portfolio. But as for declaring to her his love, or proposing marriage, why, that was out of the question. And yet, many and many a night alone in his room did he lay awake thinking of the future, and hoping for a better turn in his affairs. But the years were creeping on; Bramlette was approaching thirty; and he had not yet done anything. His notions had always crowded each other out! Think of marrying? Why, it was hard scuffling to make enough to pay his weekly board. But, the commonest clerk could do that. Does it seem strange that in such a country as this, a man of Bramlette's

talents, culture, and spotless character, and with an ambition
to succeed, should with the utmost difficulty be able to make
his board ? Probably some will have the greatest contempt
for him. Probably they have more contempt at their disposal than brains ! The truth is, some men never learn the
knack of " getting along ; " and Bramlette was one of them.
He had not failed to notice with pain, when his attention
was called to it by Fred, that Clarence Hall seemed to be
getting on badly of late, and they correctly divined the
cause. No ! he must not think of marriage, or love either,
if he could help it, until he got money. Aye, but when
would that be ? He thought once that he would have had a
competency by now ; but he was scarcely able to pay his
board. A little while ago his hopes had revived when he
thought of publishing his book ; but that was all done for
now. And the worst symptom of all with this man was, that
his self-confidence was fast leaving him. Above all things,
man, believe in yourself. On the evening we have seen
Mirabeau and Fred at his room, Bramlette was bluer than he
had ever been. Nor did he even know what he should have
done but for the following circumstance : General Clement
was a special friend of the editor of the New Monthly, just
started. This noble man, ever looking for an opportunity to
do good, and having some idea of Bramlette's affairs, came
to him the very next morning and advised him to go to see
the editor. The good General preceded him. And when
Bramlette called that afternoon, though it was not the custom of the editor to pay for articles, he at once engaged to
pay for Bramlette's ; and he never knew till long after that
an exception had been made in his favor.

13

CHAPTER XX.

" There is a tide in the affairs of men,
　　Which, taken at the flood, leads on to fortune;
　　Omitted, all the voyage of their life
　　Is bound in shallows, and in miseries."—JULIUS CÆSAR

EVERYTHING went wrong with Clarence Hall. His expenses grew heavier instead of lighter. His baby was sick
all the summer, and his wife all the winter. Do what he
would, he could not enlarge his practice; and he could not
get the money even for what he did. His butcher's and
grocer's bills had grown to a considerable amount. He had
been indulged on them once already, by agreeing to pay a
heavy interest; and they would fall due again in thirty days.
Clarence Hall was uneasy about these debts. He had not
the money to pay them; and could not now tell where he
was to get it. He had calculated confidently upon meeting
these bills with the money he was to get from a case which
he was so sure of winning that he had conditioned his fee
upon the issue. Of course, he could make his fee twice as
large in this case as if it was certain. It was his client's
offer, and he was quick to accept it. For the law was clear
—so clear that there could not be any dispute about it at all.
True, there was no statute exactly covering the point; but
in Coke upon Lyttleton it was laid down too plainly to be
mistaken. Lest there should be some mistake about his
meaning, the learned expositor had not only used up all the
English words which came within ten leagues of the main
one, but had imported large batches from France and Rome.
Of course, the client was not mistaken about what he could

prove on the trial! Nevertheless, the case went against him, and Clarence Hall lost his fee. And what made the matter particularly aggravating was, that the fault was not with the petit jury, but with the learned judge. Now, Clarence Hall had time and again said that there was not the slightest danger from that quarter. So the client was in a great huff, utterly unreasonable, would not listen to any proposition to "carry the case up." But Clarence Hall knew that the law was on his side; the best lawyers of his acquaintance all agreed that the judge's charge was contrary to law. He resolved to pay the cost and carry the case up himself; by so doing he would both vindicate his judgment and secure a considerable fee, which latter, as we know, was of urgent consequence to him. He got enough money to pay the cost, carried up the case, and lost it. Thus had he made his calculations, and had been disappointed; and the bills aforesaid, not to mention others long past, would fall due in thirty days. And what made these bills particularly dangerous was the circumstance that the homestead would not stand against them. Nothing would stop them short of bankruptcy; and to take the benefit of bankruptcy required, even if you were your own attorney, about a hundred dollars to start on. Clearly that was out of the question. But something must be done; and that in a few days. Clarence Hall seemed to be approaching insanity. One night he was walking down the street, thinking, if a man in his state of mind may be said to think, of how he was to meet the difficulties before him, when he found the sidewalk blocked up by a crowd pressing its way into a room, from which proceeded a confused noise. He stopped to listen, and he heard the voice of an auctioneer, apparently, crying, "Four hundred and ninety-five dollars still remaining in the rack, and only one dollar a chance at the whole entire lot!" "Four hundred and

ninety-five dollars still remaining in the rack, and only one
dollar a chance at the whole entire lot ! "   Clarence listened ;
he looked around him ; there was no one who knew him ;
the crowd was made up of negroes and ragged fellows ; he
was in great need of money ; by going in there and spending
one dollar he might make two or three hundred ; he pressed
in with the crowd.   This was a new kind of lottery, and was
doing a brisk business.   Behind the counter was a large rack
in which were rows of cards, each card numbered ; attached
to each card was also a common pocket-knife, worth a quarter of a dollar.   Two men were upon the counter ; one of
them, with a long cane in his hand, was explaining : " We
put five hundred dollars in the rack—there is a gentleman
who has just drawn out five dollars, leaving four hundred
and ninety-five—behind one of these numbers is a grand prize
of two hundred dollars, one hundred behind another, fifty
behind two others, and twenty numbers have each five dollars
behind them—there are but six hundred numbers—five hundred dollars in money—only one dollar a chance—and so we
are just even, counting the elegant pocket-knives at less than
twenty cents apiece, and they are worth a dollar—and our
own time and labor at nothing—you get an elegant pocket-knife worth your money, and a chance at two hundred
dollars—which will you take, sir ?—choice of the whole rack
—here's a gentleman who has just got an elegant pocket-
knife and five dollars besides."   The other man was walking
up and down the counter crying in a loud, auctioneer, mechanical voice, " Four hundred and ninety-five dollars still
remaining in the rack, and only one dollar a chance at the
whole entire lot."—" Four hundred and ninety-five dollars
still remaining in the rack, and only one dollar a chance at
the whole entire lot."   Clarence Hall had three dollars in his
pocket.   His beaver-hat, in such a crowd, attracted the at-

tention of the fast-talking man with the long cane—" This way, sir—make room for the gentleman—this way—you look like a lucky man.'" Clarence Hall handed him a dollar ; and it was not without a silent prayer that it might win the two-hundred-dollar prize.

" Which knife do you take ? "

" Give me one hundred and one."

" Ah, you are lucky, but unfortunate—that number has just drawn five dollars."

" Two hundred and two." With another silent prayer accommodating itself to the change.

" Two hundred and two does not draw any prize—but what an elegant knife ! " Clarence was surprised, but concluded his faith had not been strong enough · so he hand-ed in another dollar.

" Three hundred and three."

" Three hundred and three only gets an elegant pocket-knife—you will get all the most elegant knives in the rack—good taste—you will get a prize after a while—if at first you don't succeed, you know, as the schoolmaster says." Clar-ence Hall was blue; and with a kind of defy-fate air, he handed in his last dollar.

" Four hundred and four."

" Four hundred and four draws a nice little penknife—not a fortunate set of numbers—another line of—" But Clarence Hall, thoroughly disgusted with himself, lotteries, prayer, and fate, was already half-way out of the room. All that night he heard ringing in his ears, " Four hundred and ninety-five dollars still remaining in the rack, and only one dollar a chance at the whole entire lot." The next morning Clarence Hall saw in the newspapers that this was the last day for procuring tickets to the " Grand Library Gift Con-cert." The capital prize was one hundred thousand dollars in greenbacks; and there were many other smaller prizes. *Somebody* would draw this hundred thousand dollars; *I might* be the one, thought a great many people that day. Clarence Hall was one of them. What an amount of good I could accomplish with so much money! The city is in need of a hospital; if I had this money I would give ten thousand dollars towards building it. And that noble institution, Dr. Boring's "Orphan's Home"—I would finish it at once. I could send at least a couple of poor young men to the University, and that poor Confederate soldier that begs on the streets —by Jove, I would board him at the Kimball! And Clarence Hall rose, and walked across the room, excited with the theme. And was it not infinitely to this man's honor that all these great ideas crowded into his head before he once thought of his own poor affairs? Probably, if you had all the United States to pick from, you would not find a man who would have put to better use that hundred thousand dollars. He had just received a small amount of money from an unexpected quarter that very morning. It seemed providential. He pulled out a ten-dollar bill, and looked at it very hard. And while he looked at it he determined to buy a ticket with it, and made to himself a solemn promise of what he would do with the money—if he got it. Clarence Hall felt better to-day than he had in many—was even heard to whistle a tune; and when he started home, and saw on the corner of the street a poor old man grinding an organ, he said to himself—"poor devil—I wonder what your life has been—what cursed luck may have brought you to this?" Clarence Hall dropped a whole dollar into the old man's hat, and passed on; the poor old organ-grinder stopping and staring at him in blank astonishment.

One day Mirabeau Holmes and Fred Van Comer were at Mrs. Sutherland's. They had been speaking of a daily newspaper that Mirabeau and Fred had announced their intention of starting in the city.

"I think your are quite correct in your ideas of the enormous power of the Press. Hitherto our people have been largely controlled by their orators in politics, and by the pernicious idea of hereditary rank in all their social and industrial life. But now, the public Press has supplanted the orators; and, unless the money-power becomes too great, which is much to be feared, educated intellect will take the place of our old and absurd notions of rank," said Mrs. Sutherland.

"But if this power is all to be exerted in the cause of conservatism," said Mirabeau, "I am not able to see any great good likely to be accomplished by it."

"Why, the conservative Press will keep us where we are; it will keep us from relapsing into barbarism!" said Fred.

"But surely we should not consent always to lag in the rear of civilization. To be sure, when we were cursed with slavery we could not do better; but now we are free! And if we do not compete successfully with the foremost it will be our own fault," said Mirabeau.

"Surely, if we should fail it cannot be much our own fault, that is, the fault of the present generation especially, if what our enemies at the North say be true—that we are naturally indolent, lacking in pluck and enterprise, and, withal, scarcely emerged from barbarism," said Mrs. Sutherland.

"Begging your pardon, I do not think the Northern people are our enemies; I am sure their representative men are not—such men as Henry Wilson, John W. Forney, Lyman Trumbull, Mr. Beecher, and even Horace Greeley and Gerrit Smith. I do not think they are our enemies; I know that General Grant is now, and has been ever since the war, friendly towards us. As for these other men, surely we can give them credit for having been as honest as ourselves. For one, I am willing to believe, and do believe, that they have been through their whole lives actuated by the highest motives in the cause of Humanity. I know of no set of men, in all the history of the world, for whom I have more admiration, notwithstanding there are many things in their lives which were better out, than for those 'old-time abolitionists,' " said Mirabeau.

"I think I know of one set for whom *I* have a great deal more admiration: General Lee and the heroes who followed him," said Mrs. Sutherland.

"Ah, I scarcely thought it necessary to say that not even yourself should go beyond me in admiration for General Lee and his army. If heroic bravery and sublime endurance be the measure, all the world must acknowledge that General Lee led his noble army to a height of glory far above that attained by any Northern rival. And I will say further, that if I had the whole world to select from, and was required to point to the man of the loftiest virtue and purest character, upon which there was never a stain or a tarnish, I should point to Jefferson Davis," replied Mirabeau.

"That is a platform broad enough, certainly; especially as you are not likely to find more than one willing to stand upon it ! " said Fred.

"And that one myself? Well, so much the worse for *them*," said Mirabeau.

"As the lawyer said, when told that the facts did not sustain him ? " added Mrs. Sutherland. "But, as King Richard says, to leave off this keen encounter of our wits," said Mrs. Sutherland, resuming, "I think I understood that your paper was to be conservative."

" Not conservative ; democratic," said Mirabeau.

" What is the difference ? "

"None, in fact. But we mean to preach liberal doctrines from a democratic platform," said Fred.

"You think that a necessary precaution, in order to be heard, I suppose," said Mrs. Sutherland.

"Yes; we dress like shepherds in order that the democratic sheep of this country may not be alarmed. They would flee from anything they have not been used to," said Fred.

"For my part, I once thought there might even be a possibility of bringing that party itself up to higher ground than that of its opponents. Certain it is that no party can ever triumph over the one now in power that does not take higher ground. For example, it must at least go for universal suffrage, a national system of public schools, and a prohibitory liquor law. Speaking especially of the South, would it not be a grand thing to compel the world to acknowledge her as the champion of progress, the light of civilization, on this side the waters? I have sometimes thought that if our people would cease to wrangle over the past, abandon their conservatisms, and all come together in the great work, we might, by our achievements in art, and industry, and science, and letters, even accomplish so much. It is a shame that we should not be ahead! For rapid progress, for every conquest in knowledge, we have the best material in the whole world, except the French; and the superiority of our free political institutions makes us equal even to the French," said Mirabeau, kindling with his subject; for he never thought of it without being filled with the highest enthusiasm.

"That would be a great triumph indeed; but we can never hope for that until we have higher education, and more of it. I would not consent to a *national* system of public schools; but I think each State ought to have such a system; in spite of our poverty, I think it a shame that our State has none.   Ignorance is always more costly than knowledge at any price.   Our women especially stand in deplorable need of higher education.   No compliments.   The last census reveals a fact which ought to excite the shame of every man, and the indignation of every woman, in the State.   I doubt not you both have noticed it: that there are forty-two thousand adult whites in the State who can neither read nor write; and that of this number there are twice as many women as men.   But we need also some higher institutions of learning for our women.   There is not a single one in the State where a woman can get what would even be a passable education for a man of the most microscopic pretensions to culture," said Mrs. Sutherland.

"Let our State University be opened to women.   For three reasons: women ought to have, equally with men, the benefits of the very best institutions of learning; the State is not able to support more than one great University; the one we have ought to be much more largely endowed, and tuition ought to be made free; the two sexes ought to be educated together, anyhow," said Fred.

"The intellectual emancipation of woman is my hobby. I believe I would even agree with Mr. Van Comer, that our State University ought to be opened to women," said Mrs. Sutherland.

"Intellectual emancipation will never come before their political and social emancipation; that is, if it must come at their own wish," said Mirabeau.

"I understand what you mean by political emancipation; but what do you mean by their social emancipation?" asked Mrs. Sutherland.

"He means their emancipation from filigree!" said Fred.

"No; I mean that the wife must be the equal of the husband, not only before the law, but as an intellectual and moral being, and as a member of society," said Mirabeau.

"Though I believe it will come, and that very shortly, I think it will be a sad day for us when women go to the polls," said Mrs. Sutherland.

"Cato seems to have been possessed of a similar notion when it was proposed to allow the Roman matrons a certain liberty," said Fred.

"You mean when he made that speech against allowing them to ride in carriages, or to wear garments of more than one color?" said Mrs. Sutherland.

"Yes; and when he proclaimed a *female insurrection*, because they preferred so modest a request," said Fred.

"I reckon if, instead of such a modest request, they had ventured to ask that the law be repealed which gave the husband the power of life and death over his wife; or if they had dared to ask for the repeal of that law which classed them along with furniture, as *personalty*, making them so much a matter of property that the possession and use of them for an entire year was held to give sufficient title to them; the virtuous old conservative would have immediately demanded sentence of death against the whole of them," said Mirabeau.

"The experience of women, certainly, has been a very cruel one. And their condition now, in spite of all fine compliments, is deplorable enough. Their station is essentially low. But their great need is intellectual emancipation; and if I thought as you do, that that could not be accomplished without female suffrage, I do not hesitate to say that I should work for female suffrage with all my might," said Mrs. Sutherland.

"Plainly," said Mirabeau to Fred, after they had left, "Mrs. Sutherland is held back only by the pressure of sur-

rounding public opinion. In New York, or Boston, she
would be for woman's rights."—" Evidently."—" Now, she
thinks that at length woman has about reached her 'true
sphere.' Probably the Phœnicians thought the same thing
three thousand years ago, when, for the sake of their commercial interests, they compelled their women to stand naked
upon the beach, and by various signs entice seamen ashore."
" Did they do that?"—" Herodotus says so."—" I don't
believe it. It reminds me of one of Captain Pinter's stories: Captain Pinter says a woman was telling her experience, and made rather a bad out at it. The preacher
thought he would help her out; so he says to her, ' You believe that Christ died for you ? ' 'Why,' says she, ' I didn't
know he was dead ! ' ' Yes,' says the preacher, 'many hundred years ago, away in Palestine, on Mount Calvary.'
' Well,' says the woman, 'it's a long time ago, and a long
ways off; and I hope it's a lie! ' "

The great Library Gift Concert drawing came off. The
capital prize was drawn by a green-grocer out West. Clarence
Hall drew a blank. Then Clarence Hall saw the utter futil-
ity of all calculations based upon luck, and his trust in special providences was also considerably shaken. He took his
resolution. Once more he stood up the Clarence Hall of
yore. Nay, more. Once he had been sanguine, but resolute
too—determined to conquer in the battle of life, yet seeing
no great difficulties to be overcome. Then he had been fearless. Now he was heroic. If everything he had was sold,
even though at considerable sacrifice, he could pay all his debts,
and still have a few hundred dollars left. His creditors would
have been glad to compromise for half the amounts due them.
Clarence Hall knew this, but he did not mention it. He
determined to pay the last farthing he owed, and start anew
—this time even with the world. He was still young, not

thirty. And if, as he now saw, mournfully yet clearly, he must fight life's battle alone, still he would fight it, and conquer even the most glorious promise of his youth. If there was for him less of happiness, there was more of heroism. He would profit by the errors of the past. Calmly, steadily, slowly, if it must be, he would hold on his course. Clarence Hall went to his creditors and made the proposition to them. They were thunderstruck. This was not the usual way of doing business. What! a man proposing to sell himself out of house and home to pay his debts, and not even insisting on a compromise! It was almost unbelievable. Of course, they would not interpose any obstacles to the sale. And just here I cannot but mention with pleasure the fact that not one of these men asked Clarence Hall to pay the cost of their previous legal proceedings. The fact is, dear reader, we have a people here more kind, more generous, better and truer in all the sympathies and impulses of the heart, than any people on the earth. That evening, when Clarence Hall went home, he had already determined upon his plan and taken steps to put it in execution. Still he thought it right to consult his wife.

Mrs. Hall had greatly improved of late. But as her health grew better her temper grew worse ; which latter proceeding is frequently observed to double with the rapidity of Mr. Weller's deputy-shepherd's accounts. And this is a result which happens far from seldom, and that too in young women who, one would think, have been almost reduced to a piece of " white putty that can feel pain." Thus it was with Clarence Hall's wife. For some time after she had been married she had neither will nor temper. But then came several months of ill health ; and with it naturally came peevishness, from which to ill temper the way is short enough. When Clarence Hall told his wife of his difficulties, and proposed to her that they should adopt the plan he had already decided upon, she opposed everything. Then there were accusations, reproaches, tears. But Clarence Hall had taken his resolution, and follow it he would.

The next day Marian Malcomb went to see Mrs. Hall. Annie Dearing and Marian Malcomb had been school-girls together. To-day Marian was confirmed in what she had suspected for some time—that Annie's husband was seriously embarrassed in his affairs. She knew of the burning of his office, but not of the extent of his loss. She had more than once heard her father regret that Hall had not been elected to the office of city attorney. And to-day she managed, with the utmost delicacy, to learn the truth of the case. That evening, when her father came home, she met him in the walk and told him all about it, adding—"I have heard you say several times how sorry you were that he was not elected to be city attorney when you were trying to get the schools; and I thought maybe you might want to aid him in some way." When Mr. Malcomb said "he would send for Mr. Hall to come to his office to-morrow," Marian was content; for she believed that her father would do the very thing that ought to be done. That this man had the wisdom to discern the right, and the willingness to do the right, was the perfect conviction, not only of Marian, but of every member of his family. When he said he would see about anything, they knew it would be seen about, and well, too; and let this be said to his praise. Clarence Hall called at Mr. Malcomb's office late in the afternoon of the next day.

"I wanted to speak with you," said Mr. Malcomb, "of your own affairs. And when I have given you the reason of my wishing to speak with you, I hope you will not consider me officious. Our people carry politics into everything, and I fear that by becoming complicated in my school plans you have injured your practice. And this, coming along with the unfortunate loss of your office, and especially your library, I feared might have seriously embarrassed your business. If I am correct in my conjecture, I have sent for you, to say I might be able to assist you in some way. Perhaps a loan might be of advantage to you."

Clarence Hall was not less struck by Mr. Malcomb's delicacy than by his generosity. He desired to assist him in his difficulties, and for fear of touching his sensitiveness, pretended to make himself in some way the cause of these difficulties.

" I scarcely know how to thank your, sir," replied Clarence Hall, "for your kindness. My affairs have indeed been seriously embarrassed ; but not, I think, in any way from the cause you mention."

" True, there might be a difference of judgment there ; but no matter for that ; if I could aid you, as I have mentioned, or in any other way you may suggest, I shall be glad to do so."

Mr. Malcomb knew something of the difficulties in the way of young men struggling in the battle of life. He had been through some of them, and a good many of them, too, himself. As I have already said, this man was no born aristocrat ; he had neither wealth nor great relations to get him place and power, and help him along. He had made his way from the bottom round, and had reached the top. For many years he had been, in his State, the exponent of the feelings, and ideas, and purposes of the great mass of people who work for their living. He was now the most representative man, in his section of the Union, of the new civilization. And here was the grand reason of his success : he had learned early to work, work, and continue to work. It would not be too much to say that he had worked for thirty years without a week's rest. And this moment he was prob-

ably both the wealthiest and hardest-working man in the
State.   Evidently here was a man capable of sympathizing
with Clarence Hall in his resolution as well as in his troubles.
Clarence Hall, while thanking him warmly for his disinter-
ested kindness, thought it best to decline any pecuniary aid,
and to stick to the plan he had already decided upon.   And
Mr. Malcomb too, doubtless, thought he was taking that
course which would, in the long run, be for the best.   I
said that Clarence Hall was now heroic; and so he was.
Once he had thought of happiness; now he thought of duty.
And just here I must mention an act which I think more to
Mr. Malcomb's credit than a grand speech in the United
States Senate would be, and which I record with more
pleasure : he sent for a furniture dealer, and instructed him
to attend Clarence Hall's sale, and on his, Mr. Malcomb's
account, to make the articles sold bring their full value.
The Dearings, except the pater-familias—which is a Latin
word meaning ordinarily, pompous-un-familiar-ass—had continued to visit Mrs. Hall.   As the day approached they were
constantly making the smallest rat-biting observations; and
endeavoring to impress upon the *tabula rasa* of Mrs. Hall
what an awful and disgraceful matter it was thus to be
" brought down in the world."   Mrs. Hall declared she could
not endure the jar and bustle, and that she would go to her
mother's until it was over ; and one day, while her husband
was at his office, she went to her mother's accordingly.   The
sale had come and gone.   Once more Clarence Hall was even
with the world.   To be sure, he was somewhat disappointed
in the amount realized.   What would have been the result
without Mr. Malcomb's bidder ?   He would not have saved a
single dollar !   But, as it was, he saved enough to fit up right
handsomely a pretty little cottage which he had taken in a
pleasant quarter of the city.   He was at home.   He was

" even with the world." He was ready to begin the battle of life anew; if with less sanguine hopes, certainly with more experience and better judgment, and, probably, higher motives. He called for his wife; she was too unwell to go. He called again; the baby was too unwell. He called again; something else the matter. A week passed. Clarence Hall was alarmed.

Book 5.

GLENCOE.

CHAPTER XXI.

As to whether there ought to be, in the geography of human life, any such vale as "Glencoe;" or whether, seeing that all's for the best, every vale should not rather be a vale of laughing than of weeping; or, at the very least, seeing that nothing can be any otherhow than just as it is, whether one had not better regard all the vales, as well as every other feature of the geography aforesaid, with the most philosophic indifference; I stop not here to inquire. For which, I call the reader to witness, I have at least two most excellent reasons. First, my business in this book is to relate what actually was, and still is in great part, rather than to speculate upon what ought to be; and secondly, the American people, wishing, perhaps, to avoid the example of the fallen archangels, are not prone, in discourse sweet, to sit on hills retired, or, indeed, anywhere else, and reason high "of providence, foreknowledge, will, and fate." From which I conclude such argument might not be as intensely interesting to them as was that theological argument of the Christian

knight, Orlando, to the Giant Fenacute. But this matter of
Orlando and Fenacute may as well be related, if only to show
something of the general degeneracy of modern times, and
the special decadence of modern theologians. Charlemagne,
at the siege of Pamplona, encountered the Infidel Giant
Fenacute. This Fenacute was a great Giant, an enormous
Giant at all points; descended in a direct line, according to the
learned priesthood of that day, from Goliath of old ! He made
great havoc with Charlemagne's army, hewing down whole
brigades, as it were. The stoutest warriors, the most re-
nowned knights, were sent against him in vain. Finally
Orlando challenged him to single combat. Orlando was about
to follow the fate of all who had preceded him, when suddenly, in the midst of the fight, he thought of his spiritual
weapons. He engaged the Giant in a theological contro-
versy. This was too much for Fenacute; his strength left
him; and the gallant knight triumphantly cut off his head.

Having told what I know of the Giant Fenacute, which
may even yet serve as an embellishment for a sermon—if any
of our friends should be forced to go to preaching—I now proceed to relate the main events in the life-histories of our people. And just here may be mentioned the utter impossibility
of ever fully knowing the *life* of another. Let any one reflect
for a moment upon his own life: of the ambitious hopes,
which seem grand to-day—so high indeed, that you think even
your best friends would not appreciate them, but might even
laugh at as curious ramblings of a visionary mind, and which
you therefore keep to yourself, probably writing them down
in your diary only to laugh or wonder at to-morrow, just as
you feared your friends would; of the many headaches and
heartaches, and the disappointments and chagrin that you
have felt, even, it may be, with those nearest to you ; above
all, of the thousand inward struggles against temptation, in

which, many a time, under the hard force of circumstances, you have almost or even quite consented to yield to what has afterwards in moments of retrospection, as you lay upon your bed at night, brought to your face the rush of shame and self-contempt; let one think of these things, and many more, both on the good and on the bad side of his own life, and then say whether it is likely that another will ever know *all* of his life-history. One never knows but one's own life, that is, one's inner life, is almost totally different from the life of any other creature in the whole universe. As for these persons whose histories I am writing, I have known them all for years, and with several of them have been on terms of the closest intimacy. And yet, I dare say, there are some secret hopes disappointed, some silent cries and unshed tears for ideals vanished or turned to Dead-Sea fruit, known only to themselves and God!

Many years ago Mr. Walton, in obedience to a cursed social lie that triumphs over the laws of God, and crushes with Juggernaut wheels the life-blood from the human heart, had driven his own beautiful, unfortunate daughter forth friendless and hopeless upon a pitiless world. But it is a very hard thing to silence utterly the voice of nature. Afterwards, when it was too late; when he believed that his poor daughter was dead; when he read what he thought to be her last words—" alone, alone in the great world; without friends, without bread, without hope, what can I do but die? " when he read how she, his own daughter, had gone to beg for bread, and was driven—good God!—it may be, who knows?—even *beaten* away by servants; when he saw her touching prayer, that her father and mother—her father, he himself, her own father, the monster who had driven her forth thus to die, wretched and friendless—might never know of the depth of her suffering; and when he imagined he saw her beautiful form laid upon the cold river-bank, her innocent child tenderly bound to her bosom with plaits of her own silken hair, the pale mother's lips almost trembling yet with the beautiful prayer, "as we go to sleep to-night in each other's arms, so may we wake in the morning;" then it was that he saw himself their murderer! The dark waves of despair rolled over him. Who shall hear the cry from their depths? Or who shall interpret it? Verily, verily! The poor Indian may die even joyfully under the wheels of his Juggernaut, because the Juggernaut is to him a god. But the sum of possible misery in this world is even this, that man feels himself crushed under the Juggernaut wheels, and knows it is no Divinity, but only a hideous idol. So it was with Mr. Walton now. He saw his children disgraced and dead; he felt himself forced down to despair; and knew, too late, that it was no Divinity, but only a shapeless, sanguinary idol, a huge, hideous, social lie. The darkness had encompassed him, and all his life had he struggled and cried out for light. *But the light never came.* Mr. Walton was a sincere Christian man; and he tried hard to atone for the past. He was wealthy; he fed and clothed the poor; he gave liberally to all good institutions; his charities were large and generous. But while he regarded all this as his duty, still, doubtless, having a much stronger sense of it than if all had been clear in his past life, he did not trust to good works, he did not claim aught for his own merits; he resorted to prayer; and often long, and in anguish did he pray. Alas, alas! Mr. Walton, for what is it you pray? That the effect may not follow its cause. But this is an inexorable law, nor is there any power, on the earth or above the earth, that can reverse it. Hope not, man, to do wrong, and then by prayer or by works, by the aves of priests or by the intercession of saints, angels or gods, to get the inevitable laws of fate reversed. Know that whatever you do becomes a part of your life, and hope not to get rid of it. Thus it was with Mr. Walton; for while his theoretical faith taught him to believe he was forgiven, his feelings taught him that at least his own nature would not be appeased.

And thus the years sped on. We have seen how the last hope of his life was swept away. We have seen his youngest son, in whom the old father had fixed his last ambition, go forth in the pride and flush of youth only to fill an early but honored grave. And then we have seen how a bright promise from his oldest son, who had been long ago given up save by his hopeful mother, came to light for a moment with deceitful glare the gloom of his life. We have seen Alf Walton leave for Paris, to bring back to its own native earth the remains of his young heroic brother. He had delayed himself two months in New York; at the end of which time his father, who had heard nothing of him up to this time, but imagined something must be wrong, received a note from him, stating that he would sail for Europe that day. Two months more had passed, and no word from his only surviving son. Mrs. Walton was alarmed, then depressed, and said she could not tell how or why, but she felt like some new trouble was about to be sent upon them. Mr. Walton, too, had become uneasy and restless. Once he had written, and twice telegraphed, without getting any information. He went down in town earlier than had been his custom, anxious to get the mail.

One morning, it was in December, the streets sloppy, and a cold, drizzling rain blowing from the east, Mr. Walton, his tall, spare figure enveloped in a long, close-fitting overcoat, was seen hurrying along the street in front of the telegraph office. He was called to from within; but his head was closely muffled, and he was in a deep study; he heard not the call, and was hurrying along—hurrying from fate! But who shall escape from his fate? The messenger ran up with Mr. Walton and touched him on the shoulder. Mr. Walton turned quickly and inquiringly. "Message for you—carried it to your office, and was just starting with it to your house." Mr. Walton's office was on Wall street, not many yards off. The message was from his London correspondent, and informed him that his son, Mr. Alf Walton, had been shot the night before, and was now dead. An hour afterwards, in a pouring rain, without any umbrella, Mr. Walton, with head hung upon his breast, was seen going towards home. Mrs. Walton, already tottering from age, disease, trouble, and nervous dread of some impending calamity, was completely prostrated by the shock. All day, and far into the night, Mr. Walton watched by her bedside. Twelve o'clock. Her limbs were cold. Mrs. Walton was dying. Yes, yes. Threescore years of trial would soon be finished. Fifty years ago the roseate hues of morning had been quickly overcast. The darkness of night was approaching to shut the scene. What is the sum of this life? A brief promise in the early morning, and half a century of care, disappointment, and despair. Mrs. Walton had not yet spoken. It was past midnight. She called for Mr. Walton—called him by his Christian name, as she had in the far-off day of youthful hope and promise. All were requested to leave the room for a moment.

"My dear husband," said the dying woman, "I have been thinking of our darling child. I dreamed to-night that she was not dead. It may be, in the providence of God, that she is still living somewhere in the world; or it may be that the child is living. If not "—and her voice trembled with pathos —"if not, then all our children are gone. Lean over closer to me—I saw them both in my dream. And I want you to promise me that you will leave your property so that if they be living they can get it. Will you?" It was given. And Mr. Walton kept his promise. The freed spirit of Mrs. Walton rose upon the air with the morning hymn of the lark; and as the far-off trill died upon the ear of the ascending spirit, the sweeter notes were heard of voices angelical to many a harp in paradise.

The day after the next Mr. Walton stood beside the grave of his wife. He stood perfectly erect, and was silent. His eye was cold and dry. His thin, white hair floated in the fitful blasts of wind. His face was rigid, and he looked straight before him. For the first time in his life the old man seemed defiant of fate itself. But when they were about to lower the coffin he motioned them to stop. He bent down and gazed intently for a moment upon the face of the dead. "Farewell." And without another word, he rose, and walked away erect. All gone. A lonely old man. All of his family were dead. His hearth was desolate; his life solitary. He would go after his children. He would bring them home. He would surround himself with his dead. A little while, and the lonely old man set out upon his long, sad journey.

On the last evening that we have seen Mr. Brooke carry Emma Harlan home from his house, it was noted that he had begun to look upon her with a strange light in his eye. At first this was interpreted by her to mean no more than a watchful, fatherly affection. But there is a wonderful instinct in woman's nature, which, fairly tried, never fails to distinguish the light of love from every other. It thrills a chord untouched before by affection of family or friends. Poor Emma! She could not but be alarmed; but in moments of reflection she thought she must surely be mistaken, reproached herself bitterly, and, to atone for her unworthy suspicions of her best friend, only trusted Mr. Brooke more unreservedly than ever. We have seen how, on the night before Alf Walton left the city, defenceless innocence was armed against the most cunning attacks of that artful intriguer. So timely was the warning, and so complete the armor, that we almost regarded it as a special providence to protect this pretty, innocent flower. Alas, alas! that this very providence should turn traitor, and conspire for her ruin. Emma had not forgotten this, and when she thought of it now her cheeks tingled with shame, that she should, even in her remotest thought, harbor an evil thought against her friend and protector. "We are often," says the old Doctor, "in as much danger from the good as from the bad side of our nature;" and never was there a truer saying. So with Emma Harlan. The highest feelings of her nature were spinning around her the fatal cords which, without the interposition of providence, should bind her to destruction—the feelings of trust and gratitude. And if all that is, is for good, as surely must be, how is it that this can be? Where is the good? What is there in heaven, or on earth, or in the whole universe of God, that can demand that this poor little life be crushed? Who shall be benefited; what love shall be widened or deepened; what wrath shall be appeased; what power shall be vindicated; what justice shall be glorified; what suffering shall be diminished; what joy increased; what wisdom magnified, in all the dominions of God, by this great-small sacrifice? Just God! that the darkness might be removed, and that we might see the truth.

But what shall we say of Mr. Brooke? This girl reposed upon his protection in more than double trust; she was young and innocent, and should find a guardian in every gentleman. Mr. Brooke was the friend of her mother, and the orphan daughter looked to him with filial affection. He was her pastor, and she reposed in him the trust of confiding innocence.   He was her protector ; as it was he, under providence, who had probably saved her from disgrace and ruin. Said Mr. Brooke to her one day,

" Once it was thought that whatever was natural was wrong, that human love especially was sinful in the sight of God. But we have learned a more generous religion ; our affections were not given to us as so many snares to tempt us into sin. Our natures are God-formed.   And when the human heart is not degraded by evil intentions, then, under God, its instincts are divine.   Evil can only exist in the intention."

Emma thought much of what Mr. Brooke had said ; and while wondering vaguely at its application, had come almost unconsciously to believe in the precept. Nor let any suppose this of small consequence ; far from it.   For, although in moments of fierce temptation the mind stops not to reason carefully, yet it acts even in such cases in a kind of instinctive obedience to its theoretical beliefs, as the parts of the body act by instinctive obedience to the will, without any distinct act of the will at all.   Mr. Brooke had at first interested himself in Emma as a pretty girl, an orphan, the favorite of the Sunday-school, and the daughter of Mrs. Harlan.   But the more he knew of her the more he liked her ; he found her possessed of native intellect as rare as her disposition was sweet and amiable.   And this intellect Mr. Brooke felt a desire, common to all minds of learning and culture, to see expand and develope under his own direction, or at least according to his own ideas.   Emma, on her side, appreciated Mr. Brooke's accomplishments, gave in readily to his way of thinking, and thus they were soon in complete sympathy.   It is wonderful how completely and absolutely one mind, even of a high order itself, may be under the dominion of another stronger than itself : not in the sense that one person may control another—by means of visible power; but how, not merely its coloring, but its very cellular structure seems to proceed from the all-powerful and infinitely subtle attractions and repulsions of the stronger mind. So it was with Mr. Brooke and Emma Harlan. The girl had come to look up to Mr. Brooke as her ideal of a man.

But the girl soon became a woman. And when Mr. Brooke dwelt upon her ripe and luscious beauty; when he thought of her fine mind, well cultured for her age, and felt the incantation of her sweet temper, with the consciousness too that much in both was due to his formative hand; he naturally remembered that his wife was an invalid who could not possibly survive long, and even frequently found himself indulging in some vague imaginings that there might be for him in the future a lot that should in some sense atone for the past blank of his married life. And these vague imaginings, Mr. Brooke, knowing what must be in the near future, did not at all attempt to put down.

So Mr. Brooke soon found his love centered upon this girl; then it grew into a passion; and then he determined to possess her at all costs. From sympathy, that is, complete spiritual accord, to love, between two persons capable of loving, is a short way. Mr. Brooke already had the esteem, the confidence, the perfect sympathy, in a word, of Emma Harlan; and to get her love only needed that subtle conversion of that feeling which is made up of filial trust and friendship into lovers' love. To do him full justice, Mr. Brooke, even after he had determined to gratify his own passion, though it be at the ruin of this girl, still thought sometimes of a possible future atonement to her. From the moment that Mr. Brooke's passion became criminal, he began to lay his plans artfully. Without at all abating his parental care, he now treated her also as a grown-up woman.

Sometimes, with the rarest possible delicacy, he referred, in low tones of scarce perceptible pathos, to his own loneliness. And sometimes he even spoke eloquently, with just a slight tremulousness, of what might be done in this skeptical age by a minister of truly liberal culture and ardent zeal with a companion divinely formed to share his labors with him. Thus the weeks passed on, and the hour approached. Even in the midst of his passion Mr. Brooke's cool judgment did not forsake him; he knew the human heart; he knew the power of surprise over it. One afternoon Emma was at his house, and Miss Brooke was not at home. The two were in the parlor alone. Emma sat on a sofa, and Mr. Brooke nearly in front of her in a chair, with his elbow resting upon a table, where he had just placed a volume of Shakspeare, of which he had been rather abstractedly turning the leaves.

"Do you remember," said Mr. Brooke, in a low, tuneful voice, "when you were here one afternoon last summer and I read to you from Hamlet?"

"Oh, yes," said Emma, blushing, and not dreaming that Mr. Brooke knew the circumstances of that evening so well as he did. "I can never forget that day, any more than I can ever repay you with my gratitude for that and many others; you were, unconsciously, my guardian spirit."

"Ah," said Mr. Brooke, rising and moving across the floor, "you have uttered the very word that drives me mad. Your guardian! Good God! that I could be your guardian in fact, always, in life and eternity." Mr. Brooke walked rapidly across the room, and stood before her. "Emma, child," he began again in a tremulous voice, "I have a confession to make to you; if you love me for what I have done for you, I know you will listen to me. Child, you know—you must know—that my whole nature has gone out towards you.

Your own life has been woven into mine; each has become
a part of the other.   I could not help it—I did not know it
—I have prayed over it—it is the work of God—he approves
it."   He fell upon his knees and grasped her hands.   " Oh,
the cursed fate that separates us!   But are we divided forever?   No!   My wife is an invalid—cannot live but a few
months at most—we shall both be free.   But ah! the dan-
gers, the difficulties, that may come in our way.   We are
here now—let us bind ourselves to each other—let us leave
no escape—make ourselves wholly each other's.   See! I am
a minister—it will be lawful in the sight of God—I have
asked—he will bless us."   He caught her in his strong arms;
they rose together; he covered her face with kisses; and
rushed madly along.   " ' I promise faithfully to love, honor,
protect, and keep you as long as we shall live '—promise me
—promise—"   She struggled to free herself from his embrace; the struggle was followed by unconsciousness; the
charmed bird was in the serpent's power.

CHAPTER XXII.

"———————— here I and sorrow sit;
Here is my throne; bid kings come bow to it."
—K. JOHN.

MIRABEAU HOLMES was writing for several magazines, and had also been working hard upon his "History of the Commune." He found that it was necessary for him to take a month's rest; and he made a visit to his old home at "Ashton," and then went among the mountains in the north of the State.

"I had hardly realized before," said he to Marian Malcomb one beautiful night, while they sat on a rustic settee in the flower-garden, "how infinitely removed we are even from the near past."

"Oh, I should rather think that the true past is never away from us—that it is ever with us, to strengthen us, to add to our stock of happiness, to make us more hopeful of the future."

"You are right, too. In that sense, the past is ever with us. Nothing that was worthy, nothing that was good or true in the past, ever dies, or can die. It all remains in the world, and works for good, through endless changes. But what I spoke of was the absolute cutting off of our own actual, individual existence, even from the very last moment that we can almost catch as it flies."

"How long did you stay at your old home?"

"Not long—only a few days."

"That is a pretty name—'Ashton.' Was it long since you had been there?"

"Oh, no ; but it seemed a great while. Fifteen years ago my father died. I have told you he was a doctor. Well, I was a small boy then, but I had learned to tamper with his medicines, and I remember especially that I had just learned that nitrate of silver would turn things black. It was wonderful to me that a substance as clear as water should do so, and I marked up a great many things by way of experiment. My father's death naturally made a great impression on my mind; and I had just then got a notion of the meaning of our calendar. I was afraid I should forget the year ; and so I took a vial of the nitrate of silver and a little mop and went out and wrote under the window sill—it was an old-fashioned white house—in great round figures, 1858. I went to look at the place the other day, and there they were, 1858—looking wonderingly at me like a surprised, overgrown boy. And I looked at them—I don't know how I looked."

"Why, I heard you say once that you had no special attachment for place, that you believed it unphilosophical." Mirabeau recollected instantly to have made this remark to to her at "Elkton," not long after he had known her; and he felt glad that she should remember what he had said so long ago.

"Oh, yes," he answered; "I tried not to have; but one feels, in spite of one's self."

"So you have come to see the truth of what the old Doctor used to tell you all, have you? Don't you remember? Robert says he used to tell you that the feelings often furnish quite as sure a basis to build upon as the reason."

"No ; I did not exactly mean that; but that, owing, I doubt not, mainly to education, we cannot always get rid of a feeling, although reason should demonstrate it absurd."

"I have been somewere too."

"Where ?"

"To Elkton."

"Elkton?"

"Yes; why do you look surprised?"

"When were you there?"

"Last Thursday; we were up at my uncle's, and came by there."

"Did you go to the river?"

"Yes; alone. And the river was humming the same low sweet tune that you taught me to listen to and interpret, when we were there more than two years ago."

"And did you remember then the evening we were there?"

"Yes; and I wished I could see the sun set again; but had to come away."

"Well well. I thought the charm about the place lingered wonderfully fresh and perfect."

"Why, what do you mean?"

"That I was there myself on Friday—the very day after you left."

"You were there?"

"Yes; and I looked in the sand for your track, made there over two years ago. And when I found something that looked like it, and then stopped and thought of how long ago it had been, imagine how absurd I felt! And it was yours, sure enough. How I wish I had been a day earlier!"

"How I wish you had, or that I had been a day later. What on earth were you doing away up there?"

"Ah, I thought you could hardly have need to ask. But I will tell you. Because it was there that I felt the first thrill of a new life. It was there that my soul first saw its ideal, and made its first offering of love. I loved you then; and in all the changes that have come over me since, my love to you has been constant; it has known no change, except to grow stronger and deeper. I offer you my love, my life. And if you will give me your confidence, your love, I declare to you that I will make my own worthy of you."

There was silence for a moment. Marian looked down, and there was a faint crimson in her cheek. Mirabeau looked intensely in her face. Marian raised her great, lustrous, dark eyes, and answered, in a voice low and unsteady with emotion:

"I cannot express to you all that I feel. I cannot tell you how I appreciate the undeserved honor you do me by making me the offer you do. And I should be untrue to myself, as well as unworthy of your slightest consideration, if I did not say how much I honor and esteem you. But more than that I cannot say." Mirabeau was both startled and dismayed. He had thought that he could not be mistaken —he was sure that this girl returned his love. But he knew that these words which he heard were no idle words. Here was no fair-haired boy and thoughtless girl—no awkward declarations, blushes, chokings, timid half-avowals. These two people had some idea of the reality of life, and each felt that this was probably the most important moment in their lives. They knew somewhat of each other's character, and they esteemed, nay, they *loved* each other too! Mirabeau was not excited, and his words were measured and slow:

"You cannot say more? You do not give me your love. But you will give me a promise—of something in the future. See! I have given you my whole life—all my energies, my ambition, my hopes, my love. And will you not even give me a single hope?"

"I cannot."

"But you may change; you do not say that you may not change this decision?"

"No; I cannot say that."

"Then tell me this: is there another?"

"No."

"Then I will yet win your love." They rose, walked to the house in silence, pressed each other's hand, and parted without a word. It was a calm, beautiful night, and Mirabeau walked slowly home, thinking deeply of the events just added to his life-history. And Marian Malcomb ran up-stairs, and sat at her window, and thought too. She was not ignorant of Mirabeau's love; nor, indeed, since that evening at Mr. Brooke's, when he had spoken of the religion of the Commune, had she thought of much else.

Said Mrs. Sutherland to Mirabeau one day, "What have you done with your idea of opening the State University to women?"

"I have it yet. But I try to give everybody a copy."

"I am going to help you."

"Then the work will succeed. I knew you would. This is exactly what has been wanting. To all our arguments we have received the stereotyped answer that 'the women do not ask it, do not even want it.' Now we shall say to them—'Behold! the representative woman of the State demands it in the name of all.'"

"Now, that is the best compliment I have heard."

"That gives me an idea that it must be very good."

"No; I do not like compliments."

"Mine was to the women of the State."

"Then, as their representative, I thank you in the name of all. But where is your friend, Mr. Van Comer? I have not seen him of late. Stop—don't tell me that I have heard from him, though. I know I have. I read his pretty little poem in the last New Monthly. It seems scarcely possible that the author of such a tender, sweet little poem could write such a savage criticism."

" But, savage as it is, is there not some truth in that criticism ? "

" Oh, I dare say, much. He says my book 'begins with an exclamation,' which is literally true—'and ends with a dash,' which also has much truth in it, for I wrote in great hurry. He pronounces this inferior in power to my first book, which is certainly true ; though, as he says, the ' hypocrites and pharisees ' will not see it."

. ." He says he hopes you will write again."

" So I shall ; and better than ever. But I do not promise entirely ' to flee from conservatism.' "

" Might not Van Comer be afraid to come to see you ? "

" No ; tell him to come. I can at least thank him for one thing : he treats me as an equal in the field of letters ; and does not condescend to any of those absurd flatteries and empty compliments, which even some of my friends have called ' gallantry and manly loyalty to the sex.' I hope Mr. Van Comer was correct when he said he believed I would despise all such. Mr. Paul H. Hayne thinks he only showed in this his ignorance of the ' female literary nature ; ' but, in thinking so, it strikes me Mr. Hayne only acted upon Mrs. Poyser's notion ' that the women were made to match the men.' But the New Monthly has ceased. It seems strange that we cannot have even one first-rate magazine or review in the South."

" I do not think it strange. It is impossible that any literary undertaking of that sort should prosper in a purely conservative atmosphere. If we had a magazine in this city it would not survive six months unless it was conducted on the plan of the *Contemporary Review*."

" I understand you, and approve the plan. I hope we shall have such an one soon. It would help us in our University plans."

"We have got one first-rate Review: *The Southern Review*. But that does not belong to any particular country; it belongs to the world." . .. .

When Emma Harlan recovered from the momentary stupor which had seized her, she sat upright and stared about her with a mingled look of bewilderment, horror, and pain. Her eyes were wild and dry, and had that intense expression of wonder and pain that you have seen in dumb animals under the most scientific tortures by the knife, pincers, and battery of the scientist. Mr. Brooke knew that this extreme tension of the nervous system could not last. A revulsion of feeling must come. It might come in passionate exclamations, reproaches, curses, tears, faintings, and even delirium. And she was in his own house; everything might be found out. Mr. Brooke was frightened; the miserable villain was ever thinking of himself. Leave for a moment, reader, this scene, and recall another life-tragedy enacted near a century ago under the walls of the frowning old Castle of Joux. Think of the sad-heroic little woman, Sophie de Monnier—or rather, Sophie de Ruffey, for all the laws of Church and State could not make her the *wife* of old Monnier—and mad Gabriel Honoré. By his stormy eloquence and tropic passion this mad Gabriel, this tiger-faced god of the Tennis Court, wins the love and so-called innocence of this sad-heroic woman. Think of this man, defying alike the penalties of law, disgrace, Castles of Joux, and blood-hounds of Rhadamanthine father, scaling the walls of the garden at Pontarlier, and, Sophie in his arms, borne upon the wings of love and despair, flying over the hills towards Holland. Who says that Mirabeau, at that moment, was not a grand man? I say he was. And I should say the same thing of Mr. Brooke if he had acted similarly.

I go thus far against the hypocrites and pharisees. I

would not excuse him for what he had done. Mr. Brooke had committed a great wrong—a great wrong against this poor girl. But if he had fallen at her feet, and renewed to her the vow he had just taken, which surely was only the more sacred that it was not written down by priest or lawyer; or if he had declared his wish, for her, to defy the law, the church, and society; or if in burning eloquence he had proposed to abandon everything, and to fly into an unknown country, where they should live their life out with each other and for each other alone; whatever wrong he may have committed already, at that moment, I say, Mr. Brooke would have been heroic. Nor does it matter at all that his proposition should be scorned, as in this case it certainly would have been.

But Mr. Brooke had ruined this poor girl, and was at this moment fearful of detection and thinking of his own safety. In one sense, at least, Mr. Brooke was satisfied: he had carried his point; henceforth the girl was completely in his power. But it was necessary that Emma be got away somehow. Miss Brooke had only gone to ride; she would soon return; and there might be a scene. They sat in silence several seconds, Mr. Brooke looking solicitous, Emma the picture of doubting wonder and agony, when Mr. Brooke began: "My child—" But the girl, with a cry of horror, sprang from her seat and darted out of the room. Mr. Brooke followed her until he saw her enter her mother's gate, and returned home. He had not calculated upon this dénouement; he was too good a judge of human nature. He knew well that when one has done wrong, when one has committed even a high crime, the feeling immediately after, generally, is a feeling rather of surprise that the thing was so easily done, a kind of questioning whether there was not really much more in the dread of doing than in the act

itself. Even the cold-blooded murderer, the moment after
the deed is committed, rather wonders that so small a matter
has been so magnified. It is afterwards that he finds himself seized upon by terrors undreamed of.   Not that I would
say that Emma Harlan committed any crime, great or small.
Was this poor girl criminal or unfortunate? Is it a crime in
heaven to trust too far what you believe to be great and pure
and good? The old Doctor was right—" We are in as much
danger from the good as from the bad side of our nature."
Consider also whether this fifth act in the girl's life-tragedy
was not a necessity from all that had preceded. Verily,
verily, " is not the poorest day that passes over us the
conflux of two eternities, made up of currents that issue
from the remotest past, and flow onwards into the remotest
future ? "

There was grief in the little cottage on Ivy street.
Silent. Deep. Mother and daughter. Let the curtain be
lowered. Leave them alone. Alone with God.

Mr. Brooke heard of what was transpiring at the little
cottage. He dared not go there. He was sobered now.
He began to calculate. He feared discovery. He thought
of his family ; of his own disgrace. At first, as we have
seen, he thought that one thing was sure—the girl was now
completely in his power. And even for a few days afterwards there haunted him occasionally the ghost of a resolution to redeem, finally, his promise. But soon all such resolves altogether left him. It was unsafe to go farther.
Even possible prison-walls loomed dimly up before him in
the future.

CHAPTER XXIII.

From yonder shrine I heard a hollow sound:
"Come, sister, come! (it said, or seemed to say),
Thy place is here, sad sister, come away;
Once, like thyself, I trembled, wept, and pray'd,
Love's victim then, though now a sainted maid:
But all is calm in this eternal sleep,
Here grief forgets to groan, and love to weep;
E'en superstition loses every fear:
For God, not man, absolves our frailties here."

ELOISE TO ABELARD.

WE must now return to the little cottage on Ivy street. One doubts the necessity of giving the closing scenes. Are they not inevitable? And have they not been witnessed many a time? Witnessed? Yes; what may be seen. Felt? Never. Think what it would be if poet could ever get into language one of these life-tragedies! What can one say but, waiting for death? So it was with Emma Harlan. Sweet rose of May, blasted ere the pearl-glittering gossamer of the early morning unveiled thy perfect beauty, let thine elegy be unsung till the world shall know that it is not criminal to be unfortunate; or, better, till it shall curse all laws but the laws which love has made.

Poor Emma did not excuse herself; nay, she rather condemned herself more severely than any just judge will condemn her. And yet, there would come up from the depths of her nature sometimes a faint wail of remonstrance, that she had intended no evil. But for these remonstrances she only condemned herself the more. It is well that the all-wise and all-benevolent God of the universe remains entirely unchanged by all the hideous conceptions formed of him by

impious and ignorant men who assume to speak as his priests
and prophets. It is well that the god Emma Harlan had
been taught to serve is not the God of Heaven at all, but
only the hideous idol of the dark-minded, savage old Hebrews.
Only see: the vicious system which she had been taught,
first made her misfortune, the wreck of her young life, not
only possible but necessary, and then made her believe it the
greatest of crimes. But so it was. All the light was gone
out of her life. Even the pleasures of hope, the last stay of
poor mortals, were all gone. The glowing pleasures of
young wedded life; the serener joys of the matron mother;
the affectionate honors of venerable age—all were gone forever. The charm of music was turned to discord; the
woods and flowers grew pale in the sickened light; the
mirrory lakes and streams reflected only images of woe.
The gladness of companionship was hushed; the sympathies
of friendship were dried up; and the light of love fled from
the orbit of existence. She would be pointed out in the
crowd; simpering young ladies, her former companions and
whilome friends, would step into the stores to make room
for her; Christian women—legally above suspicion—would
elevate their consecrated skirts and give her the whole of
the sidewalk; and even the *elect* house of God was too good
for her to come to worship or ask for pardon in. But God
will protect thee, dear Emma. He will be with thee at the
last. He sees thy pure and gentle heart. The darkness
which envelopes thee comes not from him. Only light pro-
ceeds from Heaven. As the fleecy cloud, pressed down to
earth by the thick darkness, rises, dissolved from earthy elements, to mingle in celestial light, so shall thy pure spirit,
freed from material elements of misfortune and suffering,
rise and enter into the paradise of the upper air.

In all her unsung and unstoried suffering, Emma thought

not so much of her own as of her mother's woes. Poor old mother! thou too hast known somewhat of the tragedy of life. How joyously beautiful was thy morning! How stormy thy noon! How mournfully the dark curtains of evening are closing around thee. Her hair had already been richly silvered; now it was white—before the dews of late evening came to bleach it. She grew weaker and weaker each day. She too was waiting for death. And thus the weeks and months passed on.

When it was known that Emma Harlan was a mother, of course it was not any longer lawful to visit Mrs. Harlan. This with the great crowd—aristocrats, as well as honest men and women. But always there are some exceptions. Always there are some whose broad sympathies and lofty spirit raise them above the crowd. There were even a few here in this Gate City—such men as Mr. Malcomb and the noble General Clement; not to mention Mirabeau Holmes— whose sympathies knew no limit but the limit of creation— and his young friends; and such women—alas! how small, how sadly small the number—as Mrs. Sutherland. These also, the world over, no matter what their faith or what their creed, like Victor Hugo—who would be a god in a world of angels—have a maxim: *Pro jure contra legem.* Said Mrs. Sutherland one night to a question of a lady-friend as to whether she would visit Mrs. Harlan's cottage any more: "These people need sympathy. The world's, they will not get; my own, they shall have. I have heard this poor girl's story; I heard it from herself; I will not judge her, but leave it to God. If she is not so much guilty as unfortunate, all will admit that she deserves sympathy; if she be guilty, then so much the more her need of sympathy. And then there is the gray-haired, dying mother. Yes; I will go to them." She went; and I think if spirits remember the deeds of this life, this will not then be the least precious gem in her crown of memory. But some time afterwards, . when the Reverend Melancthon Brooke thought it necessary to make a public statement of the whole unfortunate affair, one of the daily newspapers, claiming to be the leading paper of the State, published a long editorial in connection with the statement, in which this representative paper said, among many other similar sayings: "This is the most unfortunate case that has ever come to our knowledge—unfortunate for the victim [the minister !], unfortunate for his family, unfortunate for the church and the cause of Christianity. We have read Mr. Brooke's statement carefully, and as it bears upon it the stamp of truth we cannot doubt it. He confesses that he was tempted, and fell. Remembering the weaknesses of our poor fallen nature, and remembering that Satan is ever present with lures and snares, whereby the best of us, taken unawares, may be tempted and fall, shall we not, following the example of the Master, who knew the weaknesses of his fallen creatures, and the many and strong temptations to which they were subject—shall we not, in the genuine spirit of our merciful religion, judge this man rather in commiseration than in wrath? For our part, though we hold him not excusable, we have for him far more of pity than blame. But as for this wicked woman, this Delilah, who by her lascivious charms has seduced a minister of the Gospel, and brought on all this shame and ruin, as to her deserts, there can be but one opinion. It seems that there ought to be some punishment more severe than death, by which she could be made to expiate, in part, her crime, and to atone for the ruin she has wrought." I have given this extract from the paper claiming to be the exponent of public opinion, certainly the organ of conservatism and orthodoxy, in the State, in its own words. For

the credit of Humanity, and for the good name especially of
my own people, I wished to omit it. For the sake of truth,
and the correctness of this history, I have given it. The
poor "seduced minister of the Gospel" deserves only
"pity." But as for this artful wretch, this Delilah, with her
lascivious charms (only poor little Emma Harlan, dear
reader, sweet as a rose of May, gentle as the softest zephyr
of spirit-land, and pure as the heavenly snow fresh-fallen
upon the mountain of the upper air, ruined by the man in
whom she had all her life been taught to repose her trust, as
the embodiment of all that was good and true, the representative of God upon earth), this seducer of a faithful minister
of the Gospel, for her, surely there *ought* to be some punishment severer than death! Just God! Allons! Times will
be better after a while.

But what to some will appear the hardest trial of all was
yet in store for Emma Harlan. She must tell the story of
her shame publicly to the world. Her own tender nature
would have shrunk from this in horror; for herself she
would rather have endured the taunts, and scorns, and lies
of the world, patiently waiting the deliverance of death and
the judgment of a merciful judge hereafter. And though
she felt and appreciated with every grateful feeling the noble
humanity of the few friends who, faithful to the divine instincts of their nature, came to offer her their sympathy;
and though urged by them to demonstrate before the country
that herself was the victim, and her reverend seducer the
criminal, she steadfastly refused to do so. But then there
was another argument. What of her child? Poor Emma!
She herself could endure all the scorn, all the contempt, all
the slanders of the world, well-knowing that outside of her
three or four friends, who already knew the truth, it mattered little whether she was criminal or unfortunate, and

believing, too, that for her, death would soon come to her relief and shut the scene. As for her dear old mother, she too was come to the river-brink, and must soon pass over. The father was long since dead; and the four gallant brothers were sleeping in the sacred bosom of Virginia. But there was her pretty, innocent child, a child of misfortune—next to the greatest crime in the social as well as in the penal code. Was not such a vindication due to him? Whatever the world might say, *he* at least would have faith in his mother; *he* would believe what she said. And he would know too that it was for him that his mother had faced this last great trial. The time would come when he would know the sad story of his mother's life; and when he reflected upon this last act of heroic devotion; when he knew how hard it was for her gentle spirit to endure this crowning torture; and when he remembered that it was for him that it was endured; then, he would forgive her everything; he would weep over her misfortunes and sufferings; he would plant roses upon her grave; and whatever she might be to the world, to him she would be a pure and gentle spirit, ever lingering near to guard him with her prayers and love. Yes; it was worth the sacrifice. For what is there to which a child, aye, or a boy, or a man, may cling, when he has lost faith in his mother? Is it not to her that he first looks as to a divinity? And is it not from hence that come those noble ideas, the striving for, and the hope of which, make life earnest and divine? How shall a child have faith in Humanity, or faith in God, if he have not faith in his mother? Such considerations, and many others, came quickly into the mind of Emma Harlan. It might be that, in the course of this child's life, he too would be forced to drink deeply the bitterness of sorrow. He might be defeated in his hopes and aims; he might be crushed to earth

by adverse fortune; he might be deserted by friends and
abandoned by fortune. Where then should he look for sympathy? To what final stay should cling his 'faith? He
should turn to the memory of his mother's love, and in her
divinity should he rest his faith. Noble young mother!
Gentle, sad-heroic spirit! Though the ignorance and superstition of men have shut thy little life in a globe of darkness, above thee is a world of light. For this act alone
thou wouldst merit immortality. For this alone the angels
would meet thee at the gates, and welcome thee with a new
song into the joys of Paradise. . . .

"Once I said," said Mirabeau Holmes to Marian Malcomb
one evening when they were seated on the same bench in the
flower-yard where we have seen them once, and where they
have been many times since. "I once said to myself, 'I am
sufficient to myself.' And I was proud in the belief. I felt
within myself the sufficient springs of my own ambition and
happiness. But I confess to you to-night how greatly I was
mistaken. No! I am not sufficient to myself. But your life
has become so interwoven with my own that I can see no
future without your companionship."

"I did not think to hear you say this. I thought you had
a noble ambition in life, and that you would fulfil it. You
will not be hindered by so small an obstacle as I."

"So small an obstacle! Ah! Do you remember that
afternoon at the river? From that hour I have had no hope,
no aim, in which you have not filled the greater part. True,
I have indulged in some hopes of doing somewhat in the
cause of truth and Humanity; how else had I dared to hope
for your love? But without you I see no future. If you
ask me what right I had so early to hope for your love, I
say I don't know, only I felt that our lives were made
for each other. I loved you then, and resolved to prove my

worthiness of you; I can only answer for my constant and complete devotion to you. And tell me, now, has there not been a time when you met my complete and full devotion with some feeling of return?"

"Must I answer that?"

"Is it too much for me to ask?"

"No; forgive me for the question. You have been so honorable to me, and I believe so true and earnest, that I could not, if I wished, be less so to you. I will not say that there was not a time when I met your love with a feeling of more than esteem."

"There was a time—there was a time—tell me, Marian, tell me, my life, my darling—if that time is not now also? or what I have done to forfeit your love. I would rather have forfeited my life. If there be anything, it shall be undone; I will unlive the day that gave it existence. But it cannot be. I have only changed in my love to you by its growing with my life, by its becoming more single and better. Long ago I said, 'now I love you best;' and many times since, I have said so; it is only now I can see how small it then was by comparison with my love for you now. Say to me that that time is now."

"And if I should?"

"Then you would name the day when we should consecrate ourselves to each other, and when our life should begin. But ——"

"No; I cannot."

"Is it, then, that after all this I am simply to be told, no?"

"Some time ago, in this very place, you remember, I told you that I could not give you any encouragement to hope for what you now ask. If I have failed, you must know how much pain it gives me; and will you not spare me?"

"Spare you pain! Good God! How willingly would

I take upon myself ten times every one that shall ever come across your life, if you might only be perfectly happy. How can you ask me that? Too often already, I fear, have I told you how willingly I would lay at your feet every energy and every hope of my life."

"No; after all that has been between us"— and she spoke these words as tremulously and sweetly as the notes of a dying harp—"after all that has been between us, I will not simply say to you, no. I confess to you that I have listened, not with an unwilling ear, when you have spoken of that exalted love upon which married life ought to rest, and I believe, too, I have felt some of your own enthusiasm when you have spoken to me of your ideal of marriage. And—must I say it—I have even felt proud of being the object of your love. But it was you, too, that first led me to reflect that there is something else essential between persons who are to spend their lives together—that their opinions and aims in life ought to be similar."

"And are not our opinions and aims in life similar? Surely you have long known that I intended my own life to be an active one. I did not think you objected to that. Look at the life of your own father and mother—surely theirs has been a happy one. And besides, when I have spoken to you of the vast amount of suffering in the world; of the great need that Humanity has of men, of men able to see the cause of justice, and to work, and die for it, if necessary; of my earnest ambition to be even an humble soldier in such heroic ranks; I think you have listened to me, not only with interest, but with approval. Once, I know, when we were speaking upon the subject, and some one present said it looked very much like a dream, you said 'if it be a dream, it cannot be denied that it is a very grand one;' and I loved you for those words, and cherished them afterwards. As to the means of accomplishing this great work of humanity, I have no opinions that may not change; I accept the best that is before me; I hope I may be willing to do whatever work is appointed. But for whatever is best in all that I have hoped to do, I have looked to you as the inspirer. Whatever honors I have hoped for, I wished to lay them at your feet; and my greatest happiness I wished to find in your approval. How then are we not identical in opinions and purposes?"

"You have not mentioned that which is of more importance than everything else—religion."

"Religion!" Mirabeau started as if he had been struck. Then he looked bewildered, as if a wall had suddenly risen up between them. All this time had he been completely, fatally in the dark; and all this time, at least since she had heard him talk that afternoon at Mr. Brooke's, had Marian been fearing that it might be just as it was. Mirabeau had not spoken to her upon this subject, first because he regarded the subject as the most unfruitful of all themes; and secondly, because he attached no importance whatever to the particular dogmas one might happen to believe in, but looked clear through all such fanciful webs, straight to the heart, and asked only if the heart was pure, and the life illustrated by good and generous deeds. But now he saw how different was the standpoint from which Marian had viewed the subject, and he was alarmed. On any other occasion than this, and to any person less religious than he knew Marian to be, he would probably have answered dryly, "I had not thought of that." But such an answer, of course, did not now enter his thoughts. He was alarmed; but still, for a few moments, he did not fully appreciate the hopelessness of the situation. Nor indeed had Marian herself ever fully appreciated it. She had continued to hope that there might be

15

some possible explanation, which she herself was not able to imagine. But of this she believed herself firmly determined—that she could not, under any consideration, marry an atheist or infidel. Having been taught that belief in certain dogmas—among them that so tersely expressed by Martin Luther: "God is above mathematics"—was necessary to the soul's salvation, it cannot be wondered at that she came to such determination. The only wonder will be if she holds to it. As soon as Mirabeau could speak, he said:

"I do not think that in religion we differ in any essential particular. As for religion in its true sense, the feelings of love and reverence with which the human mind regards the Deity, I know we do not differ. We serve, I know, the same God; we believe alike that true religion does not consist in any outward forms and ceremonies, but is a matter of the heart itself; if you trust in God, have a pure heart, and live a virtuous life, illustrated by good deeds, is not that sufficient?"

"But you know my meaning—I mean the orthodox religion of the church."

"I might say, alas! there are so many churches, and so many religions, each claiming to be true and each denouncing all the others, that one of so little learning as myself can hardly have any way of knowing which to believe. But I know your meaning; and I must answer you, before my God and my own conscience, that I cannot believe that religion to be the true one. But what of that? God knows how earnestly I desire to know the truth; and he knows that I do believe the truth, according as he has given me to understand it. Surely he will not hold us responsible for what we honestly and earnestly believe. We do not make our beliefs; we cannot will to believe that two and two make five, and believe it. But how shall this throw a single shadow across our life? Our life shall be spent in doing good; and we shall find our happiness in each other. You have said that you loved me—delicious word! Trust me, then, with your life, as I will trust you wholly with mine. Ah, then! Our life shall be joyful; and some of God's creatures shall be made happier and better for our having lived in the world." His voice was low and earnest; and when he ceased speaking, Marian endeavored to rise, saying: "Let us return to the house." Mirabeau observed that she trembled, and quickly offered her his arm, saying:

"I fear we have stayed too long. Is the air too cool for you?"

"No; the night is pleasant." They had now reached the door; and Mirabeau, she still holding to his arm, stopped to go. And then he said to her:

"But you have not answered me yet; tell me, yes, before I go."

"Do not ask me," she said, half entreatingly; "but—"

"I may hope?"

"Not that; but—come again—to-morrow."

What was Mirabeau Holmes to do? If he had had less refinement, less tenderness of feeling, he would have disregarded her half-pleading tone, and stood there until she gave him an answer. One can see what it would certainly have been. And Mirabeau knew that a promise from Marian Malcomb, given under the pressure of her present feelings, would be of infinite importance to him. But when she said earnestly, no less by her actions than by her words, "Please do not urge me," he was dumb. He only said "Good-night," and went away. And there was another reason, too, which he had often thought of in moments of calm reflection, and which was not wholly absent from his mind even in the most fervid moments of love: he did not want an answer that

was not dictated by the calmest judgment as well as the
deepest feeling.   No mental reservations, or after-regrets.
The woman he married must be wholly his, as he would
be wholly hers.   He believed that Marian Malcomb was the
woman.

CHAPTER XXIV.

"My grief lies onward, and my joy behind."
SHAKSPEARE.—*Sonnets.*

CLARENCE HALL had been at his new home some weeks, and his wife was still at her father's. Several times had he called for her to go home; and each time some excuse had been made. Clarence Hall was alarmed, as it began dimly to occur to him that perhaps they were debating at her father's whether she should come at all or not. A month passed. Gloomy forebodings of final alienation began to force themselves upon his mind. Darker than ever the clouds of fate were gathering and settling around Clarence Hall. And this was the man, who, only a short while before, on his wedding day, in the flush and fancy of generous ambition and youthful promise, had gazed before him only upon pleasant paths through Elysian fields, leading to some mystic Arc de Triomphe in the gauzy light beyond. One night he sat alone before the fire in his room at home. He had been thinking deeply of his past life, of the present, and of the future. But the rebounding mind had already left these depths, and was now far up in the thin air of revery. There was a rap at the door. He started instantly; so quickly that, one would think, there must have been some connection between his dream at that moment and the rapping at the door. He had risen from the chair, and rested one knee upon it for a second to recall his consciousness, when his eye became fixed upon the fire in the grate. The fire at that moment exhibited that phenomenon which one frequently sees in a grate when the fire is low, almost burnt out: a kind of hard crust of charred coal, looking firm enough on top, but when you look below you see that it has no support whatever, the middle having all burnt out, leaving only a ruin here and there, and a few live coals gleaming from a bed of ashes at the bottom ; the crust, being slightly in the form of an arch, supports itself, while from the under side hang small wisps of ash, giving it a comb-like appearance ; you touch the top of the crust ; it falls to the bottom, and you have only a small mass of dead ruins, of ashes and charred coal.

Clarence Hall almost shuddered as he thought he saw in the grate something like his own life. The rapping at the door was repeated, and he went to open it. It was one of Mr. Dearing's servants. " Miss Annie's baby sick, sir, and they say for you to come over there." Clarence Hall did not stop to remember that he had long ago resolved never to go to Mr. Dearing's again, and that he had, up till now, kept his resolution. He hastened hither ; and as he walked swiftly, silently along, he thought of the phantom his fancy had conjured up in the grate. When he got to Mr. Dearing's his worst fears were realized. The baby had had a cold for several days past ; on the previous night had become suddenly worse ; and by this time was in the last stage of pneumonia. All this day had the child been dangerously sick, and the father, not more than half a mile away, had only now been notified of it, and was come just in time to see it die. This was Clarence Hall's only child ; it was almost his only stay in life, and as he had felt others slipping away, he had clung only the more desperately to this. It was not intentional negligence, nor was it from any ill-feeling, that Clarence Hall had been sent for only at the last moment ; but it was mainly because no one understood that the child was dangerously ill. The doctor had been called that morning, and said he would return in the evening; and it was only when he came in the evening that they learned how bad the little Clara (the other they named Annie) was. The nurse had been accustomed to take the little girl every morning to her father's office; she had been ordered so to do by the father himself. But on this morning the father had been called away from his office on business, and supposed the baby had been to his office during his absence.

Little Clara was dead and buried; and all had returned from the grave to Mr. Dearing's.

It seems that, whatever of differences there had been, whatever grievances they had felt against each other, now, in their common affliction, father and mother would draw together to weep over their dead child, and to sustain and comfort each other. But no; they only became more bitter against each other. Words ran high between them. They accused each other. 'If the father had not made the nurse bring the poor baby to his office every morning it would not have died; for it was on one of these, a damp morning, that it had first taken cold.' 'If the mother had only been at home doing her duty there would not have been any need of carrying the baby to his office.' 'As if he had provided her any decent home to go to and do her duty; as if he had not brought her down to poverty'—angrily put in Mrs. Dearing. After all he had endured, Clarence Hall thought this was too much. He was filled with indignation and bitterness. He retorted angrily and sharply. They talked loud. Fancy, dear reader, these two, their child just buried, standing face to face and bitterly accusing each other. Was ever there sadder tragedy? Have human eyes witnessed a more mournful spectacle? And yet, dear reader, this thing hath actually been. Eyes have seen it. Flesh and blood have endured it.

At a dead hour of the night a man in a closely-buttoned

overcoat entered the cemetery, and stopped at a fresh little grave. He knelt down beside it. Maybe he uttered a short prayer. Maybe he dropped a few tears. He placed a few roses upon the little mound; and some upon a tiny tombstone by the side of it. Then he arose and walked straight and swiftly away. An hour later, and the same figure, already several miles from the city, was hurrying along, across the fields, through the woods, across valleys, and over the hills. It was Clarence Hall. Escaping from his past life. Hurrying from fate. But fate was not yet done with Clarence Hall. He had not yet fully played his part. The very night that we have seen him hasting away across the fields, his house, probably from the exploding of a lamp which he had left burning, caught on fire, and was totally consumed. All was horror and dismay the next morning at Mr. Dearing's, when it was known what had happened. Being somewhat accustomed to family quarrels, as aristocratic families always are more or less, they had not attached the greatest importance to those between themselves and their son-in-law. As for such a dénouement as this, their imagination had been utterly unable to conceive of it. Annie was wild with grief. She had been led on to where she now was mainly by the influence of her father's family. She was not unkind at heart. Once, as we know, she had loved and trusted her husband with all the little power she possessed. And if let alone, while certainly there never could have been between them any of that high and real companionship which Mirabeau Holmes's faith taught him to hope for in marriage; nay, while, for the husband at least, it would certainly have been joyless enough; if let alone, it would have been, though miserable, at least passable. As for final alienation, separation, to say nothing of the present horror, she had never thought of such a thing.

And as it is a law of the human mind, of the lowest as well as the highest, to magnify whatever good it has been deprived of, so to this poor stricken woman, so suddenly and dreadfully awakened to a consciousness of her position, her lost husband was ten times dearer to her now than she had ever known before. And in the wildness of her despair she exhibited a depth of grief, an energy of passion, which one would scarcely have thought it possible for her to possess. She accused her father and mother of everything; of the death of her child; of the alienation between her husband and herself; of the murder of her husband. For all believed that Clarence Hall, frenzied to insanity, had set his own house on fire and made away with himself. Thus it was that fate seemed to mock and glare upon Clarence Hall even as he was hurrying away over the mountains.

Meanwhile the world moved on. As also, at some pace, did that small portion of it known far and near, but mostly near, as the Empire State. But as to how far, since it is well enough to be exact in important matters, that portion of the footstool is known as the Empire State, why, seeing that the Government has not thought proper to spend a shilling even upon the Coast Survey within its limits, one must guess at it. Take a huge compass, then, and plant one foot of it somewhere about the centre, say Milledgeville, which city, I think, is probably the most eligible point for a hole in the ground, and describe a circle with a radius of one hundred miles; and far and near within this circle—except among the forty-two thousand white adults who cannot read or write, twenty-eight thousand of them being women, who, according to the statute, are the mothers of somebody's children—this domain is known as the Empire State. Of course, in this measurement no mention is made of jutts and corners; the State, being Democratic, cannot be reduced to rules and regulations. But the world moved along; and so did the Empire State. Truly, Jefferson Davis was not in the dark when he spoke of the "divine energy of our people." Even here in this State, while we have been following the histories of several of the people, one might see some evidences of the truth of the Confederate President's remark. What principally has been done during this period may be briefly expressed by saying that the wealth of the State has almost doubled.

But still there was no State system of public schools, the people still jogging along in the old belief: "Teach your bootblack Greek, and he at once becomes a rascal, or is called to preach;" the only modification in said belief being this, that many people had learned that said bootblack was likely enough to fulfil both conditions. Nor had the "State University," notwithstanding all the efforts of our friends, yet been open to the female sex; the people still going on in the belief that the highest style of education for women ought to consist in knowing how to thrum a few tunes on the piano, to tie their garters above their knees—in order that their legs might remain soft and smooth, for hard and knotty female legs are held to be out of all taste in the Empire State—and to hold themselves in readiness to be protected at a moment's notice. In the "best society" the above three were, and to the best of my skill and knowledge still are, considered the three golden rules of a young lady's education. People of enlarged views, and a kind of practical turn of mind, added two others, namely: how to make knicknacks and baby-clothes, and how to preside with dignity at the husband's dinner-table; while among a very large portion, that is, among the decidedly vulgar, including the fourteen thousand white men who were, and still are, unable to read or write, and the twenty-eight thousand white women who were, and still are, unable to read or write, there prevailed a strong notion that a regular, thorough-going, business woman ought to be able to stand in the kitchen-door and with the utmost facility kick a dog a hundred yards. Still, our friends were not the only ones who believed that the education of women was of quite as much importance as that of men, and who thought that the " State University " ought to be opened to all alike. The time had not yet come; and if any of them had daughters whom they wished to educate thoroughly, why, the only chance was to put them into breeches and bring them up in the way they should go. Mr. Malcomb succeeded in his public school plan in the city.

As for the politics of the country, Mr. Malcomb had seen with peculiar satisfaction the Conservative party " accept the situation," just as he had advised several years before and for which advice, as we have seen, even an effort was made to outlaw him. And though his opponents had now been in power some time, the Constitution, which owed its existence mainly to him, still remained unaltered. Not even jealousy, envy, could find anything in it that the people would suffer to be changed.

Acute, far-seeing, and ever solicitous for the development and prosperity of his State and section, Mr. Malcomb was now engaged in a work which promised to be of the largest consequence : he was trying to get his State to offer such terms to the discontented " workingmen " of the Northern cities as would enable and induce them to leave their crowded and starving homes and come South. Said he to Mirabeau one day, speaking upon this subject : " You say you have in New York alone a hundred thousand men, idle and homeless, but both able and willing to work. Now, to say nothing of the coal-fields, the quarries, and the ore-beds, which might be utilized to the immense wealth of the State, we have millions of acres of land rich and productive, but, like the workingmen, in unwilling idleness. Let the State invite these workingmen to come, with their families, and settle among us. Let the State furnish transportation, and to each head of a family, say, fifty acres of land with stock to cultivate it, seeds, tools, lumber, and supplies for one year—the money advanced by the State to be a first mortgage upon the improved lands and all other property the settler may acquire, payable at a low rate of interest, say, in ten years."

"It is easy to perceive," said Mirabeau, "that several things would follow if your plan was adopted and carried out. In the first place, I am able to vouch for many thousands of the workingmen's accepting so wise and liberal an offer. As to the good that would accrue to the State, the impetus that it would give to her progress in wealth, population, and power, I agree with you that it is almost incalculable. As to the workingmen themselves, there is no disguising the fact that it would be simply a clear loss of so much power to the Proletariate; for when they came here, upon such terms, they would themselves all become property-holders and many of them capitalists."

"And you make that an objection to the scheme?"

"No, I cannot say that. But while this measure would put it off for a while, the battle between Labor and Capital will come at last—*and the Proletaires will have need of all their strength.*"

It was on a Tuesday afternoon, the day on which the Supreme Court delivers its decisions, that Mirabeau and Fred, having just left the court-room, were walking down the street, and Fred asked: "What do you think of that decision?" It was the case of Mr. Brooke; the jury had found him guilty; he had been sentenced to twenty years' imprisonment in the Penitentiary; and the case had been carried to this court.

"I know it is an outrage upon decency and common sense, and I hope it is upon law; but I don't know about that. You were right, Fred, I would rather roll a wheelbarrow than be a lawyer."·

"What were the points?"

"That a woman who has been seen in the arms of a man is not a virtuous female, in the eye of the law [the reader remembers how Emma was forcibly taken into his arms by Alf Walton]; and that a woman cannot be seduced by a married man. Of course, the meaning of the whole decision is, that a minister of the gospel can't be guilty of the crime of seduction."

"That may be so in law; but I don't know of but one way of making it so in fact."

"See how the court was divided—the only one of the three who is not subject to the power of the church, dissented from this decision."

"I reckon they don't doubt that the preacher can commit the act. But then it is no crime; I suppose they think that the preacher pronounces some kind of a benediction, or may even work a Scotch miracle on a small scale, which changes the nature of the thing."

"Have you no reverence at all?"

"No. Buckle says that the origin of reverence or veneration is wonder and fear. We wonder because we are ignorant, and fear because we are weak. Veneration carried into religion causes superstition; into politics, despotism."

"Without going into that question, it rather seems to me that conscientious religious belief ought to impart something of sacredness to anything."

"Precisely! That seems to have been the notion of the Supreme Court in this case."

We have seen that Mrs. Walton, on her death-bed, under the vague impression that, possibly, somewhere in the world, her daughter, or her daughter's child, might be still living, exacted from her husband a promise that he would arrange his property so that if they, or either of them, should ever be found, it might come into their possession. Mr. Walton was faithful to his promise. He executed it before he started on his sad journey to the Old World. And it was well that he did; for the old man was not destined ever to reach the shores of Europe. He died on the passage, leaving a letter to his correspondent in London, and another to his friends in America, containing his last directions. Thus died Mr. Walton, and found his last resting-place in the silent depths of the ocean. He had started to the Old World in the sad hope of bringing home the remains of his two sons, to be deposited in their native soil, beside the dust of their mother. He hoped too to bring hither the remains of his other son, buried on the banks of the great Mississippi. And soon he thought to mingle his own dust with theirs. As for his other child, he knew not where she was; but he prayed that God would forgive them both, and bring them together hereafter where the sufferings of earth are not remembered. Thus the old man hoped. But he slept in the bosom of the ocean; his wife in the soil of Georgia; one son in the far West; another in France; the last in Britain. And Viola, too, was resting quietly in the arms of her Italian lover. God will not condemn her utterly. For behold! She too was a woman!

CHAPTER XXV.

" Treading the path to nobler ends,
A long farewell to love I gave."
WALLER.

" Come," said Fred to Olive Sutherland one night, " come, sing me a song; I am miserable to-night."

" Why are you miserable ? "

" Because there are forty-two days in six weeks."

" Do you wish there were fewer ? "

" Yes; I wish there were forty-two weeks in six days."

" You think we shall get tired of each other, and you want the time to go at a rapid rate."

" Oh, I only meant for this to last till then. You know a good rule must work both ways. After six weeks I want this one to work the other way."

" A poor rule then you wish for, by your own showing; for it will surely not work both ways, or even one way."

" There's for your wit "—kissing her hand.

" Will that do both ways ? "

" No; only one way—this way "—another kiss.

" What a sweet tune that little hand ought to play after two kisses ! "

" And what a sweet song this pretty mouth ought to sing !" and before she could turn her head, he kissed her twice on the lips. Fred said afterwards, " they were good enough to have sent a whole Puritan congregation to the State-prison for the full term of its natural life."

" What shall I sing you ? "

" Here is something your mother has just given me— ' Wicked Sixteen '—sing that."

"What, do you want to hear me say—'But alack I must own, my heart it is stone, For to love him is out of the question?'"

"Yes; and I will compare it with the truth; and amuse myself by reflecting what a fib you are telling."

"You had better watch! You don't know but that at this very minute 'even the thought makes me smile. For I frankly declare, I can never forbear, with a chance, a delightful flirtation.'"

But Fred knew well enough that here was no "delightful flirtation." For this girl's heart was as deep as her own brown eyes, and true as a star. Their love was all sunshine and roses. But that does not indicate that it was not both full and strong; rather the contrary. Is not sunlight the greatest power in nature? And what is more smooth and silent? The roused lightning is terrible in its might; but with the calm, serene power of the sunlight, it reminds one of a fallen archangel compared with the Omnipotent. The love of Fred Van Comer and Olive Sutherland was not disturbed by storms; it was smooth and genial, but deep and true. And the reason of it was this, that they had not made a mistake, there was between their deepest natures perfect accord. As for Fred, beneath an apparent lightness of disposition he carried a heart as true as truth. It would have been far from an easy task to find a clearer, better balanced, or better stored head than Fred Van Comer carried upon his shoulders. And when Olive Sutherland looked into his soul, she saw, instinctively, both deeper and clearer than many who have "studied human nature" would have seen.

She took her seat at the piano. She touched the keys. "La la la, La la la," she saucily said as she lifted her head— and here dear, reader, wishing them all manner of happiness, we must bid them an affectionate adieu.

Bramlette, with much genius, not inconsiderable learning, a generous ambition, a good heart, a large jaw, and pants a foot too short, never learned the knack of getting on in the world. Somehow, things would go wrong with him. It was always a hard matter for him to make enough money even to pay his board. Still he was never heard to murmur. And if occasionally, say on a birth-day, or anniversary of some event in his life, he could not but reflect with some sadness how rapidly he was leaving youth behind him, and how little he had yet accomplished in life, he accepted it all very quietly; wrote what he had to write, and went to the Library to read. He lived on this way some time after the New Monthly suspended publication, having no regular work. Finally he left the city; went to teach a school in a village in a different section of the State; married the daughter of a clergyman, and soon went to preaching himself. And it came to pass when the nine months had expired—of course the reader knows, from personal experience for aught I can tell, what came to pass when that notable period of time had duly expired. But Bramlette never was eminently successful at anything; and so when his first baby, according to the statute, was born, it only weighed three pounds and a half, clothesbasket and all. But if he does not grow to weigh twenty stone in so many years there in no virtue in Methodist chicken. But what was chiefly remarkable, for this latitude and time of year, was this: that Bramlette was married on the night of the second of November, about eleven o'clock—the hour for retiring on such occasions, in these parts being twelve o'clock—and this diminutive individual entered upon his duties as a baby and citizen of this Republic on the night of the second of August following, at a comfortable number of minutes past twelve. Some people remarked upon Oriental customs. Some were reminded of Arabian Nights entertainments—"it came to pass, etc." Bramlette was a very virtuous man. It has been observed, I think, that people who live in wine countries do not make drunkards.

Happening to travel through that portion of the country some time since, and hearing of a camp-meeting not far off, and feeling much in need of spiritual comfort, I went to it. I met Bramlette there. He preached a good sermon; and said he meant to put breeches on that boy before he was two years old. Bramlette always was a firm believer in the dignity of the human species. I reminded him of what I had heard him say many years before, when we were in school together, about the birth of his first baby. It was a queer notion of Bramlette's. He said he wanted his first baby, which must be a boy, of course, to be born in a splendid barge upon the Bay of Naples; on a calm night in October, under a full moon in a dark sky, music in the distance, and Mount Vesuvius in action! Born in the midst of such a scene of beauty and sublimity, poetry and action, how should the boy fail to be great? Manifestly, the theory of Goethe and the practice of Napoleon would here come together. Disappointed this time, Bramlette must still look to the future. His next child would, in all probability, be only a girl—a clear loss here. He must look to the next. Peace be with Bramlette, his wife, and his babies, *omnis et singulis*, executed and executory, of which his wife is, or may be, the mother, according to the statute.

Emma Harlan died, and her mother died also. It was on a morning in November that this notice appeared in the daily papers: "The friends of Mrs. Harlan and her daughter Emma are invited to attend their funeral at Trinity Church, at eleven o'clock to-day." And to this notice was the signature of General Clement. At the appointed time a few noble friends, of the type I have mentioned; friends of all of God's creatures, friends who had learned to feel another's woe, and to shed the tear of sympathy over every misfortune and every sorrow—gathered at the little cottage on Ivy street, now desolate in death, and the sad procession moved slowly down Marietta and up Whitehall street, in direction of Trinity Church. The church was full. The dark, rich curtains were closely drawn. And all was silent and solemn. As the pall-bearers entered, the choir sang one of the songs of Schubert. And when the faint, weeping notes had died away, General Clement, who had been kneeling the while, rose and read that grand old hymn of Dr. Muhlenberg, "I would not live alway." No !——

The few lurid mornings that dawn on us here
Are enough for life's woes, full enough for its cheer.

Only those who knew of the relations which existed between this good man and Mrs. Harlan's family could feel the fulness of this scene. Years ago, the four brave brothers had followed him to battle upon the hills and plains of Virginia. One by one he had seen them all go down in the fight; and he had borne the dying message of the youngest and last to his stricken mother. Faithful to his promise to the dying young soldier, he had never faltered in his care and sympathy for the mother and sister. In their last sad days he was frequently with them, consoling, comforting, and cheering them, and helping them to bear their great weight of misfortune and sorrow. And now he was to perform for them the last service of the dead, and follow them to the grave.

Mr. Walton named Mr. Malcomb as executor of his will, and confided to him, as trustee, his large estate. It was in the afternoon of the very day that we have seen Mirabeau Holmes and Marian Malcomb last together, that Mirabeau received from Mr. Malcomb the note written by Alberto and

Viola Simona just before their death, and which they had entrusted to the tall American, to be delivered to himself or to Mr. Walton. The note had been given to Alf Walton in New York for his father, and he had carried it with him to Europe. According to Mr. Walton's directions, all the papers found upon his son's person were forwarded by his London correspondent to Mr. Malcomb. This note was found among them, and was immediately handed to Mirabeau Holmes.

When Mirabeau last parted with Marian, as we have seen, she told him, at the last moment, "to come back—to-morrow." To-morrow came. Neither of them had slept much that night. They had both been busy thinking of what had just transpired between them, and of their future lives. Mirabeau was not without hope; but still he looked forward to the coming interview as a man looks to a trial for his life when he knows the chances are against him. He believed now that all the glow and coloring of the grand mission of his future life had been imparted by the hope he had believed in and cherished of sharing that future with Marian Malcomb.

And now, for the first time, he tried to contemplate that future without the glow and without the color. But alas! he found that not only the glow, not only the color, but also the very substance of the fabric, was largely made up of these very hopes. And at this moment, he thought that without her he could see no future whatever. But there was one thing that Mirabeau Holmes did not say even to himself; he did not say that, for her, he would renounce his faith in himself and his loyalty to God and Humanity. Then he tried to philosophize. He reproached himself: Is *your happiness* then of so much value? What does Humanity care for *your happiness?* What does Humanity expect? Every man, happy or unhappy, to *do the work* appointed him to do.

As for what Marian had thought, and what conclusion she had reached, we may judge from the following note, which she wrote and sent to Mirabeau next morning :

"Mr. Holmes: You will think me weak and uncertain, I know. That this will make you think me unworthy of you, I am almost glad, but still I am sorry, and reproach myself, to forfeit your good opinion. *You know* how much I prize it. You know the circumstances under which I told you last night to come back to see me to-day. It is different this morning, and now I ask you, for the sake of all that has been between us, not to come. I cannot say more, save to ask that I may still be your friend.   Marian Malcomb."

To which Mirabeau returned the following answer :

"Miss Marian: As to what I may think of anything you have done, let me only say, what you know well to be true, that since that October day at the river, long ago, I have loved you with full devotion; and, whatever may be the future, I shall love you so while I live. I shall come at twelve ; and by the right of the love with which I have long loved, and still love you, I ask you to see me. Remember! remember! Our better destinies sometimes come within our reach in this life, and, in our ignorance, we strike them down ; we know the truth when they lie dead before us. I declare to you that this is what you are now about to do.

"Mirabeau Holmes."

At the appointed hour Mirabeau went to Mr. Malcomb's. Marian met him in the parlor. She was calm now, and fully determined. They had been talking for some minutes ; and now both had risen and stood facing each other, he looking intently into her face, she looking down, and toying with a shell on the table.

"Will you not change that decision?"

"I cannot."

"And this is forever?"

"Yes."

He bowed his head, pressed her hand silently, and went away. Thus he gave to love a long farewell. Another crisis in the life of this man had passed. And this too was necessary to give him higher and broader views of life and its duties. He was still young. He was rising to meet his destiny. We shall see him again. The next day he started to look for the child, the Italian patriot and his American bride.

www.ingramcontent.com/pod-product-compliance
Lightning Source LLC
Chambersburg PA
CBHW051127120726
47905CB00005B/1453